A Fire in the Sky

A Fire in the Sky

Or, the Fantastical History of
James Sadler, as Related by Himself:
How the Son of an Oxford Pastry-Cook
became the First English Aeronaut

Wendy A.M. Prosser

ISBN 978-1-73997-932-4

Swervy Piglet Productions
P.O. Box 516
Abingdon
Oxfordshire OX14 9BB
United Kingdom
info@swervypigletproductions.com

Cover design by Wendy A.M. Prosser

Cover image: 'Ascent of James Sadler at Oxford 1810', photographed by the author

℗

O HAPPY Sadler! whom the Gods design'd

To scorn the Terrors of a Fearful Mind;

Enraptur'd Beings! open your sightless Eyes;

Is that a Mortal who can reach the Skies?

'Elmer', *Jackson's Oxford Journal,*
17th November 1784

PART I

CHAPTER ONE

I LOST MY TASTE FOR SWEETMEATS during the ninth year of my three-score-and-ten. 'Twas the Twenty-First Day of June—"A day for cheese-cake," according to my father, who upon that confection had built his fame, if not yet his fortune. (The secret, he claimed, being the peel, boiled for a full seven minutes—no more, no less—then mashed with a pestle and mortar 'til it be "tender as fine *marmelado*".)

Amongst our fellow townsfolk, meanwhile, the date signalled a fête of middling allure: less arduous than the Beating of the Bounds, more fun than St Frideswide's Day. The annual Amphibalian Benefaction, despite its Midsummer setting, remained just one of many timeworn traditions that clung to the City of Oxford like a November-morning fog on the River Cherwell.

My sisters, Mary and Lizzie, and I giggled in happy unison as Father marshalled us out of the shop, then lined us up by order of height on the High, for a final inspection.

"I could be no less proud," he said, when satisfied with our turn-out, "were the King himself to send for a pint of our comfits. For this is the Sadlers' greatest

3

hour, and could be improved upon only if your grandmother were here to see it."

Mother squeezed his arm. "I am sure she knows, Thomas dear."

Smiling, Father clapped his hands, and off we set— six of us that morning, for this was a family affair, and my cousin Jediah, if not a Sadler, was the next best thing.

"Be of no doubt," Father continued, "'twas her labour—and hers alone—that saved my sisters and I from destitution..."

We had heard it countless times before, of course: how Granny Sadler avoided the poorhouse by selling fruit pies from the back of the lodgings they shared with three other impoverished families. Yet the tale never failed to stir me. As we turned onto Catte Street, I glanced back at the shop—our home—snuggled between the Salutation Inn and Tillyard's Coffee-house, its green-and-gold sign rocking gently in the warm summer breeze.

"It shall all be yours one day, my son," boomed Father; any louder and they would have heard him out at Binsey.

I blushed and mumbled, "Th—Thank you, sir."

"Do take your hands from your pockets, James," said Mother. "And do not scowl—you are not in charge yet."

I heard Jediah snigger behind me, but did not rise to it. Although he was heir to riches beyond my boyish imagination, and lived in a big house in St Clement's while I slept in a garret over a pastry-shop, I pitied my privileged cousin, who had little family of his own and only his servants for company. I reassured myself that no one would ever mock me when I was grown, and as well respected as my father.

The scale of that fame was revealed when we entered the Broad. Friends, colleagues, and strangers alike detached themselves from the crowd of townsfolk converging on Alban Lane and hurried across the street to applaud him.

"'Tis a day for cheesecake indeed!" was agreed by all, then good-humoured chitchat ensued regarding the tradesman's lot, and how success in a fickle market requires a marriage of product and timing—Father being a case in point. For had a Sadler's Finest Cheesecake not stood fresh-baked upon our shop counter on the morning of the birthday of the Dean of St Alban's College, the Sub-Dean might have purchased a different gift, and said Dean, failing to taste the cheesecake, would have not, within the week, named Father his Official Supplier of Comfits, the previous holder of that office having recently expired. Amongst Oxford confectioners, Supplier of Comfits to the Benefaction was an honour akin to the granting of a Triumph to an Ancient Roman general, the tradesman being considered by his peers close to a king—or even a god—for one morning each year.

Being destined to join the trade, I followed this shopkeeping small-talk closely—until a woman I recognized as the wife of a well-to-do Witney confectioner crept upon me and patted my head so roughly, my cap was swept from my scalp to the ground.

"I'll wager you cannot wait to get your little teeth around those sweetmeats," she cackled, clamping my ear between sausage-thick fingers. "Your dada's a fine pastry-cook and a finer figure of a man. I'll wager you cannot wait to become just like him, eh?"

Between gasps of pain I explained that my 'dada' did not approve of wagering, or of me talking to strange women, then wriggled free from her grasp and dropped back to the top of Catte Street, where I found Jediah. Having no one to tell *him* to straighten his shoulders, smooth his hair, or remove his hands from his pockets, my cousin was free to trudge along in a slovenly manner.

"Do hurry up," I urged, hearing cheers from the Broad as the City Waits struck up with 'The Maid of Llangollen'. "We shall miss the best ones."

Jediah laughed, though his gold-and-green eyes and long, lean face remained as humourless as ever. "Do you honestly believe they will waste their best ones on *that* rabble?"

"The comfits are not *theirs*," I retorted. "They are Father's."

"They paid in coin so the comfits are theirs, to dispose of however they wish." He tweaked my already-bruised ear with a pitying sigh. "Dearest coz, you have much to learn about business before you come into your inheritance."

Tears welling, I shoved him aside before I embarrassed myself. I would have run to Mother, had she and Father not already passed into Alban Lane and an ocean of coat-tails and petticoats gushed in behind them. I tried to follow, but being undersized for my age I would have made faster progress swimming through egg blancmange. I yelled in vain for Lizzie and Mary. Then I, too, was swept up by the press of bodies, and towed like a rudderless tub towards the focus of all this excitement: the House of St Alban the Martyr in the University of Oxford, more commonly known as St Alban's College.

'Twas fast approaching noon—the time when, to mark the feast day of their patron, tradition dictates that the College's Master and Fellows bestow their goodwill upon the townsfolk of Oxford. Tradition further dictates that this goodwill be delivered in the form of comfits fashioned to resemble the eyeballs of the Saint's executioner (if you remember your history) and that the bestowing be done from the top of Old Crab's Tower in the East Quad of the college.

I arrived there just as the Waits sounded a fanfare, and moments later a man in a grey hooded cloak appeared on the roof: the Master dressed as Saint Alban, who had assumed the guise of his teacher Amphibalus, who had latterly fled the Romans, who had sought to have him slain. Father had explained the essentials over breakfast; I would have made neither head nor tail of it otherwise. The next act, however, was simple enough. To a roar from the crowd, the doubly-disguised gentleman hefted a bran tub onto the battlement, and reaching within it drew forth a handful of spheres the size of walnuts. Father's comfits! Swollen fit to burst with delight, I added my voice to the clamour.

"*Albanum egregium faecunda Britannia profert!*" bellowed the Master—a strange spell with which to summon sweetmeats, but it never failed. He raised his fists above the parapet, and all around me eager shouts went up: "Here—over here!", "My way, sir!", "Let the good Saint guide your arm!"

"See what I mean?" Jediah had found me. "You left before I could finish," he added. "I didn't *have* to come after you, but as your cousin, 'tis my duty to warn you."

I scanned the crowd on tiptoes, hoping Mother and Father were nearby. "Warn me what?"

"Beg for tidbits if you must—but be sure not to eat them."

"Why?" I grew impatient. "What are you talking about?"

"They are poisoned."

I pulled a face, thinking this a poor kind of joke, but Jediah remained deadly serious. An icy knot of dread seized my vitals.

"You poisoned the comfits?" I squawked.

"Not I," scolded my cousin. "Shame on you for thinking that."

"Then who?"

Jediah shrugged. "Can you not guess for yourself? 'Tis well known that pastry-cooks and confectioners are a cutthroat mob, with not a speck of honour between them. The obvious culprit is one of your father's rivals, envious of his success."

If this were true, who could it be? John Spicer, perhaps—for years, he'd put it about that Spicers, not Sadlers, were first to sell cheesecake in Oxford. Or Henry Truss of Shoe Lane, who had never got on with my father. Or the Beazley brothers, of Beazley, Beazley, & Co. of Paradise Square? Or the Witney wife? My still-throbbing earlobe attested to her violence, and 'twas common knowledge that women made the best poisoners—

"You are wasting time, James."

"What do you mean?"

"The poison acts quickly. Within the half-hour or sooner, your father's precious customers will be puking upon their shoes—and what of his reputation then? Not to mention your inheritance. I doubt he will trade in this city again, nor any other when word gets around."

Upon the battlement, the Master continued to tease the crowd. I yelled at him—at anyone—to stop, but then the bells of St Mary the Virgin began to sound the hour of noon. On the first chime, the Master opened his fists, and sweetmeats rained from the cloudless sky.

"Do not eat them!" I cried. "They are poisoned!"

I flung myself into the crowd, forcing my way to the front with elbows and shoulders. At the foot of Old Crab's Tower, I found a flock of younger children pecking like pigeons upon the cobbles; I shooed them away, then set about crushing the comfits under my heels, deaf to the youngsters' wails and their parents' protests alike. But one voice I could not ignore.

"James!"

I stopped mid-stamp and looked up as the crowd parted, revealing my father.

"Son... what are you *doing*?"

On the roof of Old Crab's Tower, several Fellows had joined the Master. I yelled again as they reached for the bran tub, and again went unheard as the comfits tumbled. A great, fat barrel of a man stepped forth, his face raised to the sky, his mouth open wider than a pancake. He lumbered this way and that like a drunkard, his antics encouraged by a steady handclap from his comrades and rewarded with a "Hurrah!" when a descending comfit dropped dead-centre between his lips. Turning away from Father, I charged him—no match for his size or weight, but the surprise alone was sufficient to bundle him over, onto his back. He clutched at his throat, whooping for breath, his eyeballs bulging so hideously I feared they might fly from their sockets, like the orbs of Saint Alban's executioner. I thanked Our Lord when a racking cough convulsed him, shooting the sweetmeat free like a miniature cannonball.

The crowd fell silent. Afraid to look upon their faces—and worse still, my father's—I slid off the fat man's belly and onto my knees, hanging my head.

"The comfits are poisoned," I whispered.

"I spoke in jest, you fool!" Jediah yelled from Father's side; my cousin seemed fit to explode, though with anger or mirth I could not tell. "Do you not understand? It meant nothing."

There came a horrid pause, then someone said, "I never did trust those Sadlers."

The speaker did not reveal himself—'twas one of those cutthroat confectioners, no doubt.

With a tearful roar I leapt at my traitorous cousin, but Jediah proved a nimbler foe than the fat man; a simple sidestep caught me off-kilter, and skidding upon a mulch of the comfits I'd crushed, I staggered buffoonishly. A cobblestone struck my skull as I fell, filling my head with white lightning.

Then I knew naught but a swirling black ocean, and the laughter of the crowd that followed me down.

CHAPTER TWO

I AWOKE CONVINCED I HAD DIED and ascended to Heaven—a silky-soft realm of white yarrow and rose, and the knell of celestial bells. Then, on no particular cue, my wits returned in a rush, and I feared I must be alive after all. For I lay, not upon a cloud, but a well-plumped sofa; the carillon I now recognized as the daily call to Evensong; and the source of the flowery smells was a poultice, bound about my head by some unknown physician. And the instant I perceived the last of these three, my head began clanging as though the bell-clappers lodged inside my skull, and I knew for certain that I was not dead, or at least not in Heaven.

I edged myself off the sofa and felt the plush pile of a carpet between my toes. I wondered what had happened to my shoes, and what Mother would say when I came home without them, as I tried to take stock of the rest of the room, the like of which I had never seen before, or seldom since.

'Twas not large—little bigger than our parlour. But while our parlour contained a hotchpotch of china knick-knacks and dainty tea-party furniture, this chamber boasted a different class of clutter. Chief in number being the books—so many books! We had books at home, of course, my father being a well-read man in matters of History and Scripture. But here every space not occupied by something else stood packed with them, and spaces that were full had somehow been stretched to hold one or two more.

I might have taken down a volume had I been older, but my eye was tempted instead by an object on the trestle-desk near the window. I had no notion of what it might be, this riddle of wheels within wheels, of circlets and spheres borne up on fine wires, finished in gold and mother-of-pearl and powered, I noted, by clockwork. The winding key recalled the mechanical mouse that Mother once brought from the Michaelmas toy fair; a favourite plaything of Lizzie's, until I took it for myself and made her cry. 'Twas with a similar wicked thrill that I brought this strange machine to life. The spheres and circlets began to rotate with barely a whisper of well-oiled gears, though I failed to learn their purpose, for then I heard voices through the partly open casement and on instinct I ducked beneath the desk.

Here lay another contraption, though in a state of disrepair, or perhaps repair, or even assembly: three horseshoe-shaped iron bands and a brass cogwheel attached to a plain wooden plate, these cumbersome parts out of sorts with the ball of blown glass also fixed on the board and the delicate golden tracery that connected them all together. As I studied this latest mystery, I fancied I heard—in the singsong voice of a child—the words of a nursery rhyme:

"The Moon shines bright,

The Stars give a light,

And you may kiss a pretty girl,

At ten a clock tonight."

The voice sounded at once both distant and close at hand—a product of my injured head, I feared. With the first set of voices now directly outside the window, I forgot the unseen singer and wriggled further under the desk.

"I heard feeding-time turned ugly this morning," said one. "Was anyone injured?"

"No one of any consequence," said the other.

They laughed—and with that, it all flooded back. 'Twas of *me* they spoke. No one of consequence, according to these two Gownsmen. And to everyone else, a laughing-stock. I fought back tears of shame and fury, and only when I was sure they had gone did I risk a peek through the window. An expanse of well-tended lawn confronted me, bordered by a cloister, from the far corner of which arose a bell-tower of honey-coloured stone. The sight seemed familiar, but it took me a moment to turn it inside-out and realize that I now stood *within* St Alban's College.

I made straight for the door, spotting my shoes beneath the sofa as I scrambled up from the floor; I pulled them on with one hand while I wrestled with the latch. To my relief the door was unlocked, and with my head now pounding far worse than before, I crept into the cool shade of the cloister. The flagstones were damp, their inscriptions obscured by dense mats of slippery moss; in my mounting delirium, I imagined these were the graves of other poor boys who'd offended the College. I spied a blue satin ribbon on one, and from somewhere ahead I heard childish laughter, first receding when I stumbled in that direction, then growing louder again. 'Tis said that every Oxford college contains a maze of concealed corridors and subterranean walkways, which might have explained my tormentor's invisibility—and why, although I saw no sign of Father in the flesh, I suddenly heard his voice.

"Gentle sir, I beg you—how might a miserable worm such as I make amends? Shall I *ever* earn forgiveness?"

I imagined him clutching his hat to his heart as he spoke, as clear as if he were cringing right there before me. Thankfully, he was not, though he would surely find me soon.

"No more beg-pardons, please!" said a new, unfamiliar voice—a Fellow of the College, I presumed from his manner of speech. "We shall mention the matter no more, and blame it on youthful exuberance, eh?"

"But the Benefaction! What will the Master say?"

"Let me tell you something I should not." The speaker chuckled. "College life is comfortable—too comfortable, many might say—but also most deathly dull. We devise diversions such as the Benefaction, but even these lose their novelty over the centuries. I am sure I was not alone in enjoying—what shall we call it? The break with tradition this year. And before I forget, I must commend you on your comfits. Quite delicious, neither too dry nor too pappy."

"So merciful, so generous!" Father sobbed. "'Tis undeserved, after the tribulations we have piled upon you. Be sure the boy will be soundly thrashed when I get him home. And he will go without supper this week."

"There most certainly is no—"

"And next week, too!"

I had always considered my father a dignified man. Never before had I heard him grovel—and how vulgar his fawning sounded! How petty those vengeful oaths! I might have surrendered without complaint, had he behaved more like the Fellow. But not now. Their voices had grown louder while I listened, and I was seized with a fear that Father might suddenly spring from the wall or drag me beneath the flagstones. Then I heard the voice of the child again, clear as a bell: "*Run!*" Panicking, I ran.

"You there—boy!" A different, angry voice rang across the cloister. "'Tis forbidden to run in the cloister! Halt or I shall fetch the Dean."

I ran faster still, the echoes of my footsteps snapping at my heels. Ahead of me, where the cloister turned a corner, I spotted a door.

"James!"

I looked back, and there stood Father. Now I knew those secret passages existed, for I had just passed the spot from which he'd emerged, and had noticed no entrance.

"How dare you run from me!" he bellowed. "Come back here at once, do you hear?"

I did hear, but I had already reached the door, and propelled by momentum and terror in equal portions, pulled the handle with all my might. Beyond, I had hoped to find freedom—Dolphin Street, I guessed, where the hosiers had their Guildhouse. But I had lost my sense of direction. 'Twas not Dolphin Street I found, but a worn and winding stone staircase. I had

15

found my way into Old Crab's Tower, and with no-where else to go I hurtled upwards in almost darkness, no more master of my actions than the orbs in the clockwork machine.

When the staircase came to an end, I felt a soft, warm breeze on my cheeks. I screwed up my eyes against the sunlight and stumbled on blindly, halted only when a hard and immovable object crunched into my chest. As my vision cleared, I saw I had run up against a merlon; had I veered just a foot to the left or right, I'd have flown straight through an embrasure. Beneath me, I saw Alban Lane, bustling with pygmy folk going about their pygmy business. 'Twas a heady moment. Beyond Alban Lane, I spied the dome of the Radcliffe Camera and the gargoyles and pinnacles of St Mary's, and beyond them the River Isis, where minus-cule boats plied their trade from Folly Bridge to the village of Iffley. I saw the road to Abingdon dotted with waggons like children's toys, and the orchards of the old priory, and a muddy stream that must be the Grandpont causeway, beyond which I fancied I saw Boars Hill, and Newbury, and Winchester, and even Southampton. So clear was the day—and so clouded my mind—I imagined I held, not comfits, but the whole of the world in my hands, and the pygmy people were cheering and calling my name rather than laugh-ing.

I was roused from this happy fantasy by the Fellow, who had climbed the tower more stiffly than I.

"Come away from there," he warned.

"Yes, come away." Father appeared behind him, red-faced and panting. "You have upset these good gentlemen quite enough already—I'll not have them scraping your brains off the street as well. Unless you believe you can fly, of course. 'Twould be no more incredible than poisoned comfits."

I staggered away from the merlon, my head in a spin; when I'd got well clear, Father grabbed my arm and shook me in fury.

"Would you have us ruined?" he cried. "You have made fools of us—and villains, too. We shall become pariahs, outcasts in our own town—"

The Fellow raised a hand. "No lasting harm has been done, I am sure." He stooped over me, his robes billowing about us both, like the sails of a great black ship. Though his face hovered but inches from mine, I could not say what manner of nose he had, or the colour of his eyes, or the size of his ears, for the Sun stood directly behind him and his face was cloaked in shade; still, I knew he was smiling. "You recovered your strength quick enough," he said, "if not your good sense."

Father grunted and shook me again. "He has always been the stupidest of my children. I shall remove him from your sight, gentle sir, and on my mother's grave, he will not trouble you again."

"Might I suggest instead that he rests here a little while longer? 'Twas a nasty knock to the head he suffered, and he is clearly not yet right in his mind. I shall return him when he is recovered, at no trouble to your good self."

I was about to say that I did indeed feel a little dizzy and perhaps another nap on the sofa would see me better, but Father responded on my behalf.

"He got no worse than he deserved. And naught compared with the price he will pay if he tries such jiggery-pokery again."

17

At that, the Fellow relented and offered to escort us both to the lodge, but Father insisted he had been too kind already, and with this exchange ended the first of my many encounters with the House of St Alban the Martyr.

Back on Alban Lane, the street remained strewn with comfits. Most had been ground to crumbs fit only for birds, but some stayed whole and had rolled into the kennel along the centre of the road. From there, the edible eyeballs watched as Father dragged me away, swinging me right off my feet when we turned the corner onto the Broad. As I tried to save the toes of my Sunday best shoes from scuffing the cobbles, I glimpsed a mangy hound, sniffing a puddle of syrupy vomit.

A sick taste rose in my own craw when I saw the half-chewed comfits it contained.

CHAPTER THREE

I SUFFERED A GOOD HIDING when we got home, then a week of early bedtimes without supper. After that, for the whole of the following month, I was barred from the family tradition of taking our pick of the unsold stock when the shop closed for business on Saturday night. I think this punishment lasted the longest because Father believed it would cause me the greatest distress. He was, however, mistaken. Not once did I pine for my favourite barberry flan nor even a slab of cherry pie, and when my sentence was served and all was forgiven if not quite forgot, I failed to regain my sweet tooth—nor have done so unto this day.

Some weeks later, Jediah came for tea, Uncle Elijah being still abroad on what Father called "one of his jaunts". My cousin sported a livid bruise on his forehead; when Mother asked after it, he scowled and blamed a copy of Plato's *Apology*, hurled at him by his tutor when he dropped off to sleep in his schoolroom.

"I hope you said you were sorry," grunted Father.

I wondered if he meant this to be funny. To laugh or not to laugh—which would offend him the least? I had Jediah to thank for my newly acquired mistrust of others' intentions, though I'd born him a grudge only briefly. On the very first Sunday afterwards, in fact, my conscience had been pricked by the Rev. Slade, with his sermon on the quality of mercy. My cousin's cruel jest must have seemed great fun, I had reasoned, to a lonely boy seldom permitted to play like other boys do.

While Mother and Mary prepared our meal, we marked time at the kitchen table; Father perusing the latest edition of *Jackson's Oxford Journal*, Lizzie being as bothersome as usual.

"Why does Jediah even *go* to school?" she demanded, having thoroughly scrutinized his injury.

Mary replied with disdain. "Jediah doesn't go to *school*. His tutor goes to *him*."

"But all the boys I know have started work, and Jediah is very much older than them. Is he not so clever, then?"

"If I were a common boy—" snapped Jediah, unaccustomed to hearing my sisters discuss him as if he were somewhere else. "—and had to attend that mare's nest of a free school, I, too, would quit at the first chance I had. What need has a smith, or a tailor, or a pastry—" He took a sharp breath. "—what need have such men for rhetoric, or logic, or music, or art?"

"But Father is a pastry-cook," said Lizzie, "and *he* needs rhetoric. I heard Mother say so—'tis for the horrid rumblings in his belly."

"That was *turmeric*, muddle-head." Mary rolled her eyes. "You should listen to Jediah. He knows rather more about these things than you."

"Well, I know what music is!" Lizzie grumbled, then treated us to a tuneless rendition of 'The Maid of

Llangollen' until Mother called a halt ahead of the third, least respectable verse.

"'Tis simple, really," I said, keen to demonstrate my own cleverness. "No common boy needs to learn music, or art, or—or the rest of it. But *Jediah* does, because *he* will become a man of consequence."

That notion had preoccupied me in the weeks since my adventure in St Alban's, but this being the first time I had put it into words, I was unprepared for Mary's sneering reaction.

"A *what*?"

"A man—a man of consequence. Isn't that right?" I turned to my cousin for support. "And when Jediah has learned all that his tutor can teach him, he will go up to the University."

Jediah nodded. "This Michaelmas Term, in fact. I shall become a Gentleman-Commoner of St Alban's, my father's *alma mater*. I shall not describe it, for you already know it quite well."

I winced, but thankfully heard no response from behind Father's newssheet. I lowered my voice. "So I shall need to learn these things too, to become more like Jediah and less like—like—"

Mary snorted before I could finish, which with hindsight, was a blessing.

"I am sure James will make an exceptional gentleman," said Jediah.

"Now you sound as ridiculous as him. What a pair of dunderheads—eh, Lizzie?"

Mary laughed again while she fetched a dish of potato pie from the range. Her mirth was unnervingly out of character, for my sister, though barely twelve years old at that time, had already grown as dour as a crone. Lizzie, of course, joined in the hilarity.

"When I am a man of consequence," I growled, "you will not dare to laugh at me."

At the head of the table, *Jackson's Oxford Journal* rustled.

"You will thank God in your prayers every night for giving you *me* for a brother. Though I might not want *you* for my sisters."

Mother joined Mary at the table, bringing with her a pot of split peas and the spicy aroma of pickled pork ragoo. My mouth began to water.

"Mamma," Lizzie giggled through her fingers, "James wants to be a gentleman's convenience."

"A man of consequence!" I barked.

Setting down the peas, Mother wiped her hands upon her apron-skirt and enquired what a man of consequence might be. I replied instantly, before Mary could even begin to interrupt.

"He is a most distinguished personage. Like—like..." I struggled again to find the right words. "Like a magistrate, but more important than that."

"Like the Reverend?" suggested Lizzie.

"No, more important than him."

"More important than Reverend Slade?" A smile creased Mother's soft, pink cheeks. "Who on Earth could be grander than that, I wonder?"

Lizzie tried again. "The Mayor?"

"The Mayor is as crooked as a zed," I retorted. "Everyone knows he bought his way into his office."

"James!" Mother's smile turned into a frown. "Where did you hear such spiteful tittle-tattle?"

Behind the newssheet, Father cleared his throat.

"A man of consequence," Jediah intervened, "is respected not due to what he has done, but because of who he is."

"That's right!" I cried "If the King were to drop his leaf tomorrow—"

"James!"

"—the Prince of Wales would reign over us, though he is still a babe, and has not yet done one thing to merit the Crown. Though neither has the King, some people would say."

Another splutter sounded behind the *Journal*. Wondering how a single newssheet could contain so much bad news, I continued: "Take Jediah—"

"I wish you would," said Lizzie. "Far, far away."

This earned her a smack on the back of the head from Mary. I ignored them both.

"Whether he pleases his tutor or not, or succeeds in college or not, he will become a man of consequence, because his father was one before him."

"Now I see the problem in your plan," said Jediah, with an odd little grin.

"Be quiet now," said Mother. "There'll be time enough for politics when you are older."

"Not to mention, the ragoo is ready and the pie is getting cold," said Mary.

Lizzie grabbed her spoon. "And I am starving."

Jediah seemed not to hear. "I am sorry to tell you this, James, but not everyone thinks as well of my father as you. Oh, they do not say it aloud for fear of offending me, but I know what they are thinking. What manner of gentleman is it, they wonder, who happily exiles himself from the land of his birth? Who would hunt plants rather than foxes? Or commits the worst sin of all—shunning polite society for the friendship of heathens and brutes? Surely no gentleman worthy of the title." He gasped for a breath when he stopped—

unsurprisingly, as he seldom spoke so many passionate words in one turn.

"Do not worry, cousin," I soothed. "Men of consequence care not one jot for such a little thing as their reputation."

"*Our* Father does," said Lizzie.

"You talk such nonsense." Mary elbowed her sister aside and started dividing the pie.

"I do not!" Lizzie rapped her spoon on the table, then dipped it into the pie dish and slurped up a mouthful of raisins and potatoes. "After Cheesecake Day, Father said his reputation was lower than a fussock's dumplings."

In the hush that followed, Father lowered the newssheet, refolded it along the crease, and placed it beside his plate. "Disgraceful child! You bring shame upon us all—and when we have company, too."

I started to beg yet again for forgiveness, but Father raised his hand and demanded silence.

"In the Sadler household, we thank the Lord for our bread *before* we eat. As well you know, Miss Elizabeth."

Lizzie pouted, but bowed her head with the rest of us.

As we tucked into our pie, peas, and ragoo, Mary turned to me and said, "You have told us where you *want* to go, little brother—but you forgot to say how you'll get there."

"With money, of course," I replied.

"Money?" Mary scoffed.

At the far end of the table, Mother frowned.

"Of course," said Jediah. "With money, a man might obtain whatever he wants—property or power, fine clothes or the best food and wine—"

"Or respect," I blurted.

He shot me an approving smile.

"If it is money you desire," said Father, drily, "I presume you'll be spending less of your time on daydreams and more helping me in the shop."

Our talk turned to other issues after that, though Mother remained aloof. When the meal was finished, and Mary washing the dishes, Father reading in the parlour, and Jediah abandoned to Lizzie's ministrations, she took me aside with a whisper: "Come with me, James. I have something to show you."

She led me down to the shop, and I wondered if this were some scheme of Father's. Would she offer me a barberry flan? A plum slice? Since "Cheesecake Day", Father had often remarked on the sure ruination awaiting a pastry-cook who baulks at the sight of sweetmeats. But then I realized Mother had her hat and shawl, and my coat in her hand.

"Put this on," she said. "It might be cold later."

"La—later?" I stammered in excitement—and not a little trepidation—at this hint I might be allowed to stay up past my bedtime. "Where are we going?"

Without a word, Mother opened the door to the High.

CHAPTER FOUR

OUR SHADOWS LENGTHENED with every stride as we crossed the Cherwell at Magdalen Bridge, then took the left turn at the toll-house and passed out of Oxford and into the parish of St Clement's. Then up the hill towards Headington; I soon lost count of the milestones and began to fear that Mother intended to walk me all the way to London, so long had we been on the move and so sore were my feet.

"Not far now," she said at each landmark, though for every step she took I had to take two or three more to keep pace, and it seemed that 'not far' for her might be an awful long way for me.

And then we had more climbing to do, and more still, and 'twas not 'til we reached the summit of Shotover Hill that we stopped.

"Here we are."

Mother led me a few steps further over the crest of the hill and down onto the westerly slope overlooking the city. I caught what remained of my breath at the view. Never before had I ventured so high. From the top of Old Crab's Tower, the townsfolk of Oxford had appeared tiny but I could see what they were about and put names to those I knew. From here, I could see no people nor any other living thing; 'twas as if a huge broom had swept them away, leaving buildings and streets but no sign of occupation. The city had stilled, like a frozen stream.

"Let us sit here and watch," Mother said.

So watch we did, side by side on the baked brown grass as the Sun went down. With naught but empty sky around us, I fancied we floated aloft in the Sun's airy realm, though I resisted an urge to wave at its bloated red face. For Mother was in a strange, sombre mood.

"Where does the Sun go at night?" I asked, instead.

"As the Earth turns about, its light falls on the far side of the world."

"As far away as China?"

"Even as far as China. During our night, 'tis daytime there. And after the Sun has set over China, it comes back to England for dawn."

"Jediah once told me that a giant black dragon swallows the Sun every night, then shats it out in the morning."

"I wouldn't believe everything Jediah says."

I silently concurred.

The heat of the day had departed along with the Sun (explaining, perhaps, why China was said to be devilish hot). I shivered inside my coat, wondering if Father had missed us. I wondered, too, if this was what Mother had meant me to see and whether we might go home now.

"See there—" She pointed Heavenward. "What is that?"

"The Moon, of course," I muttered.

"Very good. And how would it be, to live on the Moon, do you think?"

"Awfully cold, I should say." I pulled my coat tighter around me, yearning for my warm bed. "For mountains are tall and they are very cold, and the Moon is much higher in the sky than the mountains. And quiet, too, for there are no girls on the Moon, and girls love to chatter. Jediah says—" I stopped myself. "Does the Moon go to China, too, during our day?"

She nodded, her smile sketched in silver. My memory of my mother's face has faded over the years, but on silent moonlit nights, I still see her clearer than day.

"Might men travel there, one day in the future?" she asked.

"To the Moon? I should say not. No coaches run there and 'tis too far to walk. The Moon is much further from Oxford than London, I think."

Mother laughed. "You forget, James—most folk have no money for coaches and must walk wherever they go—to London or anywhere else."

"No man of consequence would traipse that far," I said. "A man of consequence would have his coachman drive him, for even the tiniest distance. And if he didn't have his carriage with him because he'd travelled to Oxford on the Dart, say, or if his coachman was drunk, he would hire a chaise from The Angel."

The silvered line of Mother's jaw hardened. "And you wish to become one of these men?"

I gazed upon the lifeless city descending into the dark; imagined seizing it in my hand and dragging it back into daylight.

"Yes, Mother," I said.

"Why?"

I hesitated. "No one laughs at them."

"'Tis not unreasonable, as ambitions go." She placed her arm about my shoulders. "But how will you achieve it?"

I shrugged. "I am sure something will come along."

"You do not think you will have to work for it?"

"A man of consequence has no need to work, not even to become a man of consequence in the first place. Whatever he desires... he gets."

Mother sighed. "A long time ago in a far-away land, there lived a young man. Just as you dream of becoming a man of consequence, he dreamed of travelling to the Moon. He studied the planets and stars his whole life, for he knew that nothing of worth is gained without work. By learning all that exists to be learned on the matter, he hoped he might one day conquer the Heavens."

I settled back on the cooling Earth, tucked my hands behind my head and surveyed the sky. 'Twould be splendid indeed to conquer it, though I wouldn't want to wait a whole lifetime. I said this to Mother, and the fairytale mood soured.

"You are always so impatient," she scolded. "Where would our family be now if your grandmother had thought that way? Or your father?"

Emboldened by the near-darkness, I pulled a scornful face.

"James! How dare you sneer! Your father devotes *his* life to his family and to the business his mother began—for all our sakes, but for you especially."

"But why must he be a *pastry-cook*?" I blurted. "What use is that?"

"What use is any man?" Mother cried. "What purpose does the butcher serve, or the baker, or the smith? Or the First Lord of the Admiralty? Or the King himself, for that matter?"

"At least they have peoples' respect," I muttered.

Mother chose not to reply to that and for a while we sat together in silence, two sparks between a pair of coal-black oceans—one a sea of stars, the other as still as a mill pond except for the puny flickers of flame that dotted the darkness here and there. It occurred to me that the stars might not be distant Suns as learned men said, but fires in the hearths and lamps in the windows of houses in the sky. I gazed upon the Moon's stony face, wondering at the nature of its occupants, and whether they ever looked up at their own night sky and thought the same thoughts as I.

"What happened to the man who wished to travel to the Moon?" I asked. "Did he get there in the end?"

"I shall give you a book," said Mother, "and when you are ready, you will know."

"Can't you tell me now?"

"Have patience, James."

She leaned over to kiss me on the head, as if I were a baby; embarrassed, I shied away, and loftily declared, "I think I do not need to read it. For if he had conquered the Heavens, I am sure I would know his name. Which means he failed, and wasted all his time and work."

"Was it wasted?" Mother asked. "Those who came after him built their own work upon his. Without the efforts of men like him, each new generation would have to start from the very beginning, again and again. Now *that* would be a waste of time. And here we are, talking about him long after his death. Can you really say that nothing came of his life? He was, I would say,

31

a man of consequence, for what he achieved had consequences for the future."

I frowned at the Moon, which seemed to frown back. "A man of consequence," I mused, "is a man whose deeds have consequence."

I had by now grown accustomed to the cold, but Mother suddenly shivered beneath her thin woollen shawl.

"Come, we must get back," she said, her usual, sensible manner returning. "'Tis late, and you should have been in bed hours ago."

I'd been dreading the long walk home, but the prospect seemed less daunting now. 'Twould not be so arduous, I reasoned, as our journey up the hill. And such was the case, though I do not remember one step of it. Even my blistered feet were forgot, for my thoughts had flown elsewhere.

~ ~ ~

I struggled to sleep that night. Each time I closed my eyes, I entered, not the Land of Nod, but the Heavenly realm of Moon and Sun—counting minutes and hours instead of sheep, and wondering where in the world the two orbs might be found at each moment. And as soon as I did begin to doze, I was startled half-awake again by a creak from the loose floorboard outside my room.

Had the man who would conquer the Moon come to take me along? I wobbled out from under my blanket to investigate, but saw naught on the stair besides a flicker of light from the parlour below. Only when I started to close the door, did I notice an object upon the floor. I stooped to pick it up: a book, with well-worn leather covers. Squinting in the gloom, I glanced inside and saw my mother's handwriting on the otherwise blank first page.

You will understand when you are ready.

Frowning, I turned to the next page, and the next, then flicked all the way through to the end. I spotted not one word of my native tongue, and though my reading was not so good at that time, I had learned enough to hazard a guess that the book was written in Latin. I could no more comprehend the close-packed text than I could the cryptic scratchings that passed for illustrations, so I closed the door, blotting out the light from the parlour, and crept back to bed in the dark, holding the mysterious volume tight.

"I shall give you a book, and when you are ready, you will know."

Know what? I mused. Know Latin? But that was surely a means not an end, and in her note Mother had said understand. If I knew Latin, I would understand the book—but what did *that* mean?

The answer arrived with the morning. I had hardly slept a wink while the Sun rolled around from China, but my mind—and my purpose—became clear with the dawn.

Something else my mother had said was the clue.

"Nothing of worth is gained without work."

Reading the book would be hard work indeed, which suggested its contents were worth a great deal. So great, in fact, that they had to include the knowledge I craved above all—the means by which a commonplace man might became a man of consequence. I hugged the book close, as I would my mother had she been there. Her pensive mood had perplexed me, but now I felt certain that, far from frowning upon my ambition, she had entrusted me with all I needed to achieve it.

CHAPTER FIVE

W E DID NOT SPEAK of that evening again, but when Michaelmas Term came around and 'twas time for me to resume my schoolwork, I returned to the classroom uncommonly enthused.

For one whole year already, I had been required to attend—on every Sunday afternoon and two mornings per fortnight—Mr Nixon's Free Grammar School, which occupied a handsome property constructed during the Commonwealth in the courtyard behind the Town Hall. Father was anxious that I should get an education, for he'd had none as a boy and all he knew he had taught himself. Surmising that left to my own instruction, *I* would learn not one whit, he had enrolled me for two years at Mr Nixon's, against my loudest protests.

My classmates were the sons of other Townsmen of ambition but limited means; our schoolmaster was an embittered old toper who believed boys to be naturally stupid and capable of absorbing new facts only when these were accompanied by frequent lashings with tongue, cane, or both. Our schooling may have been free to our fathers, but we pupils paid dearly for our reading and writing, catechizing, and keeping accounts.

Once the laziest of pupils, the start of my second year found me by far the keenest. This earned me fewer whippings, if not the affection of my classmates, and I soon got ahead of our simple curriculum and began to supplement my schoolwork with lessons at home. By now, I knew the name of the man who aspired to fly to the Moon (a certain Mr Kepler of Prague) and sorely desired to also know his fate—and through it, my own. We learned a little of the Latin tongue in class, but nowhere near enough for my needs, so I resolved to master the language for myself.

To my surprise, Mother was quick to offer her help; the source of my wonderment, I think, was not that the wife of a pastry-cook should know such things, but that a woman should. No girl had ever studied at Mr Nixon's and I had come to consider the female sex ill-fitted for scholarship. How wrong I was! My mother not only proved an excellent teacher, but also possessed an extraordinary collection of books, which she kept in a trunk beneath her and Father's bed.

I reasoned that, Mother being Uncle Elijah's sister, and Uncle Elijah being an eccentric man, their father must have been a queer sort, too—such oddities of personality often running in families—and this would explain why Grandfather Temple had provided as fine an education for his daughter as his son. I learned that my grandfather had studied the stars almost as keenly as Mr Kepler, which must have accounted for my mother's grasp of the Sun and Moon and their workings.

As my own knowledge increased, so did the hours I spent alone in my room. With Homer and Livy for company, I had little time for my sisters' bickering, less still for Jediah's increasingly frequent and tiresome calls. My cousin was now up at St Alban's, though not so busy he lacked the time to annoy me at every opportunity. On one occasion, after insisting he joined me uninvited, he prattled to such a tedious extent about so inconsequential a matter concerning his own studies, I could understand why his tutor might have wanted to throw a book at him. It took a deal of restraint not to do so myself; that, and the fact that *my* copy of Plato's *Apology* belonged to my mother, and I would never risk doing it harm.

I worked furiously through Michaelmas, over Christmas, and into January, pausing only when a fever confined me to bed for more than a month. Of the first week of my illness, I remember little except my mother's tender smile and the cooling touch of her hand on my brow. During the second and third weeks, her visits to my bedside grew fewer, and by the fourth 'twas Mary who brought my meals and grudgingly saw to my toilet. As my wits returned, I became aware that there were more people about the house than usual, though thankfully they left me in peace. With time on my hands, I took up my books and continued my studies.

'Twas on the third day of the fifth week of my illness, during the sixth book of Virgil's *Aeneid*, that I first encountered a passage I failed to decipher. Had my head been clearer, I might have persevered and unravelled for myself the tale of the Trojan's descent to the Underworld. Had I been weaker, I might have remained in my room. But restless after being shut up so long, I hobbled down to the kitchen, barefoot and clad only in my nightdress. There I found not Mother, but Lizzie, and a washerwoman of Mother's acquaintance from Horsemill Lane. In every way, that scene was amiss; not least, the pair were seated at the table, though no meal was due for hours. The washerwoman I knew to be a cold and curmudgeonly spinster who would normally cross the street to avoid a child—yet Lizzie, always the most cheerful of we three siblings, was now allowed to sob wretchedly on her shoulder.

But too concerned with Aeneas and the Sybil to care about this, I ignored the washerwoman's attempts to shush me and demanded, "Where is Mother? I must speak to her at once. Quickly, Elizabeth!"

Lizzie wailed and pressed her face into the washerwoman's bosom, just as Mary came into the kitchen behind me and hissed, "What was it that made you so selfish, James?"

From her reddened eyes and nose, I guessed Mary had been weeping too, though she spoke from behind an expressionless mask that scared me far more than her tears might have done. Seized with dread, I bolted back up the stairs, to our parent's room on the floor above. There, another neighbour I barely knew—this one got up in a black bonnet and gloves—stood guard beside the door.

"I want to see my mother."

Black-bonnet shook her head. "She is too poorly for visitors, my love."

"I want to see my mother." I advanced a step, but Black-bonnet held firm.

"I am so sorry," she said.

Then I heard Mother's voice from within, speaking my name. Without pause, I rushed Black-bonnet and charged at the door. 'Twas, of course, unlocked, and I shot half-way through the room before I stumbled to a halt, babbling about Anchises and the Elysian Fields, and how we must send all these strange people away.

"You are well again, son?"

She sat propped up in bed like a doll, on crisp, white pillows, her hands limp on the sheets, Father close beside her. Together with an elderly matron I recognized as his great-aunt from Bampton, he sat upon the couch that normally rested beneath the window, where the light was good and Mother had first acquainted me with Virgil.

"James!" Father spoke through clenched teeth. "What are you doing in here?"

"Do not send him away," Mother whispered.

My feet must have carried me towards the bed of their own volition, for I did not instruct them to do so; in truth, I did not want them to, for fear of what I would see. But Mother's face was indistinct in the half-light from the shuttered window.

"Be a good boy for your father and sisters," she said.

I heard Father stifle a sob. Beside him, the old woman opened the Bible on her lap and in a bone-dry rasp began to read aloud from the Psalms.

"'Tis time to leave," said Father softly, rising from the couch to usher me out.

Through welling tears, I snatched a last glance at the bed and its fading occupant.

"Do not neglect your studies," Mother said, her voice unexpectedly clear, though her gaze seemed focussed elsewhere.

Then I was back outside with Black-bonnet, the door shut firmly behind me, and I saw her face no more.

CHAPTER SIX

THE FUNERAL FELL ON A DESOLATE winter morning, under clouds as heavy as frozen lead and a pallid Sun without warmth or lustre. 'Twas in a weird half-twilight, though it not yet be noon, that we gathered outside the shop, then trudged across the High to lay Mother to rest in the dank, dismal Earth.

A goodly crowd joined us for the solemnities at St Peter-in-the-East: relatives, neighbours, and friends of my parents I recognized, plus many I did not. I recalled the previous year's Amphibalian Benefaction and Father's fears for the family's reputation. Fortunately, no one else appeared to remember it—'twould have only added to my grief, had my misdeeds caused a poor turnout today.

By the end of the service the day had become so dark, the verger brought a lamp to light our procession into the churchyard, where Mother, closed up in her coffin ("Best quality money can buy," Father had boasted, "finest elm with silvered handles, tin-dipped lace, and a good strong lock!") was placed in the sexton's care.

41

Father and I watched from the head of the grave as the casket descended; opposite us at the foot, Lizzie clung miserably to Mary, while Mary maintained the vacant face she had worn since the day Mother died. Jediah stood alone as usual, and for once I envied him. If Uncle Elijah were to perish, would Jediah miss him as much as I missed my mother? I doubted it. He bore a sick, pinched expression throughout the interment, though he had seemed well enough earlier when devouring the sweetmeats intended for our guests.

As we made our way back into Edmund Hall Lane, hushed voices passed comment on the weather, the Rev. Slade's sermon, and the cruel Hand of Fate, that should seize a mother so young.

"At least," said one, to much accord, "her memory will be preserved, for she has raised three sturdy children."

Jediah, who was dawdling behind me, snorted. "That would be two sturdy children, surely?"

I ignored him, being in no mood for banter.

"That is to say, just look at you, James—you are naught but a bag of bones."

I quickened my stride, but he grabbed my coat and swung me around to face him.

"I am sorry, cousin. Please do forgive." He mustered a wan smile. "I only meant to cheer you up. 'Twas just a joke, you understand?"

Then Father came alongside us, and with forced levity demanded, "What goes here boys? Not more squabbling, I hope. What would your mother say, James? Or your father, Jediah?"

Jediah muttered indistinctly and slunk back into the crowd, while Father and I walked onto the High side by side, his hand heavy upon my shoulder. The deepening gloom had already swallowed University College and the grand façade of The Queen's, but lamps blazed merrily in the windows of Tillyard's and the Salutation Inn, and squeezed between them our shop looked cold and empty. I knew a good spread awaited us ("Your mother would want no less for her family and friends," Father had said), but I had no appetite for company.

No one noticed me slip upstairs to my room. I closed the door on the muted conversation in the parlour, removed my shoes, and sat on my bed. In the roof directly over my head, a small, ill-fitted light provided the only illumination. I had dragged my bed beneath it after our evening on Shotover Hill, to follow the stars before I slept and then to dream of flying amongst them. To my delight, I'd discovered the Moon itself traversed my square of sky some nights. But this would not be one of them. I went to my writing-desk—a dilapidated fitment Mother had rescued from a bonfire last November the Fifth—and my hand fell upon the most valuable of all her gifts.

IOH. KEPPLERI

MATHEMATICI OLIM IMPERATORII

SOMNIUM

SEU OPVS POSTHVMVM DE ASTRONOMIA LUNARI

Although my studies had stalled, the title page at least no longer perplexed me: *The Dream by Johannes Kepler, Mathematician to Rudolph the Second of the*

Holy Roman Empire, a work published posthumously on the Astronomy of the Moon.

I turned its coarsely ribbed leaves, my fingertips tingling. 'Twas too dark to read. Then the doorknob squeaked and Jediah peeked round the frame.

"Friends again?" he ventured.

I said nothing.

"Excellent. Your mother wouldn't wish us to fall out, especially today." Without further encouragement, he let himself in and flopped on the bed beside me. "You did well to escape up here. In all my life, I swear I have never encountered a more wretched herd of knights and barrow-pigs... What have you there?" he added, pointing at the book.

I hesitated. "One evening last summer..."

"Get to it, coz! The sweetmeats are going like lightning."

"One evening last summer, Mother took me to see the stars. She taught me about the Sun and the Moon, and how a man of consequence is a man whose deeds have consequences."

Jediah laughed. "I'd forgotten that silly debate we had over tea. You dearly wanted *something*, you said, but had no idea what, nor how you'd get it. Have you found any answers yet?"

"She said I would understand when I am ready." I looked down at the book, holding it tight in both hands as if the slightest breath of air might blow it away. "'Twas true, what the minister said."

"Of course it was. Ministers always speak the truth."

"*Ashes to ashes, dust to dust.*" I sighed. "Butchers, bakers, smiths—all become dust. The First Lord of the Admiralty, even the King. And Mr Kepler. And Mother."

Jediah rose from the bed and placed a hand on my forearm with the barest squeeze. I supposed he was trying to comfort me.

"Do not worry, James. She will surely dwell for eternity in Heaven with Our Lord. From the highest to the lowest, He knows them all."

Whilst I had known my cousin less well than I'd thought! Jediah had always held firm to his faith, but never before had he sounded so smugly pious.

"'Tis easier," I gabbled, unable to stop now I had started, "if you are the First Lord of the Admiralty or the King. Men will write poems about you, and paint your portrait, and when you are dead you will have your tomb in Westminster Abbey. And when men of the future read the poems, and see the paintings and the tomb, they will know that you once lived."

The light had all but gone while we'd been talking; Jediah's face was now an indistinct smudge amidst shadows that had already swallowed the brickwork, the beams that spanned the roof, and even my writing desk. Clutching Kepler's book, I rocked myself back and forth, as Mother used to rock me when I was small and could not sleep.

"But who will remember the butcher, the baker, the smith? Or my mother? Or me? When everyone who knew us is dead themselves, there will be no one left to remember us and we'll all be nothing but dust."

"Take heart, James. On the Day of Judgement, we shall all rise from the grave and the righteous will enter God's Kingdom."

"God's Kingdom? Why would I wish to live in that cruel place?"

"You must not speak like that."

"I will speak however I wish. God cares nothing for me. He took my mother away."

"God loves you, and your mother too."

"My mother is dust!" I raised my face to the empty black rooflight above me. "But I shall become a man of consequence, and when people remember me, they'll remember her."

Jediah sniggered. "Not that again! The sorry truth, James, is that your father is naught but a pastry-cook, and *his* father was a gambler and a drunkard. 'Twould be easier to raise your mother from the dead, than your lowborn station in life."

I hugged the book closer still. "My deeds will have consequences. I shall become a man of science, like Mr Kepler."

"A man of science?" The mocking tone turned to horror.

"I will go to the Moon."

"You cannot go to the Moon!" My cousin's distress was obvious, even in darkness.

"I can try, at least," I said. "And if I fail, men of the future will use my work to go there themselves."

"Men cannot go to the Moon. That would be— 'twould be against God's will."

"Then why give us brains at all, if we must not use them?" I cried, and wondered how, in just a few months, Jediah's studies of logic, music, and art could have kindled such zeal.

Jediah took a long, shuddering breath, but his manner turned friendly again. "I fear 'twill be a struggle indeed, to become a man of science—more so even than a man of consequence. Where will you learn all those tedious facts, for a start?"

"First, I will read Mr Kepler's book. When I have enough Latin."

"Who will teach you? Not that idiot schoolmaster."

"I will teach myself! In fact—in fact, I have already begun. And when I am done, I shall go up to St Alban's like you."

"That would require a great deal of money. How will you pay for it?"

"I will find a way."

"And if you *do* get to St Alban's, I think you will find it not quite what you expect. One's university days are short and said to be the best of one's life, so no one wastes much time on their studies. The Undergraduates spend their mornings sleeping, their afternoons drinking and dicing, and their evenings recovering from their afternoons before their night-time amusements begin. And the Fellows are no better. No one does much work at St Alban's—or any other college. No one of any consequence, that is."

Glad that Jediah could not see my face, I replied, "Then I shall be different."

"You would spare yourself years of drudgery, if you let someone read your book for you."

"I couldn't do that. Mother wanted me to read it for myself."

"I could read it."

I shook my head.

"We are cousins. We share the same blood. It would be almost like reading it yourself."

"Nothing of worth is gained without work. Mother told me so."

"If you believe that, you have more to learn than you think."

I heard the floorboards creak, but that warning came too late; I could only protest "Hey—that's mine!", as unseen hands tore Mother's gift from my arms. An instant later, the door reopened.

"I shall read this—" Jediah hoisted the book above his head in triumphant silhouette. "—and let you know what happens."

"Give it back!" I rushed after him down the stairs and into the parlour. When I caught up, he had taken Mother's favourite chair by the fireplace, his clumsy paws all over her book. Before I could beg him to be more careful, assorted knights and barrow-pigs descended upon me with their condolences, commiserations, and insistences that I must eat *something*, be it only a sliver of bean-cake or no more than a chocolate pastil. Father saved me with a call from across the room.

"'Tis timely that you join us, son. I am about to propose a toast."

I nodded, smiled bravely, thanked our guests for their consideration, then hurried back to Jediah. He had stopped manhandling the book, but had it open at the last page and appeared so engrossed he failed to notice me.

"Please give it back."

He glanced up, wide-eyed. "I guessed you would be in a hurry, so I took the liberty of reading the end of the story first."

"I want to read it myself."

"Are you sure?" He snapped the book shut. "Your mother took this secret to her grave. Do you not want to know it? Today, of all days?"

I bit down hard on my lower lip, wary of what I might say if I let myself speak.

Then came a sudden lull in the conversation; Father had moved to the centre of the assembly, and flanked by Lizzie and Mary, he thanked our guests for coming and called upon them all to lift their glasses. Much chinking and supping ensued, and it seemed an odd way to remember a woman who never took a drink except at Christmas. Father's speech came next, followed by a round of applause, during which Jediah caught my attention. He looked flushed in the heat from the fire, idly fanning his face with his prize.

"Can I have it back now?" I asked meekly.

"Of course. I only borrowed it."

He rose from Mother's chair and leaned towards me, the book balanced precariously on the fingertips of one hand. With the flames just a wobble away, I snatched it to safety quick as a fiddler.

~ ~ ~

'Twas not the Sun or the Moon but thoughts of the grave that kept me awake that night, though once again I was lured from my bed by a sudden disturbance. I crept to the door as before, daring to dream that I'd find, not just Mr Kepler, but my mother too, both of them alive and well upon the landing. In the half-light, though, I spied only Father, and he was on his way down rather than up, manoeuvring a cumbrous object around the turn in the staircase beneath my parents' room. 'Twas Mother's trunk of books, I realized with a jolt. The books she'd preserved all her life, a testament to her singular education. And more to the point, books I would need to read myself, were I ever to master *Somnium*.

As I watched, horrified, the trunk became stuck at an angle, refusing to budge no matter how much

Father cursed it. I would have begged him to stop, had the shock not clenched my throat as tight as the stair-well. But even had it not, 'twould have been too late. With a final, almighty shove, Father, the trunk—and my future, it seemed—turned the corner and left me behind.

PART II

CHAPTER SEVEN

'TWAS APRIL IN THE YEAR OF OUR LORD Seventeen Eighty-Four when Uncle Elijah joined his sister in the Hereafter. As certain wags observed of the funeral, 'twas the first family function he had attended in fifty years. If Jediah heard these jests, he did not dignify them with a rejoinder. He spoke barely a word to anyone, in fact, remaining unmoved by the readings and sermon, silent during the Prayer for Those Who Mourn. Not even when they laid his father to rest did he shed a tear, though he spared a sorrowful glance for the graves of the elder Temple's two wives. Crusts of sulphurous yellow lichen had already partly obscured those ladies' names, and the marble headstones themselves, I supposed, would one day crumble to dust. However deep the mason's cut, no memorial to Elijah Temple—nor any one of us—would last forever.

"Try not to upset yourself, James," said Lizzie beside me. "Uncle Elijah's life was long, and more exciting than anything we timid souls could imagine."

I smiled down at her as she reached to brush a loose strand of hair from my face. The touch of her glove felt like butterfly wings; the sheerest, softest kid-skin.

"You are right, of course," I said. "Our uncle was made of sturdy stuff." I took her arm and drew her aside from our fellow mourners. "Do you remember that tale of Mother's about Jediah? How he begged over and over to join his father—*ekkipedishunning*, he called it—from almost as soon as he learned how to speak? And then, when Elijah could bear it no more and allowed him along, he repaid that indulgence by guzzling down a whole quart of the seeds they'd collected?"

Lizzie grimaced. "I heard he nearly died."

I peered over my shoulder, but the others had lined up to thank the vicar and no one stood within earshot. "What you may not have heard," I whispered, "is all the while that Jediah lay ill, our uncle defied his physician like an angry mama bear, so anxious was he to remain at his side at all times. He refused to leave for even a second."

"He must have been dreadfully worried."

"Yes, but not about Jediah. 'Twas the return of his seeds he awaited. They were rare and exceedingly precious, you understand."

Lizzie covered her mouth with a dainty hand, disguising her laugh as a cough when she caught my meaning. "Poor Jediah. 'Tis no wonder he grew up so glum. But why did he eat the seeds in the first place?"

"For attention?"

I stole a glance at our cousin, who had not moved—or perhaps even breathed—since his father's committal. His features, habitually gaunt and grey, were no more or less doleful than usual, and far from being diminished by his loss, he seemed taller than ever—like a plant that had outgrown itself looking for light.

"Uncle Elijah's favourite children lived in his garden," I said. "But who would blame him? Even a hogweed surpasses our Jediah in charm and good cheer."

"That is childish, ill-timed, and uncalled-for, James Sadler." Lizzie frowned at me as we stepped from the churchyard onto The Plain and into a raw, northerly breeze. "But now you are back to your usual, thoughtless self—" She clutched at her hat and lofty white wig. "—you must tell me all your news."

"My news?"

"I am sure the world kept turning after I left. How goes your new career, for instance? How is dear Dr Crouch? And Father—has he forgiven you yet?"

I shrugged. "Drearily. Bothersome, as always. And no."

"Well! If that is all you have to say, I am *glad* you do not write as often as you promised."

She pouted, then burst into giggles so infectious I had to join in, earning disapproving glares from behind the lych-gate.

"Oh Lizzie, I do miss you," I sighed.

"You must visit," she said. "Burleigh would be delighted to have you—wouldn't you, darling?" She raised her voice and waved to her husband.

Burleigh Barrington-Smyth, being a sensible man, had taken shelter out of the icy wind with Father, the pair of them pressed against the southern face of the little octagonal toll-house that marked the entrance to Magdalen Bridge. Between us and them trundled a herd of long-horned oxen, barely ten hands high at the withers but so fat they had to walk in single file to fit through the toll-gate. Their drovers were equally sluggish, and Burleigh had to negotiate man and beast alike to attend to his wife.

"I had forgotten how... *countrified* you are," he muttered, balancing on one foot to inspect the underside of the other. "Here in Oxford, I mean—not you personally, of course, James."

"I should hope not," said Lizzie. "For James will soon be joining us as our house guest."

"James will be going nowhere."

'Twas Father, shouting whilst he stomped through the thick of the herd like a choleric carthorse. He joined us with a nod to Burleigh, his round, red face set firm.

"I thank you for your hospitality, but my son has no time for jaunts. He already cuts his pastry too thin."

"Oh, Father!" Lizzie cried. "What about *my* pastry?" She stamped her prettily-shod foot upon the dirt, and I almost laughed again. My little sister might have acquired a well-to-do husband and a splendid townhouse in London, but to me she would always remain a girl playing ladies and gents.

"I never have guests of my own. Tell him, Burleigh."

"I will, my darling." Burleigh gathered her clenched fists in his hands. "But let us get indoors first, eh? We shall catch a chill in this breeze, and you know that old saying about funerals."

Father nodded. "'Tis true, they always come in pairs. And here we are, standing around like noodleheads in the cold, when we have a warm fire waiting at Cowley Hall—and sweetmeats supplied by my humble self, of course."

He began shepherding Lizzie and Burleigh down the turn that led to the Temples' house, but I did not follow; instead, I hastened to the toll-gate, in the steaming wake of the last of the oxen.

"James!" Lizzie called after me. "Are you not joining us?"

"See what I have to endure?" said Father, loud enough that I might hear. "Rather than raising a glass to departed kin, your brother would rather scuttle off to his beloved elaboratory."

I halted and turned about, gritting my teeth. "You mean my *laboratory*, Father. How often must I remind you? No one uses that word any more—it belongs to the last century, whilst we are almost in the next! Your elaboratories are naught but relics of the days of alchemy and turning lead into gold."

"Accomplish *that* feat," said Father, "and I might speak of your dungeon more kindly."

"'Twould take a miracle, I fear," said Burleigh. "My chymistry is a little rusty, but I do recall a lecture by Dr Wall on the transmutation of the elements, and he was of the opinion that—" He stopped with a strangled yelp.

"Come, Burleigh," said Lizzie, "we must stake our claim to the hearth seats before the others arrive. Cowley Hall is so dreadfully draughty."

She hastened down the turn, tugging a limping Burleigh behind her. Father, however, remained in the road.

"Your mother would be so ashamed," he said. "Family meant more than life itself to Anne Sadler. Will you not show her brother a little respect? For the sake of her memory, if not to please me."

I glared at him as a merry shout sounded ahead of us.

"What in Heaven's name is keeping you both? Last one to bag a comfit is a maggotty old gollumpus!"

Father shook his head in despair. "Your sisters are both such duteous children. Why must you be different? Perhaps you would be more grateful for what you have, had you suffered the deprivations *I* once endured—"

"I am late for my shift," I said, which true, though I was more anxious to avoid yet another retelling of Father's life story. "We are short-handed, so I have extra work today. And have you not told me time and again? *A man's worth is measured in the hardships of his labour.*"

"Hardships borne for the benefit of his family," Father growled. "Dilly-dallying in your elaboratory is not work—still less hard work—and 'tis not your family who benefit when you scorn the business your grandmother built from nothing."

"As you wish." I could have reminded him of my modest laboratory stipend, passed weekly straight from my purse to the family moneybox; or that I continued to serve in the shop as well and thus did the work of not one man but two. But I feared nit-picking would serve me no better than Father's obstinacy served him, so I simply said again, "I am late for my shift. I shall be back to help Mary close up, but first I must go dilly-dally in my elaboratory. It might not seem hard work to you, but to me, 'tis a noble endeavour."

I meant these to be my last words on the subject and had taken several strides towards the bridge before Father shouted after me: "A noble endeavour is sorrow and sweat, and sacrifice for flesh and blood. Not a chase after selfish dreams."

To myself, I muttered, "Like Uncle Elijah?" and looked back at the Church of St Clement, where Jediah still stood by the open grave, as if he were not yet convinced his father was dead and would not be so until he had seen him completely buried. His gaze met mine across The Plain, though he could not have heard me speak. I wondered if there were tears in his eyes. I fancied I'd caught a glimpse of something. Then a shower of soil and dust claimed my cousin's attention, as the sexton set to work with his spade.

~ ~ ~

I stopped off at the shop on my way, though I intended to spend a minute at most dashing in and out, plus another two or three to change out of my Sunday suit. Mary was occupied with a customer on my arrival (Father being of the opinion that, for my elder sister at least, raising a glass to departed kin was less important than turning a profit), but she accosted me the instant I reappeared in my regular clothes.

"Is it over already?" she asked.

"I left early," I grunted.

"'Tis not like you to be so keen. Not that I am complaining—it's been madness here all morning. I haven't had a moment's rest, nor even time for the delivery round. I shall do it now you are here." She reached beneath the counter for the big wicker basket and the cheesecloth canopy we used to keep the flies off.

"I am not stopping," I said, before she could untie her apron strings and locate her hat. "I am needed at the laboratory. Where is Billy? Can't he mind the shop?"

"He took the day off. His grandmother is sick, so he says. But anyway, you know Father doesn't like him serving the customers."

"Of course, I forgot—this is a *family* business." I scowled. "Too bad he let Lizzie get away. He didn't so much gain a son-in-law as lose a pair of hands behind the counter."

"James!"

And how I wished it were Lizzie who Fortune had cursed with unlovely looks and a foul temper, and Mary who'd married and moved far away.

"You may have to close up alone tonight," I said. "Then again, maybe not. I may be back early. Or late. Who knows? Best not wait for me, eh?"

Scant chance *she* would ever wed, I thought, as she fretted and fumed. She grew more objectionable by the day. I was spared further annoyance by the arrival of another customer, her entrance announced by a jolly jingle from the tiny brass bells suspended on a string above the door—one of Father's rare whimsies. At the very first chime, Mary snapped to attention like a soldier on parade.

"May I help Madam?"

"I hear you have fresh cheesecake today," said the matron.

I slipped away while slices were sampled and orange and lemon flavours compared. Outside, the battered old shop sign creaked in the breeze.

Tho. Sadler, Pastry-cook & Confectioner

As I hastened up the High, I was more determined than ever that it would never read *& Son*.

CHAPTER EIGHT

COME LATER THAT AFTERNOON, my time served in the *Officina Chimica*—or the University's 'Chemistry Laboratory', as it came to be known—would total exactly five months, three weeks, and two days. I knew this because I had lately started to tally the time in my head, as a convict might mark the days of his confinement upon the wall of his cell—though while the convict's sentence was sure to end in release or execution, mine could only grow ever longer, with no hope of freedom, or even death.

I could never, ever let Father know, but I detested my 'noble endeavour' with a vengeance.

My aim in taking the post had been twofold: first, to begin a long-postponed career in natural philosophy; second, to definitively assert my independence (and thereby frustrate Tho. Sadler, Pastry-cook & Confectioner). The latter had been guaranteed from the start; the former eluded me still.

For a time before my appointment, I had extended a helping hand to the gentlemen of the *Officina*, running errands and the like (in my own time and *gratis*) on the presumption that, when a paid position arose, 'twould ensure me speedy promotion through the ranks. Fool that I was! For as soon as I was employed, I went overnight from valued assistant to lowliest drudge, obliged to perform all the filthiest and most noisome of tasks. Nor could I resign, for Father would have delighted in my surrender. And so I found myself as much a prisoner in the stone-vaulted basement of the Old Ashmolean on Broad Street as in the pastry-shop on the High.

In those dark days divided between two dungeons, I had one source of light: my Philosophical Club. 'Twas not strictly my club, you understand, for I was not its founder, but I had attended its meetings for longer than any other current member—three or four years at that time—and so felt fondly proprietorial towards it. I can laugh now at our pompous airs and graces, but in the year of which I speak, our meetings were a precious respite from a world where those who toiled the hardest and asked the fewest questions were best rewarded. In the smoky backroom of Harper's Coffee-house, a man's worth was measured only by his capacity for intelligent discourse. Or so I naïvely believed.

'Twas our custom that, during one meeting in each University term, a member chosen by lot would chair a discussion on a theme of his own devising. This Trinity Term that honour had fallen to me and I was anxious to make a good show of it, though with two jobs to juggle I had little spare time for invention. The constant interruptions in the shop had proved too distracting, so I had written much of my thesis at my work-bench in the laboratory, where I hid my papers inside the order book (of which I was custodian) and pretended to be doing the work I was paid for when anyone came too near. I had laboured in this way for three days short of a month, but just as I applied the finishing touches to my address, on the very day I was due to deliver it, my luck expired.

"What are you doing there, Sadler? Reading? No time for reading in *my* elaboratory!"

As Dainty Lecturer in Chemistry (and could one imagine a less-fitting epithet?), Solomon Crouch served as Dr Wall's deputy in the Department. 'Twas rumoured he started out as amiable as any other young man of science, but lost all faith in his peers when a rival stole his work and passed it off as his own. Since that setback, Crouch had harboured such a violent mistrust of natural philosophers, one wondered how he accommodated this view with being one himself. Perhaps 'twas some resultant inner turmoil that accounted for his many disturbing proclivities.

Especially irksome was his habit of creeping up behind an unwary subordinate, waiting for circumstances guaranteed to cause an upset, then bellowing at his victim through the narrow end of his ear-horn, as though the poor fellow were as deaf as Crouch claimed to be. My own hearing being excellent, I seldom fell prey—except on this occasion, when I was so caught up in my speechifying I failed to notice his looming bulk.

"I wasn't reading!" I yelped, barely able to hear myself above the ringing in my ears. "I was writing. In my journal."

"Journal? What journal?" Crouch lowered his horn, but his voice remained loud enough to rattle nerves and bottle-stoppers alike. At his post by the reverberatory, my colleague Nugent winced.

"My laboratory journal."

"What laboratory?"

"Your laboratory. I mean—your *elaboratory*. You instructed us to record the details of all that we do each day. So you might decide who will stay and who to let go, should economies be needed."

"Do not think I have forgotten!" Crouch yelled. "But I must deliver three lectures on the pneumatic chymistry this week, and the operations are in a parlous state. Test-glasses—filthy. Florence flasks—filthier still. Air-pump—failing for the dozenth time this year. How am I to instruct and inform, given such shoddy equipment and idle, drunken operators? One might think they *wanted* my lectures to seem second rate—"

I pushed my speech back inside the order book and hurried to the washbowl in case Crouch launched upon a rant concerning the malign intentions of Dr Wall (who neglected to appreciate his genius), certain Regents of the University Convocation (who had conspired to thwart his promotion), and natural philosophers throughout Europe (who schemed unceasingly to suppress all his greatest discoveries). As I set to work, my own mind began to wander—as it commonly did when not required—while my hands, reduced to unsupervised machines, scrubbed scorched earthenware crucibles and grubby green glass phials.

Should I open my speech with an illustration of my argument or an anecdote? Should I invite questions from the start or request that my audience wait for the end? My subject was both close to my heart and sure to excite much interest, and I did not want to become sidetracked by a barrage of irrelevant queries. Perhaps I should intercept William Tench before the meeting and recruit him to raise the points I wished to address...

At this juncture, my hands—as untended machines are wont—malfunctioned, and a fine (and extremely expensive) Venetian-glass retort slipped through my fingers and smashed on the flagstones.

"You clumsy sapscull!" roared Crouch. "Is there no end to your incompetence?"

"I shall fetch a broom," I mumbled.

"You shall stand aside and touch nothing—not one thing, do you hear? Mr Nugent!"

Nugent jumped at Crouch's shout, his shovel wavering between the coal scuttle and the reverberatory's firebox. I glanced at the old brass lantern-clock on the wall above the door. This venerable timepiece did not have a minute hand, as was the fashion when it was made, but 'twas clear that the end of my shift was approaching. I hoped Crouch would send me home and have done with it.

"Take over here, Mr Nugent. Sadler will sweep the furnaces—even he can do no harm there."

I gnashed my teeth and clenched my fists, but Solomon Crouch was not so easily defied as my elder sister.

Of all the chores I despised, sweeping the furnaces was the worst. The soot took days to scour from the skin and the ashes found their way everywhere—skin, hair, ears, eyes; I once found grubby smudges inside my smallclothes. To save myself from airborne filth, I had taken to wearing a strip of linen around my nose and mouth, but my lungs felt begrimed nonetheless, my throat parched like a month-old meringue.

I started with the smaller furnaces at the western end of the chamber, shovelling their contents into a heavy wooden pail and lugging them into the yard outside. Here, they swelled a heap that not only grew more noxious with every addition, but took a seemingly conscious delight in belching unwholesome fumes at every slightest agitation. 'Twas Hellish work—and worse still, my shift had almost finished. If I stayed much longer, I would be late for my meeting, though I could hardly mention that to Dr Crouch.

I had stopped for a moment to wipe my soiled brow when a voice called down to me from the stairway outside the *Musæum Ashmoleanum*. In those days, the refuse-strewn yard with its single, narrow door provided the *Officina Chimica*'s sole means of access, while the museum, which occupied the three floors above it, boasted a rather grander frontage, with gilded double doors and steps hewn from Headington hardstone. 'Twas claimed this arrangement served as a safety measure. Were an operation to end in disaster, and the laboratory and all within it reduced to ash, Mr Tradescant's collections at least would survive. Although, in my opinion, the museum's refusal to share so little as a door with the laboratory, together with the latter's location—hidden away underground like a mad maiden aunt—revealed an attitude all too typical of the 'old learning' towards new ways of thought.

But back to the voice on the steps.

"Hey, you down there! Boy!"

I squinted up at the speaker—a tall, thin, angular man in a billowing black cloak and wide-brimmed hat that blotted out the Sun.

"I have an appointment with the Keeper of the Museum," he continued, failing to recognize me until I'd removed the rag from my face. "Ah, James— 'tis you. I'd wondered where you had got to. You do know your father is livid?"

I leaned on my shovel, catching my breath. "Were I one of your guests, I might wonder the same about you. Or have they left already?"

Jediah shrugged. "*I* left. Cowley Hall depresses me."

"Do not trouble yourself to explain," I said. "For you are not the only one—the servants feel it too, I have heard. 'Tis said it began when your stepmother died, that the house would never again be home to joy, as if the very bricks and timbers had gone into mourning. Can you imagine? All those years without—"

Jediah made a low, rumbling noise in the back of his throat. I changed the subject.

"So, you are looking for Dr Sheffield?"

"That may be his name. Where might I find him?"

I yelled at the open door behind me, "A visitor to the Museum demands my urgent assistance!" then bounded up the steps to my cousin's side before anyone could object.

"I have often wondered," Jediah said, appraising me from head to toe, "how you occupy yourself, down in your grotto. As I wonder, too, whether natural philosophy be a pastime fit for respectable men, or only for rogues. Now I have answers on both counts."

"With respect," I retorted, "I fear the answers you *think* you have, are almost certainly incorrect. Amongst the multitudes of mankind's achievements, natural philosophy ranks with the very highest—perhaps the highest of all—yet any man may pursue it, be he honest and industrious, and open to the spirit of curiosity with which all men are born."

"Fine words indeed—for a scullery boy."

"And what if I were a scullery boy?" Dr Crouch would be on my heels if we lingered much longer, but I stood my ground. "A clean laboratory is as essential to a natural philosopher as a clean kitchen to a cook. Our experiments would be next to impossible otherwise. Can you imagine—cooking plums in a pan one had lately used to boil apricots? Without a thorough scrubbing between, 'twould court disaster."

"It hardly bears thinking about," said Jediah. "But I have an appointment, if you remember. Or would you return to your cinders?"

Remembering how filthy I must appear, I self-consciously beat the soot from my waistcoat and breeches. Jediah may have been kin, but he was also a miserable frig-pig, and I was already regretting my offer of help.

"Is Dr Sheffield expecting you?" I asked, as I led him through the gilded doors at the top of the steps.

"I very much hope so, for 'twas he who requested this meeting."

"He is showing visitors around the collections to-day, so we shall soon find him. Have you viewed them yourself?"

Jediah did not reply, or spoke so softly I did not hear him. I turned to repeat my question, but a queer change had come over my relative; cowed—nay, *shrunken*—within his great cloak, he trod gingerly in my wake, darting nervous glances left and right as if menaced from every quarter.

"You have nothing to fear in here, cousin," I said. "This floor is made from strong local stone—" I stamped my heel by way of demonstration. "—and will shield us from all but the deadliest blasts from below."

Jediah removed his hat to waft his face. "'Tis close in here," he muttered—though with its lofty windows and sparkling stucco ceiling, the *Schola Naturalis Historiae* seemed a bright and airy para-dise compared with the stinking, stygian murk of the *Officina Chimica*.

"This is the School of Natural History. 'Tis where the great men of science come to share what they have learned. Dr Hornsby you will be aware of, and Dr Wall—"

"Can there be such a creature as a great man of science?"

"—all disciplines are represented. Astronomy, chymistry, the study of animals and of plants—"

Jediah seemed to shudder. "Who would want to know such things?"

"Oh, they are very popular," I said. "Dr Wall charges thirty guineas per term!"

"He overvalues himself."

"The operations add to the expense, of course, but simple instruction is considered drier than dust these days. No forward-looking scholar would part with his coin for a lecture lacking an electrical machine or the Countess of Westmorland's lodestone—"

A heavy thud sounded over our heads as I spoke, causing Jediah to clutch at his hat as though the very Heavens were collapsing upon him.

"No need for alarm, cousin." I ushered him onto the staircase. "'Tis naught but Dr Sheffield and his visitors."

Hoping to lift his mood, I pointed out the glass cabinets fixed to the walls while we climbed.

"See this butterfly from the island of Java? Who could ever imagine such a creature? An insect the size of a crow! And see how its wings change colour as we pass. First ruby, now emerald, amethyst, gold... Is it magic? The artifice of some crafty fairground trickster? Neither! 'Tis lately explained by a phenomenon called 'iridescence' that—"

"It looks shrivelled and grey to me, pinned to that board."

"See this skeleton of a dragon? Or at least, 'tis labelled *A Dragon*."

"Dragons exist only in fairytales for children."

I smiled approvingly, as though Jediah were a child himself and I the indulgent father he'd never had.

"Oh, I could not agree more! 'Tis absurd, the very suggestion that fire-breathing behemoths once prowled the parish of Iffley." I lowered my voice. "Indeed, if Dr Sheffield were not so wedded to the idea, I would laugh aloud. In my opinion, this so-called dragon is nothing more fabulous than a large lizard, the distant cousins of which walk the Earth as we speak, in the Holy Land and other arid parts of the globe. Which suggests to me that the county of Oxfordshire was, perhaps, warmer and drier in ages past than we find it today—"

Jediah interrupted me with a single sharp inhalation. "God made the Sun in the sky to shine as He wilt and the rain to fall at His pleasure. There is no warmer or drier."

I shrugged, well accustomed to my cousin's occasional preachifying. "Anything may change, time allowing."

"*God* allowing."

Our debate stuttered to a halt at the top of the stairs, where the scene that greeted us made me wish I had remained in the yard, so poorly did it reflect upon what I'd just done my best to extol. Of the seven visitors in Dr Sheffield's retinue that morning, four were boys not yet in breeches and the remainder their custodians, a slovenly trio of nursemaids. 'Twas not the presence of boys or even nursemaids that appalled me, however. 'Twas the insolence of boys who dared to play tag between the exhibits; the negligence of nursemaids too busy tittle-tattling to control their delinquent wards; and the wilful indifference of all to the wonders of nature.

Dr Sheffield, meanwhile, played his usual role, though in a manner so heavy-hearted, the words seemed to drop like lead weights from his tongue and drag themselves like dying animals along the gallery floor, syllable by weary syllable.

"...in the next case," he droned, "we find a jar containing blood that gushed from the sky on the Isle of Wight, a bottle containing a witch, and the right thigh of a giant..."

This excited lewd remarks from the nursemaids, best ignored.

"...these dried worms and precious stones were collected by our founder Mr Tradescant in Russia, in the Year of Our Lord Sixteen Eighteen..."

Jediah spoke close to my ear. "You allow women in here?"

"Anyone may enter, on payment of sixpence."

I led him down the central columned aisle, where the meagre remains of a Dodo sat alongside the skull of an elephant (together with the spear that killed it) and a robe that had once belonged to the King of Virginia.

"I would come down from there, if I were you," I called to one of the brats, who had somehow got himself onto a chandelier and was rocking it to and fro like an ape in a storm-tossed rowboat. "If that chain works loose, you will surely fall and spill your brains, and it seems you have few to spare."

I shall not repeat the curses he heaped upon me. Then a second whelp grabbed the caps of the third and fourth and began a merry chase around the geological displays, deaf to his fellows' demands for the return of their headgear. I readied myself to intervene for the minerals' safety, when Jediah spoke up again.

"Do you remember the day of your mother's funeral?"

The boys' pursuit held his gaze as he spoke, though his gold-and-green eyes seemed to dim and lose their lustre, like stained-glass windows in need of a dusting. Beneath the broad black hat and sharply steepled eyebrows, his countenance appeared chiselled from slabs of white marble, so hard was the set of his jaw, so cold the curl of his lips.

"I was so envious of you that day." His voice grated, as if he were inching aside the lid of an ancient sarcophagus. "For I knew that when my father died, I would not mourn his passing in the way you mourned your mother, or your own father in his time."

"I recall," I replied, "feeling much the same about you, cousin, and for a similar reason."

A twitch raised one corner of his mouth; a sour smile, perhaps. "Did you finish that book?"

"Kepler's *Dream*?" I forced a breezy laugh. "Now, if there ever were a fairytale for children!"

"So you did not finish it?"

"Well... After Mother died, everything changed, and so quickly. I thought I might take it up later, but after I'd finished my schooling, and Father put me to work in the shop, I simply never had the time. And then..." I tailed off miserably.

Jediah huffed. "You did not miss very much. I read the last page if you remember. The narrator failed to reach the Moon and became a laughing-stock—a warning to all who would seek to know the Mind of God. When our First Parents ate of the Tree of Knowledge, they found not wisdom, but the shame of sin and death—as your men of science will also come to learn. I fail to understand why you—my cousin!—would wish to consort with them, *down there.*" He dipped his bony chin at the floor, indicating the laboratory, I supposed, though he might have been alluding to the lowest Circle of Hell. "Now you know Kepler's fate, I mean."

I scowled and hailed Dr Sheffield. The Keeper seemed to welcome the interruption as much as I; more still when I introduced my cousin. Grasping Jediah's right hand in both of his own, he flushed an unbecoming shade of pink and cried, "My dear, dear Vice Sub-Rector Temple! 'Tis an honour to make your acquaintance at last."

Jediah snatched back his hand as if stung by a wasp. Strange behaviour, I thought, for such a very important appointment. But I'd done my job, and had an engagement of my own.

I got half-way up the aisle before the Keeper called me back.

"Sadler! Be so good as to show out the visitors."

"But—"

Shielding his mouth with his hand, Sheffield added, "And be sure they have not had away with anything, eh?"

Jediah smirked at me. "I wish you well, cousin."

I waited until he and the Keeper were out of sight, if not hearing, before I shouted at the rabble: "Hey! Over here!"

This went unheard by the nursemaids, while the boys took it as a signal to start scrambling, one after another, up the sides of a tall, narrow case containing a hoard of gold medals and coins. I began to wonder if sixpence were perhaps too small an entrance fee.

"The viewing is over!" I yelled.

With every added weight, the case grew more unstable, until, to the boys' delight, it toppled over onto its side and showered the tiles with its glittering contents. Like carrion birds, they swooped upon the treasure in an instant, their nurses not far behind.

Mindful of Dr Sheffield's instructions, I sighed. It seemed my thoroughly wretched day could only get worse.

CHAPTER NINE

'TWAS LONG PAST NOON when I made it to Harper's. I stopped running at the top of Edmund Hall Lane to wipe the sweat from my face and collect my wits before I entered the establishment, but as I marched through the lobby and across the well-swept floorboards to the bar, my nerves remained thoroughly jangled.

"Is everyone here?" I demanded.

Molly Bonnet, acknowledged by all as the best coffee-woman in Oxford, frowned as she bustled out from behind the counter. "More or less."

"I trust you have put out the latest newssheets," I continued, too stuffed full of self-importance to wonder what troubled our hostess. "And a pot of your finest Mocha. 'Tis Mr Osborne's favourite—"

"There is something you—"

"—while Mr Piggott enjoys a well-roasted Batavian, as you know—"

Molly drew a breath through the carious gaps in her teeth. "Will you stop blethering and listen?"

"'Twill have to wait. The Club is expecting me."

She did not budge so I stepped around her and zig-zagged through the close-packed tables in the lounge towards the back room, ignoring the insults that flew my way as wigs were dislodged and elbows jarred. As I had feared, the Club had already assembled.

"Gentlemen!" I skidded to a breathless halt and whipped off my hat. "Please do forgive my—"

Only then did I realize why Molly had tried to restrain me. In my absence, the Club—*my* Club—had convened of its own accord. A sensible move, I supposed, given the time spared for our meetings seemed to grow shorter from month to month. And at first appearance, 'twas business as usual: our favourite table; the aromas of good, hot coffee and tobacco smoke; the rustle of newssheets and the thrum of intelligent discourse. *Un*usual was the sight of a stranger, perched upon my stool at the head of the table.

He put me in mind of a peacock with his flashing black eyes, unmusical laughter, and coat of blue-green brocade with gold buttons, all topped off by a black solitaire and a silver pin—the latter set with a diamond of striking proportions. His long, lithe hands primped and preened as he spoke and 'twas quickly clear he had stolen not just my seat, but my thunder as well.

I had arrived at the *denouement* of some salacious item of gossip ("...the way this lady comports herself, you would believe not even butter could melt in her mouth—but cheese would not choke her, I'll wager!") that occasioned a round of applause and pleas of "Do tell us more, dear Ambrose, please do!" I tried to call the meeting to order, but my voice went unheard amidst the commotion.

"See this diamond?" The intruder tapped the pin in his solitaire. "I shall relate the tale of how I came by it..."

Only William Tench seemed to notice me, and moved along the bench to make space for me to sit down. He greeted me with a fretful smile, his mortar-board clutched like a shield to his breast.

"What is happening?" I hissed.

"Edwin Osborne brought him along," William whispered. "He is a distant friend of the family from Yorkshire, I hear."

"Family friend or no," I said, "this is a Philosophical Club, not a Fellowship of Scandal-mongers." I stood and rapped my knuckles on the table. "Silence please! 'Tis time to turn our attention to the business of the month."

The intruder stopped mid-sentence. "I believe we have not been introduced."

From his traditional position slouched in the back-room's only armchair, Edwin Osborne raised a languid hand. "Mr Ambrose Bean... James Sadler... *et cetera, et cetera...* Forgive the interruption," he added, to Bean. "Do continue with your tale."

I spoke up quickly. "We are happy to have you here as a guest, Mr Bean, but even guests must abide by the rules of the Club—rule number one being that socializing comes *after* the meeting's main business."

"I have never heard that rule before," said a Servitor of Exeter College.

"What are rules for, if not to be broken?" Edwin lounged back upon his bolster. "As for this month's business... 'Tis my understanding that the purpose of this Club be not business, but amusement. Is that not so?" He glanced around the table.

"Bang up!" said the Exeter man.

"This is surely the best meeting in years!" enthused another.

Bean waved a lace-cuffed arm to summon the coffee-boy. "Will you join us, Sadler? The Mocha is excellent."

"With respect, sir," I said, "I do not have to join. I am a member of this Club of longer standing than anyone present. And these gentlemen wish me to deliver a discourse today. Which I shall now do." I squared my shoulders, cleared my throat. "The matter in question this term is *A Peregrination through Interplanetary Space, or A Novel Procedure for Travel to our Most Proximate Heavenly Neighbour, namely, the Moon.*"

"Travel to the Moon!" Bean almost received his Mocha in his lap, so badly did he startle the coffee-boy with this exclamation. "I fear 'twould make a terribly long and tiresome voyage. Though not nearly so perilous, I would wager, as my own journey to Old Cathay—"

I raised my voice. "Concerning the Moon—"

Edwin drummed his fingernails on the rim of his empty dish. "Sadler, no one is interested in the Moon."

"I am interested," piped William.

Edwin snorted. "That says more about you, William, than the Moon."

"I imagine it must be a fearfully dry and dusty place," said Bean.

"Dry and dusty or lush and green, it matters not one jot," I growled. "'Tis the going there that counts."

"My dear Sadler!" Bean laughed, and my Philosophers laughed with him. "What is the point of going somewhere just for the sake of it? Unless the Moon be filled, not with cheese, but lusty Moon-maidens!"

"Sadler!" Mr Piggott raised his voice above the merriment. "Is that Moon-dust on your coat?"

I looked down at myself, baffled, then spotted the furnace ash on my coat skirts. And was that icing sugar, too? I felt my cheeks redden.

"Stand down, James." 'Twas William, muttering at my elbow. "You can speak another time."

Bean, however, refused to desist. Peering at me from over the top of his Mocha dish, he asked, with sudden sincerity, "So you propose to fly to the Moon? By what magic, may I enquire?"

"My method involves no magic," I replied, hoping this question—at last!—signalled the start of a sensible debate. "Natural philosophy shall furnish our wings."

"No philosophy—natural or otherwise—could do *that.*"

"To the contrary! Men of science can achieve anything, given ingenuity and hard work."

"As we are making new rules today," said Edwin, "may I suggest another? No member of this Club may ever, under any pretext, mention that filthy word 'work'—and still less, the hard variety—on pain of a damned good hiding!"

He looked at Bean as he spoke—expecting a chuckle, perhaps—but Bean did not react.

"Men might dabble in natural philosophy when their moneybags are bulging and their bellies full." Bean patted his own belly, across which snaked a thick rope of golden watch-chain. "But when they are cold, or sick, or starving, they turn to superstition to deliver them from their woes."

"If they do," I said, "they are dolts. For by means of invention, they could build a world where no one would want for food, good health, or shelter."

"Invention never succoured a grieving widow, nor a sailor aboard a sinking ship, nor a child afraid of the demons that lurk in the dark. Life is short and cruel, and superstition man's only true solace."

"But natural philosophy can raise men *out* of the dark. How less bright would be our lot, had Mr Cavendish never discovered his inflammable air nor Mr Franklin his lightning rod? Or our own Dr Wall not devoted his life to the study of metals and salts?"

"Those are, I trust, rhetorical questions," said Edwin.

"I have heard," ventured Mr Piggott, "that the great-grandfather of the present King of France retained the services of a Court *Électrician*—a showman of no mean skill, they say. 'Tis also said—though this may be fabulation—that on one occasion, for the amusement of the Dauphin and his guests, this fellow assembled a mile-long line of monks, made them link hands like children, then conveyed an electrical force to the first, the magnitude of which caused them all, one by one, to leap into the air—like a chain of startled rabbits!"

"I have heard a similar yarn," said Bean, "from a high-born *Parisienne* of my closest acquaintance—but 'tis a tale for another day." He waggled a well-manicured finger in my direction. "So there be your natural philosophy—a diversion for the idle, party tricks for the rich."

"I assure you, Mr Bean, I am neither idle nor rich."

"Did I not mention it?" Edwin yawned. "The Sadlers are shopkeepers by trade. But this disputation bores me. Ambrose, you promised to share the story of your diamond pin."

Ignoring his friend yet again, Bean asked me, "How frequently do you Philosophers meet?"

"On the fourth Tuesday of every month, excepting Christmas Day," I replied.

"I have a proposal." Bean's eyes glittered, like twin dark reflections of his diamond. "When you assemble here one month hence, we shall settle this dispute once and for all: superstition or natural philosophy—which is the greater? What say you, Sadler? Are you up for it?"

"I most certainly am." I was so annoyed with Bean, I would have agreed to just about anything that might wipe the smile from his handsome face. "And I have no doubt that natural philosophy will prevail. But how will we measure their worth?"

"By the only measure that matters," said Edwin. "Money!" He was suddenly more alive than I had seen him all afternoon. "You shall both endeavour to raise hard cash: Mr Bean by dint of superstition, Sadler through invention. The details we leave to you—though should they exceed the bounds of the Law, we thank you to keep our names from the magistrate's ear."

"That will not be a problem," said Bean.

Edwin clapped his hands. "Then we are set. At our next meeting you will both bring your purses and he whose spoils are the greater will be declared the victor."

"Bang up!" The Exeter man bounced about with such enthusiasm, my own rear was juddered at the opposite end of the bench.

"But what shall be the forfeit for the loser?" asked Mr Piggott.

"No one mentioned a forfeit," I said.

"I have a suggestion." Bean treated me to a chillingly amiable smile. "The loser will swear—under solemn oath—to never again darken the doors of this Club, nor will he disrupt, interrupt, or by any other means obstruct the business of its meetings."

"That is hardly fair!" I protested. "You are only visiting and unlikely to ever return. Whereas I have been a regular member for years."

"I agree with James." William gripped his mortar board tighter still, his knuckles white as marbles. "We must think of a different forfeit."

Edwin ignored him. "That is an excellent suggestion, Ambrose. If Sadler disagrees, perhaps he is not as confident as he claims?"

"You misunderstand me, Mr Osborne." I could have quite cheerfully ripped Edwin's throat out at that instant, even as I placated him. "I simply indicated a possible flaw in Mr Bean's proposal. But if these are the terms of our wager, I shall accept them, of course."

William half rose to his feet, his face flushed. "Wait—if the loser must suffer a forfeit, should not the winner receive a prize?"

Why had I not thought of that? I was about to suggest a waiver of the next year's Club subscriptions, when Bean spoke up again.

"May I be so bold as to make another suggestion? If Sadler risks expulsion from this Club, which he seems to hold most dear, justice dictates that I, too, must hazard a cherished possession. So let it be agreed—" Nimble fingers brushed the black cloth at his neck. "—that at your next meeting, be it by way of natural philosophy or by superstition, whosoever might win this wager... will have my diamond."

My jaw would have dropped had I not been struck rigid.

"If—if you wish," I croaked.

"Then the deal is done." To murmurs of approval, Bean stood and extended his hand across the table. I shook it firmly, surprised—and gratified—to feel a film of cold sweat upon his palm.

Edwin looked equally pleased with himself. "A most constructive meeting—thank you, gentlemen. Now, if there be no further business, may *I* suggest we call a halt to proceedings and adjourn to Bagg's— the only place in town that serves a truly decent Mocha."

"And while we are there," trilled the Exeter man, "we must tell everyone about Mr Bean's bang-up wager!"

The back room cleared in seconds, leaving naught but myself, a stack of empty coffee dishes and unread newssheets, and William Tench, who vacillated between leaving and staying, his mortar board half on his head and half off.

"I brought this for you," he mumbled at last. "Bacon's *Opus Maius*."

He placed a book on the table. I did not inspect it.

"You asked to borrow it, do you remember? For the next meeting? I shall need it myself shortly, though—I must dispute with Dr Fyshe on the logic of Bacon and Abelard—so if you might return it as soon as you can..."

I nodded, barely registering his words. The folly of what I'd just done had begun to dawn.

"I may see you tomorrow. I hope to attend Dr Crouch's new lecture on the pneumatic chymistry. He was a little abstruse for my liking on the metallic and earthy bodies last term, but still..."

I nodded again.

"Cheer up, James." William roused himself and patted me on the shoulder. "I cannot wait to see you knock Edwin down to size. He has been getting far too big for his boots lately."

I managed a smile.

"I'm sure you have some spectacular scheme in mind."

I laughed a little deliriously and began tidying the table so my hands had something to do while my brain composed a reply.

"You do *have* a scheme?"

He was spared my scathing response to that question when my gaze fell upon the front page of that week's *Jackson's Oxford Journal*, lying crumpled and stained beneath a dish of cold Batavian. 'Twas a pure accident of fate, though Ambrose Bean might have called it proof of his hypothesis, that natural philosophy alone cannot explain all that is in this world. I was not Ambrose Bean, however, and to me this happenstance was nothing more or less than an extraordinary stroke of good fortune.

I folded the newssheet, tucked it into my coat, and smiled at my anxious companion.

"Shame on you, William," I said, with a wink. "Do you really believe I'd have taken the bet, had I not?"

PART III

CHAPTER TEN

MY NEXT SEVERAL DAYS at the laboratory found me once again neglecting my work and now with no fear of sanction (save Nugent's occasional frowns of reproach), for Dr Crouch was busy lecturing upstairs. When I was not constructing little open-based boxes of paper and attempting to levitate them in the hot air arising from the portable furnace on my bench (furnaces were, after all, good for something), I was planning my future, which would begin, of course, with my education. I whiled away entire shifts on quandaries such as the number of terms the diamond's sale might finance, what course of study might serve me best, which college, which tutors... I had to choose wisely, if I were to become a man of consequence and cheat Fate of the commonplace life it had dealt me.

Before very long, I was prepared to advance a stage further.

At noon I announced to Nugent that I was finished for the day and that the reagents Crouch had requested I'd left on his desk, all labelled and weighed.

"Would you rather not wait a half-hour and tell him yourself?" said Nugent. "Heaven knows, you must regain his good favour somehow. What is that?" he added, indicating the tea chest in my arms.

I hastened past him, replying over my shoulder, "This? Oh, 'tis nothing of any importance."

On Broad Street I encountered William Tench. With a party of his fellow Undergraduates, he was heading from the *Schola Naturalis Historiae* towards Bagg's Coffee-house on the corner of Catte Street; he fell behind when he spotted me struggling up the stairs from the yard. Although William was my good friend—and remains so 'til this day—I cannot say he ever learned when to engage in a man in conversation, and when best to not.

"Dr Crouch is in a wretched mood," he burbled, oblivious to my impatience. "Three times did he hurl his ear-horn at poor Carstairs! *Smack, crash, thud!* I cannot tell you which was worst injured—Carstairs's head or Crouch's dignity—though neither was dented as much as the ear-horn I think, for Crouch would have surely blown his breeches had he heard what Carstairs called him. They say his temper is shorter than ever—Dr Crouch, that is, not Carstairs—because he must bear the brunt of Dr Wall's recent ill humour, while Dr Wall in turn endures the wrath of Dr Sheffield."

"I fear that may be the fault of my cousin," I said. "He defied the museum over some promise made by his late father, and they have not stopped sulking since."

William's eyes opened wide. "Your cousin defied Dr Sheffield? How thrilling! Is he a Philosopher too? You must bring him to our next meeting. Everyone is talking about your wager." He gestured west along the Broad and north up Parks Road, as if every man, woman, and babe in the city would rather mind my affairs than their own. "I cannot wait to hear about your scheme."

"You must wait just a little longer." Had I a hand free, I would have appended a conspiratorial tap to the side of my nose. But William needed no prompting.

"Understood," he whispered. "Least said, soonest mended, eh? What is in the box?" he added, noticing my burden as if for the first time.

I leaned in close. "You will excuse my bad manners if I decline to answer that question—and if I tell you I have to dash. I am on business of the most extraordinary importance."

From the thatch-haired crown of his head to his scuffed shoes, my friend quivered with excitement.

"Then be about it quick," he cried. "Heaven forbid I should delay you!"

~ ~ ~

I waited on the Broad until William had found his way into Bagg's, then hurried down to Magdalen Bridge via Holywell and Longwall Streets, avoiding the High and the risk of being spotted by Father or Mary. Though such was the traffic, I doubt I would have been noticed. The cause of this congestion was the fortnightly Gloucester Green market, and livestock and vehicles alike clogged the road, withers to wheels in a discord of mounting frustration.

During interminable days behind the counter, I often occupied my mind watching coaches passing the shop on their way to The Plain, wondering enviously where their occupants were headed and what adventures they'd have when they got there. Today, however, 'twas incoming transports that seized my imagination. Passing a near-stationary carriage from London, I peered inside rather longer than might be considered polite, awestruck to think that any one of those impatient passengers could have witnessed in the flesh a feat that I had only read about (although *Jackson's Oxford Journal*'s account had no dearth of stirring detail). They'd be blessed if they had—doubly so, if they knew what I had hidden in my tea chest!

I left the road at the turnpike, hastening down the slope from The Plain to the pasture we called Angel Meadow. In those days, The Angel being Oxford's foremost coaching inn, it rented the land east of the Cherwell to graze its customers' horses, so I did not have the meadow to myself. I recognized an ostler from the inn eating a pie beside the riverbank; he waved so warmly on seeing me, an onlooker might have mistaken me for a regular at his pothouse. I dared not imagine what Father might say.

The tea chest settled upon the grass, I extracted my latest handiwork: a miniature aerial globe no more than sixty inches around, painstakingly fashioned from *papier mâché*. I had decorated its equatorial regions with scrolls and ribbons in imitation of Signor Vincenzo Lunardi's vessel, and with three light ropes had secured an old sewing basket of Mary's beneath its southern pole. This I now filled with an assortment of straw, scavenged wool, and threadbare stockings, and then with trembling hands set to work with my tinderbox. As you will know, it can take a deal of effort to get a decent blaze going, but time seemed somehow shrunken on that day. Half an hour might have passed in actuality, but my memory insists that my very first strike birthed a flash like the Spark of Creation, and that the rags in the basket caught fire at once with no need for blowing or fanning.

Exhilarated, I cast the globe upon the breeze. And Good Heavens, did it fly! I had attached a fourth rope to the sewing basket, which I grasped as the aerostat rose—a prudent measure as it turned out, for the little traveller was itching for its freedom. I found myself walking it up and down about the meadow, like a fashionable lady with her lap-dog upon a leash. The ostler stopped eating his pie to watch, while his horses sounded a curious chorus of whinnies. My confidence growing by the second, I returned the ostler's earlier wave.

"Watch carefully, my man! You will never forget what you see here this day, nor the name of James Sadler. 'Tis the stuff from which history is made!"

And thus, like reckless Ikarus, did hubris prove my undoing. For while I looked elsewhere, a sudden wind snatched the rope from my hand, and dancing a gay minuet in the sky, the aerostat scudded away down the meadow.

"Oi!" the ostler yelled as his horses bolted. "You are scaring them!"

I had other worries; my globe looked certain to escape the Earth's bounds, so fast was it rising. With a despairing leap I managed to grab the trailing end of the rope, but hit *terra firma* off balance. Turning my ankle in a pile of equine sirreverence, I pitched forwards and landed head first in the river.

Then time played tricks yet again. 'Twas hours, it seemed, before the ostler hauled me out.

"Are you drowned?" he demanded.

I spat out a mouthful of duckweed. My beautiful globe had gone, reduced to a glutinous lump of paper and paste, shedding teardrops of red and blue paint into the Cherwell. Had the ostler not been staring at me so keenly, I, too, would have wept.

"Your—your—whatsoever it be, 'tis sinking," he added. "Would you have me fish it out?"

I shook my head—and wished I had not, for the water in my ears sloshed about as though a storm at sea were confined inside my skull. Then I heard a worse sound.

"Who is that?" I cried. "Who is laughing?"

"Laughing? Not me." The ostler looked offended.

"I heard someone laugh. Overhead..." I squinted up at the bridge, but if there had been a spy behind the balustrade, he was long gone by the time I had blinked away the river water and scraped my sopping hair from my eyes.

"You must've hit your head when you fell," said the ostler. "Wait here while I get your father."

I jumped to my feet and thanked the ostler for his concern, then caught the rope as it drifted past, to drag my aerostat out of the depths.

CHAPTER ELEVEN

MY SISTER MARY ALSO HAD BUSINESS east of the city that day, though I knew naught of this at the time, learning the details only after the strange events that were soon to befall us. We missed each other by minutes; as I plodded back onto Magdalen Bridge, my spirits as low as my footprints were muddy, Mary had just left The Plain, taking the turn for Cowley Hall.

On the doorstep at the front of the house, his hand upon the knocker, stood a man she knew by the name of Wyndham Rudge, a relic of Uncle Elijah's jaunting days. Dressed like a farmhand in long trousers and an uncocked hat, with a farmhand's weathered face, he followed her approach with eyes as bright and sharp as a pair of new pins.

"Is no one home?"

Rudge shrugged. "I've been knocking here a good five minutes."

"A *good* five minutes?" Mary shrilled in exasperation. "I am glad someone sees the good in time wasted, for there is none in my experience—unless you have plenty to spare, of course."

Rudge struck a pose unexpectedly grand for a man so humble by birth. "I would not presume to know how busy *your* diary be, but full or no, 'tis clear you are not short of cheek."

My sister would have replied to this with some cutting barb of her own, had she not caught Rudge's sly grin.

"Were I rude," she said, "I had cause. My days are already too brief, and the few hours I have, I cannot expend on needless journeys."

"No journey *need* be needless. The end may disappoint, but in my experience there is always cheer to be found on the way."

Was he teasing her still? Mary wondered. "Are you implying I should make the best of my lot? 'Twould be impossible, I am afraid. Cheer could be got as easily as a sweetmeat—" She rattled her basket. "—but I'd still want for time to enjoy it."

"Then for both our sakes," said Rudge, "I shall knock again."

As he spoke these words, the door creaked open, and a weary voice demanded, "What do you want?"

'Twas Matty Prout, Uncle Elijah's sorry excuse for a manservant.

"Mr Jediah sent word he would see me today," said Rudge. "'Twas a promise he made on the death of his father."

"Was it, now?" Prout sighed, as if Rudge's very existence was an unconscionable imposition, and why was it *he* who had to answer the door and deal with his master's affairs? "He never told me. Mind you, he never does. And you?" He turned to Mary.

She raised the basket.

"Deliveries go round the back."

"Your master and I are family—as you well know," Mary bridled. "And this is a gift, not a delivery."

Prout scowled. "Then I suppose I must let you off—but just the once, mind."

He slouched back inside without further discussion, leaving Mary and Rudge to admit themselves. Another protracted wait ensued.

"'Tis always so cold in here." Mary shivered. "I trust Jediah's rooms in St Alban's are warmer. And these ugly curios in every corner. 'Tis no wonder he was an anxious child—the bravest soul would tremble at sharing a home with such nightmarish nonsense."

With a sigh Rudge removed his shapeless hat. "The last sparks of fire that warmed this house, guttered and died along with its owner. As for these *ugly curios...* They tell the tale of half my life."

He had until now seemed spriter than his advancing years might admit, but with this speech 'twas as if the whole weight of those decades fell upon him. So suddenly shrunken was he, so forlorn, Mary regretted her initial spite. "You were a loyal friend to my Uncle, I have heard," she said, in a gentler tone.

"I like to believe so. Thirty-five years I followed him, from jungle to mountain to desert and back, and every voyage we marked with a keepsake. Elijah had a taste for the out-of-the-ordinary. See that beauty strung over the hearth? 'Tis the snout of a saw-shark, won in a battle that still be legend amongst the pirates of Nosy Mangabe. And here—the death mask of Shu-Nammu. Now that *was* a nightmare. Only the Good Lord Himself knows how we survived."

Spying a glass-topped bureau tucked in the shadows beneath the stairs, Mary stooped to examine its contents. Now she looked more closely, she saw that every item, however small or apparently insignificant, bore a label recording the how, where, and why of its acquisition.

"This is how James describes the museum. He often talks about it—though I do not often listen."

"Your brother?" Rudge chuckled. "He reminds me of Elijah."

"Never say that in Father's hearing! 'Tis already his firm conviction, that James will make such fools of us one day, we shall become outcasts, the Sadler name reviled throughout the county."

"So we were fools, eh? Your Uncle and me."

Mary blushed. "I am just repeating what Father says."

He crooked a finger. "Come with me," he said, and led her across the hall.

"That is Uncle Elijah's study," Mary whispered. "We cannot go in there—we've not been invited."

"If Elijah and I had waited for invitations, we would never have got anywhere. And besides, you are family."

He opened the door and marched inside; Mary, meanwhile, had to halt on the threshold to catch her breath.

"That smell!"

"Elijah's tobacco," said Rudge. "And his Portuguese snuff—ebulum, flavoured with clove and best Burmese ginger. 'Tis hard to believe he is gone."

Mary had never been close to her Uncle; he'd been absent for much of her life, and even when present, not quite there. Like the rest of Cowley Hall the room felt cold, and the musty smell of neglect would soon extinguish the scents of tobacco and snuff. Elijah Temple himself gazed down from the wall behind the desk, witness to his own dissolution—his likeness caught in a portrait framed with gilded plaster mouldings. He seemed younger than Mary remembered—in his prime adventuring days, she supposed—dressed ready for action in an open-neck shirt and a practical, wide-collared frock coat.

"The scene behind him—does that also mark one of your voyages?"

Rudge snorted. "'Tis no land I ever saw—and that be quite a few, let me tell you. For sure, the cove who made it had never strayed south of Abingdon. And Lord, what a fuss that painting caused. Elijah could never sit still for long, and Becky—Mrs Temple—thought it most hilarious to pull faces at him from across the studio. Of course, it fell to me to keep order, but she was so full of fun, so full of life, 'twas like trying to tame a whirlwind. And then all three of us would fall about in merriment. *This is too impossible!* I can still hear that blasted painter's bleats. *I am an artist, not a nursery maid!* Of course, we just laughed all the more."

"'Twill not be so funny, I think, if Master Jediah finds you in here."

A sneering Matty Prout had appeared in the open doorway behind them.

"We were just—" Mary gasped, "—just—"

Prout grinned disagreeably but did not press the matter. "Master Jediah says he will see you both in the garden. You know the way, I presume? If not, I'm sure you can find it—you have managed so well this far."

Red-faced, Mary hastened back to the hall. Rudge was not far behind, but with every step they took towards the sunroom at the rear of the house, his swagger grew less pronounced, his stride a little slower.

When they reached the *porte-fenêtre* onto the terrace, he came to a stop altogether, removing his hat to smooth what remained of his wiry grey hair and wiping the palms of his hands on his threadbare trousers.

"Ladies first," he said.

Well pleased at this show of good manners, Mary obliged and lifted the latch, but before she could take a step outside, or draw a single breath of fresh air, Rudge's swagger returned a flash.

"Jediah! What are you doing?" he yelled.

Jediah looked up from the border in which he was crouched, in his hand a muddy trowel, poised mid-excavation.

"Is it not obvious?" he replied. "I am doing a little weeding."

"Weeding? Those are not weeds!"

All niceties—not to mention his years—cast aside, Rudge barged past Mary, hurdled the low colonnade that divided the terrace from the garden, and raced across the lawn towards the border. It was, however, too late for most of the blooms. Their destruction had been ruthlessly thorough.

"I am no gardener, I admit," Jediah continued. "But is a weed not simply a plant, growing in a place where it is not wanted?"

"But these plants are beautiful! Unique. Irreplaceable." With shaking hands, Rudge cradled the ravaged leaves, the fractured stems. "They are your father's."

"They *were* my father's. And now they are mine, to do with as I wish. As is this house and all that is in it. And I am the one who decides who comes and goes, and what he may say and what he may not, and how long he might remain before my manservant removes him."

He smashed the trowel against a paving stone, flinging clods of earth in all directions. Then he sighed and his anger seemed to ebb. He pulled a cloth from his sleeve to pat the sweat from his high, pallid forehead.

Rudge lowered his gaze. "Forgive me. I did not come here to argue. It has been a long time."

"Not long enough." Jediah unfurled from his crouch, dwarfing Rudge. "Yet here you are now."

"And much obliged for your invitation. I was sorely troubled to have missed the funeral, but I feared there might be a scene between us."

"I have rather more dignity than you credit me," Jediah growled. "However, that does not mean you would have been welcome."

"I see." Rudge gave a single, slow nod of acceptance. "Your father promised me his expedition notebooks."

"I know, you idiot. That is why I summoned you here. Though 'tis a strange gift—writings for a man who cannot read." With a laugh, Jediah returned to his weeding. "Yes, yes, take them. Take them. Take the whole damn library if you wish! It means nothing to me."

"And regarding his seed collection—"

"I. Said. Take. Them."

Rudge hesitated. "Jediah?"

"Yes?"

"There is something I—"

"Do not stretch my patience, Wyndham Rudge. I tolerate your existence out of respect for my late father, but I am not your friend and never will be. Is that clear?"

Rudge met Jediah's icy glare with narrowed eyes, as if seeking something—or someone—long lost. Then abruptly he spun about and returned indoors, stranding Mary, alone and embarrassed, upon the terrace.

"Forgive me, cousin." Jediah sank his trowel up to its tang in the ravaged earth. "I did not mean you to see such unpleasantness. That trumped-up hired-hand brings out the worst in me. Come, may I offer you some refreshment? We shall take it inside—the day grows uncomfortably warm."

Mary struggled a moment to find her tongue. "'Tis kind, but I must refuse. Father will be frantic, worrying where I've got to. But here—" She held out the basket. "He sends his good wishes and hopes you will visit us soon, but 'til then perhaps you'll accept these modest supplies, with his compliments. Lemon biscuits, almond loaf, walnut preserve—and more! I picked them out myself."

She could not remember the last time she'd seen him smile.

"'Tis a pity you cannot stay. But I thank your father—and you—for your consideration, and I shall certainly pay a visit when time permits." Jediah sighed. "House, garden, legal affairs... It seems my own father needs me more in death than he ever did in life."

"I understand," said Mary. "Do not trouble yourself to come indoors. I shall leave the basket with Mrs Prout and return to collect it later."

On returning to the sunroom, she happened upon a furtive Matty Prout.

"'Tis most disloyal to spy on your master," she scolded.

Prout stepped aside from the *porte-fenêtre* and lowered the hand he'd had cupped to his ear. "I plight my troth to no one," he growled, "'til I know where *his* loyalties lie. Did the miserable goat say aught of his plans for the house? The missus swears he will sell, and then we shall both be out on our arses." He lifted a corner of the canopy atop Mary's basket and sniffed at the contents. "Now, Mr Elijah... you always knew where you were with him. He was a strange old cove, but he never bossed us about nor interfered in our work, and we miss him sincerely—hey, do I smell caraway cake?"

Before she could even begin to object, he snatched the basket and shooed her into the hall with a lordly wave.

"Such frilly fancies are wasted on that kill-joy in the garden. Leave them with me and I shall find them a happier home."

CHAPTER TWELVE

"WHERE IS THE SEEDCAKE?" I shouted, for the tenth or twelfth time that afternoon. "Father said there would be seedcake today, and I've turned away half a dozen customers already."

"Begging your pardon, Mr James, but he said no such thing." Billy loped through from the kitchen, rubbing his thick-knuckled hands on his apron. His shirt was speckled with flour, an unwelcome reminder of Harper's, and I am afraid I may have scowled at him, though he was far from the cause of my displeasure.

"There will be seedcake on Friday," he continued in his ponderous way, "but today we have Queen's cake."

"Well," I harrumphed, "people are asking for seedcake."

"They must be mistaken."

I clapped my hands to my hips, and with a withering glare demanded, "Billy, will you never learn? The customer is *always* right." Then I cringed within myself, for I sounded just like my father.

Billy shrugged. "I cannot explain it. But Friday is seedcake, today is Queen's cake."

"If today *is* Queen's cake, as you insist—where is it? I see none on the shelves."

Billy turned his back at that and stomped back into the kitchen, sniping over his shoulder, "I'd bake faster without all these interruptions!"

There followed a great deal of clanging and clattering, a cacophony of cake tins and pans opportunely joined by the mantle-clock in the parlour. Another hour over and done, its expiration marked by a chime. 'Twas normally sweet music to me, but now I had no time to spare, the loss of yet another sixty minutes vexed me greatly. Denied any further laboratory shifts (Father having no need, it seemed, of the extra wages I'd earn), I had found inventioneering even harder home than under Dr Crouch's watchful eye. Troubling, too, was my failure to find a secluded location for future ascents. God forbid I should ever suffer an Angel Meadow fiasco again!—though absent a functioning aerostat, that particular problem was, perhaps, moot.

With all these miseries crowded upon me like wasps about a jam-jar, all I could do was bat them aside with mindless distractions. But having already counted every last dragee—violet, coffee, and French alike—and weighed all of our stocks of flours, fruits, nuts, &c. to the nearest ounce, I had been reduced to polishing the little brass bells above the doorframe, when events took a unexpected new turn.

It began with the arrival of a customer so eager for admittance, I had scarcely the span of an eye-blink to register his approach through the window-pane and snatch my ladder—and my person—out of harm's way before he burst in.

"I am sorry, we have no seedcake," I said, loudly for Billy's benefit. "We may have Queen's cake, though I cannot say when it might appear."

"I have no especial affection for cakes of any kind," said the newcomer.

I glared at him and strode back to the counter. "Then what, might I ask, has brought you so gaily into a cake shop?"

I knew the man as Wyndham Rudge, a labourer in the Physic Garden and former assistant to my late Uncle Elijah. I was in no mood for chat, but I suspected his avowed aversion to cakes was genuine, for I had never before seen him in the shop.

"May I help you in some other way?" I grated.

"Perhaps." He smiled mysteriously, his button-bright eyes a-twinkle. "Or more to the point—may I help *you*?"

These words, though pleasantly spoken, chilled me for some reason I could not explain.

"Is it work you are after? For if that be the case, I am afraid you will be disappointed. We have no need—"

"You most assuredly do have a need," he said, placing his grubby palms upon the counter-top I had just an hour ago buffed to a spotless sheen. "Though I should not blame you if you would rather stay here with your pastries. 'Tis an easy life, I dare say. Dry, as well."

He laughed then—and I learned at last who had mocked me from Magdalen Bridge.

"I trust you enjoyed yourself at my expense," I sniffed. "What a pleasure it must be, having time to stop and stare while other men toil."

Rudge shrugged. "'Twas but a brief amusement."

"*A brief amusement?* Well—if I might say, what you lack in manners you more than make up for in ignorance. 'Tis fortunate some men, at least, have the wit to dream and the mettle to act—and aspirations loftier than grubbing around in the mud for a living!"

"I'd bid you tell my father—" Rudge bristled. "—or my grandfather, or his father before him, that there be shame in their labours. You!—a Sadler, whose kin have done naught of greater account, than plunder the purses of gluttons and clodpoles."

In other circumstances I might have agreed with him, but my temper was worn thinner than a butter-paper. "So, we are likened to bandits? Is that what you are saying?"

If he were, I would never know, for my outburst prompted a shout from the parlour, enquiring after our customer's welfare.

I went to the foot of the stairs to reply. "'Tis but a misunderstanding, Father. No matter for any concern—though our signage could, perhaps, be made more informative."

I returned to the counter to find Rudge jabbing a soil-stained finger into a tower of ratafias I'd spent hours constructing that morning.

"Can I help you or not?" I barked.

"And again I must respectfully ask, can I help you?" Rudge lowered his voice. "If I might speak plainly—fire, as a means of elevation, is all of a piece with a scalded slattern: cheap and plentiful, but fickle, foul smelling, and ofttimes deadly. You learned that your-

106

self, the hard way. You will learn quicker, and better, from me."

'Twas an age before I grasped what he meant.

"*You* want to help *me* build an aerostat?"

He puffed out his chest, inflating with self-admiration. "At last you get my meaning. Since the death of your Uncle, God rest his soul, I have had some spare time—"

"You have some impertinence, too! How dare you come into my shop, insulting my family and scorning my methods? You—a *gardener*!—presume to teach *me* about pneumatics? *I* work with Dr Wall."

Rudge glowered. "I do not doubt you are well-schooled. But not so wise as to take up my offer, it seems."

"At last we agree."

He chuntered under his breath in response; I failed to catch the drift, but he meant me to hear his parting jibe, for he looked me straight in the eye before he doffed his hat and took flight.

"You Sadler whelps are a saucy brood. Your father must be proud to have sired such ingrates!"

Said parent he missed by seconds, my father having bestirred himself on hearing the door-bells chime.

"I truly hope," Father said, "'twas not in anger you just raised your voice."

"Less in anger," I replied, "than out of a reasonable desire for respect due to my station. 'Tis lucky he left when he did, for he was testing my patience.

"*Your* patience? Respect?" Father slammed an open hand upon the counter, scattering my begrimed ratafias in all directions. "Have I not told you a thousand times? Your desires are neither here nor there. The customer is always—*always*—right."

"But he wasn't a customer—"

"Nor ever will be I expect, given such service!" He shooed me towards the delivery basket. "A little fresh air might sharpen your business sense. I shall take over here, lest you drive away all of our trade."

I groaned. "Can't Mary do it?"

"Mary is helping me balance the ledgers—would you do that instead? No?" Point won, he reached for his apron. "Besides, this customer is a college man and requested the order be brought directly to his rooms."

"Very well, very well." I marched towards the stairs. "I will fetch my coat."

"So do not try leaving the sweetmeats with the porter."

"As if I would," I growled.

~ ~ ~

At St Saviour's, the Porter denied all knowledge of any "Staircase Six Society", though the college did harbour, he conceded, innumerable clubs, leagues, and circles, and also a Staircase Six. "On the left," he directed at length. "Be sure not to tread on the grass."

There being a market at North Gate that day, the streets were a madhouse—in North Bailey alone I'd been stalled by a flock of fat geese, three cheese-mongers' carts, and the snags of a furious hog. What bliss, then, to catch my breath in a realm ruled not by Mammon, but Mind. 'Tis true that idleness and de-bauchery prospered throughout the University in that period and 'twas a lean time for learning. But consci-entious scholars were still to be found—not least my own Dr Wall, and even Dr Crouch on a good day.

I ambled around the quads to enjoy the silence as long as I dared, then located Staircase Six and commenced a serpentine ascent to the topmost floor. From above I heard laughter, the tinkle of glasses, and cries of "Bang up!" and "Pay the Banker!", all of which led me to a solitary attic set, squeezed beneath the roof-beams. The heavy outer door without a handle was closed—a sign among students that the occupant is working and unable to receive visitors, though that was clearly not the case here. I knocked loudly.

"Refreshments for the Staircase Six Society!"

I heard the inner door open, then the outer oak swung aside—revealing, to my horror, Edwin Osborne.

"'Tis the pastry-boy!" he exclaimed, adding, as he waved me inside, "We were wondering where you had got to."

I had entered upon a convivial scene: Edwin toasting crumpets over the fire, Mr Twining and Mr Piggott enjoying a round of Pharo, and reclining upon the sofa, a little apart from the rest, a personage I had not expected to meet again for weeks—or perhaps, I had hoped, forever.

Edwin extracted the basket from my unresisting hand and placed it upon the sideboard. A pretty piece in the Adam style, I noted, all in a daze. He certainly lived well up here on Staircase Six, with his Axminster carpet and expensive Chinese wallpapers.

"I see you admire my rooms," Edwin said. "I rent these three from the Dean, plus another for my servant. Three hundred guineas a year all told, and the decorations cost another small fortune. But what am I to do? A gentleman cannot live in squalor." He took up his lorgnette, to inspect the basket's contents. "Ratafias, comfits, sweet carrot pie... All in order, it appears, and looking simply scrumptious, too! But wait—where is the seedcake? I expressly requested seedcake. How *very* disappointing."

"I detest seedcake," said Mr Piggott from the card table. "If God had intended us to eat seedcake, He would have given us beaks."

"What say you, my friend?" Edwin turned to the occupant of the sofa. "Seedcake, yay or nay? Nay, I'll wager."

"A guinea says yay," said Mr Twining, barely glancing away from his hand.

"I am sure Sadler's treats—" Ambrose Bean raised his glass to me in salute. "—will all be quite acceptable regardless."

"More than acceptable, I should hope," said Edwin. "Sadler's father is the finest *pâtissier* in all of Oxford. Is that not so, Sadler?"

I nodded, quite speechless.

"Oxford's finest, you say? Then *savoir-faire* demands I sample his vendibles, seedcake or no." Bean bared his teeth in a Mephistophelian smile. "Tell me Sadler, how goes our wager from your perspective?"

I shifted from foot to foot. "Well... I have been quite busy... making plans and... such..."

Edwin tut-tutted in sympathy. "It must be a struggle, finding time for invention when one has to work for a living. I hear you plan to fly."

"To fly?" chirped Mr Twining.

Edwin turned to his friends with a grin. "Sadler will need his seedcake, for he hopes to join the birds. Do you remember that pair of Frenchies we heard so much about last year? Whatever happened to them, eh?"

"Some calamitous disaster, I expect," said Mr Piggott, "—pass the claret would you, Charlie?—though for entertainment, I doubt it would have outshone Sadler's performance, right here in our own Angel Meadow."

Mercilessly, they laughed. I squirmed, pinned as if I were a bug, and Edwin's luxurious carpet a tin tray in the Ashmolean. Of all the muscles and joints in my body, just those in my neck seemed to function—and then permitting me only to nod my head at every word my tormentors uttered, like an inflated pig's bladder bobbling atop a jester's baton.

"How adventuresome!" said Bean. "You will never find me courting danger, I am afraid. I value my comforts too much." He yawned and stretched, sinking deeper into the cushions of red silk velvet. "And by happy chance, I have plenty of time to enjoy them."

He glanced, perhaps unconsciously, towards something I had not noticed before: a boxy object resting upon a wooden tripod beneath the window.

"What is that?" I asked, despite myself.

Bean slid off the sofa to join me by the box, patting it fondly. "Come along to my show and you will find out."

"Your show?"

"I am expecting a sizeable audience." He reached into his pocket, withdrawing a slip of paper. "Here—allow me to give you a complementary ticket. I appreciate funds might be a little tight."

I did not take it, being too busy scrutinizing the mysterious box. The object of Bean's affection was roughly cuboidal in shape, a hand's length or so in its greatest dimension, and made from polished walnut with corners and catches of brass. An angled handle projected from a small hole in one side, and in what I supposed to be the front, a larger hole contained a circle of glass resembling a telescope lens. I had never seen anything like it.

"If I may say so, sir," I ventured, "this contraption appears to me more like an instrument of natural philosophy than of superstition."

Edwin was beside me in an instant. "Are you suggesting Mr Bean intends to break the terms of the wager?"

"Of course not, no, I—"

"For that would be the gravest insult to his honour."

"I only—"

"A slander, in fact, demanding restitution. In the traditional manner, you understand."

"I meant nothing by it, I swear."

Bean patted my shoulder. "Dear Edwin, you must stop teasing poor Sadler. I'm an easy-going fellow and seldom take offence."

I was glad to hear it—'twould have been out of all proportion, had a tiff at the Philosophical Club ended with pistols at dawn in the town ditch. The current state of affairs was quite dire enough.

"Might we cease this pointless chatter?" grumbled Mr Twining. "'Tis becoming distracting."

"Oh, do ignore him, Edwin," said Mr Piggott. "He is on a winning streak."

"Is he, now? We shall see about that! And we must also stop wasting Sadler's time. I expect he has many more deliveries to make." Edwin took a coin from his purse—I did not see its worth—and dropped it into my coat pocket. "That is for you. I will settle up with your father at the end of the month, as usual."

Then all four of them returned to their amusements, with no further word nor even one glance in my direction. Quick as I could, I unpacked the sweet-meats and grabbed my basket.

Being delayed so long inside, I blinked to see the Sun again as I trembled in the shadows at the foot of Staircase Six. Edwin had placed that order with a single, obvious aim. And it had worked—though not, perhaps, entirely as he'd intended.

CHAPTER THIRTEEN

DESPITE THE SETBACK AT ST SAVIOUR'S, my spirits were high when I reached Trinity Lane and passed under Danby's stone arch—though the points and stares of two gardeners knocked me rudely back to Earth.

"Well look here!" cried one of the pair. "'Tis Little Red Riding Hood."

I shifted the basket behind my back.

"Are you looking for the Big Bad Wolf?" asked the other.

"I am looking for Wyndham Rudge."

The first gardener plucked a twig from the espalier on the wall behind him and stuck it between his teeth, chewing thoughtfully. "If I were you," he said at last, with a vague wave of the hand, "I would try the East Quarter first."

"But mind yourself," warned the second. "He is in a right old crotchet and might gobble you up!"

"His humour will improve," I assured him, "when he hears what I have to say."

'Twas a commonly heard gibe that, in the Physic Garden's creation, so much was spent on the buildings and walls, a mere pittance had remained for the pur-

115

chase of plants. And seeing the grandeur of the Danby arch, the magnificence of the Keeper's residence, and the ingenious construction of the various conservatories and glasshouses, one might well concur.

Lately, however, the current *Horti Præfectus*, one John Sibthorp, had procured for the vacant beds a wealth of vegetables gathered from every part of the Globe. And so the search for my soon-to-be aide was all the happier for the scents of Indian Tobacco and African Rhubarb, the play of light upon Cedar of Lebanon, and not least the strange doings of the South American Sensitive Plant. The world seemed at last set aright—a wonder in itself, given recent events.

The garden was then, as now, arranged in four equal parts, each quadrant enclosed by dense yew hedges and a stout iron gate. The entrance to the East Quarter I found unlocked and Wyndham Rudge within, pruning a long, low row of lavender bushes. He missed my approach, distracted perhaps by the odd little tune he was humming.

"I have reconsidered your offer," I announced, quick to the point.

Betraying no hint that he'd heard me, Rudge paused to pat his brow with the sleeve of his smock.

"And you will be pleased to know, I have decided to accept it after all."

He grunted and carried on working.

"I admit, I might have appeared somewhat... hasty. Maybe even a little short—though 'twas not intended."

The pruning knife twitched in his hand.

"But now we shall put that behind us and start afresh. 'Tis the sensible thing to do, for I shall see you are well rewarded."

With a single flash of sunlight on metal, a fistful of ragged grey stems sprayed the ground at my feet. Somewhat anxiously, I added, "If you wish me to apologize, I shall gladly do so."

Rudge spared me a glance as sharp as his blade. "Do *you* want to apologize?"

"Of course!" I beamed. "At last we are getting somewhere. I am sorry—nay, *very* sorry that I was... hasty. And short. Now—may we get down to business? I fear my opponent Ambrose Bean has rather more than a head start on me."

Rudge grinned. "It pleased you to waste *my* time, James Sadler. Now I shall return the favour. You may wait here while I finish. Or take yourself off and come back later—'tis naught to me, either way."

"But—"

"Stand aside, please. You are blocking my light."

During the half hour that Rudge delayed me there, how I yearned to tell him where to take *himself* off! Along with his trug of prunings, his ridiculous hat, and even his help with my aerostat. Only the pastry-basket on my arm—or rather, the thought of how foolish I looked carrying it—kept my tongue in check as the aged gardener shuffled from plant to plant with an agonizing want of haste.

How I grew to detest that tuneless hum! And the pointless way he buffed his knife upon his trouser-leg after every cut! To this very day, the smell of lavender renders me fractious. And then, as the bells of Tom Tower struck five, my torment was blessedly ended.

"Follow me," was all he said.

He led me on a circuitous path that skirted the East Quarter, circumnavigated the West, doubled back through the North, and ended up at a row of rude

117

wooden sheds beneath the southern wall of the garden. They stood in stark contrast to the splendour of their surroundings, like a line of shrivelled potatoes in the shadow of a great English Oak. We stopped at the end of the row, where Rudge admitted me to a cubby hole—'twas too small to describe as a room—containing a bed, a chair, a stove and a tiny table. Rudge sat on the chair, leaving me no choice but the bed, which was occupied by a large grey-and-white cat that dug its claws into the mattress when I tried to edge it aside. Rudge laughed and reached across me to ruffle the animal's ears.

"I am curious to know," he said, "what a hasty man like yourself might want with a balloon in the first place. If it's timely transport you're after, 'twould be better to purchase a horse."

I hesitated, for I had expected our dealings to proceed more in the manner of a business transaction than a cosy *tête-à-tête*, but if Rudge's aid must be bought with conversation, 'twas a price I would have to pay. And so I told him at length about the Philosophical Club, Ambrose Bean and his diamond pin, and the wager I hoped would make me a man of consequence.

"And your father? You have spoken with him, I trust?"

I failed to see how this mattered, but by now I had warmed to my theme. "Goodness, no! He would send me early to bed without supper for months, if he ever found out I'd been gambling. Especially on the value of natural philosophy, and worst of all to escape his precious shop. If only he were more like Uncle Elijah."

Rudge raised his eyebrows. "Dead, you mean?"

"Indifferent." I sighed. "How I envy my cousin Jediah! His father expected nothing of him. He was free to live as he pleased."

"And look at him now." Rudge spoke, not to me, but the cat. 'Twas not a surprise, I supposed, for he must seldom receive many guests, or for very long, unless they be as Lilliputian as their surroundings. I suffered a twinge of guilt for snubbing him earlier.

"Do not make an enemy of your father, James. He is an honourable man, ever loyal to his kin."

I scowled. "He does not know the meaning of those words. To Father, family is pastries and pies, and loyalty lies in their selling for maximum profit. And as for honour... They say there is no honour amongst thieves. Well, 'tis much the same for shopkeepers."

I vented my frustration by slapping the mattress; startled, the cat jumped onto the floor and yowled in indignation.

"I am not fond of sweetmeats, as you know," Rudge said as he patted its head. "But it seems to me that a pastry-cook earns more than many men, and spends less in sweat and blood than those who must labour with their hands for their bread."

"There is more to life than money!" I sprang upright, cracking my own head upon the ceiling. "Where is the beauty in baking? What truth does Sadler's Finest Cheesecake reveal? It could be the finest, most toothsome cheesecake in all the World, but it would still, at base, be naught but sugar and orange peel, and finished in just a few bites. *Thomas* Sadler's dreams extend no further than the end of a pastry-shop counter. His son's go far beyond."

Having slunk beneath Rudge's chair, the cat hissed in rage at this outburst, though Rudge himself seemed unperturbed, so I continued, "The *Officina Chimica* was my first hope for escape. But they work me harder than Father, if that be possible, and with even less chance of advancement. So now I plan to best Ambrose Bean, and with the funds raised from the sale of his diamond I shall purchase a place at St Alban's College."

"Now *that* sounds like hard work."

"Hard work? You would not believe the mountains I must climb, day upon day! Father has always thwarted my attempts to better myself. Even now, he does his utmost to distract me. 'Tis odd, you must agree, that I need but glance towards a pamphlet—God forbid I should ever read a book!—and the Lady Chester requires her macaroons post-haste, or the butter-factor is at the door and there is no one but me free to deal with him."

"At least you will have your balloon."

"My aerostatic globe," I corrected. "'Tis not a child's plaything. But yes—and lest we forget why we're here, you promised to help me construct it. So quickly—tell me all that you know and we'll trade talk for industrious action!"

"If we are trading in talk—" Rudge took a long-stemmed clay pipe from the table and slotted the bit in the side of his mouth, where it dangled unlit. "—then *you* must first tell *me* what manner of action you've taken so far. And none of your *quickly*, mind. I have not as many days to spare as you, and must choose wisely where I spend them."

"Obviously," I replied (being careful to conceal my increasing annoyance). "But I, too, have no wish to waste time. You have, I trust, heard the recent news concerning Vincenzo Lunardi?"

Rudge shook his head.

"Perhaps you know him better by his nickname? *The Daredevil Aeronaut*, as the newssheets will have it. No? But how could you not? He is the talk of all London, not to mention— Oh, never mind. Suffice to say: Signor Lunardi is an exemplary man. A diplomat from Naples by profession, but also a pioneer of aerostatics. By means of which, he latterly ascended from the old artillery grounds at Finsbury and thus shall ever be known as England's first aeronaut—though not, of course, the first *English* aeronaut. 'Twas *Jackson's Oxford Journal* that alerted me to this feat, and of all the accounts I have collected, theirs remains the most instructional."

"That was a stroke of luck," said Rudge.

"If only the rest came so easy! 'Twas a labour fit for Hercules, finding detailed reports in our native tongue on the past year's advances in Europe. Even the Montgolfiers are skimpily treated, and the ascent of Monsieur Pilâtre de Rozier and the Marquis d'Arlandes—man's first free flight!—merits less than a footnote. However, I persevered, for the record abounds with tales of the earliest aeronauts—the likes of *Les Frères Roberts*, Professor Charles, the Duke of Chartres—"

"That is indeed a peck of reading. And grand-sounding names."

"'Tis not the least of it! I have acquired the first volume of Dr Priestley's *Experiments And Observations On Different Kinds Of Air* from my colleague Mr Nugent, and have committed to memory the attributes of alkaline air, nitrous air, phlogiston and dephlogisticated air, the production of inflammable air from the decomposition of water—"

"So many airs, and none of them any good for breathing. 'Tis a wonder God put them there at all— No, do not trouble yourself to explain it. You have not answered my first question yet."

I had to admit I'd forgotten.

"*What*, exactly, have you *done*?"

"Done?"

"What do you have to show for all of your learning?"

"Ah," I said, my cheeks beginning to burn. "You have seen it already, I think. Though I have also fashioned numerous small boxes of paper and raised them with great success from my work-bench in the laboratory."

"Hmm," said Rudge. He stood, and with the unlit pipe still clenched between his teeth took the two short steps from the chair to the bothy's door.

"Come with me. I have something to show you."

~ ~ ~

Our destination was but a brief stroll through a side-gate—blessedly so, my patience having already been tested to breaking point (as would, within the year, the aerostat of the bold Monsieur de Rozier, who Fate had decreed to be first to fledge, but also quickest to fall).

"In here," ordered Rudge.

"Here" being the occupant of an otherwise empty tract of land on the riverbank; I shall call it a glass-house, though 'twould scarce compare with the crystal-line mansions we see in great gardens today. Plate glass was expensive then, far beyond the means of even John Sibthorp. Rudge's construction, though of decent size, was instead fashioned from a multitude of small panes held together by thick black glazing bars; not one sat square against its neighbours and so the whole presented a patchwork of mismatched reflections. A sliver a sky here, a chink of Cherwell-water there— 'twas as if some whimsical landscape artist had cut his favourite painting into a million tiny fragments, flung them all into the air, then rejoined them together at random wherever they fell.

I hastened within for the sake of my sanity, though the interior of the glasshouse proved almost as disquieting as its façade, with its hoard of broken-down wheelbarrows, cracked flowerpots, and rusty shovels and shears. The entire assemblage seemed on the brink of disintegration, held together only by the spider webs that blanketed every surface. And yet, at the very centre of this decrepitude, stood an easel, clean and intact, and beside it a cherry-wood table bearing a brush and three saucers of pigment.

"You paint?"

Rudge grunted something indelicate, then for no obvious reason fell upon a nearby mountain of sackcloth, tearing into it for several minutes before I spied the object of his exertions: a battered ebony chest, lodged deep within the morass. As he heaved and hoed it free, a massive cloud of dust sprang up, causing him to stop and blow his nose. I supposed that while he was, by necessity, well ordered in his cramped living quarters, the spaciousness of the glasshouse nurtured some natural penchant for chaos.

"I offered to help you build a balloon," he wheezed. "Not to fetch and carry while you stand around watching."

Matters might have gone smoother between us, had I explained there and then that fetching and carrying was precisely the manner of help I required. But I leapt to his aid without comment, alas, and cheek by jowl we loosened the chest and hauled it into a clearing amidst the clutter. Rudge paused to wipe the palms of his hands on his trousers, then cracked open the lid and removed a roll of paper, which he unfurled with some solemnity.

"You painted *this*?" I exclaimed, on seeing the contents.

"Many years ago, yes."

"How can that be? Not even *one* year has passed since de Rozier's ascent. I know this for fact—the Marquis's account is quite clear on the dating!"

Rudge treated me to a gap-toothed grin. "Well read you are, James Sadler, though that does not mean you know everything. Pilâtre de Rozier was the first to find fame for his deeds—that, I cannot dispute. But the first *aeronaut*... well, *he* had no wealthy Marquis to make him famous, nor any desire for such."

I snorted in derision at this, and scanned the offending tableau intently in search of some telltale discrepancy, some fatal flaw that would prove the gardener wrong.

"You tell a pretty story with your paints—"

"Ah, you are too kind—"

"—but 'tis *only* a story. That you painted it, does not make it true, however much you might wish it otherwise."

And yet... So vivid was Rudge's brushwork, I almost forgot my own advice. It took an effort of will, not to squint in the glare of sunlight on scorched white sand, or cup a hand to my ear to hear the men speak—these men who were not of England nor even of France. And that skinny, half-naked boy who watched from the wings... Doubt gave way to envy, part of me wishing I were he, as the man at the centre of the action (the lad's father, perhaps?) cast off the ties that have hitherto bound all mankind to Earth. I wondered for an instant what he might find at his destination. And then, thank goodness, my good sense brought me back.

"Everyone knows the Montgolfiers conceived the first aerostat."

"Do they now? I trust they also know the name of Leonardo di ser Piero da Vinci."

I cursed under my breath; no gardener dare best *me* in a contest of knowledge.

"Leonardo's inventions were as fantastical as your painting. No man could build a flying machine in his day. Only now do we have the knowledge. Only in this time, in this place, have the means and the opportunity come together, by Fate or Providence."

"So men are cleverer now than they were, and cleverer in England and France than elsewhere?"

"That is right. We understand each other now."

"Hmm."

Having noticed that this simple sound often led to some grave proclamation, I feared I had pushed him too far and that he meant to renege on his offer.

I added before he could speak, "'Tis good to know our differences are so slight and so easily settled—"

But Rudge had now disappeared behind an immense and perilously unstable-looking tower of packing crates at the rear of the glasshouse. Part curious, part fearful for his safety, I followed him and continued, "It proves how well we are suited to working together."

"It proves how much you have to learn," Rudge grunted.

"I—Whatever are you doing down there?" He scowled up at me from the floor, where he had crouched over a crumpled mound of fabric that resembled nothing so much as a gigantic pastry puff, though dusted with dirt rather than sugar. "What does it look like I'm doing?"

I shrugged.

Rudge sighed, but bounced to his feet with surprising agility. Then, with a grandiose twirl of the arm—like a fairground magician pulling not just a rabbit from his but an entire warren-full of the creatures, plus a dozen head of cattle and a donkey for good measure—he drew my gaze to the formless mass on the floor.

"You were telling me," he said, "how the Montgolfiers made the first aerostat...?"

CHAPTER FOURTEEN

N EXT MORNING, I AROSE AN AGE before my natural waking time, though still not so early as Mary. The door to the kitchen burst open the instant the tip of my toe touched the landing.

"Who goes here?"

She looked me up and down with eyebrows raised, delighting as always in foiling my plans.

"'Tis a ghost, surely? For it cannot be my brother. *His* day is but eight hours long, not the eighteen or more that the rest of us toil."

"Not a ghost," I said, though I did feel half-dead with exhaustion. "Nor even your brother, as you knew him before today. You see here the *new* James Sadler: reformed, restored, and ambitions rekindled."

I saw her stifle a laugh, and tensed.

"You look no different to me."

"But I am thoroughly changed inside. As cousin Jediah would probably say, *by their fruits ye shall know them*."

Her expression softened, though only for a moment. "I have less need of fruits than of a helping hand around the house. If this new James Sadler is as improved as you say—I presume you mean 'improved',

127

for you surely could not be worsened—might he see fit to lay the table while I finish his father's breakfast?"

"Well—"

"Now there's a surprise."

She stepped back inside the kitchen, grabbed the lump of bread dough she'd been pummelling and slammed it back onto the tabletop. 'Twas time I took my leave.

"Tell Father I shall be back within two hours."

"Of course." She thumped the dough so hard, I winced. "You never change, do you?"

"I swear it. Upon my honour!"

In the pause while my sister contrived yet another insult, I spun about and bolted down the stairs. Her words had cut deep. Of course, I had erred—too many times to count, let alone mention. But that, I promised myself, was all in the past; in the present, Father's good favour was vital, for without it 'twould be next to impossible to manage my labours in the shop, the laboratory, and now Rudge's glasshouse as well.

To my surprise, I found the streets almost as busy then as later in the day, though with different sorts of people—the hawkers' stalls on the High surrounded by builders gobbling steaming-hot pies; the farmers bound for the vegetable market with waggons full of fresh green-stuff; the cook-house keepers and housemaids; the gummy-eyed floozies dodging the Proctors; the butchers and bakers, coachmen and boatmen—all those who keep a town running, in fact, instead of the late-rising types who merely provide decoration. The scholarly life seemed vainglorious by contrast—until I happened upon the night-man's cart on Holywell Street. Such people may be useful, I decided, but higher-minded men smell much the sweeter.

As I'd expected, the laboratory was empty—and would remain so for hours, I hoped. My aim was to whisk through my chores for the day and still be back at the shop for the morning deliveries. But confronted by my work-bench, littered with scorched paper boxes, I almost erred before I could start. I swept them into the furnace, but my thoughts had already drifted to the shrivelled aerostat, and the thrilling prospect of restoring it to life.

Rudge—that kill-joy!—had been quick to crush any notion that my wager with Ambrose Bean was now good as won. After mouldering in the glasshouse for so many years, the Chinese aerostat—the 'Little Emperor', as Rudge called it—would be in no state to fly without an immense amount of work. And money, too. "We need paper to make a new lining," Rudge had explained, "and rope and timber to build masts to suspend the globe as we fill it. And a good length of pipe fashioned from leather, and a stout barrel to hold the iron filings—of which we shall need a prodigious amount—and, of course, much Spirit of Vitriol, from which we will make our inflammable air."

My father once baked a bride-cake for the youngest daughter of the Lady Turbot, and I swear the shopping list for that commission was child's play compared with Rudge's demands. I'd suggested to my new 'helper' that my method of burning old stockings in a basket, though less 'scientific' than his proposal, was simpler and very much cheaper. "'Tis a matter of lift," Rudge had said, adding darkly that I might be of a different opinion when I found myself a thousand feet above ground reliant on naught but a paper balloon and a large open fire.

But how will we raise the money? I had persisted. And where will we obtain all these items? Rudge had shrugged in an irritating manner and muttered something about this being "your wager", "your balloon", and "your problem". And thus concluded our first "strategical meeting", as Rudge liked to call them. I might have conceded victory to Bean there and then, had I not suffered a terrible dream that night in which certain Philosophical Club members, shrunk to the size of schoolboys, laughed in my face when Ambrose Bean showed his box to contain naught but dust.

I sighed heavily, a hollow sound in the vaults of the *Officina Chimica*. Then I set my worries aside as best I could and went to work. First on the list was a hastily scribbled note from Dr Crouch. Blue Vitriol, Sal Ammoniac, Alum, Tartar, Spirit of Salt... and on and on and on it went; an endless inventory of powders and waters and oils for me to weigh and mix and stir. If there was anything I hated more than cleaning the furnaces, 'twas preparing Dr Crouch's reagents. But this was the first day of the 'new James Sadler', I reminded myself, and the greater good demanded I endure such tediums with a willing heart, if not good cheer.

With another sigh, I made my weary way to the eastern end of the laboratory, where a glass-fronted cabinet spanned the wall from ceiling to floor, on its shelves a profusion of pots, bottles, and jars. I scanned their ranks for the first item on the list. Blue Vitriol, Blue Vitriol, Blue Vitriol... one brown glass bottle looks much like any other, and it took me a good ten minutes to find what I wanted. After repeating this process for Sal Ammoniac, and then for Alum and Tartar, I cursed the bottles for not being arranged in a more logical manner. Then I remembered Dr Crouch saying the very same some weeks ago, and assigning me the task of reordering and relabelling the entire collection, and how I had prevaricated so long, he eventually forgot about the matter, and thus I avoided that dreary chore. I assured myself that such a thing would never happen now, and continued my interminable task.

'Twas on the nineteenth or twentieth ascent of the stepladder that my gaze fell upon one of the few clearly labelled containers in the cabinet. Not a reagent on Dr Crouch's list, but a chymical that had been much on my mind during the past several hours. Spirit of Vitriol—stored alongside Mercury and Lime, I noted, not with the other spirits as one might have expected, or even with the other vitriols. I recalled my protest to Rudge. *From where will we obtain these materials? And how will we raise the money?* I reached for the bottle, dropping Crouch's list as I did; it drifted to the floor like a crushed butterfly.

So many reagents, so poorly catalogued. Would anyone notice if I took just a little? Or even a lot? I thought of the laboratory order book on my bench. Requests were supposed to be approved by Dr Wall but were never refused, or even questioned. Who would know if I placed an order of my own? Each of us toiled in our own small world; no one knew what anyone else was doing. I could tell Crouch the iron filings were for Nugent, and Nugent they were for Wilkes. No one would guess their true purpose.

And, I thought, why should I *not* divert to myself a minuscule portion of the laboratory's wealth? 'Twas not as though my aim was personal gain (not entirely, anyway). My aerostat would be no less a feat of natural philosophy than Dr Crouch's operations—and of a greater sort than the mere mixing of chymicals to entertain Undergraduates with the smell they might make, or to observe whether their precipitate be yellow, green, or pink. My aerostat would lift me into the atmosphere, where no Englishman had gone before, and what greater contribution to mankind's progress could one make!

My loins only slightly girded by these mental contortions, I gripped the frame of the stepladder with one hand, lest it overbalance and toss me back to Earth (which would have been fitting), and inched the other towards the shelf—

"Sadler! What are you doing here?"

With a strangled squawk of pure terror, I somehow spun about on my perch without falling.

"Nothing, I swear! I mean, that is to say—"

Ignoring me, Nugent consulted his pocket-watch. "Well, that's a relief. For a moment there, I feared I must be late."

"You are punctual as always," I croaked. "I am the one out of step."

"But coming to your senses." Nugent marched across the room to retrieve Crouch's list from the floor and handed it up to me with a self-satisfied chortle. "I see you have taken my advice."

"I certainly have. And shall continue to do so. You will excuse me if I do not stop to chat." I swivelled back towards the wall, pretending to study the list until Nugent—grumbling at the very notion that *he* might want to *chat*—had withdrawn to his bench.

My cheeks were surely redder than the belly of Nugent's reverberatory, so close had I come to disgrace. Would I have taken the Spirit of Vitriol, had my colleague not entered the room at the very instant my hand touched the glass? I cannot say for certain, though for the sake of my eternal soul, I remain thankful that he did.

CHAPTER FIFTEEN

"TWO GUINEAS. NO MORE, NO LESS."

The pawnbroker put down his eyeglass and pushed William Tench's *Opus Maius* back over the counter towards me. I left it there, dismayed.

"But this is a rare edition! And in excellent fettle, as well. See—there is not a mark upon that lambskin."

"'Tis goat, not lamb. And hardly a rarity—quite the opposite, in fact. 'Tis obvious this volume comprises the off-cuts of various misprints, assembled into a whole worth even less than the sum of its parts." He sniffed in disdain. "Besides, there is little market for books."

"Little market for books!" I spluttered. "Do you take me for a fool? This is Oxford! Turn any stone and beneath it you'll find a scholar."

I had not intended to liken Gownsmen to woodlice, but the pawnbroker merely shrugged.

"Turn a stone and you'll find a *student*—and there he might remain, for all I care—but *scholars* are rarer than an honest lawyer these days. Two guineas is my final offer. Take it or leave it."

"You drive a hard bargain, sir."

135

With a tight smile—and me looking on glumly—he swiped the book off the counter and perused his crowded shelves for a space to display it.

"While you are here," he breezed, "may I interest you in a box of French pins? Or a splendid matched pair of duelling pistols?"

"I am here to make money, not spend it," I muttered.

I slunk away head bowed, as if I carried the two guineas not in my purse but about my neck—thirty pieces of silver could not have weighed heavier! The pawnbroker had his shop on Butcher Row, once home to every slaughterman in the city, where the kennels used to run red with blood and gore. In recent years, the Corporation of Oxford had moved them all to the new covered market, out of the sight and smell of sensitive eyes and well-bred noses, but the cobbles still bore the stains of their trade. And now 'twas I who wielded the knife, both betraying the trust of a friend and scorning the guiding principle of all men of science (for, to paraphrase Professor Newton, no Dwarf who feared a stab in the back would dare mount a Giant's shoulders).

I stopped by the Carfax Conduit to cool my face with a splash of water from the stone ox's pizzle. On the pedestal above me, facing North, South, East, and West, stood stern-faced effigies of Fortitude, Temperance, Justice, and Wisdom—virtues it seemed I'd already lost, and I'd not yet even begun to raise the funds for our iron filings. That was my next task. Heaven help me.

As I dried my cheeks on my sleeve, a scrawny youth flashed by and pushed a handbill into my palm. I was about to dump it straight in the cistern, but the word

Emperor caught my eye. And then *Golden Box of the Emperor*, swiftly followed by *Golden Box of the Emperor, He who Reckons the Heavens, Counter of the Stars and Measurer of the Earth*. I tried to call the youth back but he was already halfway down Fish Street, darting between the old butter-bench, with its congregation of vagabonds and laggards, and the crowd of aldermen and corn-dealers bustling outside the Town Hall. I stared hard at the crumpled slip of paper, remembering Ambrose Bean and the Staircase Six Society. *"Come along to my show and you will find out...I am expecting a sizeable audience."*

"The Proctors must hear about this," rumbled an ominous voice behind me. "'Tis nonsense, of course, but dangerous nonetheless. I trust you are not a subscriber."

I turned to find my cousin Jediah reading the hand-bill over my shoulder. I stuffed it into my coat, unnerved less by the sudden appearance of the very person I was now on my way to see, than by the tenor of his words, which seemed more a question than a statement of fact.

"Of course not! Such flim-flam might be in vogue amongst melancholics, ladies, and the gullible, but it holds no appeal for a natural philosopher."

"'Tis a Godless age we inhabit when even the dead are not safe in their slumber, lured blasphemously from their graves for the sake of spectacle and the avarice of the peddlers of these *Phantasmagoria*." Jediah heaved a doleful sigh. "But you must forgive me, if I spoke amiss."

He looked as though he meant it, which surprised me—as did his apparent acquaintance with a form of entertainment I had only read about in the London newssheets.

"I, too, read the newssheets," he added, "for my sins. Good day, cousin."

And thus with my unasked question answered, he tipped his hat and took off on the path of Wisdom.

"Wait!" I scurried after him. "May I speak with you? I was hoping to find you at college today."

"You would have been disappointed, then, for I am here, and about deanery business."

"Then may I walk with you? Your father's death has reminded me how little time we have on this Earth and how much of it we waste."

Jediah shrugged. "Come, then. What is it you wish to say?"

For such a tall man, my cousin had an exceptionally short stride; so short, in fact, I could have twice traversed the entire length of North Gate Street in half the time it took us to reach the pillory opposite Bridewell Lane, though this did at least give me time to prepare my approach.

"You will know about my wager, of course."

"Your wager?"

"The one I contracted recently with a certain Mr Ambrose Bean."

"I am afraid I do not."

"Everyone is talking about it."

"*You* will know that I never listen to gossip. Or perhaps you overestimate your own consequence."

I bit back a peevish rejoinder.

"If you *have* been gambling, however," Jediah continued, his staccato pace unfaltering, "'tis incumbent upon me to caution you that—"

"'Twas done with the best of intentions, I assure you. And if I win—when I win—the proceeds will be used wisely."

"Will they, indeed?"

"Indeed! By their careful investment, I shall soon have the wherewithal to join you."

"Join me where?"

"At St Alban's, where else?"

As I spoke, two leery coves crossed our path; on seeing Jediah, one of them nudged his companion and cried, "Bugger me! 'Tis the Reaper hisself!"

"More like a death's head on a mop-stick," sniggered the other.

I sidestepped to let them pass without further insult, mindful of Jediah's mood, which was already less agreeable than I'd planned for.

"I loathe intemperance," my cousin said. "Almost as much as I detest nepotism. God bestowed upon man the capacity for pleasure, so 'tis fit and proper that he might enjoy in moderation the society of his fellows or his kinsman's promotion, if rightfully earned. But the drunkard and the nepotist alike exalt their pleasures above all else, neglecting the true purpose of life, which is to delight in God Himself, accepting gratefully the joys that He provides."

He glared at his ungrateful slanderers, who now appeared on course for The Plough, still jeering and jibing at any and all they encountered.

"In short—never ask me for favours, for my answer will always be no."

"As I would expect from a man of principle such as yourself," I replied, relieved that my cousin's sermon had not lasted as long as it might. "However, 'twas not my question—"

"And what of your languages? You have a school-boy's grasp of Latin I grant, but unless you enjoy considerably more leisure time than the average working man, I doubt you have any Greek."

I grinned. "Cousin Jediah, you know as well as I that every college makes exceptions for the wealthy."

"The wealthy—you?" Jediah scoffed, though with grudging curiosity. "Might I ask what exactly this wager entails?"

At last I had his attention!

"It entails—and since you keep abreast of the news, you will appreciate the significance." I took a deep breath. "I shall soon become an aeronaut, God willing—the first amongst our English race."

Jediah stopped dead, like he'd trodden in something spilled from the night-man's cart.

"Thrilling, is it not? Like a knight defending his lady's honour, I shall champion the cause of natural philosophy while mounted upon an aerostatic globe of my own creation. See here—" I scrambled in my pocket for the page of *Jackson's Oxford Journal* I'd taken from Harper's, but Jediah waved it away without touching it.

"Please get to the point," he said.

Within the voluminous folds of his cloak, I could have sworn he was trembling. Perhaps he had noticed the same, for he started walking again, and faster this time, catching me unawares.

"'Twould be a formidable task for even the best-connected gentleman—" I hastened after him. "—and all but impossible for a lone pastry-cook's son. Cousin Jediah, I beseech you... St Alban's is the best of colleges, famed throughout the county—nay, the country—for the brilliance of its scholars. Can you inform me, if there be any Fellow amongst you who might be inspired by my adventure? And being inspired, aid me with materials or advice?"

"Or money?" Jediah glanced down at me, narrow-eyed.

I squirmed. "Any gentleman who might wish to invest will be welcome to do so, of course."

"Ha! There are no such gentlemen in St Alban's, or in any other college. Fellows are not, by and large, as rich as you seem to suppose. And if they were, not one of them would be so witless as to find inspiration in an *aerostatic globe*." He spat out the latter two words, as though they tasted unpleasant upon his tongue.

"They might refuse *me*," I replied, "but what of their country's needs? We are already outpaced by the French, who excel in aeronautics—and much else besides, in every field of natural philosophy."

"We have nothing to fear from the French. They are far too fond of their fine wine and rich food."

I might have responded that the same could be said for any number of Oxford men, but did not wish to upset him further.

"I mean no offence, cousin, but the men I seek *do* exist in St Alban's. I encountered one myself—or his rooms, at least. You know the day of which I speak," I added quickly, in case Jediah mentioned it first, and in more detail. "The items I saw in his study suggest a man who might be at least a little curious about my scheme."

"I know of no such Fellow now. He must have died years ago and long returned to dust. Perhaps you are the only person alive who remembers him."

I shivered at the thought. Then we reached the Turl, and I had to step into the kennel to avoid a group of gentleman-commoners, the thread-of-gold tassels on their mortarboards bobbing in the sunlight as they meandered upon some business of interest only to them. They occupied half the breadth of the street with their idle swagger, their vacuous conversation.

"It does not please me to beg," I cried, all at once overwhelmed by the injustices of my own sorry existence. "But believe me—*I* am not the one demanding rope, or iron filings, or Spirit of Vitriol. *I* am not the one insisting we fly by inflammable air, though 'tis obvious a fire balloon would be cheaper, and easier too. We are surrounded by all the fuel we need—old rags, bits of wool, and the like—and all cost-free, or bought for next to nothing!"

Now 'twas I that passers-by swerved to avoid, but I barrelled on regardless. We would soon reach the side-gate of Exeter College, and close upon it the entrance to the Old Ashmolean, then before I knew it, I'd be back at the steps that led me daily down into purgatory.

"Yet will Rudge ever listen? Oh, no!" I waggled my fist in mocking imitation of my partner. "The Little Emperor was once a gas balloon and so it must remain for all time, commonsense be damned—"

"What did you say?" breathed Jediah, halting again.

"Forgive me, I did not mean to curse."

"Before that!"

"The Little Emperor? 'Tis an aerostat—or the remnants of one. Wyndham Rudge claims he acquired it while jaunting with your father. Do you know of it? He has kept it all these years at the Physic Garden."

Jediah closed his eyes and his skin, already ashen, developed a frightful deathly hue. I feared he would faint and looked around for somewhere to lay him, but he steadied himself with a shuddering sigh.

"'Tis clear to me," he said, "that your problem has but one, simple solution."

"I would like to hear it," I muttered.

He cleared his throat and continued, "My father had his failings, as does any man, but in financial matters he was faultless. Might I confide in you?" He drew closer and lowered his voice. "Certain shrewd speculations on his part have left me with an inheritance that borders on the embarrassing, given the simple life I lead. I could leave the deposits untouched and no doubt accrue a greater fortune still, but what would become of it? For of course, I have no heir."

I dared to begin to hope that I might understand him. "You wish to give me... a gift?"

In the shadows beneath the brim of his hat, his eyes glittered like diamond dust. "Not a gift—'twould be too easy. You may consider this a business proposal."

"A loan?"

"An investment." He raised a forefinger in warning. "Let us be clear, I would demand a substantial return. For we are, after all, family."

Needless to say, this development filled my head with all kinds of extravagant imaginings. I saw the Little Emperor rising Phoenix-like from the glasshouse and myself hailed a hero throughout the civilized world; I saw Ambrose Bean and the treacherous Edwin Osborne forced to admit my preeminence; and Nugent insisting that furnace-cleaning was his job alone from now on; and Mary promising likewise for the delivery round. Dazzled by this tantalizing bauble, I snatched at my cousin's proposal without a thought for his own intentions, and was nodding my agreement even as he spoke again.

"There is one condition."

"Name it!"

"Rudge must go."

"Go where?"

He stooped a little to look me straight in the eye. "No kin of mine must ever work with that man."

I was dumbfounded. "What about the Little Emperor?"

"'Tis no concern of mine, or of yours now. Why settle for an old man's cast-off, when you can have a brand-new globe all of your own? And fresh, sprightly assistants—you will have your pick of the best of them."

"Rudge is not my assistant."

"Is that so?" Jediah grimaced. "If you consider that poisonous farmhand your friend, I advise you to think again. Wyndham Rudge has no concept of true friendship. Respect, loyalty, constancy... all are foreign to him. Oh, I am sure you find him endearing—who could fail to warm to that gruff façade or the kindly heart beneath? Which is the true Rudge? Neither, I would hazard, for both the ill humour and the good are fabrications, designed to confound and confuse."

Confused I certainly was. "You say Rudge is not to be trusted?"

"I would no more trust that wretch than a snake in the grass."

Jediah sliced a hand through empty space—despatching in his head a serpent, I hoped, rather than Rudge.

"I am surprised you need so long to decide," he sniffed.

I fidgeted this way and that in a miserable quandary; lifted my hat to smooth my hair, tugged a loose thread from the elbow of my coat, wriggled my hands deep in my pockets as though I might find my answer there. What I did find was the handbill given me by the youth at Carfax. I took it out and read it again, disheartened and beguiled in equal measure. How I ached to discover the contents of Ambrose Bean's box! And how could the son of a pastry-cook compete with the Counter of Stars? I had but two guineas to my name; that, and a small mountain of canvas.

Jediah's tone softened. "I have read that there are a great many... *aeronauts* at work on the continent. Some in London, even. With my backing, you could purchase a vehicle from one of them. Think of the all the time and hard work you would save."

He was, of course, correct, and who in sound mind could refuse him? Yet I struggled to find a reply, being lost for words of any sort, let alone the right ones. Then, as we neared the Ashmolean, fate offered a helping hand in the apposite form of William Tench, who sprang upon me with an exuberant punch to my ribs that sent me reeling.

"James—where have you been all these days? I feared you had taken fright and resorted to self-rustication! Not that you ever would, of course. I suppose you have been busy with *you-know-what.*" He winked in a theatrical fashion while I continued to splutter, then extended a hand to Jediah. "This must be your relative. I see the resemblance. Pleased to meet you, sir." He did not wait for Jediah to reciprocate—though I doubt my cousin would have done so—instead, he turned back towards me and waved a handbill in my face. "Have you seen this?"

Between wheezes, I nodded.

"'Tis Ambrose Bean's handiwork. It all sounds rather intriguing, I have to confess. But rest assured— I, for one, shall refuse to attend. You are my loyal and constant friend, and that presumptuous popinjay will not have a farthing from me!"

I swear I would have wept for shame, had he gone on much longer.

"Now I must bid you farewell, I'm afraid, for I have a lecture on Logic today and must get up on my *Analytics*." He nodded to Jediah. "Good day, sir. And James—next time we meet, do remind me to drop by the shop to collect my Bacon."

I mouthed something indistinct in reply to his cheery wave.

"I must also take my leave," said Jediah. "When *we* meet again, we shall discuss the details of our arrangement."

"No," I said.

"No?"

"You are more generous than I deserve, but I cannot accept your proposal." I spoke hurriedly, anxious to get the words out before the sensible side of my brain realized what the other half was doing and put a stop to it. "For Rudge has been generous too, and your investment would require me to do him a great disservice."

'Twas Jediah's turn to be dumbstruck. "You prefer that—that... You prefer *him* to me, your flesh and blood?"

You prefer him to me. Bemused by this oddly childish presumption, I hastened to reassure him. "I have no preference one way or the other—'tis merely a matter of timing. You do understand? I am grateful

146

for your offer, but you cannot deny that Rudge was there before you."

"Would that *he* ever felt the same," growled Jediah, but under his breath, and clearly not for my consideration.

"Please do not take it personally. We shall, as always, continue to meet, to talk, to sup, to—" I stopped before I said *jest*; with Jediah, that was never likely. "As you said, we are family."

"Family? What remains of my family lies rotting in St Clement's graveyard."

"I am sorry, I swear," I continued. "But do not fear for your legacy, cousin—I guarantee you will soon find another deserving recipient. Should I encounter one myself, I shall point him in your direction. Now, if I may, I would beg one favour before you go."

Jediah said nothing, though while I spoke he seemed to have shrivelled, crushed within his cloak like a wounded raven.

"Father will learn of my wager before very long—he is not so well guarded from gossip as you—but until that moment, if you find him in earshot, I trust I can count upon your discretion?"

"Of course," Jediah said, with the ghost of a smile. "My lips are sealed."

I would have thanked him, had the Earth beneath our feet not suddenly quaked with a thunderous din. Jediah made off in some haste, while in the yard below, the door to the *Officina Chimica* burst open with a sulphurous belch, and a pillar of roiling black smoke spewed out and shot skywards. Much panicked wailing and howling followed, none of it more terrifying than the bellows of Solomon Crouch.

"—you half-witted bull-calf! You dull-swift! Be damned what it said on the label—"

'Twas time, I decided, to follow my cousin's example.

"God's teeth!—is that Sadler up there, gawping like a loon?"

I turned about with a sigh.

"Get him down here this instant—and put out that fire!"

I longed to explain I might gawp as I please, being off duty—but preferred not to be hauled off the street by Nugent, Wilkes, or anyone else. With a wistful glance at my cousin's retreating back, I descended once again into the pit.

CHAPTER SIXTEEN

"**Y**OU LOOK LIKE YOU LOST seven guineas and found a Scotch fiddle."

"And what, precisely," I growled, "is *that* supposed to mean? No—do not bother. I doubt you would look any better than I, had you endured the merest fraction of the hardships I have suffered already this day—and 'tis not even teatime!"

I slumped upon the nearest pile of sackcloth, while Rudge continued to chortle.

"Hardship? Why, you slugabed youngsters! You barely know the meaning of the word. When I was a boy, we rose at dawn and toiled in the fields all day without rest. To bring in the harvest before a storm struck, we worked through the night as well—babes, infants, and all!"

"You must be thankful, then, that your present employment is naught but a little light pruning."

"Hmm."

Rudge shambled to the centre of the glasshouse, beneath the highest part of the roof, where we had cleared a space and unfurled the Little Emperor in all his tattered glory.

"I suppose you have been too busy to search for supplies? If you remembered them at all, having so many hardships in need of attention."

"'Tis in hand," I replied, my annoyance disguised with a feigned fit of coughing. "Zounds, you keep it so dusty in here—ofttimes I can hardly breathe. It cannot be good for our health."

"It suits me well enough," said Rudge. "But feel free to return to your shop, if you'd wish somewhere cleaner."

I was back on my feet and at work in a flash. In truth, those chymicals, ropes, and the like would be of no more use to us than Rudge's Scotch fiddle if we failed to repair the Little Emperor first. The outer skin of the globe was fashioned from gores of lightweight canvas, these elements sealed against leakage by the surprisingly simple means of countless bone buttons and fabric loops. Over the years, however, many of the buttons had become loose—their threads gnawed by mice, no doubt—and the fabric torn; our first task thus demanded a great deal of sewing. Or should I say, *my* first task. Rudge had an admirable knack of avoiding work whilst giving the orders.

"Use a double thread—'tis stronger and quicker," he barked, impressing me yet again with his knowledge of the seamstress's trade. "And wind it half a dozen times around the shank to secure the button."

I would have bridled at such interference had it come from my father or Dr Crouch, but I found myself gladly accepting Rudge's advice—even inviting it, on occasion.

During a rare break from the needlework, I decided to discover more about my colleague's adventures in China.

"The man in your painting—the aeronaut—did you and Uncle Elijah know him well?"

"Well enough."

"Did he build the aerostat himself?"

"Aye, he did."

"Then where did he learn the skills he would need? In our scientific endeavours we Europeans stand on the shoulders of giants. On whose shoulders did the aeronaut stand?"

"Foreign lands breed their share of giants, too," Rudge replied in a mildly exasperated manner.

"And what of the boy?"

"What boy?"

"The boy in your painting. Did he follow his father into the atmosphere?"

The gentle smile turned into a rather less merry expression. "That is not the aeronaut's son. 'Tis your cousin Jediah."

I'd assumed the boy was a native, given his state of undress and tanned skin; to learn we were kin was both startling and intriguing.

"I've heard he hardly ever joined you on your travels."

Rudge nodded. "That was the only time."

I wondered if I might ask him whether the story concerning the seeds was true, though his mood suggested that might be reserved for later.

"'Tis peculiar," I mused instead, recalling Jediah's visit to the museum, "that a man who has seen something of the world—especially at such a young age—should profess so little... so little *curiosity* for what is in it."

"As I said, 'twas just the once. Now, let me see those buttons." Rudge came alongside me to squint at my handiwork. "Passable, I'd say—for a beginner."

"I wish 'twere me in that painting." I gazed upwards, through the glass roof and into the darkening sky beyond. "When I was that age, I'd convinced myself I would one day fly to the Moon."

Rudge grasped an edge of the canvas with a vigorous shake, dislodging a huge puff of dust and yet more buttons for my collection. "From where, in Heaven's name, did you pluck *that* fanciful notion?"

"'Twas thanks to my mother." I smiled at the memory. "One evening she walked me all the way up from the High onto Shotover Hill. It took us forever to get there, it seemed, and my feet were so terribly sore. What misery must my whining have caused her?"

"No more than it usually did, I suppose."

I ignored this and continued, "I dreamt of that night many times after she died. The pair of us back on the hill, the sky a boundless crystal inscribed with the planets and constellations, like points on a map. Then a fire-bolt flares in the blackness—a flaming arrow, shot from the bow of Orion. In the dream, Mother always told me 'twas an aerial traveller, roaming alone between the worlds, and that the beam I saw was a signal meant for others of its kind, like a ship's light in the night. I have since heard such flares described as falling souls, or exhalations of fire and air, but I liked to imagine that Mother was right—that there is a way to travel through space. She named the seas and the mountains on the Moon for me, and I dreamed that I was there, borne on the tail of the fiery wanderer."

"Your mother was an exceptional woman," Rudge said, with an air of embarrassment. "I once heard your father say she bewitched him the moment they met."

"My father has always favoured the women in his life." I sighed. "His mother over his father, his daughters over his son, his wife above all."

Rudge smiled understandingly, and had I been within reach I fear he might even have ruffled my hair. Happily, I was not.

"I do not doubt he loves you too, in his way. But here is your chance—" He indicated the Little Emperor. "—to make him *proud* of you."

"I fear it is too late for that," I said, but deferred to Rudge's optimism by waving my needle and thread in the air, as a swordsman might brandish his sabre. "Into battle, then!"

We laughed long and loud in a comradely fashion, disturbing the sleep of the grey-and-white cat, who had been dozing upon a nearby stack of lining paper. He hissed in irritation, then yawned, stretched, and decamped to some quieter spot.

CHAPTER
SEVENTEEN

A S USUAL, COME SUNDAY OF THAT WEEK, my father and sister attended St Peter-in-the-East for the late-morning service. Also as usual, I did not accompany them. Although the perils of my impiety had long troubled my relatives, they had accepted my miserable prospects in the Eternal Life to come, and Father seldom compelled me to worship except on occasions like Easter and Christmas, when 'twould be scandalous for a family not to present a united front. I often wonder if he indulged me, not so much to avoid a weekly row, as to hide me from public view, it being better to have a Godless son than an ungrateful one.

That particular Sunday, however, 'twas this world and not the next that commanded his attention. For the pastry-cooks of Oxford had recently agreed that, being short of influence within the Corporation, they must organize themselves in the manner of the older trades—the butchers, bakers, blacksmiths, &c.—and by doing so might secure lower taxes, better conditions, and all the other perceived advantages these occupations enjoyed. And when the pastry-cooks had decided their demands would have greater impact if they joined forces with the city's confectioners, my father—being both a pastry-cook and a confectioner—had been quick to suggest himself as the obvious choice to lead the new guild. To his credit, many concurred, though many more remained undecided.

'Twas this latter group he now sought to sway to his cause, during the convivial interlude that follows every church service, when the congregation spills outside for discussions on the sermon, pressing news from home and abroad, and who might be rangling whom.

"We have a new cheesecake this week," was the bait, "and shall be offering complementary samples all round. You will find us under our sign on the High—bring your families, too. All are welcome!"

Mary shuddered, embarrassed that our father—in other respects a virtuous man—should use for election-eering, if not quite Our Lord's house, then at least His garden.

"Delicious your cheesecake may be," trilled a voice of dissent—a confectioner from the Turl who (in Father's opinion) desired the Mastership for himself but feared humiliation in the election and was gauging his popularity before throwing his hat in the ring. "However, according to my contacts in London—of which I have many, as you know, and all well con-nected—such heavy sweets are now considered... may I say it—a little *old-fashioned*. The modern appetite is for lighter desserts in the French style. And of course, pastry-cooks as well as confectioners must move with the times."

Several other sweetmeat vendors nodded in agree-ment, freezing Father's smile upon his face, though before it could slide away completely, his stoutest ally hastened to his aid. This was the wife—now widow—of the Witney confectioner who once so heartlessly bruised my nine-year-old ear. Having inherited her late husband's business, Mrs Winstable (as I must call her from now on) had thrown her not-inconsiderable weight behind my father's campaign, and 'twas a brave pastry-cook or confectioner who would go up against her.

"Your Londoners are welcome to their Frenchified fancies—they have less taste than a sugarless syllabub. We know better here in Oxfordshire. Sadler's Finest Cheesecake is the King of Confections! No other sweetmeat can rival its savour."

"Indeed," someone else opined. "I heard the Bursar of St John's praise it most highly just last week. Although I must admit, I have not tried it myself since boyhood."

"Nephew!" Making a great show of importance, Father turned to greet the speaker. "Then that *was* you, hunched in the choir stalls. Mary insisted she'd seen you."

Jediah bowed, the hem of his cloak sweeping gravel onto the grass from the well-kept path. "Observant as always, dear cousin."

Mary kept her counsel, responding with a thin-lipped smile.

"What brings you here?" asked Father. "Not a hunger, I hope, for intellectual sustenance. Our parish fare is hearty, but no match for the meat of a college sermon, I am sure."

Jediah nodded. "'Twould be akin to comparing a choice dressed ham to a dish of cold pottage. But—like your cheesecake and your associate's foreign desserts—each has its place in God's scheme. Your vicar was admirably succinct on the Sins of the Fathers. However..." He took his uncle's elbow and drew him aside from his colleagues. "...I came here not for theology but to speak with you—in private."

Father's smile had all but gone now, for no audience with Jediah was ever light-hearted. "Is there a problem?"

"You might say so, yes." Jediah edged still further away from the church, towards the part of the graveyard where my mother's body lay. "I see James is not here," he added.

Father shook his head in exasperation. "Your cousin cares no more for God than he does his family, the business that feeds and clothes him, or aught else that does not serve his selfish ends. In his contempt for his elders and betters, he is quite as bad as the Prince of Wales—" He stopped and looked about guiltily, as though His Royal Highness might have hidden himself behind Jediah's back or been concealed within his cloak.

"Were it not I who must inform you!" Jediah sighed. "But people are talking behind your back, and the news will come better from a relative than some gossip on the street."

Father blanched. "What has happened? Tell me at once!"

And so, with sincerest regrets, Jediah obliged.

CHAPTER EIGHTEEN

HAVING REACHED THE CONCLUSION
THAT, to beat Ambrose Bean I would have
to join him, the Lord's Day found me at the
North Gate end of the Broad, in my pocket a bundle
of hand-lettered chits announcing *The Greatest Show
In The City!*, along with a guarantee of *Your Front-
Row View, Secured For Only 6d.!*

I could have chosen a better time—Gloucester
Green market day, for instance—for many of my potential customers were, of course, at church. On the
other hand, Father was at church as well, and thus unlikely to witness his only son trading upon the Broad
like a common hawker. Still, I kept a close eye on the
clock of St Mary Magdalen and prayed that the Rev.
Slade had penned an especially rambling sermon that
week.

I glared hard at all who passed—the old maids, the
families out for a stroll, the young men in their Sunday
suits with their ladies upon their arms—hoping to steer
them towards me by sheer force of will. This was no
match, however, for the hurdy-gurdy man with the
dancing monkey, who occupied the prime spot in the
middle of the street, where the Oxford Martyrs met

their end. It occurred to me that I should have brought along a banner to advertise my wares, or at the very least fashioned a stall from a stack of boxes and maybe a tablecloth, to make clear I had something to sell and was not merely begging or preaching some dissident creed. Though were I to do so, none would have heard it—the blare of the hurdy-gurdy rendered my pronouncements all but inaudible, and swelled in volume when I dared to raise my voice. Even the monkey's screeches grew louder, adding to a hellish crescendo that ended only with the approach of my first customers. As they turned from Magdalen Street East onto the Broad, only a barely perceptible break in their stride suggested the slightest glimmer of curiosity, but 'twas excuse enough for me to pounce.

"Might I interest you in a ticket?" I gasped, being by then quite out of breath with all that shouting.

The pair looked disappointed. "You are not a crawthumper, then?" said the man, a plump and pink-faced young fellow of the commonplace sort—an accountant's apprentice, I guessed, or a solicitor-in-training. "Nor even a croaker? 'Tis a shame, for Ellie loves a chuckle. Is that not so, my sweet?"

"I cannot provide chuckles," I responded. "But I do offer a privileged location from which to view the most important event you may ever witness."

"Did you hear that, Johnnie?" cried the young man's sweetheart, a plump coquette in a frothy yellow frock. "A privileged location—how exciting!"

"Certainly sounds so," said Johnnie. "Come on then, man—do not keep the lady waiting. Spill it out."

I squared my shoulders. "You are doubtless aware of the many excursions into the atmosphere undertaken by our continental neighbours, this year and the last."

"Not the foggiest idea what you are talking about, old chap."

"I refer, of course, to recent advancements in the field of aerostatics."

Both shook their head.

"Flight by means of a globe filled with air?"

"Ahh, I see your meaning now." Johnnie grinned. "Balloons! I am right, am I not, my dearest?"

"As always," Ellie simpered, adding, to me, "Johnnie read all about them in *Jackson's*."

I nodded. "'Twould have been their account of Signor Lunardi's departure from Moorfields, the first such venture in *England*. What I shall accomplish here in Oxford..." I paused for dramatic effect, "will be no less than the first ascent—and descent, of course!—by an English*man*."

I thought I had astounded Johnnie, for he hesitated before he spoke again. But then, 'twas only to ask, "Is that it?"

I frowned. "What more do you expect?"

"Excuse me if I have this incorrect. You say that you will ascend, and then descend."

"There will be some sideways motion, also."

"Ah, I am clearer now. And where will that motion take you?"

"That, I cannot say. 'Tis the winds that decide the direction, not the aeronaut."

Ellie giggled, though at least she had the manners to cover her mouth. "That seems awfully silly. What is the point of setting out on a journey, if you do not know where you will end up?"

"'Tis not the destination but the journey itself that's important," I said, now scarcely containing my irritation. "Especially a journey as momentous as this one. Front-row tickets are just sixpence apiece."

Johnnie raised an empty hand. "Sorry, old chap—not today. Come along, my sweet. You wished to pet the monkey."

"You are all as bad as each other!" I bawled after them, forgetting what Father had taught me. "Happy to part with sixpence to scorn the world's wonders, but not to see history made. I expect you'd pay a tidy sum to see me cold and dead."

"I beg your pardon?" said Johnnie, half turning back.

"Were I to fall, for example," I mumbled, immediately abashed at my theatrics. "From the aerostat, I mean."

"Is that likely?" Ellie demanded.

I shrugged. "'Tis not impossible. New philosophies are by their nature unpredictable. A rope could snap, throwing me from the basket. An unnoticed rent in the fabric of the globe could expand to disastrous proportions. In the worst case, the aerostat could catch fire and both it and I be burned to a crisp in an instant."

"Good Lord!" gasped Johnnie. "That would be a spectacle."

Ellie clutched at his arm. "Johnnie—you must buy us tickets at once. I have to know what happens to him!"

I took Johnnie's shilling and pressed the tickets into Ellie's eager hands before they could change their minds.

"You will not regret it," I said.

"I am sure we won't," said Johnnie, "though I fear *you* might. Good luck!"

They resumed their promenade in the direction of George Lane—planning, perhaps, an amble along the river—but had not gone far before they stopped to exchange pleasantries with another young couple, and moments later I saw this new pair hasten towards me.

"We hear you will almost certainly die," they trilled, "and are selling tickets to view!"

A passing popinjay, overhearing these words, was quick to inform his companions, who relayed them with excitement to a nearby party of matrons, whose parasols quivered like a swarm of silken butterflies as they, in turn, alerted a clan of wide-eyed country-folk enjoying a day in the city. I was soon surrounded by would-be witnesses to my demise, all waving their sixpences and clamouring for their tickets. I had to call upon them to quieten down and form an orderly queue, but none objected. Indeed, merry conversations soon struck up all along the line—farmer with factor, *friseur* with fop—and everyone was agreed on the perils of progress, and how seldom Oxford played host to such thrills.

My modest stock of tickets was soon running low. I feared announcing this might spark a riot, but I was spared by the arrival of a college porter—I recognized him from St Saviour's—with a Proctor in tow.

"This is the one," said the porter to the Proctor. "He's been causing a disturbance all morning."

I started to object that the disturbance had begun only minutes ago and I was doing my best to contain it, but the Proctor cracked his rod upon the cobbles, striking sparks.

"Statute Eleven, Section Three," he barked. "It will be an offence to impede, obstruct, or otherwise delay on any grounds a Member of the University coming or going from College pursuant of his lawful business."

"I am nowhere near any college!" I cried.

"And even if he was," added one of my customers, "your fat old Fellows are greater obstructions than he."

The Proctor scanned the assembly for the speaker, but failing to spot him returned to me. "Would you have me call the Bulldogs?"

I sighed, my shoulders slumping, though mostly from the weight of coin in my pockets. 'Twas time to beat a dignified retreat—to a round of sympathetic applause, I hoped. But my customers were also moving on. Within a second or two, my spot near St Mary Magdalen was deserted save for the Proctor and porter.

"See you don't come back!" the porter said with a shake of his fist.

I considered making some clever riposte (reckoning I could outrun him even carrying a small fortune in silver), but before I could devise one, caught sight of a Gownsman, standing half-in, half-out of St Saviour's lodge, his arms folded upon his chest.

I recognized him with a start.

'Twas Edwin Osborne, and he was smiling.

~ ~ ~

I opened the door to the smell of boiled beef—an obvious warning of trouble ahead, though I had reached the door to the kitchen before I realized I wasn't alone.

"Sneaking upstairs to our room, are we?" Father spoke from his seat at the table without looking up. He had the ledger books and moneybox in front of him, a pen in his hand, and continued to write as he added, "Hoping to get home ahead of us? Something to hide, perhaps?"

I could have answered yes to all three questions, but instead ignored him and asked Mary what was for dinner. Before she could answer from her station chopping carrots by the stove, Father raised a hand to silence her.

"Nothing. To each shall be given, according to his contribution."

I groaned. "You sound like Jediah. Though you should have said *need*, not *contribution*."

"Do not test me, James. I mean what I say."

"I pay for my keep."

He laid down his pen, blotted and closed the daybook, and fixed me with an icy stare.

"A family is bound by more than money alone."

"Is that so?" I snorted in derision, causing Mary to jump and lose hold of her knife. "Then you will not be wanting my wages this week, I presume?"

"This is not about your elaboratory."

"'Tis a *laboratory*. A laboratory!" I flung my hands in the air. "How many more times do I have to tell you, you backwards old fool?"

"James!" Mary gasped. "You cannot speak to Father like that!"

"I am not a child. I can speak however I please."

"Not whilst you dwell beneath *my* roof," said Father. "Though your insults are the least of the matter. In your selfish and unnatural pursuits, you bring disgrace upon the entire family."

"Employment in the *Officina Chimica* disgraces a pastry-cook?" Like the bubbling pot on the stove, I was close to overboiling. "Surely the shame is the

University's, for appointing the son of a common tradesman in the first place."

"The shame is mine—that the ingrate I must call my son, should vaunt himself for all the world to scorn. Gambling, begging—are these the worst of it, or should I steel myself for more?"

I could think of no reply, nor do anything other than seethe with indignant self-pity. After my morning on the Broad, I could hardly deny that my secret was out or that Father would have to be told—and sooner rather than later. But I'd hoped to break the news in a manner of my choosing. No chance of that now, and I marvelled at the speed with which gossip could travel.

There was, however, a simpler explanation. Jediah had betrayed me. And worse, I had trusted him.

My cheeks began to burn distressingly; I convinced myself 'twas the heat of the fire, and with this arose the incongruent notion that Mary should check on the pot, for it would soon boil dry and our meal would be ruined.

"You do not deny it, then?"

"Would you rather I lied?" I managed to croak.

"You mean to exhibit yourself for payment, like some tawdry fairground freak?"

"Better a freak than a nobody." He shook his head, his anger turned to sorrow. "What would your mother say, James?"

"She would say I am right, for she wanted more for me than *this*." I spun about with a scything gesture, encompassing in a single sweep the kitchen, the parlour, my attic room, even the shop. Especially the shop. And even as I did it, I knew I had gone too far; I heard a tiny yelp from Mary, then came a long, terrible silence during which only the stew-pot dared to make a sound.

"You are right, I am a fool," said Father at last, his voice now shorn of emotion. "A fool to have ever believed you might one day be grateful for all I have done. You have never disguised your malcontent, but at last I understand why. However—" He raised a forefinger to emphasize his point. "—the fault is not entirely mine. You are not, nor have ever been, obliged to accept my charity."

I frowned. "What do you mean?"

"Father..." Mary abandoned the chopping board and came alongside the table to grasp his shoulder. "There is no need—"

"There is every need. Too long has your brother abused our goodwill." He pointed towards the door. "Collect your belongings if you wish, but do not dawdle in the hope I might change my mind. You have already outstayed your welcome many times over."

~ ~ ~

I refrained from taking a detour up to my room, for that would have meant passing the kitchen again on my way out, and having Father watch me leave while he tucked into his dinner. Or worse still, not watch me. Better to rise above such provocations, I decided, though at the very last I faltered and slammed the shop door behind me. In the resulting tremor, one of the chains on the shop sign's wall-bracket snapped, dropping that half of the board by a foot and leaving the whole to dangle perilously from the unbroken chain alone. 'Twould not hold for long, I observed with a grim smile, and would have thrust my hands into my pockets had they not been fully taken up by the morning's receipts. So with my fists clenched at my sides, I marched dauntless up the High.

I wore that smile until I reached Carfax, where the gravity of my misfortune hit me at last, bursting my bubble of bravado as swiftly as a popped button might bring down an aerostat. My swagger became a round-shouldered trudge, and without much thought I took the first turning I came across—a choppy passage that descended to The Crown, the shadiest den of repro-bates and topers this side of the West Gate. Having naught else to occupy my day, I took a deep breath and entered within.

Father, of course, abhorred such establishments, and though he had never forbidden me to drink, he had not encouraged it either. I felt instantly out of place—less from lack of experience than due to the sudden abundance of jollity and good cheer I found inside, which were so at odds with my own sorry mood. Nevertheless, I took a seat by the hearth, laid a handful of coin on the table before me and ordered a glass of ale when the potboy approached. When it arrived, I downed the frothy, bitter liquid so thirstily, I soon had to shout for another.

I scanned my surroundings while I supped, unsettled by the laughter, the incessant, vulgar banter, the overpowering stench of beer and sweat. How I yearned for the civility of Harper's and the gentle hum of phil-osophical debate. Then my gaze alighted upon a post-er pinned to the beam above my head, this bearing a passable sketch of a fat, grinning sow entitled *Coming Soon To These Premises, The Pig Of Knowledge, A Remarkable Prodigy of Nature Renowned Across Three Counties*, followed by an announcement that said Pig would be available at The Crown a short while hence and for the sum of sixpence would answer any question put to it by patrons. I was clearly selling myself short, charging no more for people to see me die than a swine, however erudite, levied for chitchat.

In a nook on the opposite side of the hearth, a parched old twig of a scoundrel fell silent. 'Twas only then that I realized he had previously been singing, and that the half-heard words of his rhyme held a timely meaning.

"Again, old man!" I ordered. "Sing for me!"

He pointed at the heap of coin on my table, so I tossed him a penny. He pocketed it with a smack of his crusted lips and crooned once more:

> *"As the high-towering Eagle flies,*
>
> *Majestically through the skies,*
>
> *So did the brave Lunardi soar,*
>
> *Aerial regions to explore.*
>
> *And when he came*
>
> *To Earth again,*
>
> *Each British dame,*
>
> *To crown his fame,*
>
> *Below her knee, or round her thigh,*
>
> *His dear enchanting name did tie,*
>
> *And showed the bold adventurer more*
>
> *Of Heaven than ever he saw before."*

I straight away emptied my glass, now determined to drink myself into oblivion rather than endure another moment sober in this cruel world. But before I could yell for the potboy again, a shadow fell across the table, and I heard a familiar, supercilious sniff.

"I must say, I would have paid him to stop."

I sat bolt upright. Ambrose Bean, dressed in a red velvet suit with gold embroidery, might have gone unnoticed at a Corporation Ball, or even the Port Meadow races, but stood out like a dog in a doublet in the public bar of The Crown.

"Wh—what're you doing here?" I slurred.

"My lodgings." Bean pointed at the ceiling, then pulled up a stool beside me, unbidden. Perhaps he perceived the surprise on my face, for he added, "The accommodations much surpass the bar."

I nodded, wondering if this were true, or whether Bean might be less well-moneyed than his appearance suggested. But still, he possessed the diamond pin—an asset beyond priceless in my estimation.

"I see you do well from our wager," he said, indicating my own puny fortune.

"Oh, this is nothing," I breezed. "Just a tiny portion of all I have raised. A very, very tiny portion."

"I am glad to hear it. 'Tis never wise to carry all you possess in your pockets—you do not know who might be lurking around the next corner." He peered over his shoulder, as though the bar might be crawling with cutpurses. Which on reflection, it probably was. "You must avoid drinking it away, too." He nodded at my almost-empty glass. "Though I do understand the temptation to celebrate your success. I myself have earned precisely nothing. In fact, my printing and other sundry expenses have left me out of pocket. But as they say, one must speculate to accumulate. And the balance will swing my way three days hence."

I gulped more ale. "What happens then?"

"Surely you must have seen—" Bean glanced at the beam above us. "Tsk! That stub-faced pig farmer has been replacing my posters with his own again. No matter. My fame is already assured." With an extravagant twirl of the hand, he continued: "On Wednesday eve, my dear Sadler, the world will witness my show. A night of wonderment awaits! You will be attending, of course."

I started to mumble that I did not have a ticket, but the return of the potboy interrupted me.

"Another glass for my friend," Bean commanded, adding, "On me," when I tried to protest. "We shall not let you sup *all* your takings."

The ale arrived, and Bean paid not only for that glass but for the previous two as well. He would not join me, however, explaining that he had an urgent appointment for which he must keep a clear head.

"Now I remember." He stood and straightened his coat. "You refused a ticket last time we met. But here— I have no hard feelings. Take this one instead."

He placed a slip of paper on the table, weighting it down with a shilling.

"Do not forget—Wednesday, at the sign of the Golden Cross. Be sure to arrive in good time—and prepared for the night of your life!"

~ ~ ~

Rudge welcomed me back with a withering scowl when I staggered into the glasshouse many hours later.

"I never took you for the God-fearing sort," he said, rising from his seat upon the ebony chest and folding the gore he'd been repairing into a neat bundle with his needle and thread tucked inside. "You *have* been to church, I presume?"

"I would've, except—"

"Then you spent the day in rest and prayer."

I burped. "Not exactly."

"Hmm. And I wonder why I so often feel I am fighting a hopeless cause."

"More hapless than hopeless! Perchance my luck will improve someday."

Unexpectedly seized with emotion, I tottered open-armed towards my accomplice—intending, perhaps, to embrace him as my sole remaining friend—but taking such pains to avoid the many obstacles on the floor, when I eventually reached the chest I found he had slipped past me and gone elsewhere.

"Sadly," Rudge said, from the door, "luck alone will not launch our balloon. You said you would bring fifty yards."

"Fifty yards of what?"

"What in Heaven's name do you think? Fifty yards of broken promises? Fifty yards of hot air?"

Vague recollections surfaced of a promise, made late last night, that I would obtain a good deal of rope before our next meeting. But at the time I had been so exhausted, I would have agreed to procure fifty had-docks stuffed with snaggs and a five-legged duck, had it won me a brief respite from my labours.

Rudge donned his hat with an exasperated huff. "Do not stay on my account. I am done for today and off to my bed. You'll do likewise if you take my advice."

I tried to explain that I hadn't forgotten and would bring the rope tomorrow, but Rudge was out of the door by then and did not—or would not—hear me.

I sat on the chest and tried to pick up where Rudge had left off, but the tribulations of the day—not to mention the surfeit of ale I'd quaffed—swiftly caught up with me. Having no bed to go off to, however, nor any other place to retire, I fashioned a blanket and pillow from two still-to-be-patched segments of canvas, and thus huddled amidst the tattered makings of the Little Emperor, fell into a restless and dream-raddled sleep.

PART IV

CHAPTER NINETEEN

NEXT MORNING, I PAID A VISIT to the High—exhausted, aching from head to toe, but hopeful that, after a good night's rest on his part, Father's temper would have cooled and I might be allowed home that evening.

My sister, of course, had other ideas. Spotting my approach through the window, she rushed from behind the counter and flung her entire weight against the shop door to prevent me entering, refusing to speak with me except through a tiny gap betwixt door and frame, and then in naught but a terrified whisper.

"He does not want you back. 'Tis no use trying."

"But I am his son! He cannot simply throw me out like a stale cake or a spoiled sack of flour."

"Well, *he* would say he can. And I say you made it easy for him." What little Mary could see of my expression must have betrayed my feelings, for her manner softened then, and she added, "When he is calmer, I will try to speak to him in your favour."

"Mary, you surely are my favourite sister. No man could wish for better."

She returned my grin of relief with a scowl. "Do not mock me, James. I could just as soon speak against you, and then you will never return."

She glanced towards the staircase and began to close the door still further.

"Wait—I have one question."

"Quickly, then."

"How did Father find out?"

"Not from me, if that is what you are implying."

"I implied no such thing!"

She sighed. "Jediah told him at church."

I had already guessed the answer, of course, but had not quite believed it—or perhaps not wanted to believe it.

"But why?"

"That is two questions." Mary flinched at some disturbance out of my earshot. "You must go," she hissed. "Father is coming."

"But I—"

"Go, James! 'Twill be the worse for both of us if he finds you here."

She forced the door completely shut, and though she mouthed some cold comfort through the window, I failed to catch the words. I tapped on the pane to regain her attention, but she waved me away as if ejecting some irritating insect. Still exhausted, still aching, and now genuinely hopeless, I turned aside from *Tho. Sadler, Pastry-cook & Confectioner* and trudged on towards the laboratory.

~ ~ ~

Despite our dispute the previous night, that evening found me in the glasshouse as usual, in the company of Rudge, the Little Emperor, and the grey-and-white cat (whose name, I had learned, was Buttons—though perhaps Rudge had spoken in jest).

"You are quiet today," said he. "Not that I am complaining, mind you."

"I didn't sleep well last night." Nor will I tonight, I brooded while yawning and stretching. Or any other night, 'til Father admitted his error.

Rudge shuffled over to our stove—a prized acquisition from an empty bothy and much appreciated on chilly evenings. "Would you like a dish of tea? I have a tin of Bohea somewhere."

"No, thank you."

"Or something to eat? Some pickled pork and bread?"

"I am not hungry, thank you."

He sat down again, cross-legged upon the floor with a fresh segment of canvas in his lap. "You did well, fetching the rope."

I grunted.

"When we have the chymicals we need, we will be ready for our first launch, eh?"

I barely managed a nod, drawing a troubled glance from my partner.

"James, I fear you may be coming down with worse than barrel fever. You're as pale as an 'otomy, closer than a pair of inkle-weavers, and not once have you complained about your father, your sister, or even the shop."

I shrugged. "I have nothing new to complain about. Having not been home in a while."

"You missed your shift at the counter? Your father will split his puddings."

"Perhaps."

A few more minutes dragged by in this uneasy manner before Rudge had had enough.

"I welcome a break from your blather," he said, "but this silence is upsetting Buttons. You are plainly out of sorts, but why?"

I sighed. "I have been most cruelly wronged, and not once but twice—first a confidence betrayed, then disowned and made a vagrant... and both thanks to my treacherous cousin."

"Hmm. So, not only out of sorts—out of a home, as well." He peered at my makeshift bed. "What does Jediah have to say for himself?"

"I have not seen him since," I replied, "though it wouldn't be much, I expect."

"He has become a man of few words, our Jediah." Rudge frowned at his handiwork, unpicked a wayward stitch. "Few pleasant ones, anyway. When he was a boy, he was almost as much a chatterbox as you."

"Perhaps he ran out of things to say."

"Perhaps."

"Though he did venture an opinion on *this*." I indicated our work space, the Little Emperor, the hoard of bits and pieces that littered the floor—canvas, paper, needles, thread, buttons, buttons and more buttons, wooden struts awaiting assembly, nails, hammers, barrels, and all. The makings of fortune and fame.

"Why does he hate you?" I blurted.

"'Twas not always the case." Rudge did not continue straight away, focussing instead on his sewing, and when he did speak again 'twas in the manner of someone divulging a terrible secret. "Young Jediah never wished for aught, 'cept his father's love and attention. Like any son, I suppose. But Elijah had another claim on his heart."

"Ah, I understand." I nodded sagely. "Jediah's stepmother. I should've guessed it."

Rudge laughed, but it was a bitter sound devoid of humour. "Then you would've guessed wrong. I meant his natural philosophy."

Abashed, I remarked by way of deflection, "How Father used to rail against those jaunts of yours."

"He might have had cause, looking back. Elijah came home in body from time to time, but his mind was always elsewhere. He was never suited for family life. When Jediah was growing up, when he most needed a father's strong hand, he had none. I tried to be a friend to both—not to fill your uncle's place, but to build a bridge between them, as it were. To give them common purpose."

I remembered Rudge's painting. "Like the expedition to China," I said, certain that this time I had it right.

Rudge put down his sewing and stared straight ahead, into the distance. I followed his gaze. By day, the panes of the glasshouse provided glorious—if fractured—views of the Cherwell and Magdalen Tower. By night, they became a blank veil of darkness, impenetrable to our sight but affording a fine view of *us* to passers-by. I had never before thought on this, and doubted John Sibthorp would ever take callers so late. But still, 'twas unnerving—like I'd been bottled and shelved for display.

"We always travelled alone. Explorations are dangerous and cannot be compared with an outing to Cheltenham or even the Vaux Hall Pleasure Gardens— as your uncle would remind Jediah whenever he begged that we take him along. So imagine his joy when his father relented."

Rudge seemed unaware of my disquiet, or even my presence. From the grimace of pain on his face, I surmised he was lost in the past.

"I promised them both I'd look after him," he sighed.

"Both?"

"Elijah insisted his new wife join the company, too. He wanted to make it a family affair."

"As you will know by now," I said, "I rank thought above deed, and am largely unversed in the niceties of jaunting. But 'tis clear even to me that women and children are ill-suited for such pursuits, and must be still less so when befuddled by unfamiliar customs and climes."

"'Tis clear with hindsight," Rudge huffed. "Elijah set out with the best of intentions, but he'd never before played the father so long, and what started out an adventure soon became a vexation. Jediah's excitement, his eagerness to help, his endless questions—all ignored. It fell to me to find amusements for the boy."

"Such as the Little Emperor?"

Rudge nodded. "We came upon them in the desert south of Tulufan. Men in flying machines. Men navigating the air like birds—but no chattering rabble of starlings or sparrows. Slow and stately they wandered their realm, like eagles on the wing. 'Twas a marvel to me—me, Wyndham Rudge, who had travelled so wide and thought I had witnessed most things. As for Jediah... I saw the danger, but how could I refuse him? He was happy, perhaps happier than ever before—"

"Or since," I muttered.

"—and with the boy occupied, Elijah could work without distractions. 'Twould be best for everyone, I thought. I was wrong."

A marvel indeed, I thought, to have cheered up my dolorous cousin—though I understood how, for a pious child, fear and fascination could combine to pernicious effect. With their flying machines, these men had defied both God and His natural order, and as Rudge continued his tale, I understood also Jediah's anguish when his new companions proved, in the end, as indifferent to his existence as his father. 'Twould have been more surprising to hear that he *hadn't* leapt into that basket.

"The ropes had already been cut," said Rudge, "and 'twas too late to eject him, for the balloon was rising too fast. He took us all by surprise... Still, no harm would have come of it, had he not all at once lost his reason. Looking back, I would explain it this way: his heart was set on leaving the Earth but his head would have none of it, and the discord between the two unbalanced his judgement. Rational thought deserted him and madness took its place."

"But what caused this madness? The heat? Unfamiliar food?"

Rudge sighed. "Jediah had earlier swallowed some prized seeds we'd collected nearby. He took to his bed with a terrible sickness—Elijah refused to leave him even once until he recovered."

I squirmed in discomfort. "I think I have heard that story before. Uncle Elijah's concern was for the seeds rather than Jediah's health."

Rudge shook his head. "Then you heard it not quite right. Elijah's first concern was his son's good health. Of course he was happy to have the seeds back, but had it come to a choice, he would've exchanged them for Jediah without hesitation. He was not a monster!"

"I am sorry. I did not mean to suggest—"

"Elijah had the sharpest mind of any man I have met," Rudge continued, less testily, "but his thoughts became muddled whenever he tried to speak of his feelings. I fear Jediah misread his father's joy and convinced himself that the truth was as *you* described it. 'Twas that false and horrid realization, that drove him to escape his lot on this Earth."

I nodded, my conscience pricked at the thought of the jokes I had shared at my cousin's expense. "What happened with the aerostat?"

"Jediah turned upon the aeronaut like a savage beast, and might have tossed him to his death had the man been weaker or Jediah stronger. I feared he would throw *himself* from the basket, so frantic was he to escape. 'Twas then he remembered a little of what he had learned, though it did him no good."

"What do you mean?" I asked, even as I began to guess the reply.

"He grabbed the rope that opened the vent."

I winced. I, too, had learned enough about ballooning to know that, done carefully, the release of the inflammable air that keeps an aerostat aloft is the best means to a safe and leisurely landing. Done in haste, on the other hand...

"I cannot say whose God we must thank, but 'twas a miracle that neither Jediah nor the aeronaut died in the fall. Though your cousin suffered a great gash to his head." Rudge rapped his knuckles upon his skull. "Worse still, his blood became poisoned, and he entered a feverish sleep from which we feared he would never awake. As soon as he was recovered enough to travel, Elijah sent him home with Becky, and swore 'twould be the last time he indulged the boy. Jediah survived the affair, but it left him as you see him today—injured in heart."

"I understand what occurred," I responded. "But not why it earned you such disfavour. 'Twas Jediah's decision to jump aboard the aerostat, not yours. From what you have told me, it seems you always bore his best interests in mind."

Rudge returned to the stove, rubbing his palms and stamping his feet. "By Jove, 'tis cold in here tonight. We must work harder to warm ourselves up. Here, you can help me with this." His back creaked as he bent to the ground then straightened, in his left hand yet another section of canvas, in the right a fistful of buttons. I shook my head.

"'Tis late, and I must rise early come the morning."

I feared Rudge would drive us 'til dawn if no one made a move to stop, though I expected him to chunter at my suggestion; to call me a work-shy sluga-bed, or an intolerable twiddle-poop, or any one of the hundred colourful names I had come to know so well. But no insult arrived, nor even the slightest complaint.

"You are right," he said, "time marches on. To bed it is, then. I shall see you tomorrow?"

This was his usual farewell, though tonight it sounded more like a question.

"I should think so," I said. "Now I am barred from the shop I have more free time than previously and little else to do with it."

"Then this—" Rudge flung both canvas and buttons back upon the floor, the latter rebounding with such velocity, I had but an instant to duck or risk losing an eyeball. "—all of this—to you, is *little else*? Best to know where we stand, I suppose."

185

I sighed and rolled my eyes. "I didn't mean it like that."

"Do not mean, do not say." With a scowl, Rudge returned to his seat and snatched up his needlework.

"If you remember," I said, "we had agreed to adjourn for the day."

Rudge continued to toil. "Can you not see the problem? Your being here will keep me from sleep, and if I cannot sleep here, I must look elsewhere."

"I trust you will find some comfortable lodging-house."

"Any old hovel would be an improvement." I glowered at the heap of canvas that had served as my bed the previous night. "God forbid Father should know, but I am already pining for that garret above the shop."

"Then 'tis to be hoped you are soon reconciled, lest your living expenses claim *all* of the monies we've raised."

"*We?*"

"Though before you part with a penny in rent, I might ask that you purchase our chymicals first."

"Would you rather I slept on the street?" I cried. "'Tis thanks to you and your damned Little Emperor I am homeless in the first place. And why is it always *I* who must buy and sell, and fetch and carry? I am worked like a horse, while you do naught but sit about preaching. You are every bit as bad as my father."

Rudge sniffed. "Go back to your garret, then—and your father's shop counter. I am sure he'll be overjoyed to have you behind it again."

I muttered, "Do not tempt me," then reached for my needle and thread.

CHAPTER TWENTY

COME WEDNESDAY EVENING, I attended Bean's show not so much to redeem my free ticket, as due to a desperate urge to escape from the glasshouse, if only for a few hours. Even then, I nearly stayed put, for the weather turned cold and unwholesomely foggy that night, and upon reaching the Golden Cross I discovered that most of the city had shared these misgivings. The crowd I encountered at the entrance could not be described as teeming, even by someone less partial than I—though the sight caused me more terror than joy. If an indoor attraction might fail or succeed at Nature's whim, how much greater the risk for an aerostat launch!

I showed my ticket to a youth guarding the door and made my way to an upper assembly room, where a diverse assortment of townsfolk filled the seats, perhaps favouring the female and more antiquated faction, with no sign of Edwin Osborne or any other member of the Philosophical Club. 'Twas no surprise, for according to the University's statutes, all taverns and inns were barred to Undergraduates, upon pain of rustication. This did not stop them drinking, of course, but their preferred hostelries were those of

Headington and other villages beyond the reach of the Bulldogs.

A hum of excitement pervaded, largely due to the curtain that hid the front of the room from view. To further focus their students' minds on their studies, the University had also outlawed dramatic arts of all sorts, but in this case throughout the city. For generations, no theatre had operated nor any travelling player performed in Oxford, sparing Town and Gown alike the mawkish melodramas of the day, but also denying them Sophocles, Shakespeare, and even the soberest Scriptural works. And hence the *frisson* at the Golden Cross that evening. Did Bean intend to stage a play? Would the Proctors find out? What would they do if they did? The University Court never dealt gently with Townsmen who flouted its laws—especially outsiders.

I found a vacant space at the rear of the room, betwixt a lanky fellow and a well-made but veiled woman clothed all in black. I wondered what kind of widow might frequent a public house—and for entertainment, at that. But I thought no more of her, for at that moment the bell of Tom Tower began to strike nine, and on this signal the youth from the door came into the room and snuffed out the lights. (The Golden Cross, being a better stripe of establishment than, for instance, The Crown, provided candles rather than rushes.) He did this so quickly, many of those present failed to notice what was happening before darkness swallowed the room, and more nervous members of the audience responded with cries of astonishment or even fright. I pursed my lips and folded my arms, silently challenging Bean to surprise *me*.

With a swishing sound (doubtless the curtain brushing the floorboards, though someone ruined the drama by screeching, "A wyrm, a monstrous wyrm! Heaven help us all!"), Ambrose Bean himself appeared, illuminated from below by a lamp placed on the floor at his feet. The view up his nostrils was startling, as was his manner of dress: from the pointed silk slippers to the bejewelled turban upon his head, he sparkled like the Trill Mill in moonlight as he raised his hands, palms uppermost, in welcome. Many audience members gasped, as though he had materialized out of thin air and not simply had the youth pull aside the curtain. I gritted my teeth.

"Greetings, O ye seekers after truth!"

He spoke an octave lower than I remembered and with a peculiar accent, the like of which could never before have been heard by Oxfordshire ears, or perhaps by any in the World. More curious still, despite the chamber's modest size and the abundance of draperies, a booming echo rebounded.

"The frail and the faint of heart should leave while they may," he said. "For I cannot be held responsible for aught that might befall us this night."

"If I do, will I get my money back?" came a call from the side of the room.

Bean ignored this and spread his arms wide, raising his powdered face to the ceiling and emptying his lungs with a shuddering sigh. A distraction, clearly, for with another swish a polished wooden box on a tripod appeared beside him—the contraption I had first encountered on Staircase Six.

"O ye seekers after truth, have no doubt—as we live and breathe, this very night, we shall open a door onto the world of the *dead*."

Bean circled the box like an eagle eyeing a rabbit, his slippers tippity-tapping in time with a chorus of *ooh*s and *aah*s from the crowd. Then he stopped abruptly, grasped the handle in the side of the box and began to turn it, slowly at first.

"The spirit world interweaves with the world of the living. 'Tis likened to a mirror, that captures the deeds of all men in life, and especially in their death. And like a mirror, it duplicates those deeds, rendering them visible to those who know how and where to look."

The handle emitted a squeak with each revolution, but nothing else. Someone sniggered, another patron laughed aloud; Bean stared straight ahead, his eyes black pools in his white-powdered face.

"Events of the greatest consequence reverberate eternally—reflections of the past, concealed from human eyes."

All at once, the hecklers fell silent. For with oddly little ado given the circumstances, the likeness of a lake had sprung into view, in appearance as broad as a horse is long, though 'twas impossible to know the scale due to the absence of trees, boats, fish, or any other features against which to gauge it.

Had the youth delivered another surprise while Bean's squeaky box diverted our ears and eyes? Logic said it must be so, yet the canvas depicting the lake confounded all reason. First, despite its size, it had no clear means of support, neither frame nor easel. More remarkable still, the image somehow contrived to depict not a single instant frozen in time as a normal painting, but a succession of such instants. Inspecting it as closely as I might from my distant location, 'twas clear the waters ebbed and flowed as if stirred by a ceaseless breeze, while beneath these waves I glimpsed a shadowy undertow—a monstrous wyrm after all, perhaps.

Bean, meanwhile, had completely recovered his stride. "'Tis a perilous business," he breathed, "but these spirits of the dead—these unseen vibrations impressed upon the atmosphere—are sometimes persuaded to fashion a shell from the ether, and thus might step into the light."

At this instruction, the lake in the painting split apart like the Red Sea before Moses, and the roiling walls of water disgorged a mountainous rock that burst into flame. To shrieks of terror from those on the front row, numerous members of the audience overturned their benches and raced for the door in a crush. I feared 'twas but the start of a soon-to-be-famous catastrophe, except Bean quelled the panic by raising his fist, and with this latest cue returned the flames, lake, and rock to nonexistence. While the faint-hearts slunk back to their seats, he opened his hand to reveal a tiny glass pyramid.

"O mighty spirits! I invoke thee! Wilt thou appear? Art thou there? Wilt thou manifest thyselves in this smoky mirror?" He paused, then dropped his voice to a quivering whisper. "The spirits are here with us now, in this room, but a heartbeat away—"

"What blasphemous nonsense is this? I refuse to listen a moment longer!"

This latest interruption prompted a frown from Bean, and a satisfied smile from me. Sounds of pushing and shoving ensued, then elbows connecting with faces, general blundering about in the darkness, and a furious hiss: "Sit down and shut your bone-box, you moon-eyed hen!"

"The spirits are calling!" Bean yelled above the disturbance. "Louder, I cannot hear you—What is it you say? You have a message? Can you tell me for whom?

Somebody here, tonight... they know who they are, you say, for they came here in search of a sign—great or small—from their loved one so recently lost. Will that person reveal his- or herself? Speak up now— no need to be nervous."

"My old dog Pip dropped dead last Saturday week. If he wants to leave me a sign, can you tell him to do it outside?"

This drew laughter from the crowd, another scowl from Bean, and an ever-broader smile from me. Then the mood about-faced yet again, with an ominous thump so heavy as to judder the floorboards, followed by another, and another still, as if the youth had some petulant, foot-stamping giant concealed behind his curtain.

"Can that be—No, I cannot believe it. Is that Archie? Tell me 'tis true!"

This new voice—elderly, quavering, and female— emanated from the front of the room. Another of Bean's accomplices, I decided.

"Eleven years he's been gone," the woman continued, "and not a peep have I heard from him, though Heaven knows I have listened."

"Now is your chance," said Bean. "What is it you wish to say?"

"Will you not get him out here? I want to see him."

"*I* can see him. He stands with one foot on the Earth and the other upon a cloud."

The woman sniffed tearfully. "That must be him. He always was a dreamer."

Another thump sounded, raising murmurs of consternation. I fidgeted in my seat, longing to expose Bean's deception to the increasingly riveted audience.

"He dwells in paradise now, where he waits for you to join him."

"Is that it?" The woman sounded disappointed. "Will you not ask him a question for me?"

"You may ask him yourself," said Bean. "He is here, waiting for you."

"He can wait all he likes," she huffed. "I'm quite happy where I am for the time being, thank you very much. Though I would like to know if he's seen Sam on his travels."

"Sam is here also, and at peace."

"But I left him in the Lamb and Flag half an hour ago."

The man who had sniggered earlier laughed aloud. Before anyone else could join in, Bean rapped his knuckles upon his box and trilled, at an ear-splitting pitch: "Open to me, O ye gates of the Netherworld! Spirits come forth! Present yourselves!"

I covered my eyes. Much as I disliked Bean, 'twas hard to watch a full-grown man make a fool of himself. Indeed, it became so embarrassing, I wondered if I should leave, and how I might do so without causing another disturbance. Then mercifully, the shrieking stopped.

"I hear the name *James*," Bean moaned, somewhat hoarsely. "Is there a James here tonight?"

I froze, disconcerted. 'Twas a common name, of course, but no one else volunteered.

"I know you are with us," Bean chided. "Pray, do not be shy."

Much to my relief, a young woman half-rose from her seat, then sat down again and ventured a trembling hand.

"My brother Jimmy," she whispered. "He died of the King's Evil not one week ago. But how did you—?"

"You wish to see your Jimmy again."

"I don't know... I'm not sure..."

"You doubt there is life after death?"

"No... Yes—I mean... that is to say... perhaps we best not meddle—"

"Get on with it, girl!" called the sniggering man. "Else we'll *all* be cold in our graves before he's finished for the night."

'Twas a turning point in the show, for from that moment Bean brooked no dissent. He grasped the brass handle with steely resolve, and what came next transcended all that had gone before. Even I can find no words to describe what we saw, and *I* knew 'twas naught but a trick of the box. But what were its workings and how did Bean command them? As all Hell broke loose around me, I could only sit silent and wonder.

~ ~ ~

I stayed in my seat at the end of the show, as the youth passed around the room with a taper to relight the candles and the audience began to disperse. Too weary in heart to stir, I gazed miserably at my shoes while the crowd bustled about me, my gloom deepening with every new plaudit I heard. Bean, meanwhile, basked in their adulation, their blubbering gratitude, their predictions of glowing reviews in *Jackson's* and demands for a second performance at once, "For none should miss the chance to witness your genius!"

Bean accepted all this praise with an engaging display of modesty, surely feigned. While I could do naught but watch and gnash my teeth at the arrant unfairness! The only person who seemed the slightest bit disenchanted was the woman in black, who hurried out of the room without stopping to thank the showman. She no doubt regretted her impropriety, though I did wonder why she had not called upon Bean to summon her dead, as had so many others in the audience.

Eventually, I was the only person left in the room save the youth, who handed a bulging moneybag to Bean before departing two shillings richer. Then Bean sauntered in my direction, the caked powder upon his cheeks cracking like a drought-stricken riverbed when he grinned at the sight of me; both cosmetics and costume appeared less dazzling with the candles lit. Not that it mattered now, of course.

"Sadler! So glad you could make it." He greeted me with his usual voice restored and an overdone bow, almost losing his turban. "Will you tell me your opinion of the show? Do not spare my feelings!"

If only I could oblige, I thought. But 'twould have been pointless to lie.

"I found it most... enjoyable," I croaked.

Bean beamed as if I had paid him the most fulsome of compliments. "You did not find the shades too gay? 'Tis difficult to achieve a balance—people imagine the Underworld as a drab and dreary place, but for entertainment's sake I must fill it with flashes and bangs, bright colours, and clamour."

I swallowed. "The shades were quite perfect."

"Then the screams of the souls of the damned— they struck you as anguished? And the succubi, not uncomely?"

"They were all quite perfect," I said again, though now through clenched teeth. "I cannot imagine them any better."

Bean's sleeves billowed like the wings of a huge silky bird as he clapped his hands and said, with a wink, "As a true Philosopher, you are yearning to know how I did it, I'll wager."

I tried to respond in an offhand manner, but he was, of course, correct, and I sprung off the bench and trotted after him as he returned to the makeshift stage.

"You have met my Thanatoscope," he said.

Having seen it in action, I now understood the instrument's name. Microscope. Telescope. Thanatoscope—a tool to view the dead.

"Would you like a demonstration?"

Anticipating my reply, Bean turned the handle again. Behind the lens at the front of the box, a tiny incandescence sprang to life. In the near-dark, it had seemed so much brighter; cries of *"Your box is ablaze!"* and *"Call the fire-pump!"* had briefly halted the show. But what manner of fire was this? A strange blaze indeed, lacking heat, flame, and crackle. I could not hide my curiosity, which Bean was happy to stoke.

"To those ignorant of its source," he said, "the glow appears miraculous. But this is no thaumaturgy. 'Tis an expression of the vital force that you, as a man of science, will know as *electricity*, generated by the action of this handle."

"You built this?" I could no longer hide my admiration—though it immediately proved unwarranted.

"Me? Good Lord, of course not." Bean chuckled with no hint of humility. "As I explained previously, such bagatelles are but toys for the rich and idle."

"'Tis a game to you, maybe, but the stakes are high."

I stooped to put my eye to the lens, to study the box's interior.

"Pray do not do that. The effects can become... perplexing."

From the folds of his robe, Bean produced what I supposed to be a spare lens, though I'd never before seen its like—'twould have been worse than useless in a microscope or telescope, being not just scratched and chipped, but blotched all over in red, blue, and green, these colours not painted on the surface of the glass but embedded within it, placed there deliberately in its manufacture.

It pleased Bean well enough, for he stopped turning the handle (which did not interrupt the beam of light, I observed) and deftly swapped this second lens for the first. Without delay the wall behind us sprang into life, the phantasms released from Bean's box sweeping around the room as he rotated it upon its attachment to the tripod, soaring to the rafters when he angled it upwards.

"See here—our spirits!" he cried. "Are they not glorious?"

They were flimsy vestiges of the beings that had so terrified his audience in the darkness, but spectacular nevertheless, though I was loathe to admit it. Bean produced several more lenses of differing patterns and hues, but I declined a further display.

"If you did not make this *Thanatoscope*," I demanded, "who did?"

"I cannot say." Bean caught my doubtful frown, and added, "Truly, I cannot say. I inherited this machine from another, and never met nor even knew the name of the man who fashioned it. I know only that it came to England from a faraway land of mystery and magic."

"It may have *come* from a land of magic, but this is an instrument of science—as I said when I first saw it.

Edwin Osborne silenced me, but I was right. Your takings tonight—" I pointed at the moneybag. "—are the product of natural philosophy, not superstition. You have broken the terms of our wager."

"Are you sure about that?" Bean countered, with an overly friendly smile that dislodged a slab of his crumbling face paint, dusting the toes of his slippers with powdered chalk. "Do you not remember our agreement? We shall both endeavour to raise hard cash: I by dint of superstition, you through your philosophy?"

I had to agree those were Edwin's words.

Bean hefted the moneybag. "This coin was undeniably raised by dint of superstition—the superstition of my audience, the good folk of Oxford."

To this, I could find no riposte. Bean had turned science against me, and cost me my chance of advancement. As he straightened his robe upon his shoulders, I glimpsed the diamond pin at his neck, and my own reflection, trapped in the stone's glazy facets.

"I suppose," I said forlornly, "you owe your close acquaintance with recent deaths to *Jackson's Oxford Journal?*"

Bean patted me on the shoulder. "Very perspicacious, my dear Sadler. We may make a magician of you yet. But now I must get on. I have use of this room for another few minutes only and much to pack away. Will I see you at a future performance?"

I took my leave without a word, and only a single glance back at the Thanatoscope. Deprived for too long of Bean's cranking, the light inside the box had begun to die.

~ ~ ~

I left the inn fuming at—in equal measure but no particular order—Ambrose Bean, my father, Rudge, my
idiot fellow Townsmen, and the sheer, senseless gall of
this cruel existence and its countless injustices. I might
have paced the city all night in that state, had my exit
from the Golden Cross Yard to North Gate Street not
been blocked by a black-garbed figure I recognized as
the widow-woman from the show. She had left so long
before me, I presumed the non-arrival of a carriage
had stranded her there, though when she turned her
veiled face in my direction, I had an uneasy suspicion
that *I* was the one she awaited.

"Good evening, Madam." I tipped my hat and tried
to edge my way around her, but she shot out a hand as
I passed and took hold of my elbow.

"I saw you talking to that man," she hissed. "Is he
your friend?"

"Ambrose Bean?" I snorted. "He is no friend of
mine. Though I know him both too well and hardly at
all. Why do *you* wish to know?"

She raised the veil with a nervous glance round
about, revealing if not quite a perfect exemplar of feminine loveliness, certainly such a pleasing visage that I
briefly forgot my misery.

"Tell me all you know of him," she urged, her dark
and anxious gaze boring deep into mine. "'Tis a matter
of greatest importance."

"Unfortunately, as I said Madam, I have little to relate, except that we are bound by fate in a wager that
has thus far ruined my life, though it could have
changed it for the better. And that he is quite possibly
the queerest gentleman I shall ever meet."

"A wager?" 'Twas the woman's turn to scoff, though
she did so most prettily. "I would not trust him, sir.

And he is no gentleman, either. He is but a fairground showman, and before you accuse *me* of lying, I know because I am one too, as was my father, and all of our family."

At this she became tearful and tugged a lacy handkerchief from her sleeve to dab at her eyes.

"There, there," I said, awkwardly. "Are things really so bad?" I patted her on the arm, then thought the better of it and jerked my hand away. I realized she was much younger than her widow-weeds suggested; in fact, I began to wonder if she were a widow at all.

"May I ask your name?"

"I am James Sadler, a native of this city. I presume, by your accent, you are not?"

"Forgive me that I accosted you," the woman sniffled, lowering her handkerchief to peek up at me through thick, black lashes. "My name is Serafina D'Bonaventura. I have no home for my life has been spent on the road. My father Enrico was the greatest of all entertainers, and taught Ambrose Bean everything he knows about how to hold an audience."

"He taught him well," I said, relieved that a weeping fit had been averted, though the woman had not yet put away her handkerchief. She clutched it in both fists as she spoke again, crushing the delicate fabric as if it were Ambrose Bean's neck in her grasp.

"My father trusted that man like a son. And I—I began to love him as more than a brother. I dared believe we might marry one day. Then not long ago, my father fell ill and unable to work. Ambrose abandoned us." She pressed the handkerchief to her lips but maintained her composure. "Worse, he took all our savings and the machine you saw tonight, which belonged to my father and was the heart of our show."

I shook my head, both vindicated and saddened. "The wretch said he inherited it!"

"Lies spill from his lips as easily as—as—" She sighed, and in a small voice, added, "'Twas not the only treasure he took."

She turned aside as she spoke, but I grasped her shoulders and spun her about to face me, my own gaze unflinching.

"My dear, you must not blame yourself. And nor would anyone else, I am certain. 'Tis obvious the scoundrel took advantage of your sweet and trusting nature."

"After Ambrose had gone," she went on, stifling a sob behind her handkerchief, "we found our most precious family heirloom gone with him—a diamond so large and so rare as you could not imagine, fastened upon a silver pin—"

I heard not a word she spoke next; this woman's predicament, however bothersome to her, seemed suddenly nothing compared with my own. The bauble for which I had sacrificed so much was not Bean's to give, and in my mind's eye I saw the already half-closed door to my future slam shut with a dreadful finality.

"—friends on the road, so I followed him here." Serafina laid a dainty hand over mine, returning me to the present with a start. "Getting back the money, even the Thanatoscope, means nothing to me compared with our diamond. 'Tis all I have left to remember my father."

Her sobs turned to bitter tears, and she laid her cheek on my chest. I hoped she could not hear how fast my heart was pounding, but she must have done so, for she sniffled, "Did you know, 'tis said the heart is the seat of the soul?"

I placed an arm around her shoulders and hugged her close. 'Twas an unseemly situation; at any moment, someone might have entered the yard on their way to the inn.

"Shall we walk?" I suggested. "Let me accompany you to your lodgings."

She shook her head and demanded, "Does Bean still have the pin? Has he sold it?"

"He still has it." I sighed. "'Twas meant to be the prize in our wager. I had hoped, if I won, to sell it, and use the proceeds to buy a place in the University and become a man of consequence."

It sounded ridiculous now, but Serafina did not laugh.

"Then he has betrayed us both, and so we are also bound. Let us make a deal of our own, Mr Sadler—"

"James. Please call me James."

"—the terms being so simple, not even such a snake as Ambrose Bean could find room to wriggle." Her eyes gleamed, though now with devilry rather than tears. "First, you will win your prize, with my help. You will then return the pin to me, its rightful owner, and after that you may become whatever you wish—I shall see to it!"

I hesitated, not to consider Serafina's proposal, but to savour the flush of excitement that had bloomed upon her porcelain cheeks, the rosy lips half-parted in expectation, the impassioned dark eyes. Her loveliness could not be denied, but I doubted she'd be of much help in building an aerostat.

"Nothing could please me more, gentle lady!" I gushed. "And be certain I am both honoured and touched by your offer. But my needs, being of a technical bent, cannot be satisfied by womanly wiles."

"I think you underestimate my wiles, Mr Sadler."

She pushed me aside quite unkindly, given our recent intimacy, though what they say about furious women was amply confirmed (Mary being the exception that proved the rule). I swooned, and in that instant she was suddenly gone from my sight, and with her the inn, the arch onto North Gate Street, the rainy weather, and even the time of day—all vanished without warning, as if I were back in the assembly room, and the whole world had been hitherto hid by a curtain, now torn to the ground by a hired-hand for the handsome sum of two shillings.

And what weird new reality dawned in its place? A sunny morning on Angel Meadow, an aerostat soaring into the sky—and Ambrose Bean, waving at me from its gondola, his bejewelled turban glowing like a fiery crown upon his head.

I wailed and clutched at my own head, fearing I had suffered a rupture of the brain, or gone mad, or been granted some cryptic Divine revelation. Though if God had indeed delivered my vision, He was no expert in balloon-craft, for as I observed the rising globe, it struck me as far too small in girth for the weighty load it supported; in truth, it should never have got off the ground, let alone surged so swiftly. Rudge would have roared had he seen it.

The instant I spotted this flaw, the illusion proved no more solid than Bean's face paint, and crumbled as dust all about, returning me with a jolt to the cold, dark, damp of the Golden Cross Yard.

"Forgive me," I gasped, supporting myself against the gatepost. "I took a strange turn."

"I know," said Serafina. "For I caused it."

I could only gape at her.

"You saw the balloon? Ambrose Bean?" She grinned in a most unladylike fashion. "Do not look so afeared. I mesmerized you, that is all."

"Mesmerized?"

She gave me a pitying look; had I been able to fashion the words, I'd have left no doubt that I knew what she meant.

"Mesmerism," she said very slowly, as if I were the stupidest of creatures. "'Tis the artful direction of will and intention. Of making men do what they would not have done and see what they have not seen."

I managed to gasp, "But how did you—? And how did you know what—?"

She shrugged. "I am a *prodigy*, so they say. Father called me the star of his show!" Those rosebud lips trembled, as if tears would again overwhelm her. But she gathered herself, took my hands in hers, and continued, now deadly serious: "You saw what I can do. With time and circumstance, I can make the whole city believe you have flown in your balloon. You will be famous! Just help me get back what I lost to Ambrose Bean—my enemy, and yours."

Still scattered between two worlds, I failed to find a reply. Meanwhile, Serafina lowered her veil and slipped through the arch.

"I'm sure we shall meet again."

"Wait!" I cried at last. "How shall I find you?"

"I shall do the finding," drifted my answer from out of the darkness. "And soon, so do not think on the matter too long."

~ ~ ~

I headed immediately for the Physic Garden, keeping a close eye on my surroundings as I walked. Not for fear of rowdies and cutpurses—who had largely disappeared from the centre of Oxford in recent years, since the Corporation introduced street lighting. I simply wished to confirm to myself that I had returned to the real world and not re-entered Serafina's imaginary one. I reached the glasshouse in double-quick time and slammed the door firmly behind me, well aware that 'twould not be so easy to safeguard my mind. Nevertheless, the fabric of the Little Emperor felt reassuringly solid in my hands, and I stood there for many minutes clutching a portion of it to my breast.

However much I relished the prospect of further secretive meetings, Serafina's proposal would have me cheat on a solemn oath I had sworn of my own free will, if somewhat begrudgingly, and witnessed by the entire Philosophical Club. And worse, in resorting to deception and someone else's fairground tricks, I would become no better than Ambrose Bean, when the moral high ground was currently mine.

Except, would it really be a trick? Mesmerism could not be magic, for magic did not exist. Yet mesmerism *did* exist and therefore, I reasoned, must be explainable by rational means. I knew of its basis—an essence contained within all living creatures termed "animal magnetism"—and of its popularity at that time amongst the London *beau monde*, its practitioners ofttimes reckoned as skilful as doctors at healing the body (to the chagrin of my brother-in-law Burleigh) and even more so for ailments of the spirit.

Even in Oxford, a certain Dr Holloway had lectured at length on the subject just two years past. The only scandal had been the exorbitant price of admission—five guineas, a small fortune for a single oration. Those with the means to attend had spoken highly of his philosophy, among them Dr Wall. And who was I, to gainsay Dr Wall?

My decision thus made—almost for me, it seemed—I was wondering how to locate Serafina despite her instructions, when the door burst open and Rudge strode in, bearing a lantern and an anxious expression that turned to relief when his gaze fell upon me.

"I could not sleep," he said, "and saw movement in here. I thought you were a thief."

"I'd make a poor thief," I said. *But an excellent traitor*, a voice in my head remarked. Ignoring it, I held up the section of aerostat I'd been clutching, and with a faint laugh, added, "Who in his right mind would want to steal *this*?"

"You are working on the Emperor?" Rudge beamed with delight. "At this time of night? Why, James... Perhaps I have misjudged you!"

I could have explained that he'd caught me, not working on the aerostat, but simply looking at it. That, however, would have required an explanation in itself, and *that* would have led to Serafina, and my vision, and the offer she made. And the fact that I planned to accept it, and that the Little Emperor—and by extension, Rudge—had all at once become redundant.

And yet, I hesitated. Watching Rudge battle tears of joy, I realized, for perhaps the first time, how much our enterprise meant to him, and that even if I wanted to, I could not betray him.

"I will join you," he said, setting the lamp down on the floor. "Let us burn some midnight oil together, eh?"

I nodded, speechless with shame. Then I sat upon the floor at his side, drawing a curtain in my mind over Bean's success, the provenance of his diamond, and especially Serafina D'Bonaventura.

CHAPTER
TWENTY-ONE

THROUGHOUT THESE EVENTS, I spared not one thought for my sister, though 'twas Mary who suffered the worst for the sake of my own advancement. Pale and pinched at the best of times, within the week her cheeks bore a sickly pallor, the circles under her eyes evincing too many nights of too little sleep, and days too full of cooking, cleaning, delivering, serving, accounting—in sum, running here, there, and anywhere Father might send her.

When late one morning Father announced he had guests for tea that very afternoon, rather than buckling under this latest imposition Mary rallied and served up refreshments so splendid, all present concurred they could not have done better themselves, even had they tried.

'Twas Father's good fortune that, for all his faults, his daughter's loyalty never wavered. "You must understand their position," urged Mr Robinson, of Robinson & Robinson of Ship Lane, clutching his plate of ratafias in one hand and his cup and saucer in the other, so he could partake of neither. "They fear for the Guild's reputation."

His fellow guests murmured their agreement. As she moved amongst them with the teapot, Mary winced to see the anguish Father concealed behind his smile. While his adversaries openly questioned his fitness for office, even his most stalwart supporters had become more quarrelsome than before.

"They are, of course, entitled to their opinions," Father replied. "But in *my* view, they fall behind the times. What harm is there in a little progress now and then? Why, without progress we would still be making macaroons from mashed potatoes!"

Mr Robinson sighed. "Those are not the words of the man I have known and respected these twenty years past. Is it contagious, perhaps, this disorder that ails your son?"

Father blushed at the hesitant chuckles this raised.

"Do tell us, Thomas," prodded another some-time ally, "might we soon see you, too, horsing around Angel Meadow, up to queer business with that odd little gardener?"

The laughter came louder this time.

"My son's disorder, as you call it," Father huffed, "is naught but opposition and contrariness for their own sake—a modern malady, sadly not uncommon amongst the younger generation. 'Tis reported that the King himself is likewise troubled by the Prince of Wales."

Mrs Winstable nodded. "I have heard that, too. I cannot say from experience, but 'tis well established that children are born depraved and can only get worse as they grow."

"Even if that be the case, which I doubt—" Mr Robinson paused to take a sip of tea, balancing his plate upon his knee. "—giving instruction on how to know right from wrong is surely what parents are for."

"With respect," interposed a weedy confectioner from north of the city, "the personage in question is hardly a child, and should have learned that particular lesson long ago." He glared accusingly at Father.

"More cheesecake, anyone?" Mary interrupted.

"Thank you, but I must decline," said Mr Robinson. "I find cheesecake a little too slow on the innards of late."

Though they dawdled awhile to finish their tea and talk business, all too soon only Mary remained. With the parlour to herself but still no time to call her own, she gathered the teacups and half-empty plates, fetched a broom to sweep up the crumbs, then replaced the chairs against the walls and made her way back to the kitchen.

CHAPTER TWENTY-TWO

WITH OUR DIFFERENCES PUT BEHIND US, Rudge and I entered a period of quiet but productive endeavour, completing the sewing of the aerostat and making preparations for our public launch, for which we had now set a date. I produced a poster for display in the hostelries of the city and handbills that I spent hours distributing at the markets, in Butcher Row, and elsewhere that people gathered in numbers. Rudge, too, did his part, persuading his fellow gardeners to purchase tickets, and we even started work on the Little Emperor's successor—the large aerostat in which I would make my first ascent. As the materials we needed arrived upon their carriers' waggons, what had often seemed a dream began to feel real—and certainly more believable than Serafina's mirage.

On Serafina herself, I dwelled as little as possible—partly for fear that, if I allowed her into my thoughts for even a moment, she might seize control again; largely in an attempt to forget her proposal, and how close I had come to accepting. For although I now enjoyed my labours more than previously, I still found them arduous, and often wished for an easier life come the end of a wearisome day. At least Rudge seemed less inclined to lash out with his tongue, though when he did, I had to bite my own, for fear of letting slip resentments I had hidden from even myself.

Each morning on my way to the *Officina Chimica*, I stopped to hang one of our posters from the lamp-post at the junction of Catte Street and the High. I had done this every day for a week, and every night the lamp-lighter removed it; I persevered nevertheless, reasoning that more people would see it by day than by night, and for the cost of a poster and a moment of my time, any attention was useful. One particular morning, however, as I negotiated a flock of sheep that had blocked the High at that juncture (to the ire of every coachman with a schedule to keep), I saw the lamp-lighter had surrendered this losing battle, for the poster still hung there, waving like a pennant in the breeze. I congratulated myself on this small triumph—until I reached the corner, then my pleasure turned to dread.

Not To Be Missed!!! shrieked a crude, barely legible script. *The World Famous Pig Of Knowledge!!!! Back Soon By Popular Demand!!!!!* Piling injury upon insult, it glibly went on to inform me the date of the sow's return: the very day Rudge and I had selected for the Little Emperor's launch.

I tore it down—as I did with all the others I spied around town that day. Later, Rudge tried to console me, opining that, it being human nature to seek out new pleasures, people would find room in their hearts and minds—and more importantly, their purses—not just for our balloon, but for a whole farmyard of well-informed livestock and even, dare he say it, Ambrose

214

Bean's brand of hogwash. But the prospect of losing our audience to the Swine of Superstition gnawed at me and my good cheer unravelled as the day of our launch grew closer. My wits were also strained to their limits—as Rudge informed me whenever I arrived at the glasshouse late, exhausted, or both, or made some simple error that annoyed him. Living on the job, as it were, afforded minimal time for rest, and though our work proceeded faster as a result, I suffered for want of sleep.

One afternoon, while scouting for suitable launching spots in Angel Meadow, I heard a shout—clearly aimed at me—from the bridge above. I squinted into the sunlight, remembering my first encounter with Rudge and anticipating more mockery. But the Townsman on the bridge smiled and waved when he saw I had seen him, and bellowed, louder still, "Mr Sadler—we are all hanging upon tenterhooks to see your show! Best of luck to you, sir!"

From that day onwards this happened increasingly often, until whenever I visited the meadow, whether to make preparations or simply to take the air, I was met with good wishes or even applause. On occasion, half-a-dozen or more would gather to watch my most humdrum doings, as if I were the grandest person in town.

And as time passed and the launch drew ever nearer, I began to think that perhaps I *was* such a person. For whom else would dare attempt what I meant to do? Who else would risk so much for the sake of his principles?

I was not there yet, I decided, but perhaps I was, at last, *becoming* a man of consequence.

~ ~ ~

The day of the launch dawned cool, dry, and windless. When Rudge tested the air with a moistened finger, he declared conditions to be ideal, not for the start of a great adventure, for we had already done that, nor for the end, as we had much further to go, but for the raising of a waypost that would live long in the memory of all who bore witness.

I had sat up throughout the night in the meadow, both to guard our apparatus and to supervise the Little Emperor's inflation. Aided by a pair of ostlers from The Angel whose services we had secured at an extortionate rate, we had brought our materials from the glasshouse late the previous afternoon and erected a framework of wooden beams, to which we roped the limp aerostat. Ostlers and horses alike looked on curiously while we attached a rubber tube to the Emperor's neck, then joined this with four others that each led to a lidded metal box resembling a large biscuit tin. I promised the men a surprise—and an extra shilling apiece—if they returned promptly for work the following morning.

Many long, lonely, and worrisome hours ensued, fraught with checking, and fretting, and checking again. Was the Emperor filling evenly? Were the ropes becoming tangled or the globe contorted? Were the generators well supplied with iron filings and Spirit of Vitriol? The product of their reaction was the inflammable air that, being lighter than regular air, would provide the lift required to raise the globe into the atmosphere at the appointed time. This was all an achingly tedious process, and when Rudge arrived at dawn, refreshed after a cosy night in his bothy, he found me cold, stiff, tired, and in no sort of state for adventures.

"How fares my dearest old gas-bag this beautiful morn? Growing fatter by the minute, I trust?"

I assumed he did not mean me, and scowled as I watched him bound through the dew-sodden grass, like an overexcited babe on his way to a sweet shop.

"Of course—how else?" I snapped. "'Tis *me* who's in danger of shrinkage. I cannot remember the last time I ate."

"Then you'd best get your breakfast," Rudge laughed. "I shall keep watch while you're gone—but be sure you mind the time. 'Twould be a pity to start without you."

~ ~ ~

When I returned to the meadow a short while later, I marvelled at the change. The chilly mist had lifted, re-vealing a cheerful, sunny morning that matched the improvement in my mood after a nap, a wash, and a belly-full of the good food that Rudge had left me.

The High now teemed with traffic, and as I hurried over Magdalen Bridge I saw we had already attracted a crowd in the meadow. They welcomed me with a little *Huzzah!*, which boosted my spirits still further as we began our final preparations, checking the tension of the globe, the direction of the wind, and the myriad other provisions that would ensure a faultless ascent.

Then—all of a sudden, compared with the endless wait overnight—the aerostat was ready and we had naught left to do but set it free.

"Shall I cut the ropes?" I asked Rudge, eyeing the expectant crowd.

"Perhaps you should say something first," Rudge replied.

217

I hadn't considered this, and had nothing prepared. "Could we not just... surprise them?" I whispered.

While we dithered, the crowd grew restless.

"Hurry up!" someone yelled. "I can't wait around here all day."

"You must speak!" Rudge hissed. "They are expecting a performance!"

I cleared my throat and stepped forwards. I noticed that, in addition to the paying crowd in the meadow, we had attracted a sizeable audience on Magdalen Bridge—curious passers-by who had lined the balustrade to stare and point at the aerostat, now fully inflated to its maximum diameter of thirty feet and straining at its tethers like a gigantic rotund child craving adventure.

"Thank you all for coming," I said.

In the front row in the meadow, someone yawned. I registered neither their age nor their gender, seeing only a bottomless pit of teeth, tongue, and throat that threatened to swallow me whole.

"Greetings!" I cried, somewhat alarmed. "Greetings, O ye seekers after... after the genuine truth, not all manner of lies and confabulations that only the stupidest gull could ever believe!"

The yawning stopped mid-gape.

Encouraged, I continued. "The frail and the faint must leave straight away, for I refuse to take the blame for any mishaps that might occur—"

"No one said 'twould be dangerous," came a tremulous cry from the back of the crowd. "We should have been warned. If I'd known, I would never have come—"

I raised my voice further still. "O ye seekers after the genuine truth, this very morning, we shall open a door to the world of the... the world of the atmosphere. That place where few men have been, but... more shall go in the future! How close it appears—" I waved my hands above my head. "—but only thanks to recent advances in the pneumatic chymistry have a few brave souls left our Earthly home to explore the mysteries of the aerial realm. What will they find there? What secrets will they learn? Who could possibly not want to know?"

"I want to know what simpleton spewed up this pigswill!"

I frowned at the speaker, a coarse-faced cove in a stonemason's apron. "With respect, sir, if you cannot listen politely, perhaps you should not have attended. But since you have done so, best you leave before I go further, and stop spoiling the occasion for everyone else."

I pointed towards the bridge amidst murmurs of discontent from the crowd, followed by not a few cries of "Shame!"

Rudge elbowed me sharply in the ribs. "You are meant to be entertaining them."

"That balloon," observed another man, "seems very small. Can it really lift you into the atmosphere?"

I smiled, glad of the diversion. "You have misunderstood, sir. I do not intend to ascend on *this* occasion. What you will witness today—and are privileged to do so—will be a demonstration of the *principle* of flight."

The howls of disappointment that greeted these words knocked me aback.

"I came to see you fall from the sky!" cried one protester.

"I fear," said the man who had queried the size of the Emperor, and seemed to have some knowledge of ballooning, gained from the newssheets perhaps, "that even if he *were* to ascend, there'd be scant chance of disaster. The weather is far too clement."

"Pah! What kind of spectacle is this?"

"Not one worth sixpence."

"I would pay sixpence *not* to watch."

"They should pay *us* a shilling apiece for the waste of our time."

"I told you those posters were over the top," murmured Rudge.

I removed my hat and ran a shaking hand through my hair; nothing short of my death, it seemed, would please this barbarous mob. Then the situation became immeasurably worse, as I spotted Edwin Osborne and a band of his cronies descending from Magdalen Bridge.

"I must apologize for our late arrival," said Edwin, striding to the front of the crowd. "I feared we had missed the excitement. But I see you have not even started yet." He appraised the bobbing globe through his lorgnette. "You *do* plan to ascend, I presume? We have numerous other appointments to keep."

"Your timing is perfect," I replied. "For we were just about to begin."

"About time too!" was the general response, as Rudge and I raced about disconnecting the tubes from the globe and securing its neck so none of the precious inflammable air might escape.

"And now," I declared, tugging Rudge's pruning knife from my pocket, "I shall cut the cords that bind the Emperor to Earth and allow him to rise to the Heavens."

I grasped the nearest rope and began to saw, but had barely bruised it before Rudge stayed my hand.

"Wait!" he whispered into my ear. "We have a problem—look!"

I looked, and saw, and felt a cold, indigestible lump in my throat like I'd swallowed a gobbet of bread dough. The balloon looked less pleasingly plump than it had just a moment ago.

"'Tis leaking!" I hissed through my teeth.

"Releasing the tubes must have loosened one of the buttons," said Rudge.

"But how could that happen? We checked and double-checked them all." I risked a glance at our increasingly agitated audience.

"Having trouble?" Edwin called. "Anything we can do to help?"

I feigned a smile. "'Tis merely a hitch, as might occur with any new philosophy. This one in particular, being reliant upon the forces of Nature."

Edwin smirked. "But is that not the very purpose of natural philosophy—to harness those forces? Whereas you two, 'tis clear, would struggle to harness a little girl's pony."

I saw something beyond simple scorn in his eyes, as if he knew more about our "hitch" than he cared to let on. But 'twas no time for accusations, for our audience had begun chattering amongst themselves, their interest in the aerostat all but evaporated.

"Go back to the glasshouse and fetch our needles and thread," said Rudge, with admirable *sang froid*. "I will hold the fort here."

How?" I squealed. "Look—they are leaving already!"

"Can you blame them?" Edwin said, then cleared his throat to declare, above the chatter, "I suggest you all take off to The Crown. The Pig of Knowledge is playing today, and must surely provide a better show than this puffed-up swine's bladder."

He himself lingered, no doubt anxious to see my reaction as more of my audience drifted towards the bridge.

"Wait!" I stumbled after them. "History will be made here this day. You cannot just walk away!"

"Better run then, hadn't we?" someone quipped.

I jerked to a halt, my arms falling limp to my sides.

"Hard luck, Sadler," said Edwin. "Although, as you must have known from the start, good fortune alone can never make up for a lack of good breeding."

I gathered my breath to scream some taunt of my own, but was saved from further embarrassment by a small, hesitant voice, and turned to see a small, hesitant damsel standing behind me.

"Excuse me, sir," said she, "but did I hear you mention buttons? Needles? Thread?"

I was about to congratulate her on her eavesdropping skills when Rudge darted between us.

"I am a seamstress, you see. I have my tools with me." She indicated an embroidered case at her feet. "And references, too, if required."

"We have no need of paperwork," said Rudge. "Just a quick hand and a ready heart, and I reckon you lack neither."

She smiled shyly in return.

Turning to me, Rudge ordered, "Find the source of the leak and set our good helper here to work. And try to be polite," he added, under his breath. Then he raised his voice and addressed the departing crowd: "Ladies and gentlemen—see here! The flower of Oxfordshire womanhood! As lovely as she is valiant, and modest to boot!"

The pretty young seamstress was certainly better attended than the Emperor. As the crowd returned to their places, a lively debate ensued regarding how she might be lifted to repair the rent in the fabric (which I had located on the upper hemisphere of the globe) and especially how her modesty might be preserved once she got up there. Never had the simple act of sewing occasioned such fascination; breath was held and fingernails bitten as the seamstress teetered atop the stack of boxes, trunks, and other items supplied by the crowd for her elevation, a scarf bound around her ankles to keep her petticoats in place and save her blushes as the breeze picked up.

Meanwhile, Rudge and I hastened to reconnect the tubes to the neck of the balloon and restart the inflammable air generators.

"Let us refill it as quickly as possible," said Rudge, "and get it in the air."

To cheers and a round of applause—and a race amongst the bachelors in the crowd to be the one to help her down—the seamstress descended from her makeshift tower, and without further ceremony, I cut the ropes. As the final strand parted, the Little Emperor trembled for an instant, as if, after so many years shut up in its box, then so many days inert on the floor of the glasshouse, then so many hours tethered to its scaffold, it could not quite believe its freedom had come. Then, with a great whoosh of air, it ascended—thankfully clearing the top of the frame before being caught by the breeze and tugged eastwards.

From our audience in the meadow and the crowd on Magdalen Bridge, came naught but stunned silence.

Then a tremendous cry went up, and though they could have numbered no more than a hundred, they made the noise of thousands with their whooping, hollers, and screams. I saw a lady faint, a man clutch his chest and go pale. I felt weak at the knees myself, dazzled in my mind's eye by a vision of another balloon. Unlike that miserable night at the Golden Cross, however, this aerostat carried *me* in its gondola, and was not an illusion but a reality that would come to pass, if I strove for it.

"To the future!" I bellowed. "And the triumph of natural philosophy!"

The crowd roared in agreement, the liveliest giving chase as, gaining further height, the Little Emperor careened across the bridge and towards the High. In the road, chaos erupted—coaches stalled, horses rearing—and shrieks of wonderment sounded as a multitude of children joined the ever-swelling crowd, laughing and leaping into the air like little frogs as they tried to snatch the globe, though it had long risen beyond the reach of grasping hands.

The last I saw of it, 'twas still gaining height. I turned to Rudge, overwhelmed.

"We did it!" I cried. "We did it!"

"Aye, that we did," said Rudge, his gruff old face moist with tears.

CHAPTER TWENTY-THREE

LOUD AND PROTRACTED CELEBRATIONS ENSUED, progressing first from the High to the Turl, then hours later onto The Crown. Our supporters seemed in no hurry to resume their own lives and businesses. Indeed, the crowd continued to grow throughout the day, so that by evening we numbered so many as to fill all the inn's public rooms, with more spilling into the courtyard and onto North Gate Street beyond. The ale flowed without cease, the innkeeper's joy knew no bound, and for once, life felt sweet—so much so, even my erstwhile porcine rival felt the benefit. The Pig of Knowledge, I learned, having drawn a meagre audience in competition with our aerostat launch, risked being turned into Ham of Oblivion if her takings did not improve soon. To tide them over, I gave the swine's manager half-a-crown towards her upkeep.

With dusk falling, a hubbub arose as a waggon drew up outside the inn and was found to contain the Little Emperor—or what remained of him. We learned the globe had returned to Earth near the village of

Wolvercote, three miles northwest of Oxford. Terrified country-folk had mistaken it for a monster dropped in from the sky, and attacked it with their pitchforks until a local farmer, better acquainted with modern life, had realized its true nature and saved it from further abuse. Reasoning by the direction of its flight that the aerostat had come from the city, the farmer had loaded it onto his waggon and set off in search of its owner.

Rudge's joy turned to sorrow at this news. I paid the farmer for his time and quick action and bid him a glass of ale, which he declined, saying his wife would be expecting him. When I'd waved him goodbye, I found my partner still caressing the mangled fabric, as if the aerostat were a sick animal that he might somehow stroke back into health.

"Do not worry," I said. "'Twill be repaired. We can employ a whole army of seamstresses."

I did not jest—during the day's festivities we had collected enough subscriptions, and promises of the same, to purchase the materials for a new aerostat many times over. When we re-entered the inn, we found waiting for us yet another queue of subscribers, all eager to part with their coin for the promise of further aerial adventures.

How easy it had been, in retrospect, I mused. I had become a man of consequence without the University, or even making my name as the first English aeronaut. For all those people who'd be disappointed (not to mention out of pocket) if I failed to fly again, I spared not a thought, being as drunk upon success as ale that night.

Whilst processing from admirer to admirer like a lady of the second estate at her coming-out ball, I spotted Ambrose Bean, sitting alone at the table by the hearth where I had encountered him before. He raised his glass of porter in salute when he saw me.

"Congratulations are in order, I hear." He smiled with not a hint of dismay once I'd shrugged off my suitors to join him. "I regret I could not attend, but 'tis clear your launch was a resounding success."

"'Twas indeed," I replied, slurring only very slightly. "You missed a great *shpectacle*."

Expecting naught but mockery in return, I reminded myself that, for all his airs and graces, Ambrose Bean was no better than I—and a thief, besides. But to my surprise, he rose to his feet and extended his hand.

"I am well aware of that. And accordingly, must admit defeat."

I gaped at him, slack-jawed.

"Come on, man!" Bean laughed long and loud, earning curious glances from all who were drinking nearby. "Let us shake on it before I change my mind."

As on that fateful afternoon in Harper's Coffeehouse, I grasped his long, slim fingers—although this time, 'twas my own palm that felt clammy.

"The next meeting of your Philosophical Club is but a few days hence," Bean said, retaking his seat. "And I could not raise as much money by then as you have collected this single evening. Or win as many hearts," he added, as a tearful stranger sprang upon me from behind, embracing me like his dearest friend and thanking me repeatedly, though for what, I could not say.

"Here," Bean made a show of withdrawing the diamond pin from his neckcloth, then wrapped it in a handkerchief and offered it up to me with an untypically earnest expression. "'Tis yours. Guard it carefully." And with that, he emptied his glass in a single gulp and took himself off to the back of the inn, where the stairs to the lodging rooms were located.

For several minutes after he'd gone, I could do nothing more than stare at the square of folded linen in my hand, hardly daring to imagine what this meant (and my trophy's rightful owner long forgot). I barely noticed Rudge shuffle up beside me and tug at my sleeve.

"I've been asking around," he said in a low voice, "and 'tis as I thought—our setback this morning was no accident. One of the 'prentices swears he saw a light in the glasshouse two nights past, when neither you nor I were present."

Had it come earlier in the day, I would have raged at this revelation. Now, however, I struggled to muster much concern at all.

"Let us discuss it tomorrow," I said. "I'm in too good a mood tonight."

"Too drunk, you mean" said Rudge with a wry smile, as yet another well-wisher pressed a glass in my hand.

The bitter suds slid down like the sweetest of spa waters, so accustomed had I become to their dubious charms. While I supped, I sneaked a glance at Rudge, who had cut a melancholy figure since the Little Emperor's return, though he brightened on hearing a song strike up in the tap-room.

"Listen, James. They are singing about you!"

Before I held the diamond pin in my hand, I might have pronounced myself the happiest man on God's Earth, and all my dreams fulfilled. But with Bean ceding victory, I had new dreams, and troubling decisions ahead—especially the future of our aerostatic adventures, now they no longer served me a purpose. How would Rudge react if I quit? I told myself 'twould be best for him in the long run; for all his attachment to our enterprise, the effort it cost him had taken its toll.

Even as I thought this, Rudge yawned and said, "'Tis time for bed. I am too old for such frolics." He reached inside my coat and removed my bulging purse. "I shall look after this. 'Twould be easy pickings, the state you are in."

"Spend a little on yourself, if you wish," I said. "You deserve it. But *I* shall keep this." I slid the diamond pin from Bean's handkerchief and fastened it onto my own neckcloth—a well-deserved badge of triumph.

Rudge's eyes widened. "Be careful, James. There are worse than pickpockets prowling the streets."

"I will, dear Wyndham."

I felt suddenly snivelly, overwhelmed with emotion like a lovesick maid, and unable to help myself hugged my partner with such passion, an observer might have thought it our final farewell.

Fortunately, he shrugged me off straight away. "Enjoy yourself while you might," he grunted. "I shall get the Emperor back to the glasshouse and clear up there."

We parted with a firm handshake, after which I rejoined the celebrations with renewed zeal. During my conversation with Rudge, the Pig of Knowledge had wandered into the public rooms, and was now enjoying a bowl of beer on the floor. Several Undergraduates had also joined the throng, having heard of the morning's events and being anxious to meet me. So again I was fêted, and fed, and watered, and the merriment continued for another hour or more, until the cry of

"Bulldogs!" went up and a whirlwind of fluttering gowns and stampeding feet let loose, as the Gownsmen made themselves scarce.

Being already as unsteady as a newborn lamb, I was tossed and turned from pillar to post in the chaos, and when it subsided found I was sat on the floor in the sawdust, beside me the Pig. A Bulldog came past and cast a suspicious glower over the pair of us.

"I'd thank you to keep your eyes to yourself—" I belched. "—for the lady is mine."

And with these words I flung my arms about the Pig's neck, and kissed her sloppily full on the snout.

CHAPTER
TWENTY-FOUR

ITH THE APPEARANCE OF THE BULLDOGS, the party stuttered to a halt. I left not a moment too soon for the sake of my health, not to mention my dignity. Even then, 'twas only my supporters' encouraging shouts that kept me upright, and moving in the required direction down North Gate Street. It had seemed to me a perfect time to catch up on my *Officina Chimica* work, which I had neglected sorely in the days approaching the launch. Although upon entering the Broad, I wondered if resignation rather than overtime was in order, me being a man of consequence now, and such menial toil better suited to a young fellow of limited means just starting upon his career.

On my way down to the basement, I thought I heard a cough—or perhaps a whisper, or a sneeze—from the street above. But being fully occupied by the complicated task of descending the steps, I simply halted for a moment to scan the entrance to the museum, then finding no explanation promptly forgot it.

Given the peace and quiet of that late hour and the absence of interruptions from Dr Crouch, I'd expected to breeze through my chores. But the vast amount of ale I'd consumed had left me sluggish and clumsy. I realized that what I could not break, I would miscalculate, and what I could not miscalculate, I would break, and perhaps 'twould be best all around to do neither. So lacking other employment, I pulled up a stool at my work-bench, removed the diamond pin from my neckcloth, and spent the next half-hour or more admiring it from every possible angle.

I had not much experience of diamonds and certainly none of this magnitude, but now, on closer inspection, its oddities struck me as much as its size. In cut, 'twas neither shapely nor symmetrical—nor even very attractive—with an unsightly delve hacked in one end where the silver pin was affixed. Its clarity also suffered for the presence of many minuscule dots, which crowded its interior and twinkled like tiny stars as I rolled the pin between my fingers. Yet those limitless depths harboured beauty beyond mere appearance.

By this point quite smitten, and eager to see to the heart of the stone, I pressed the diamond to my eye in the manner of a lorgnette and leaned at full stretch across the bench towards my lamp. This awkward manoeuvre ended in horror, when my prize somehow detached itself from its mount, dropped with a splash into the beaker of Aromatic Spirit Vegetabilis that I had earlier failed to divide into equal measures, and vanished with such totality, I might have believed I'd imagined the gem, had I not still been holding its pin.

"Dear Lord!" I wailed aloud. "It has dissolved!"

But how? How could a *diamond* simply discompose, like table salt in water? I dropped to the floor for a clearer view of the beaker, but then I heard a thud at the door behind me, and swivelling upon my knees beheld two large, scruffy, ill-countenanced men jammed shoulder-to-shoulder in the entrance. It occurred to me that, if they stayed there, I would have no easy means of escape. And straight away I knew I would need one, for the look in their eyes promised mayhem.

"Don't get up on our account," said the first of the pair, a pudgy specimen with a grey and lumpen face like an old potato. "We like you better where you are."

I doubt I'd have rushed to attack them, even granted their permission. "Who—who are you?" I stammered from the flagstones. "What are you doing here?"

"The first is none of your business," the ruffian growled. "As for the second..."

"We saw the old man take the moneybag," said his partner, whose purplish cheeks and flattened skull put me more in mind of a turnip. "But we know you kept the jewel."

I shook my head sharply, and wished I had not, for it sent the whole room into motion around me, yawing and pitching to such a sickening degree, I feared I might topple over. "You are mistaken," I babbled. "I have no valuables on me. You can see for yourself." I spread my arms wide, both maintaining my balance and proving my point.

"That we will," promised Potato-face. He advanced around the tables towards me, while Turnip-head hung back as though he feared I might make a break for it. I would have scoffed at the very notion, in safer surroundings.

"You have no valuables, eh?" Potato-face glowered down at me. "What's this, then?"

He swiped the pin from the bench and waggled it in my face, the sliver of silver dwarfed by his finger and thumb.

"Just a pin," I quailed. "For sewing. Our aerostat has many buttons."

"I shall ask you again," he growled. "Where is the diamond?"

"I don't know," I whispered.

He nodded with an air of satisfaction—as if he had hoped for that answer all along—then bunched his massive fingers into a proportionately massive fist and punched me in the face.

My head hit the corner of the bench as I fell, but far from knocking me senseless as I might have hoped, the double impact jolted me instantly back to sobriety. I slumped in a pitiful heap on the floor, groaning in pain and frustration, the good cheer and fellowship of The Crown but a distant memory.

"Careful now," said Turnip-head. "We want him to talk, remember?"

Potato-face reached down to wind his hands in the front of my waistcoat. "In the end, maybe," he replied. "But I'm not in a hurry."

And with that I was hauled to my feet and flung with contempt at the nearest wall, which happened to be the one that housed our chymical stores. I managed to brake before I hit it—imagining the mess I would have to clean up if the whole assemblage came down—but my reaction triggered a change of tack in my assailant.

"Hey! I've heard about these places." A slow, misshapen grin took form as Potato-face scanned his surroundings. "Now what do they call them...? Elab—Elab—*Elaboratories*, that's it. I'm right, aren't I?"

I was surprised that he could handle so many syllables all in one word, though I simply nodded in fright.

"And these elaboratories, they're dangerous places. Stands to reason, doesn't it? All these poisons, just sitting around. Should be under lock and key, I say. A cove could get hurt." He ran a finger along the nearest shelf. "I don't know what these labels say." He turned to me, his eyes gleaming in childish thrill. "But you do, don't you? You know which are nice..." He took a bottle of Oil of Cloves and placed it on my bench next to the Aromatic Spirit Vegetabilis. "And which are not." He unstoppered a bottle of Spirits of Hartshorn, took a wary sniff, and recoiled with a jolt. "Phew! Smells like the Devil's own fart."

I glanced towards the door, but Turnip-head still blocked it. I looked to the one-handed clock, but not even Nugent would turn out this early. I was, quite simply, helpless—and all the while, Potato-face continued to browse the shelves.

"I reckon some of these could make a right royal mess of the physog. Or the eyes."

I jerked backwards as he jabbed the bottle stopper at my face.

"The chitterlings, too." Nose wrinkling, he poured a measure of the Hartshorn into an empty beaker. "Fancy another drink?"

I shook my head.

"Had a skinful already?" Potato-head laughed. "I'm sure we'll find something to tempt." He snatched another bottle from the shelf. "How about this one? Or this one? Or this?"

At the third I could no longer hide my horror. Concentrated Spirit of Nitre. Dr Crouch had once described how one of my predecessors—having spilled barely a tablespoon on his forearm while stocking the shelves with a dearth of due care and attention—had required immediate amputation at the elbow to save the rest of the limb. The corrosive had sizzled unstoppably up his arm, devouring flesh, nerves, bone, and all in its path. 'Twas fortunate, Crouch had concluded, that anatomists from the Medical School seized the chance to lend a hand. And then he had laughed at his own, poor but grisly pun.

"So this is a nasty one, eh?" Potato-face jiggled the bottle in my face like a boy might torment his sister with an especially large and horrid spider. I shied away, which only increased his enjoyment.

"*Very* nasty, by the look of you. But there's only one way to be sure." Then to Turnip-head, he said, "Hold him steady."

'Twas my last chance. I raced for the door, but Turnip-head moved faster than I'd expected. Before I'd covered a yard, he had grabbed me with an elbow around my neck and the other hand twisting my right arm behind my back. I bucked and heaved, choked, protested; all in vain.

With an unpleasant, black-toothed grin, Potato-face leaned so close, I could smell his rancid sweat, mingled with an earthy scent that reminded me of Rudge. Then his big hand shot out and grabbed my face, squeezing hard between my jaws to force my mouth open. I flailed and thrashed as he reached for the Spirit of Nitre, but my assailants held me firm between them.

"Now, for one last time—where is the diamond?"

"It disappeared!" I cried.

Potato-face smiled happily. "We shall have it your way, then. Bottoms up!"

He opened the bottle an inch from my face, the fumes searing my throat and filling my eyes with burning tears. I panicked, lashing out blindly with my free arm, and with terror lending me strength, dashed my elbow at Turnip-head's face. The speed and violence of my reaction took my captors by surprise—before either knew what had hit him, I'd managed to kick Turnip-head in the shins as well, and followed up with a shove that flattened Potato-face and sent the Spirit of Nitre sputtering over the flagstones.

Now free to move and enraged to distraction, I overturned my bench with a deafening crash of shattering glass, grabbed the portable furnace from the wreckage, and with a roar of inchoate fury hurled it at the smaller brute as he swung at me. It connected with a gratifying clang, and Turnip-head staggered backwards, swearing and clutching his skull. Meanwhile, Potato-face had crawled towards the reverberatory; as he dragged himself to his feet against the flue, he screamed and flapped his left hand.

"I'm on fire!" he howled. "It burns!"

His palm had already turned yellow and blistered, and was, indeed, smoking. I grabbed a bottle at random from Nugent's bench and advanced on my attackers, the chymical in one hand and the furnace in the other.

"You think that hurts?" I yelled. "Try this!"

I pulled the stopper from the bottle with my teeth, then made as if to douse them with its contents. That did the trick. Like bullies the world over, the smallest taste of their own medicine proved them cowards; they fled as quick as they'd come, but with rather more shrieking and sobbing. I replaced the bottle on Nugent's desk, though not without reading the label first. *Aqua.* Purest water.

My knees gave way beneath me and I crumpled back to the floor, gasping for breath. Spots of red spattered the flagstones before me; I hadn't noticed my nose was bleeding, and I fumbled in my waistcoat for a handkerchief to stem the flow. As I did so, a glimmer of light caught my eye near the upturned bench.

Heedless of the broken glass and puddles of nameless chymicals splashed all around me, I hastened towards the object and snatched it up. The diamond! It had been there all along, somehow rendered invisible by the vegetable spirit. I thanked Providence that neither ruffian had noticed it during the struggle, and congratulated myself on having survived with no more than a nosebleed, though my joy was short-lived. I'd stuck to my story when threatened with torture, and even quarter-wits such as they would surely realize, sooner or later, that I really did not have the diamond. Would they conclude instead that I'd secretly slipped it to Rudge? And once they had nursed their wounds, would they trace him back to his bothy?

My heart pounded with fear for my partner, but I had the presence of mind to hide the diamond before I ran to warn him. The obvious place was another flask of Aromatic Spirit Vegetabilis, a simple enough procedure, even with hands as unsteady as mine—a little Potash in a flask containing Oil of Bitter Almond, a few second's stirring, then I dropped the diamond into the colourless liquid and once again it vanished as if it had never existed. I shook the flask gently, and heard the stone scrape the inner face of the glass. 'Twas a puzzle, but one I had no time to solve.

I placed the flask behind several others at the rear of the least accessible shelf, retrieved the silver pin from where it had fallen, and raced back into the night to alert my friend.

CHAPTER TWENTY-FIVE

I FOUND THE BOTHY COLD AND DARK, and in silence save for Buttons the cat, purring in his sleep on the undisturbed bunk. I ran next to the South Quarter, where I burst into the glasshouse with no other plan than to play the hero again if I must, though I hadn't thought to bring my weapons. Again no Rudge, and no ruffians thank goodness, but instead, seated atop the old man's ebony chest, was a sight for very sore eyes indeed—albeit not someone I might have expected to find in that location.

"Mr Sadler! 'Tis so lovely to meet you again!"

"What are you doing here?" I demanded. "And where is Rudge?"

Serafina D'Bonaventura greeted me with a smile so blithe, we might have been crossing paths upon a Sunday morning stroll in Christ Church Meadow; she seemed oblivious to my frayed appearance.

"I promised I would find you." She had been poring over one of Rudge's watercolours, which she now laid on the nearest packing crate and instead picked up the moneybag that had been sitting on the floor alongside the chest. Our takings from the previous day. I marvelled at Rudge's innocence—leaving valuables in plain sight, with criminals like Potato-face and Turnip-head on the loose.

"I wish I had seen your performance! You are quite the talk of the town. And much richer than before." She let the moneybag fall with a thud then rose from the crate, patting the dust from her sombre petticoats and peering at my face with, for the first time, a look of concern.

"You are in a state," she said. "And you reek of ale. You have been celebrating perhaps too well, I think."

"So I was," I replied. "Until a pair of cutpurses took a liking to your family heirloom. I won the wager, you see." 'Twas almost an afterthought now, with all that had happened.

She clasped a hand to her mouth with a gasp of dismay. "You were assaulted? And I am the cause."

"Do not blame yourself, Miss D'Bonaventura. 'Twas simple misfortune, no more nor less. The ruffians themselves said they saw me with the pin. The fault is theirs only." And perhaps a little mine as well, I thought, for not heeding Rudge's advice to keep the diamond out of sight.

Serafina refused to be consoled. Brushing a tear from her eye, she sobbed: "You are a gentleman to say such a thing, but I fear I truly *am* to blame. When we spoke before, I... Oh, it sounds so bad of me now, but—but I did not tell you the absolute truth."

"Pray do not upset yourself, my dear." I motioned her back to her seat, but she shrugged me off and began to pace back and forth in agitation.

"You must believe I meant you no harm. I only hoped to save you from danger—and look what has happened!" She indicated my nose and torn clothes. "Oh, what a fool am I!"

She covered her face with her hands and began to weep, the tears subsiding only when I held her close, as I'd done in the Golden Cross Yard. Having the chance to do so again 'twas a pleasure, whatever the circumstances.

"There, there," I crooned. "You must tell me everything. Or not, if that would please you better."

"Oh, James." She managed a tearful giggle. "You are so sweet. And so undeserving of the trick I have played on you. But now I will tell you the truth, and perhaps one day all might be well between us again."

"Miss D'Bonaventura—Serafina, we have met only once before, but already I feel I have known you all my life. And that will never change, whatever you tell me now."

"Then let me see to your injuries while I explain."

She sat me down on the chest and tore a strip from my mangled shirt, dipped it in the pail of water Rudge used to soak our sewing thread before use, and set about cleaning the blood from my face. It hurt tremendously, but I bore the pain like a man, so as not to distract my nurse from her tale.

"The diamond," she began, "is not a diamond."

"Not a diamond?" I gagged.

Of all the blows I had suffered that night, this hit me the hardest—Divine retribution, no doubt, for planning to take the pin for myself. Though had I done so, any diamond merchant or jeweller would have laughed me off their premises. My hatred for Ambrose Bean, extinguished by victory, flared once again.

Serafina soaked the cloth a second time. "But neither is it a cheap trinket made from glass or paste. 'Tis a precious crystal, from the land of China."

"China? Like the Little Emperor—?"

I winced as she dabbed at my nose.

"Tis said to be but a fragment of a larger stone, cut by a priest of the old religion for an ancient line of magicians, and passed from father to son until *my* father—Enrico D'Bonaventura was his name—brought it to Europe." She sniffled unhappily, but gathered herself to continue her task. "Now the stone is mine by rights, for I am the only child he had."

"Of course you should have it," said I—indistinctly, for she had begun working the cloth in a soft, circular motion around my lips. "'Tis only fair."

"You are my dearest friend to say so." She treated me to a smile, before her expression hardened. "If only everyone else were the same. 'Tis also said, you see, that this stone is as old as the world itself—'twas in fact the first ray of light, which fell upon a desert and turned the sand into glass. Such a stone, they say, is a prodigy of nature—as am I!—but as a woman I am found wanting, and must be robbed of my own birthright. They will stop at nothing to claim the stone for themselves—even violence if they have to."

"'Twas they who attacked me, you mean?" I cried, appalled at the thought of Serafina in the grubby hands of Potato-face or Turnip-head. "But they were just common thieves, not—not—"

Not what, exactly? Words failed me, as did Serafina as a source of further intelligence.

"Let us hope so," she said, somewhat doubtfully.

"And Bean—is he also one of... *them*?"

"Oh my, no! And if he had known what I have told you, he would never have dared to so much as touch the stone, and none of us would be here now—not you or me, or my enemies, or their servants. If only they had found him and not you."

As she spoke, she turned her attentions to my blood-smeared chin, her face so close to mine I could feel the warmth of her breath on my skin. I knew not what to make of all this preternatural piff-paff, but my fear of another encounter with my attackers—or worser villains unknown—felt very real indeed.

"We must go to the laboratory," I said. "'Tis where I have hidden the dia—the stone. Then we shall put you and it on the first coach to anywhere in the morning, and get you to safety."

Serafina shook her head. "I do not run away. 'Tis not in my blood."

"Your courage does you credit, but this is hardly a time for—"

She sprang upright to silence me, striking a defiant pose with her hands on her hips and her chin tilted upwards. "My father would have me stand firm, no matter the fight. You had a good look at the scoundrels who attacked you, I hope? Once we know the name of their employer, we shall use it to our advantage."

I might have argued further, but the night's events were by then taking their toll.

"'Tis agreed, then," said Serafina. "And meanwhile, best the stone be out of my hands. You have it well hidden?"

I nodded. "No one will see it, I guarantee. But—" After Serafina's brave speech, I knew I would sound chicken-hearted; however, it had to be said. "What shall I do if the scoundrels return?"

"Dear James." She cupped my cheek in her hand, a sorrowful smile upon her rose-pink lips. "I am a scoundrel myself, to have brought you such grief. But now, I promise to help you. As for these men... why would they wish to come back, having nothing to gain? You are safe, I should think. For the present at least."

For the present? 'Twas the future that concerned me. I swallowed and enquired, "What will *you* do?"

"Do not fret for me," she said, and kissed me lightly on the tip of my throbbing nose. "Do all you can to keep yourself safe, and when I have news, I shall find you again."

PART V

CHAPTER
TWENTY-SIX

THE KNOCK ON THE DOOR dragged me out of my bed though not from any dream, good or bad—for I'd slept not the briefest wink since the night of the Emperor's launch. As I removed the stack of chairs, table, and trunks with which I had barricaded the entrance to my dreary lodgings in Blue Boar Lane, I hoped the caller would tire and leave me in peace. But instead the knocking continued, growing more insistent with every rap.

"Open the door, you fool! I know you are in there."

Having made enough space that I could open the door a crack, I squinted into the gloom beyond. "Please do not shout. It might annoy the other residents."

"I will shout as much as I please!"

Cursing colourfully, Rudge elbowed aside the remains of my bulwark and barged straight past me into my bedchamber. I had eaten no better than I had slumbered in recent days and lacked the strength to stop him, or to defend myself when he turned upon me, wagging his finger as if chastizing an errant schoolboy.

"Where in God's good name have you been these past three days? And none of your clever talk, mind."

"Nowhere but here," I mumbled, hanging my head.

"Nowhere is where we are getting at present, 'tis true." Rudge peered at my swollen nose; he seemed about to remark upon it, then changed his mind and instead exclaimed, "After all our hard work, all *your* sacrifices! 'Tis no time to slack! Come back with me now and we'll soon have you up in the air."

"I cannot come back! Not now. Perhaps in a little while. Or maybe longer. 'Tis hard to say for sure—"

"Have you lost your mind? Why, for Heaven's sake?"

"Why?" I wrung my hands in anguish. "'Tis... complicated. Please try to understand."

"I understand there are cosier homes to be had than the floor of the glasshouse." Rudge began to pace about the room—examining the stack of furniture, fingering the threadbare fabric of my bedsheet, blowing dust from the tightly latched shutters. "But this is more a prison than a palace, and if you cannot—or will not—leave, how do you pay for its upkeep?"

I thought this must be a rhetorical question and that Rudge had already guessed where the money had come from. Then I thought on *exactly* where I had found it, and on the old man's candour in matters financial. And as I thought all this, I saw the truth dawn upon his weathered face, and his genuine curiosity turn to rage.

"You are living off our subscriptions!"

"I had no choice!" I cried, my cheeks afire with embarrassment. "I shall pay it back, I swear—"

"Pay it back? Take it all if you wish. 'Tis of no use to me."

"Do not leave!"

I did my best to intervene as he made for the door but in my haste fell afoul of my own defences, first stumbling over a trunk then stubbing my toes on the frame of my washstand. By the time I reached the door, my partner had stormed halfway down the hall and refused to look back when I bellowed his name, regardless of who might hear me.

"Come back, please! I can explain—"

I hoped I had won him around, for he paused at the top of the stairs, but 'twas only to catch his breath before he descended.

"Your deeds speak louder than words," he yelled from below. "Ballooning is beneath you now, *man of consequence*. Pah! I'd sooner be a man of no account, than a false-hearted *thief*."

~ ~ ~

I was a popular fellow that morning, for barely half an hour after Rudge's angry exit, I received a second visitor—this new call announced by a soft, feminine knock that set my heart racing. What a let-down then, when, after hurrying to remove the barricade I had only just reassembled, I found Mary on the threshold.

"You cannot come in," I said, fearful of another tongue-lashing. "I am busy."

"Busy at what?" She peered suspiciously over first my shoulder, then her own. "Do let me in, James. I hate this sort of place. And I hate the thought of you living amongst such people."

Her voice softened as she spoke, and against my better judgment I waved her inside.

"Are you expecting someone?" she asked, with a glance at my movables.

I managed a nervous laugh as I closed the door behind her, shoving the table across it as a temporary measure. "One can never be too careful. Not with all these *people* around."

"But 'tis not one of *them* you are waiting for, I would guess."

"Whatever do you mean?"

"'Twas obvious—that hopeful look on your face." She smirked. "And the disappointment, when you saw me."

"Disappointed to see my favourite sister? How could that ever be so?" I pressed my lips to her forehead to prove it. "Would you like to take a seat?" I indicated the bed—all of the chairs being stacked against the wall ready to go back behind the door—but she scarcely glanced at it.

"I shall stand, thank you."

I remained standing myself, still jittery after my set-to with Rudge. "I am afraid I have no refreshments to offer."

"I am not hungry, thank you."

"So..." I shifted my weight from foot to foot. "What brings you here, dearest Mary?"

She folded her arms upon her over-stuffed bodice—a fearsome sight at the best of times—and replied, with a touch of reproach, "Everyone is worried about you, James."

I smiled wryly. "I very much doubt that *everyone* is worried."

"Well, I am worried, at least. Look at the state of you. Have you been fighting?"

My hand flew instinctively to my nose. "This? Oh, 'tis nothing. A gang of drunkards chanced to relieve me of my purse. Four or five of them, maybe six all told—I can only guess at their number. But I fought them tooth and nail, and they fled empty-handed."

"You never used to attract such attention. Your fame has changed you, and not for the better. Father says..." She trailed off and looked again at my make-shift barrier; I could not deny the concern in her eyes. "Perhaps you should swallow your pride and come home. 'Twould surely be much... safer for you there."

"Did Father say that?" I cried, indignant. "No? Of course he did not! You know as well as I—he will never take me back. I could have died at the hands of those brutes and still he would have renounced me, for shame that a Sadler might find himself so indisposed."

"James!"

"'Tis true! I have ruined his reputation once too often. And perhaps..." I took a deep breath. "Perhaps I do not *want* to return. Perhaps I shall find a new home, with a new life of my own design—and a less demanding name to suit. God willing, I might forget I was ever a *Sadler*."

"What sorry solution is that?" cried Mary. "Running away, denying your family and all they have done for you, all that they stand for? You might wish it were that simple, but it isn't, I warn you. Look to cousin Jediah—eaten by despite from the inside out. Would you become like him? A hollow, dried-up husk of a man, with not one soul in your life but yourself?"

"I would mend your own ways before you criticize others', sister." Her high-handed tone had annoyed me, and I spoke with little thought and not one ounce of consideration. "Else *you* will be the one who dies on her own."

Mary looked dumbfounded. "How—How can you say such a horrible thing?"

"Rather easily, thank you. For 'tis not the least of it."

"I should never have come." She flung up her hands in exasperation. "I offer you my help, and you repay me with insults."

"I didn't ask for your help. And you are right, you should not have come, though doubtless 'twas not for *my* benefit. You have grown tired of running the shop on your own, I expect, and whatever Mary desires, Mary gets."

"Does she? I had not noticed. Though what you say explains a lot." She regarded me through narrowed eyes for a moment, then laughed with a bitter dearth of humour. "You are envious of me. Of *me*! Look at me, James. What are you envious *of*? A worn-out, ground-down drudge? I must serve like a scullion in my own home, yet I'll never see a penny in payment, nor much gratitude, either. You think life has treated *you* unfairly, but what can I possibly have, that would make yours better?"

I stared at the wall above my bed, determined to avoid her wounded glower. "Father has always favoured you over me," I muttered.

"And Mother favoured you," she shot back. "From the moment you were born—no, from before you were born. 'Twas always all about you—her *treasure*, she called you. She never spoke of Lizzie that way, nor of me, of that I am sure. Even Father fell under the spell. Mother's lying-in is my earliest memory. It seemed to last forever, and Father would sit alone at night in the parlour, watching the mantel-clock by the moonlight, as if that might make you come sooner."

I continued to study the wall, wondering idly where the greasy stains had come from, not to mention the furrows gouged in the plaster.

"You can pretend to ignore me. But you *will* listen to what I have to say, because you need to hear it. Mother said she had feared I would burst with excitement, the day she brought home her treasure—so long had I waited to see it! What a let-down, then, when I sneaked a look in the crib, and saw naught but a mewling babe, no more precious than any other." She paused. "Did you know, James—Jediah once had a baby half-brother?"

I finally met her gaze, which had turned venomous. "No, I did not," I murmured.

"He passed away around the time you were born. Perhaps you would prefer that he had lived and *you* died instead?"

These words came as more of a shock than even Potato-face's fist. What manner of monster was I, that my own sister would wish me not just dead, but to have never existed at all?

"Mary—"

"Goodbye, James."

"No! Let me speak—"

Mary dodged behind the table, though before she could reach for the door it swung open again, revealing yet another visitor. The two of them looked askance at each other, tensed like a pair of alley cats.

"Am I too early?" the newcomer called, waving at me over Mary's shoulder with a slender, black-gloved hand. "I didn't expect the domestic would still be here."

I closed my eyes, expecting violence, but heard only an indignant sweeping-up of petticoats, followed by a bang as the door slammed shut.

"That was my sister," I groaned.

"Really? I saw no resemblance." I opened first one eye, then the other. Amidst the dismal surroundings of my bedchamber, Serafina sparkled like a ray of mid-winter sun, melting away my misery for the pure joy of her presence.

"Nice and firm," she observed as she dropped upon the bed, and bounced up and down several times, somewhat distractingly.

I grimaced. "'Tis not a patch on my old room in the attic. Or even the floor of the glasshouse."

"When you spend your whole life on the move, you make the most of a bed when you find one." Her knowing wink left me speechless; 'twas a relief when her attention switched to my barricade, and her tone to consternation.

"Oh, James... 'tis wretched to see where I've brought you! But you'll soon be away, I promise. For I have a plan."

"You do?" Spying a flicker of irritation, I added, "I mean—of course, I expected no less. Please continue."

"'Tis simple but cunning, though I cannot tell you all of it yet." Still seated upon the bed, she glanced quickly left and right, then leaned forwards and lowered her voice. "Fetch the pin—the whole pin, mind, mount and all—and I shall meet you on the towpath beneath Folly Bridge at ten o'clock. I have arranged an escort, and safe transport out of Oxford to a secret destination."

"Meet you at ten o'clock?" I hadn't expected so much so soon and struggled to take it all in. "Ten o'clock when?"

"Tonight, of course."

"*Tonight?*" My innards lurched. "Why so soon?"

"'Twould be sooner, if I could." She indicated the heap of furniture. "You cannot live this way, not even for another day."

"'Tis not so bad," I mumbled. "And not worth you acting in haste on my behalf. Let us wait until you have a solid plan. I can help," I finished, hopefully.

"Dearest James! I would keep you close to me always, if I could." Tears of sympathy welled in her depthless sable eyes. "But we are set upon different paths, and following mine you'd find nothing but grief—which I could not endure."

A little part of me broke with those words. Had I been the hero of some low romance, I would have flung myself at Serafina's feet and begged her not to leave, or demanded that she take me with her at least. But I was not, so instead I said, glumly, "I wish I could follow your path."

"You would not, if you knew what that meant."

"But *my* path has come to an end. I've lost my home, my family, work, friends. My life is over."

She smiled and took my hand in hers.

"Perhaps a new life awaits you, just around the corner."

I shrugged. "Perhaps."

"So you will meet me under Folly Bridge tonight?"

With heavy heart, I nodded. "At ten o'clock, yes."

CHAPTER TWENTY-SEVEN

RATHER THAN HEADING STRAIGHT HOME to salve her wounds, Mary continued past the shop and went to the Physic Garden instead. Here she located Rudge in the South Quarter, planting seedlings in a freshly dug bed.

"I will be with you in a moment," the gardener said, without looking up.

"This is important!"

"As is this. And it cannot be hurried."

Rudge pricked out another tiny shred of greenery, made an equally tiny hole in the soil, and tenderly settled the miniature plant in its home.

"And *I* cannot be delayed—Father will be furious if I stay away much longer. 'Tis about my brother," she added, a little less harshly.

Rudge paused, a seedling pinched between finger and thumb. "Go on."

"I want to know what you have done to him."

"What *I* have done to him?"

Rudge huffed in annoyance, and convinced that would be that, Mary turned for the gate with a curt nod of acknowledgement. But then she heard him sigh behind her, and when she looked back he was on his feet and motioning her to follow him.

"Come along."

As they walked towards the glasshouse, she spared him no sordid detail of her excursion to Blue Boar Lane.

"Having seen him myself just this morning," the gardener said, "I am as mystified by your brother's affliction as you."

"Whatever it is, 'tis not new. He began behaving oddly around the time—the time he started associating with *you*."

Rudge raised an eyebrow. "Is that so? I wonder why?"

"When I was very young," said Mary, not entirely changing the subject, "Father warned us to keep our distance from you. He said you were not to be trusted. Of course, James has forgotten—he never listens or takes advice, unless he can turn it to his own advantage somehow—but my cousin Jediah says you are a trumped-up hired hand and that you always bring out the worst in him—"

"And what do *you* say?"

Mary fell silent, containing her fears 'til they stopped outside the glasshouse. "James is seeing a strange woman, I think," she said, in a rush.

Rudge chuckled as he opened the door. "I thought I'd smelled perfume in here. The saucy young buck!"

Mary followed him inside, and at last felt free to speak. "I worry most that James... that James has put this woman in the family way. 'Twould explain the bruises. He said he was attacked by robbers, but I do not believe him. And 'twould explain why he is afraid to leave his lodgings. This woman's family want retribution. And who could blame them—"

Then her gaze fell upon the Little Emperor, which remained an impressive sight despite being torn, deflated, and hung from a hook in the roof like a scrawny pheasant.

"This is what you raised from Angel Meadow?"

"'Tis our balloon, yes," said Rudge, with obvious pride.

Mary crept closer, as though it might bite if she woke it, and she a pitchfork-less peasant.

"May I touch?"

Rudge nodded.

"I heard about it from Billy." She prodded the lifeless machine with one finger, causing it to sway listlessly. "He said it reached Wolvercote."

"Where it had an unfortunate encounter with the locals. But it can be repaired."

"Then James will fly in it?"

"Not the Emperor. To carry a man into the atmosphere, a much larger globe is needed. I have the makings of it here—" Rudge indicated the crates stacked in rows against the glass walls. "—but no pilot, since your brother hid himself away."

This was, of course, the reason for Mary's presence, but her attention had by now shifted elsewhere. "Is it true," she asked, "that there has been no English aeronaut?"

"That is the case," said Rudge. "There was a Scot by name of Tytler, out of Edinburgh, then Lunardi of Naples in London. But no English aeronaut."

"And James will be that man," Mary marvelled. "To think of it—my very own brother!"

"If he ever climbs out of his rat-hole," Rudge muttered, then nonchalantly added, "Although to my mind, why must the first English aeronaut be a *man*?"

"I should get back," Mary blurted. "I've already been out too long."

"You will visit again?" Rudge accompanied her to the door with a greater spring in his step than he'd shown on their arrival. "I'll boil a pot of water and we shall have tea—if you might supply the biscuits."

Mary frowned at him. "I expect I will not have the time. Father needs my help throughout the day—every day—and we are shorthanded since James... well, you know about that."

To Rudge's regretful farewells, Mary made her second awkward exit of the morning.

CHAPTER TWENTY-EIGHT

OLLY BRIDGE PROVED AN APTLY NAMED MEETING PLACE, though my initial pre-occupation that night was not my poor judgement, but Friar Bacon—the wisest of all Oxford men. He had lived upon the bridge in long-gone times, at that very location composing his *Opus Maius* (and as I crept under cover of darkness from my lodgings, my visit to the pawnbroker's shop seemed decades ago). The old philosopher's tower had been demolished only a few years past, and coming off Fish Street I spied Serafina standing atop its foundations, veiled in black lace, and so still in the moonlight, she might have been one of the Friar's famous automata.

I hissed her name, but she shushed me and waved me down onto the towpath beneath the bridge, where I ventured a swift embrace when she joined me moments later. To my delight, she did not resist; in fact, she drew me closer than was strictly decent, given the late hour and our lack of a chaperone. I relished the rosewater scent that sweetened the dank, dark stench of the River Isis.

263

"Do you have the pin?" she breathed.

"'Tis here." I tapped my coat pocket, a little crest-fallen that she hadn't thought to ask about my own safety first.

"Then give it to me now," she said, darting a glance along the path. "We have no time to waste."

I did as she asked, under protest. "Are you sure? This all seems so rushed. Let me find us somewhere to hide while you think it through—"

"Us?"

She raised her face to regard me, and I fancied I discerned a glimmer of admiration behind the veil. Or amusement, perhaps.

"I cannot abandon you to your fate, Serafina." I clutched her by the shoulders, close to shaking her in my desperation. "We are in this together!"

"Forgive me, James," she whispered, "but there is more to this than you and I."

As if on cue, I heard the thud of many footsteps. Before I could ferry either of us to safety, three hefty brutes sprang forth from around the northward bend in the river, and seeing us upon the towpath charged in our direction. Fearing the worst, I pushed Serafina behind me and raised a hand in warning.

"I advise you to stay away from the lady. Or you will have me to answer to."

The trio froze on the spot. Even at that distance, I could smell the sewer upon them.

"What goes here?" demanded the foremost, who I took to be their leader. Was this, I wondered, the power behind Potato-face and Turnip-head?

"I could ask the same," I retorted. "'Tis a strange time to be out for a stroll."

To my surprise, Serafina broke cover as I spoke, and approached the chief brute with an air of familiarity.

"Did I say you could bring those two dolts?" she barked, with a scowl at his henchmen.

"You never said I couldn't," the chief replied, with a roguish grin.

It occurred to me that this might be the 'escort' Serafina had mentioned, though why she would entrust her safety to such men I could not fathom. These filthy curs were clearly trouble incarnate from head to toe, although that was, I supposed, a useful trait in a bodyguard. Then I ceased worrying about the men's appearance, as I realized what their arrival meant— Serafina would soon pass out of my life, and I could do nothing about it.

"Please reconsider, just for a moment," I begged.

The chief brute sniggered. "Is this your new puppy, 'Fina? 'Tis touching, the way they attend you so faithfully, tongues drooling and tails a-wagging."

"Do you mind?" I snapped. "I am trying to have a conversation with your employer."

This raised a guffaw from the two underlings, while their chief said to Serafina, "Employees are we, eh? Then what of our wages?"

"You have your lives," Serafina replied. "If those be a poor reward, 'tis no fault of mine. Now stop your yattering—you as well." The last three words were directed at me. "Get under the bridge and wait for my signal."

She bundled all four of us into the cramped, clammy space against the stone abutment, then took herself into the open on the towpath, as if expecting someone else to arrive.

"What is happening?" I hissed at my unwanted companions. "Who are you? What are we waiting for?"

The chief brute put a finger to his lips. "Don't go upsetting the Princess. A whey-faced gull like you— why, she could suck you drier than a dead man's bawbles, then spit you out like a pip."

I would have cut him to the quick for that particular vulgarity, except... Princess? *Serafina*? 'Twould explain her beauty and gentle bearing, but what of her life as a travelling player? And her enemies? And the supposedly magical stone—could it be a diamond after all? I knew not what to believe and had little time to decide, for that already perplexing evening then took a turn for the utterly bewildering, with yet another arrival upon the riverbank—and this one no stranger.

"There you are—at last!" he called, his pace quickening when he spotted Serafina on the path ahead of him. "My dear Lettie! Or are you Lottie? I never can tell you apart. What better proof could one need for the goodness of God, that He should design the perfect female in form, face, and performance, and then make two of her."

Bean chuckled lewdly; Serafina remained silent.

"I must say, your invitation surprised me. Neither of you seems the outdoor type—not that I am complaining, of course. But where is your twin?" he continued, with a hint of disappointment as he looked beyond Serafina and saw no one. "The note said you would both be here."

"I am never alone," Serafina murmured.

"You are a busy girl, eh?"

His arm snaked around her waist as he spoke—a sight so revolting, I would have called him out in a flash, had the chief brute not restrained me and been none too gentle about it. I was thus compelled to watch Bean's lecherous gropings, which ceased only when he lifted his victim's veil in search of a kiss. What sweet satisfaction, to hear his reaction! A yelp of fright, a plaintive protest, then a dull, repeated thud of flesh against bone when he inexplicably started smacking his hand against the side of his head, as if trying to dislodge an insect trapped in his ear.

"What subterfuge is this?" he cried.

Serafina giggled girlishly and stood upon her toes as if to kiss him. "Dearest Ambrose," she cooed. Then she shed all pretence of affection, as a snake might discard a superfluous skin, and shot out a hand to deal him a blow to the chest. Bean tottered crazily backwards, his mouth gaping ever-wider in a silent scream of protest until his strength deserted him, and he slumped like a broken doll upon the riverbank, slack-faced and empty-eyed.

Beside me, the chief brute drew a sharp breath.

"Was that poison?" grunted a henchman.

"Worse than that," the chief replied.

Dumbfounded, I said nothing. If Bean's duplicity had indeed driven Serafina to murder—which seemed to be the case, for I'd glimpsed a flicker of moonlight on metal the instant before her hand struck the showman—why do it here and now, and with so many needless witnesses? I hoped she might explain herself when she joined us beneath the bridge, but the defenceless damsel I'd once presumed to defend had disappeared, replaced by an ill-mannered stranger.

"Darkin!" she barked, as though taking a roll call.

The chief brute stepped forwards. "Yes?"

She nodded at me and said, "Grab him."

I struggled, but all three brutes got their arms about me, so tightly I could hardly draw breath let alone wrestle free. Potato-face and Turnip-head had been amateurs by comparison.

"Serafina!" I choked. "What is happening? Please—"

A tiny smile played about her lips, and I saw cupped in her hand the diamond pin, on its needle-sharp point a drop of Bean's blood.

"One little prick," she said, reaching out with her other hand to tug open my shirt, "and a thrilling new life will be yours, just as you wanted."

I am not ashamed to report that I howled when the silver slid into my flesh; I would challenge any man to endure such unnatural horror in stoic fashion. And in fact, I thereby spared myself a calamitous fate (although what did transpire was ghastly enough), for my wailing caught the attention of the night-man, whose cart had just trundled onto the bridge. Fortunately, 'twas only Serafina and the three brutes who were stayed by my scream, while the night-man leapt into action. Through a haze of terror, I glimpsed a face peering over the parapet, then heard him thudding down to the towpath.

"What is this?" he demanded, his coarse voice perhaps the sweetest sound I had ever heard.

Sliding the pin from my shoulder, Serafina stepped back and addressed the chief brute with unconcealed contempt.

"Get rid of him, Darkin."

With a better view of my face, the night-man now bellowed in rage.

"You dare to assault Mr Sadler? Oxford's finest son? Unhand him this instant!"

As he spoke, I realized I knew him, too, though not by name—for 'twas he who had embraced me so tearfully in The Crown on the long-ago night of my triumph.

"What are you waiting for?" Serafina hissed. "Throw him in the river and let us be done here."

"Go quickly and fetch help!" I gasped. "These are dangerous criminals."

Thankful though I was for the man's intervention, 'twould do neither of us any good if he were to end up as incapacitated as I.

But the night-man refused to obey. "Unhand him," he repeated, "or I shall not be blamed for aught that happens." With that he rolled up his sleeves to reveal thewy forearms, and adopted a prizefighter's stance.

Throughout all this, the three brutes remained silent. Although they still had hold of me, I sensed they were weighing up the situation, perhaps wavering in their support for Serafina.

"I would listen to him, if I were you," I cried. "For he is more beast than man when provoked."

The brutes looked between themselves.

"Come on, Darkin!" Serafina mocked. "Can you not count? I see three of you and but one of him."

The night-man, in reply, delivered a short, sharp jab to the ear of the henchman on my right, who immediately proved more mouse than man.

"Yow—he *hit* me!" he squealed, letting go of me and clutching his head. I seized the chance. Recalling how well it had gone in the *Officina*, I flung back my now free right elbow, hoping to connect with some part of the chief brute, who stood behind me. I missed, and wrenched my injured shoulder, but 'twas diverting enough—with a roar, the night-man fell upon the chief and his remaining henchman, fists flying. Both dropped back, leaving me suddenly unsupported. I realized my legs had lost their strength, as well as all other sensation—and not just my legs. My whole body felt weak and wobbly.

From a very great distance—as if beholding the Earth from the roof of Old Crab's Tower—I watched my body crumple onto the cold, damp soil, as the chief brute—Darkin—raised his hands in surrender.

"This isn't worth the bother, boys. Come on, we're going home."

"We had a deal!" Serafina shrieked.

"I thought you'd have learned by now," Darkin said, with a grin. "Never make a deal you can't walk away from."

And then he made an almost-fatal mistake, for instead of departing as smartly as possible, he dawdled to blow her a kiss.

"You bastard!" Serafina screeched again, and flew at him like a vengeful raven.

Still immobilized on the ground, my hearing and vision were next to abandon me, plunging me into a devilish realm where a gale howled without end, and a multitude of forms with the likeness of birds chittered and chattered. I barely heard Darkin's scream, and watched through a falling curtain as he clawed at the stone jammed tight in his reddening shirt. Serafina hastened to rip the pin out, and like a punctured balloon, Darkin's body dropped to the Earth, lying head-to-toe with my own. I saw Serafina's rosebud lips part wide in a vengeful smile, before the throb of giant wing beats overtook me, engulfing all that was left of my being, until only the flapping remained.

CHAPTER TWENTY-NINE

OPENING HIS EYES FOR WHAT FELT like the first time in weeks, Ambrose Bean found himself lying upon his back, spreadeagled and facing a ceiling. The ceiling appeared familiar, though on the last occasion he saw it, he'd been laid low by a wench from Marsh Town, not a hammering pain in his head. He wondered how much he had drunk the previous night. And the name of the girl—Lettie, was it not? She of the twin sister who was more than double the fun...

Then at last, he remembered. The invitation to meet at Folly Bridge—no need to guess who sent *that*—Serafina, her face veiled... the silver pin invading his body...

He gasped as if the shaft still dwelt within him, and tried to sit up. 'Twas then he saw he'd been stripped to his breeches, and bound to his own bed by his ankles and wrists. His stockinged feet wiggled helplessly at the other end of the mattress, and beyond them stood Serafina D'Bonaventura. She had the Thanatoscope on the table, and hummed softly to herself as she probed its inner workings.

"Serafina," he croaked, "my dearest. 'Tis good to see you again. I have missed you terribly."

"Really?" She spared him not even a glance. "I am surprised, knowing how keen you have been to avoid me."

"Avoid you? Whatever gave you that idea, my sweet?"

With a mocking laugh, she said, "Did you seriously think you'd escape me by passing the Soul-Eater onto another?"

"But you have it back," Bean protested. "So let's put all that business behind us, why don't we?"

Serafina laughed again and pulled the stone from her bosom, holding it up to the lamp to catch the light on its roughened facets.

"I am surprised—but eternally grateful—you let me out of there," Bean said. "So you care for me, after all. Even just a little?"

Serafina looked up with a wicked smile. "Do not flatter yourself. I never intended to keep you. Only to... exchange you."

"How very imaginative. And who was to be this fortunate man? An exceptional fellow, I trust."

"'Twas the highwayman Isaac Darkin. I engineered his escape from gaol by mesmerizing the keeper."

Bean shuddered at the thought, but maintained his jocular manner. "Not only imaginative, but considerate as well. I would have spent the rest of my days—presumably small in number—evading the law, then died horribly upon the gallows."

"Most certainly." Serafina closed and latched the Thanatoscope's cover then came to stand beside the bed, sadly out of reach of his bound hands. "But on second thoughts, I decided you did not deserve such a swift and famous end, and besides, I had come upon a much better alternative."

"Ahh... someone rich and successful but ancient, no doubt. The good life in abundance, but no strength or time to enjoy it. That would suit your sense of humour."

As he spoke, Bean tried to sneak his right hand free from the cord that secured it to the bedstead; he had almost succeeded, when Serafina's reply all but stopped his heart with the horror.

"'Twas your wagering friend James Sadler."

"My God, Serafina, that is beyond cruel."

She giggled. "A long life, I should expect, and not uncomfortable. But my, how so deathly dull."

"I would have withered away to naught," Bean groaned.

"And I would have loved to watch you." She took his right wrist and retightened the cord. "Not so quickly, dear Ambrose. I have not finished with you yet." She dragged a long, sharp fingernail from his collar bone down to his waist.

"Now, now, dearest," he said. "We mustn't do anything hasty, eh?"

"Oh, I do not think haste will be the problem. Just *deciding* what to do with you will take me a while, I expect. And then comes the doing it."

Beads of sweat pricked Bean's forehead. "'Twill be gratifying, I'm sure, to dispatch me out of revenge. But it can only take so long, and who will entertain you when I'm gone? You could have much more fun with me, than without."

"Could I now?" Serafina breathed, her teeth uncomfortably close to his neck.

"Let us work together again. My fortunes are on the rise here in Oxford. Why, I am almost part of society. And what a wealthy and influential society! 'Tis where the highest in the land send their sons to earn their spurs."

He could tell by the glint in her eye that he had caught Serafina's interest.

"You always wanted to be a princess. I could help you achieve that dream."

Her thoughts seemed to drift at those words; back to her childhood, Bean supposed. He let his taut muscles relax, to enjoy the rhythmic motions of her fingertips on his skin. Then the dandling stopped and her nails dug deep, wringing a gasp of pain, before she leaned close and breathed in his ear.

"Do that and I may consider setting you free. But tell me the truth, mind. I shall know if you are lying."

~ ~ ~

"Father! Come quickly!"

As usual, he did not. 'Twas an age before Mary heard a reluctant creak from the parlour door and even then he failed to commit to further exertions, hovering instead upon the lower landing, peering up at her with suspicion.

"I think he has taken a turn for the better," she added, hoping to stir him.

"'Twould be a blessing if true," Father huffed. "For the sooner he recovers, the sooner he can crawl back to his hovel, and we can return to normal."

Normal? Mary scarcely recalled what that meant— nor the last time she slept or enjoyed a square meal.

Her nights and days had blurred into one, and now, in the spare time she did not have, she must serve as her brother's nursemaid as well.

"You could have left him with the night-man, lying senseless amongst the filth in that cart," she snapped. "Why did you take him in? Why pay for a doctor?"

And waste that payment, she thought, though she did not remind him. The physician had found no cause for James's ailment nor even a name for it, and had asked more questions than he answered.

"I was sorely tempted," Father said. "However, I could not be seen to turn away a family member in need, still less by the night-man."

Mary wondered how he accorded this view, with his flat refusal to summon Burleigh for help. "If that is what you thought—" she began.

"Thinking and doing are not the same, my girl. And neither are seeing and wishing to see." Father glanced into the attic but did not enter, as if he feared his son's affliction might be catching. "He is quite unchanged since the last time I saw him. Now leave the wastrel to himself—" He raised a hand to silence her protest. "I have a business to run, and the books will not keep themselves."

Mary sighed and started to follow him out of the room. She turned around on the threshold to take a last look at her lifeless brother, and had an unwelcome memory of her mother, lying cold and grey in her deathbed. She shuddered, imagining she had heard Mother whisper, then realized 'twas James who had spoken.

He had done this many times since his return; at first, Mary had tried to make sense of his words, hoping they might reveal his attackers' names. And names he provided, though they meant no more to her than any other part of his ramblings, which gave no hint of what had befallen him. Indeed, they gave no hint of anything, being merely nonsensical babbles. But whereas those previous episodes were accompanied by sweating and groaning, and thrashing so energetic she sometimes needed Father's help to hold him down, today James's limbs remained still and his breathing steady.

"I *said* he was better!" She rushed back to his bedside just as, with a cough and a rustle of sheets, he sat bolt upright and stared straight at her. "James!" she cried, overjoyed.

That joy was quickly extinguished when he crumpled back to the bed.

"What has happened?" he gasped in horror. "Where am I? How did I get here? And who the devil are you?"

~ ~ ~

My first mistake was to open my eyes. The pain in my head was daunting enough, but what disconcerted me most was the realization that, although I was tucked in a warm and comfortable bed, said bed was in neither my lodgings nor my room above the shop. Startled, I sat up, and when the sickness had subsided, took stock of my surroundings.

Although 'twas not *my* room, this was clearly *someone's* garret. From the dressing-table, mirror, and pottery trinkets, I guessed that a woman dwelled here, while the muffled, merry babble below suggested a hostelry of some sort. Hung before the window, a sheer orange drapery bestowed upon the room a cosy air that cheered me a little, and I thought I might risk a look outside and determine where I might be. I slid my feet from beneath the blankets and placed them on the thick woollen rug by the bed—another homely touch that might have further eased my anxiety, had I not noticed then that my usual clothing was gone. Indeed, I wore no clothing at all, save a knee-length white cotton nightshirt as unfamiliar to me as everything else in that place.

Embarrassed at the thought of someone other than my mother or sister undressing me, I scanned the room for my missing clothes. They were nowhere to be seen, though I did spot a coat flung over a side-chair, and this I grabbed as I made for the door. I did not get there.

As I donned the shabby garment (which fit surprisingly well, given its cut), I realized I was not alone in the chamber; a long-legged, sallow-faced man was lurking behind the dressing-table, reaching into his own coat as I delved into mine—for a weapon, I feared. I scrambled back towards the bed, casting around for something with which to defend myself; this unnerved the stranger, who backed away himself.

Only when I tripped on the rug and the stranger followed me down, did I realize that he was in, not the room—but the mirror. Bewildered, I watched him tiptoe back towards me, as I approached him. Of all the bizarre events that had plagued me lately, surely the most absurd was finding a man confined in a looking-glass.

Except mirrors merely reflect what stands before them by means of incident waves of light, as Mr Huygens had shown a full century past. They did not entrap people. Chiding myself for entertaining such nonsense, I placed my fingertips on the smooth, cold surface. And the man in the glass did the same.

'Twas my reflection. But not my face.

I recoiled with a terrified yelp, just as a roar of laughter burst into the room, followed by a fresh-complexioned young woman clad in the simple garb of a country girl. She carried a basin of water, which she almost dropped in fright at the sight of me.

"Who—who—?" I rasped.

"Who am I?" The woman smiled sympathetically at my confusion. "I'm just your Kat, my dear. And pleased as punch I am, to see you on your feet again."

"Not who are *you*," I gibbered. "Who am *I? Who am I?*"

I raked my fingernails down the stranger's cheeks, as though the face that goggled back at me were merely a mask I might strip away.

"You are Isaac Darkin, of course." The woman put down the basin, but before she could steer me towards the bed I grasped her forearms and spun her around to face me. "What has happened to me?" I cried.

Her expression remained both calm and kindly.

"You've been raving like this for a night and a day—since the boys brought you back from Oxford." She tugged one arm free, and in the mirror I saw her stroke the strange dark hair. "Poor dear," she murmured. "Look what prison has done to you. But I'll get you better, I promise."

The only graspable part of all this, was the news that I was no longer located in Oxford. But if not there, where? And why? I made for the door, but felt suddenly weak as a babe; a hand against my chest was enough to halt me. I shrank from the woman's touch.

"They've been asking for you," she said, with a frown. "But time enough for that when you're well. You don't want them seeing you like this, do you? Come now, let's rest."

Powerless to resist, a minute later I was stripped of the coat and back in the bed, the blankets tucked beneath my chin. To my horror, the woman slipped in beside me, pausing only to remove her shoes, and began stroking my hair again and making a soft, cooing sound that I presumed was intended to soothe me.

I lay unmoving on my back, my body as taut as a bowstring as my mind replayed the events that had brought me there. Folly Bridge, the Full Moon, Serafina. Ambrose Bean sprawled lifeless in the dirt. And the image of a face. The face of a stranger, though now I knew his full name. Dirty black locks, green eyes, large ears but a strong chin; features more humorous than handsome, but haunted, too—testament no doubt, to his recent incarceration and forthcoming death.

As the woman called Kat whispered tender words in my ear, I raged against Serafina, cursing her duplicity, cursing the diamond pin. I knew not how she had done it, but she had stolen the most precious thing I possessed—my life. I was no longer James Sadler, son of a pastry-cook.

I was Isaac Darkin, highwayman.

PART VI

CHAPTER THIRTY

ISAAC DARKIN WAS ALSO DISMAYED BY EVENTS. But having the sturdy mental constitution of a man who dwelt perpetually in the hinterland of peril, he was already planning his escape. He spent a single night recouping his strength (and overhearing his hosts disagree on their brother and son's best interests, and whether he might be moved to Hook Norton and "boarded out" humanely at a discreet establishment there). Then at dawn, he arose and donned the clothes he found about him. They sat strangely upon his new form, but were better than the rags in which he had fled from Oxford Gaol.

He chuckled to himself, thinking he might have changed into smarter attire, had he known the gaol-keeper planned to unlock his shackles then fall asleep at his post. But even as he smiled, his mood changed. For although Serafina D'Bonaventura had broken him out, she had also traded his body for that of a whey-faced twiddlepoop—and gratitude for the one would not spare her his wrath for the other. He would find her and force her to return him to his person; only then could he take back his life and put prison behind him.

But Darkin, being by nature a late-riser and un-accustomed to the habits of working folk, had not allowed for Mary, or her industrious nature. For she had arisen while Darkin still snored, and lit the fire and dusted the parlour and scrubbed the kitchen before he was dressed, and was only then taking a guilty break before she set out to sweep the shop floor.

Unaware of Darkin's presence, she rested her broom against the counter and reached into the 'seconds-jar', where misshapen sweetmeats were placed to be sold at a hefty discount. At random she pulled out a currant pie and devoured it with unseemly haste, plucking out the fruits with her fingers and stuffing them 'twixt her teeth with scarcely any time for chewing. And this was clearly not the first she had thus consumed, for the counter was littered with crumbs.

When Darkin cleared his throat, she whirled around to face him, her cheeks blazing red amidst a fountain of buttery fragments as the pie case shattered in her hand.

"James! What do you think you are doing, scaring me like that?" She grabbed a cloth to dispose of the crumbs. "What a mess!" she cried, as she sneaked a sidelong glance at Darkin, her eyes darting about like a startled rabbit's. "I was peckish, that is all. I've been up for hours, and 'tis hours more 'til breakfast."

Darkin shrugged, unperturbed, and joined her at the counter. Seeing him wearing his coat and hat, she swiftly changed the subject.

"And where are *you* going, at this time of day?"

"I am looking for a woman."

Mary gagged on an unswallowed morsel of pastry. "I beg your pardon?"

"She goes by the name of Serafina D'Bonaventura. Small of stature and hard of temperament, however soft she may act. Black hair, black eyes, rotten heart."

"I *knew* this was her fault." Mary grimaced. "What is it between you and that blowen? Tell me the truth now James, for I will not accept any lies."

Darkin smiled at the woman's bravado. She reminded him of Kat, if a milder, more innocent version.

"There is nothing between us," he said, firmly. "Except that she has stolen something from me and I want it back."

"What do *you* have that's worth stealing?" Mary sighed and shook her head. "Father was right to warn us off Wyndham Rudge."

Perhaps, Darkin thought, the Sadlers might not be as boring as they appeared on first acquaintance. "Go on, please," he prompted, intrigued.

"About Rudge?"

He tapped his temple. "I still see only flashes of the past, and they seldom make sense. Who is this Rudge and why should I avoid him?"

"I'm not sure I should say."

"In my experience," Darkin persisted, "there are only two reasons a man prevents his children befriending whomever they wish—fear, or guilt. Or both."

'Twas the first time he had heard Mary laugh.

"Of course, that is three reasons," he added.

"Oh, do forgive me." She patted his arm, still chuckling. "I didn't mean to make fun of you, 'Twas just the thought of *you* having *experience*."

Darkin feigned indignation. "I have rather more experience than you realize, young lady. I think 'tis you who wants for knowledge on how the wider world works."

On impulse, he reached across the counter to brush a pastry crumb from her cheek. She raised her own hand to push his away, and for a simple act this occasioned much embarrassment. Blushing again, she turned aside and grabbed the broom.

"Once, during my delirium—" Darkin swiftly returned to business "—I heard you and... our father discussing this man Wyndham Rudge, and some manner of scheme we had."

"'Tis what turned your mind." Mary glared at something unseen as she swept. "The aerostat."

"An aerostat? A *flying* machine?"

"Father ordered me not to mention it." She glanced at the staircase, as though he, too, might be watching her. "He hopes that by forgetting about it, you will be cured."

"Will I?" Darkin mused. "Tell me, Mary, is this Rudge also an early riser?"

"I should expect so," she replied, with an offhand wave. "Don't men of the soil always wake with the dawn?"

"Then take me to him."

Her guilt-reddened face turned suddenly pale. "Now?"

Darkin grinned. "'Tis time I met my aerostat again."

~ ~ ~

During their brisk walk down the High, Mary related the facts of the story as she knew them, with regret that she could not explain her brother's predicament.

"Do not scold yourself, dear Mary—'tis others who bear the blame. And who knows, perhaps seeing Rudge and the aerostat will bring me back to myself."

His tone was good-natured—kindly, even—but this only added to her unease. James wheedled and whined; he mocked and misled her. He was never *kind* to her, nor ever in any other manner attempted to lighten her load. Mary began to wonder whether she wanted the old James back.

They found Rudge perched on a stool outside his bothy, a sketchpad on his lap and a pencil in his hand. He froze when he saw his visitors approach, the point of his pencil hovering over the skeletal outline of a yew tree.

"Why have you brought him here?" he demanded of Mary, with such ill will she took a step backwards.

"I—I must beg your help," she stammered. "James has been injured again—"

"No more than he deserves," Rudge muttered.

"—and worse this time. He has lost his memory, and he—*we* believe seeing you and the aerostat might restore it."

As she stumbled over this speech, Rudge peered at her brother, as if weighing the truth of her words. "'Twould be better, perhaps, if you stayed ignorant of yourself," he declared. "A clean slate you can write anew, with good deeds rather than ill."

"What did I do to upset you, old man?" James advanced upon the gardener boldly, ignoring Mary's pleas not to antagonize Rudge, to leave the talking to her.

Rudge regarded his former pupil with distaste. "'Tis more a case of what you did not do," he growled. "You flit from here to there like a butterfly, you never finish what you start, you care only for yourself and what you can gain from other people. I wish I had never offered my help, for it has been sorely exploited and then cast aside when no longer needed."

Mary held her breath, fearing her brother's reaction to these home truths, but James merely nodded as though he accepted each word.

"If I have upset you," he said, "I apologize. Perhaps we can draw a line under all that has gone before and make a new start."

He extended his right hand, but Rudge did not take it.

"Not all slates are easily wiped," said the gardener.

Mary took her brother's arm. "Come, we have outstayed our welcome. Father will soon awaken and wonder where we have gone."

James, however, pulled away. "Not so hasty, my girl. We have not yet done what we came for. I would dearly love to see my—*your* aerostat, Mr Rudge, having heard so much about it. Will you lead the way?"

A reluctant grin brightened Rudge's face. "*Mr* Rudge. I like the sound of that." He considered a moment, then crooked a gnarly finger. "Very well—follow me."

Mary trailed behind the two men, no less unsettled than before. Had her actions improved or worsened the situation? When they reached the glasshouse, she saw little had changed since her previous visit. In its lack of substance, the balloon rivalled the tree in Rudge's sketch, but James's excitement more than made up for that, as he circled the half-made globe.

"'Tis magnificent," he breathed. "How does it fly?"

"By means of inflammable air," Rudge replied, "which being lighter than normal air rises through the atmosphere until it finds its level. The inflammable air we generate by the action of Spirit of Vitriol upon iron filings." He scratched his head. "But you should be the one explaining this."

"Natural philosophy has always been a mystery to me."

"But you are a man of science!" Mary cried. "You have ever said so. Natural philosophy is your fascination."

Her brother looked suddenly furtive, more like the old James. Then he laughed and said, "I meant, of course, 'tis a mystery to me now. Perhaps my knowledge will return with my memory."

"You take it well," Mary said. "I should have thought losing your knowledge would be your worst fear."

"Fear is for children. I thumb my nose at it—" And this he did, by way of demonstration. "—for 'tis a waste of time and energy, and frustrates doing for the sake of thinking."

Rudge concurred. "A sound philosophy. It seems those bumps to your head might have knocked some sense into you."

He clapped James on the back and they joshed like long-lost comrades, 'til James demanded to know how one might steer the aerostat, and Rudge said to Mary, "How is it he never showed such fire before?"

Mary smiled tightly, and while her companions discussed aerial navigation, wandered over to the ebony chest, which had been pushed against the wall to make space for the aerostat and stood laden with Rudge's watercolours. She flicked through them absently, witness to the gardener's long life and his versatility as an artist. Exotic landscapes were the least of them, being outnumbered by portraits of her uncle and his family, and those surpassed again by works that could be described as still life, though their subjects were never mundane—from weapons of war to gemstones and jewellery, masks, musical instruments, and more.

Gazing upon the faces of Jediah as small child and a woman she remembered as his stepmother, Mary recalled with dismay her unkind words to James. She should apologize, she told herself, for she had not meant what she said. But if James had forgotten his natural philosophy—his greatest passion—surely he would not remember one particular clash with his sister, especially when they had had so many. Perhaps, she decided, losing one's memory might not be such a terrible thing.

With a start, she realized James had once again crept up behind her.

"These are excellent," he declared, inspecting the paintings over her shoulder. "Did you make them, Mr Rudge?"

The gardener mumbled a self-effacing reply.

"'Tis a pity he only draws plants these days," Mary said.

Rudge shrugged. "These days I prefer plants to people."

"Perhaps we can change that, eh?" James said to Mary, with a wink that compounded her unrest.

"Change is for young men," Rudge retorted, reclaiming his paintings and stowing them back in the chest.

CHAPTER THIRTY-ONE

I WAS CONFINED TO MY NEW ATTIC ROOM for the next several days. My nurse, Kat, insisted I must rest and regain my strength, though I suspected she also wished to keep me from something—or someone—on the other side of the door. I did not argue; Kat was a tough woman, and anything that frightened her was worth taking seriously.

I used the time to make my acquaintance with the unfamiliar body in which I now found myself. Isaac Darkin was older than I, but fitter and stronger, his agile frame packed with lean muscle—and pocked with many scars, the origins of which I could only guess at. According to Kat I had lost much weight while imprisoned, but it took only a few hearty meals to restore my vitality. I soon began to enjoy making use of my new capabilities, and even yearned to leave the room—a snug and charming prison, but a prison none-theless—and test them under more exacting conditions.

With time on my hands, my thoughts also drifted to my own body, and what had befallen it after our parting at Folly Bridge. If Serafina's devilish device had done what I feared, and my present situation were not the product of some feverish dream, did Darkin's soul now occupy *my* mortal form? The prospect troubled me greatly. Had the highwayman assumed my identity, as I had reluctantly assumed his? Had anyone noticed the difference? My sole certainty was that I had to return to Oxford as soon as possible and persuade Serafina to reverse her procedure (I dared not call it "sorcery", for fear of where that admission might lead).

To that aim, on the third morning after my awakening, I donned the clothes of Isaac Darkin—which were hardly to my taste, being of a flamboyant style unflattering to a man of moderation such as myself—and set about my escape. Although the inn was quiet at this early hour, I dared not leave by the normal route for the risk of encountering Kat and being shown back to bed (or worse, encountering that which Kat feared I should meet). Also, having never once ventured beyond the threshold of my room let alone downstairs, I might delay myself while searching for the exit.

So instead, I considered the window. The roof was steep and in poor repair, but I believed I could find a safe way down, and would then head east back to Oxford as fast as my feet would take me in their clumsy-feeling shoes. I had learned that the inn— The Jolly Bull—lay on the Oxford-to-London road near Stokenchurch, a considerable distance on foot, but exceptional circumstances demanded exceptional endeavours.

The previous evening, Kat had mentioned a trip into town the following day, to shop at the weekly market and for other such female diversions—all the better for me, I had thought. But not for long. I had just got the casement open and climbed upon a stool to squeeze my over-large form through the frame, when the door was opened (as always, without a knock) and Kat reappeared not five minutes after she'd left.

"Well, that was a stroke of good luck," she announced. "See what I found—Isaac! What are you doing?"

I almost fell off the stool, overcome with surprise and guilt—the latter inexplicably, for I was a free man, and had the right to depart if I wished.

"Just taking the air. It gets stuffy, shut up in here all day long."

"You are leaving, aren't you?" Kat dropped her basket onto the table—I glimpsed a loaf of black bread, potted beef, and golden, russet-skinned apples. Then she dropped herself onto the bed, and placed her elbows on her knees and her face in her hands.

"I thought you cared for me," she sobbed. "I thought you had changed."

I inched towards her. "I—I *have* changed."

"Rubbish!"

I'd been right to be cautious, for as she spoke she snatched an apple from the basket and hurled it at my head with such force, 'twould have knocked me cold had it connected. I was saved by my own right hand, which to my surprise—and Kat's frustration—shot forward as if of its own accord and plucked the fruit from the air with aplomb.

"See!" Kat wailed. "You are the same old Isaac Darkin—king of the highway, subject to none. Go then, go on!" She gestured tearfully at the open window. "Do what you wish. Just don't expect I will always be here waiting for you. For some day I will not."

"Kat." I laid a hand on her trembling shoulder. "Katherine."

She looked up, sniffling.

"I'm not who you think I am," I said, gently. "I don't belong here."

"You have found another woman, then."

I shook my head, attempting a smile. "There is no other woman, I swear."

These words reignited her anger. "Serafina D'Bonaventura!" She spat the name like poison. "Of course, I should've guessed when I heard the boys gossiping... So that stuck-up dishclout is back? The shameless baggage!"

Though shocked to discover Kat knew the woman, I hid my surprise in case she misread it as a guilty secret.

"She means less than nothing to me," I vowed. "But she has done me a great wrong and I must return to Oxford to find her and put it right."

Kat took a deep breath, scrubbed the tears from her face, and said, "Then take me with you."

"What?"

"You said there is no one else. Then prove it. Let me come with you and see this great wrong righted."

Before I could respond, she was on her feet and flinging her arms about me, pulling me close to her soft, warm bosom.

"And then we can start again. Just us two, together. A new town, a new life."

"I do not think—"

Then the door burst open again, and my gaze fell upon the first persons other than Kat I had seen since the night on the towpath. Four mean-looking men, full of beer and bad intentions. I knew immediately 'twas they that Kat had sought to spare me from. I also knew why, for two of them I recognized as Darkin's henchmen.

All four laughed lewdly at the sight of us.

"So sorry to interrupt," sniggered one. "We didn't know you were busy."

Kat rounded on them. "Who invited you in here? He is not yet recovered, I tell you!"

Another one snorted: "If he's fit enough for play, he's fit enough for work. Is that not so, Isaac?"

He gave me a broad grin, then all four surrounded me to slap me on the back and applaud my escape from justice. Without further protest Kat left them to it, head bowed and gaze averted. I wanted to shout, *Come back! Send these ruffians away! I shall take you to Oxford, I swear!* But 'twas too late; my nurse had abandoned me.

"'Tis long-past time we got back to business," said a third man.

At last I found my own voice. "Now? What's the hurry?"

The fourth guffawed. "Coves have gone soft while you loafed at the magistrate's pleasure. They think they are safe—let's teach 'em otherwise, eh? You'll be needing this again," he added, producing an unfamiliar object from his coat. "I kept it in good order for you."

I shrank within my able new body. The object was a pistol.

"And this, too," said the first.

From his hand dangled a silken black mask.

CHAPTER THIRTY-TWO

"**I** AM HERE TO PRESENT MY PURSE," announced Ambrose Bean, with an elegant bow. "My opponent, I note, is not."

The thud of a moneybag hitting the table caused Edwin Osborne to jump in his seat, his attention having been hitherto focussed on Bean's uninvited companion. Her arrival had elicited much scandalized grumbling amongst the regulars, though no attempt had been made to remove her. Even in her concealing black cloak (secured about her neck with the diamond pin), she provided a comely diversion from more serious issues.

"Indeed, that is the case." Osborne cleared his throat. "Sadler has failed to abide by the terms of the wager—are we agreed?" To almost a man, the Philosophers raised their hands in accord. "'Tis decided, then. If there be no objections, I shall declare Mr Ambrose Bean the winner by default."

"Gentlemen—" Bean began the speech he'd prepared, but his moment was interrupted by a voice from the end of the table.

"I object," said William Tench, with a timorous wave of his mortarboard. His cheeks reddened as all eyes turned to him. "James may not be here in person, but no one can deny that his efforts exceeded Mr Bean's. People still discuss James's aerostat from Banbury to the Hendreds, whereas Mr Bean's show earned scarcely an inch in *Jackson's Oxford Journal*. And I heard that Mr Bean had surrendered the diamond pin—" He darted a suspicious glance at Serafina's cloak. "—thereby admitting his defeat. I move that we defer declaring a winner until both parties are present."

"Your objection is noted, Mr Tench. However, the terms of the wager were shaken upon. If one party won't trouble himself to turn up and argue his own case, that is his concern, not ours." Osborne stood and rapped on the tabletop with his coffee-spoon. "I hereby proclaim James Sadler, pastry-boy of High Street, Oxford, banished from all future meetings of this Philosophical Club, forever and in perpetuity."

A round of applause ensued.

"Gentlemen," said Bean, "thank you all for your support. I trust you found the contest entertaining."

Osborne returned to his armchair. "'Twas fascinating, indeed," he said, "to witness the clash of two parties so evenly matched, who nevertheless believed themselves as different as night from day."

Bean knew not what to make of this, but took it as a compliment.

"At our previous meeting," he continued, "I hinted my sojourn in Oxford would be but a brief one. Now, however, I'm minded to linger a while—"

Feeling fingertips at his elbow, he looked over his shoulder. Behind him, Serafina tipped her chin towards the exit. He shook his head, annoyed.

"Forgive me. As I was saying—I feared on my arrival that your *démodé* little town would prove too provincial for a man of my citified tastes. Whereas, in actuality, 'tis in every way quite charming. So much so, in fact, that I have resolved to extend my stay until further notice. I shall, of course, attend many future meetings." He waited—in vain—for a happy reaction to this news, then pressed on: "I may even treat you to a demonstration of my Thanatoscope. Few men in the world know its true workings."

"That will not be necessary," said Osborne.

"But the Thanatoscope is a marvel of man's invention and ingenuity! Is that not the very *raison d'être*, for Philosophers such as we?"

"Perhaps," Osborne conceded. "If there *were* a *we*."

Again Bean felt a tug at his arm; again, he shrugged it off.

"What do you mean?" he asked, a sickly sensation seizing his gut.

"'Tis not obvious? If the son of a pastry-cook is unfit for this company, how shall we accommodate the likes of a vagabond player?"

As Bean began to tremble, he wished he, too, had an armchair to sit in, or even a space on the bench.

"Mr Somerfield."

At Osborne's invitation, a rotund man in a tiny chequered waistcoat rose from the bench and pointed a chubby digit at Bean.

"I was certain at our last meeting that I recognized this interloper—"

"You *invited* me here," Bean appealed to Osborne. "You *told* me play your relative."

"—but where I had seen him before, I could not recall. Then it came to me, this Thursday past. 'Twas two summers ago, on my return from a visit to York, when I lodged the night at an inn south of Newark. Though weary from my journey, I was intrigued by the promise of unusual entertainment that evening and so postponed my bedtime to view the same. This—" He waved the finger again. "—was the show. And his harlot, as well!"

To Bean's surprise, Serafina winked at the man.

"I shall never forget..." Somerfield continued, clearly shaken. "...the indecent nature of her costume... God help me, I have tried."

Gasps of horror rebounded around the table. "Disgraceful!" cried one, "Disgusting!" another.

"With no disrespect to Mr Somerfield," said Osborne, "one would hardly expect to encounter the Comte de Buffon at such an establishment. Nor the Marquis de Condorcet. Nor Mesdames Roland and Geoffrin, unless they were sorely down on their luck. Yet I do not know where else Bean might have met them, for despite his claims, I doubt he has ever been to Paris. Is that not so, Bean? Those tales of the high life in Versailles are as fanciful as your gentle birth."

With the sole exception of William Tench, the Philosophers burst into laughter; then laughed some more, and more again, and continued to crow until the proprietress herself came to ask if they might not consider the other patrons. Meanwhile, Bean had lost his voice, his will to move, and his wits, unprotesting when Serafina thrust her arm through his and dragged him out of the room. As he staggered to keep pace, he heard Osborne addressing his cronies: "How sweet that Batavian smells, free from malodorous rabble at last!"

Back on the High, Bean raged with shame and gross self-pity. Ignominious though it might be, for a grown man to weep in public, he was quite prepared to do so until Serafina delivered a sharp slap to his face, shocking him back to his senses.

"The Philosophers of Oxford may be intelligent." She raised her hand to his cheek again, but with a reassuring pat instead of a blow. "They are not, however, as clever as they think..."

CHAPTER THIRTY-THREE

'TWAS SOON OBVIOUS TO DARKIN that his definition of bedtime—and of morning—was at odds with that of his hosts and, he assumed, the man whose body he occupied. By habit the highwayman slept and rose at his leisure, but life with the Sadlers meant rude awakenings daily due to the hustle and bustle of commerce. Were it not for his affliction, he was certain he'd have been forced to keep the same godforsaken hours. All the more reason to escape as soon as possible, he thought, as he dressed yet again in the drab garb of the pastry-boy and descended into the shop.

He was greeted by discord—although in *this* house, that seemed to be always the case.

"If I must do the delivery round *and* serve tea to a dozen confectioners, how shall I find time to do the books and cook the dinner?"

"I do not know or care, so long as you do. If you wish to complain, take issue with that shiftless brother of yours—"

Then Sadler saw him on the stairs. "James! Good to see you up and about. And 'tis not even teatime yet!"

Mary muttered something under her breath and took the basket from the counter. Before she could reach the door to the street, however, Darkin snatched the sweetmeats from her grasp.

"Allow me," he said.

"No—you still need to rest!" She tried to snatch the basket back, and a farcical tug-of-war ensued.

"Stop that!" Sadler snapped. "You will damage the pastries!"

Mary, being the more startled, lost her grip on the unwanted prize. "If you are sure..." she murmured, clearly hoping that Darkin was.

"I have been a liability far too long." Darkin straightened his coat and settled the handle of the basket over his elbow—where it had sat countless times before, given the worn patch in the fabric. "And 'tis nothing new, for I sense it predates my current predicament. But no more! I intend to pull my weight from now on."

The Sadlers' reactions told the story: Sadler stared without a word, while Mary's dejection melted into a smile.

"Thank you, James," she said. "But what of your memory? How will you know who to serve—or even where to go?"

"I shall find my way, do not fret." Touched by her concern, Darkin suspected the real James would not have deserved it.

He tipped his hat to the pair of them as he left—and promptly collided with a sturdy young fellow decked in student robes who appeared to be heading inside.

"James!" the student exclaimed. "I heard you had become indisposed—is that why you missed the meeting? No matter, I am on my way to tell you what happened. Though you might like to take a seat first. I could stand you a coffee at Bagg's—"

Darkin raised his free hand to stem the tide of chatter. "Slow down! You are making my head hurt—and it aches quite enough already."

"Is it true you were assaulted in the street?" The student peered at the fading bruises on Darkin's face. "'Tis scandalous—this used to be a safe town. Now rowdies lurk around every corner, and 'twill only get worse with the escape of that wretch Isaac Darkin—"

Darkin raised an eyebrow.

"But back to the meeting..." the student continued. "You must be aggrieved at losing the wager—and your membership. Did you realize that Bean would win if you didn't show up? But have you heard the truth about Bean? He is no one special at all, it turns out—just a wandering play-actor. And that woman of his—I saw her wearing the diamond. How did Bean get it back from you?"

Darkin had started edging up the street, intending to excuse himself at the very first opportunity.

"What woman?"

The boy flapped his hands about wildly—a diversion, perhaps, from his glowing cheeks. "Oh, you would know her if you saw her. Small, dark. Exotic, some might say."

Darkin grinned. "Do you know where I might find her?"

"I'm not sure that would be a good idea, James. Think of your reputation."

"I shall risk it." The student frowned.

"Well, I do not know the location of the woman, but Ambrose Bean lodges at The Crown. Although of course, you knew that already."

Darkin patted him on the shoulder, then indicated his basket. "I should love to gossip all day," he said, "but business calls."

"As for the Club," the student said, by way of farewell, "Let us get you reinstated, eh? They are not all like Edwin Osborne, though they fall over themselves to flatter him."

Darkin walked into another delay as he left the talkative student behind, this time a tall man in black. The stranger's deliberate pace seemed out of sorts with his air of anxiety, and when Darkin attempted to skirt around him, he stopped and became more anxious still.

"James! I was coming to see you at home. I had not expected to find you out."

Darkin waited for some clue to the man's identity, but none was forthcoming.

"Then again, according to your father, 'twas not an affliction of the body that confined you to your bed, but your mind."

Darkin frowned. "Indeed. And that affliction has robbed me of my memory of many things, including names and faces."

A hopeful light dawned upon the stranger's. "Did you say you have lost... your *memory*?"

"'Tis catching, I fear." Darkin grinned, but the stranger missed the joke.

"For names, you say. And faces?"

"Aye, even the most distinctive of faces."

"And for... events?"

"Events too. All gone. 'Tis as if I were born a full-grown man just these few days past. Some may call that an affliction. *I* prefer to call it a new start, a clean slate, freed from the baggage of the past."

The stranger's response was, Darkin supposed, as close as he ever got to a smile.

"That is... an example to us all—for blessed is he, who endureth under trial. I should introduce myself. I am your cousin, Jediah Temple."

"Ah, yes. I have heard your name mentioned."

The look of alarm reappeared.

"On all occasions fondly, do not fear." Darkin slapped him on the back and began to walk on. Sadler's cousin, however, followed him.

"May I walk with you?"

Darkin eyed his clerical garb with concealed distaste. "You may, and you will be of help to me if you show me the way. I have important business at an inn by name of The Crown."

And now 'twas horror that filled the man's face. "I accept your mind is not functioning as normal, cousin, but I do not think you have business at such an establishment."

"I assure you I do."

Jediah frowned. "Very well, I shall lead the way. And we shall catch up on our news while we walk."

~ ~ ~

'Twas quickly apparent, to Darkin's perplexity, that the whole of the city of Oxford considered James Sadler its dearest friend. No man, woman, or child he encountered failed to find words of goodwill or hopes for his health; had his cousin's funereal presence not put off the worst of them, he might never have reached his destination. Meanwhile, Jediah Temple made conversation on this and that; Darkin could tell that such chit-chat came hard, as if there were more the man might say, but dare not. That secret, whatever it be, Darkin would leave to the parson's real cousin to deal with.

The Crown proved a respectable place compared with The Jolly Bull, though one would not have thought so, seeing the look on Jediah's face.

"You need go no further," Darkin said, taking pity on his guide as he opened the door.

Jediah's reaction to the belch of beery air suggested he would like nothing better. Nonetheless, he replied, "If it is no trouble, I should like to accompany you."

Darkin raised an eyebrow.

"To—to see that you are safe. You said yourself, you are not yet fully recovered. And you have already been twice assaulted. 'Tis my duty as your kin to see you come to no further harm."

"Well, then." Darkin paused. "Follow me."

The innkeeper's welcome was lavish—as were the discounts and other incentives proposed, should the aeronaut choose to visit The Crown to celebrate future ascents. Darkin promised to weigh this offer with all of the rest that he had received, then escaped upstairs to the lodging-rooms, Jediah still shuffling in his wake. The tall man's eyes widened when Darkin reached for Ambrose Bean's doorknob.

"You would enter unbidden?"

"I never stand on ceremony. Besides, the person I am here to see was happy to enter *me* without my permission."

The scene inside came as no surprise, though Jediah muttered some prayer at the sight; Lord deliver us all from the sins of the flesh, no doubt. Besides the bed with its stained, torn, and crumpled sheets, the room contained an abundance of gaudy clothing—far too many to fit in the meagre storage space—along with a tripod, hung upon which was a gay feathered hat, and in a space cleared on the tabletop, a contraption of wood and brass. Jediah came into the room and headed straight for it, staring dazedly at its open lid and its innards, laid bare on display.

"What—what—"

"'Tis nothing to fear," Darkin said. "Just a box of tricks."

Jediah reached out with a trembling hand, but before he could touch the box, they heard angry voices approach.

"These Gownsmen are all the same. So depraved, yet so precious, so prudish. You heard that walking, talking grotesquerie, Somerfield—" The speaker spat the name, before he adopted a mocking squeak: "*I was intrigued by the promise of unusual entertainment.* How *disgusting*, how *disgraceful*—but neither so much that he would not watch, mind you. I'll wager his piggy eyes were all agog. Hypocrites they are, to a man!"

"You shall have your revenge when I have had mine," said a calmer, female voice, "and then you may— Wait! The door stands ajar."

"A thief?"

"Most definitely."

Tossing his basket onto the mattress, Darkin stood squarely in the centre of the floor as the door swung aside.

"I did not order desserts," said Serafina D'Bonaventura.

He looked her up and down in silence. Still dressed like a layer-out in her black veil and cloak, with the prettiest sneer on her lips, and the source of his plight unashamedly worn in plain sight. Ambrose Bean sidled up behind her, careful not to place himself in the line of Darkin's glare.

"I see your Bean-stalk is back in the fold," Darkin said. "It must be the ceaseless supply of cheap bonnets that pleases, for he certainly has neither brains nor balls."

"How dare you!" Bean spluttered.

"While you, I presume, are amply endowed with all three?" Serafina stepped closer, returning Darkin's appraisal with a giggle of wicked delight. "May I ask why you are here? Or shall I guess?"

"You know why. I want my body back."

Bean dared to join her then, his swagger recovered. "My God," he breathed, with the ghoulish fascination of a schoolboy inspecting a circus freak. "To think this could have been me."

"It may be yet, if you dally with this one too long." Darkin glowered at Serafina. "Well?"

Serafina placed the tip of a pointed fingernail over his heart. "Now *that* would please me, for this body does not suit you. But I cannot restore you without your own person to hand, and the last I saw of that, 'twas vanishing into the night with your boys. You will know better than I where they took it."

Darkin frowned. "What are you saying? If I bring my body to you, you will do as I ask? As easy as that? 'Tis not like you to give service for nothing."

"I'm sure I shall think of something."

She ran the finger further down his torso, until Bean could endure no more and elbowed Darkin aside.

"I am surprised you want it back," he sniffed. "Your style of life might seem thrilling to some, but one must tire of having to constantly look to one's rear, for fear of the hangman."

"You may have your opinion," growled Darkin, "but I alone shall decide my best course."

"And you, thief." Bean suddenly rounded on Darkin's companion. "Who are *you*? Speak up!"

"I—I am Jediah Temple," Jediah stammered, blinking at the brightness of Beans' coat and hat. "I am Vice Sub-Rector of St Alban's."

"A University man?" Bean snarled. "Let's turn him out on his ear, shall we? Serafina?"

Serafina ignored him.

"I think I have thought of something already," she said, and moved to the table. "You remember this, do you not? And this."

She rested a hand on the box, then moved her hand to the gem at her throat. Jediah opened and closed his mouth several times, but finding no words, simply nodded.

"And me."

At that, he lost whatever volition remained, pinned in her gaze.

"You remember *me*."

"Come, come Serafina," laughed Bean. "You are not so important that *everyone* must remember you."

Before she could speak again, Darkin stepped up and took Jediah by the arm. "Stop your sorcery, woman. My cousin may not know what you are about, but I do—and only too well."

"*Your* cousin? You have made yourself at home, it seems."

"I knew it!" cried Bean, who had by now flopped on the bed and begun to rifle through the basket. "He says he wants to return to his previous life, when all the while he prefers his cosy new one. He is just too afraid to admit it."

"We are done here." Darkin snatched back the basket. He considered reclaiming the pie from Bean's gullet as well, but decided against it.

"So soon?" Serafina pouted. "I thought you wanted to deal?"

'Twas hard work, hauling Jediah out of harm's way. The tall man, though thin, was still heavier than he appeared, and showed no intention of helping himself. Darkin cursed James Sadler's feeble form almost as much as his shiftless cousin.

"I think—" he gasped, "—we must meet without distractions. Just—the two of us, alone."

"As you wish." Serafina's hand strayed back to her throat. "I shall look forward to it."

~ ~ ~ ~

It took an hour of clicking of fingers and shoulder-shaking—not to mention dosing with rum—to restore the Vice Sub-Rector Temple to his old self. Or at least, Darkin hoped what emerged was his self, having no prior acquaintance to go on.

"What degenerate manner of Hell is this?" were the parson's first words, his gaze darting wildly from drunkard to dragsman to brandy-faced dasher and back.

"'Tis the public bar of The Crown."

"The public attends this incommodious hovel? For *pleasure?*" Jediah shuddered and screwed shut his eyes. "I could never imagine such high-smelling men nor so many low-born women."

"Well," said Darkin, "I could, I suppose, have deposited you at that *less* incommodious hovel across the road. I expect it smells more acceptable, but you seemed about to slip off your perch and I thought I had better not risk it. Besides, rum is not cheap, and the innkeeper here strikes a generous bargain."

"You made me *drink*?" Jediah gagged.

'Twas Darkin's turn to close his eyes. "Thinking on it again," he said, after slowly counting to ten, "I would have saved you from all these privations, if only I'd let the sorceress and her not-so-lovely assistant see you right."

Jediah shuddered. "I should thank you, of course. 'Tis simply that... I felt not quite right in my reasoning." He jumped when the potboy came close; only when Darkin had waved the lad away did he continue, his voice dropped to an undertone: "She said I remember her, and I did. She was a child. And I—"

"She wants you to *think* you remember. Why, I cannot guess—'tis all a game to her, though a deadly one for some."

"That infernal device, and the stone... I sought God's forgiveness, but He did not respond to my prayers."

"'Tis no cause for shame." Darkin smiled with heartfelt sympathy. "Wiser men than you and I have fallen for her deceptions. 'Twould be best for you now, if you took yourself home—wherever that may be—and rested awhile. Think on happy thoughts. Allow yourself a dash of whatever you fancy."

Jediah seemed as shocked by that as by anything else that afternoon.

"Shall I accompany you?" Darkin added, for the parson swayed when he managed to find his feet, and when he unwound to his full height cracked the crown of his head on a rafter.

"I need no assistance," he said, though he nodded with weary thanks when Darkin sprang to open the door, and even accepted a steadying hand at his arm as they stepped through the ruts in the yard.

Hearing a whistle, Darkin turned to see the inn-keeper, smiling and waving farewell from the door. And then they were back on the street, and the friendly attention resumed as before. Jediah regarded it all with alarm.

"I beseech you, as your cousin," he muttered. "Do not breathe a word of this. Man, woman, child—not a soul can ever know."

"Of course, you can trust me," Darkin replied. "We are family—and is that not what families are for?"

CHAPTER
THIRTY-FOUR

I REMAINED IN A DAZE as the "boys" bundled me out of the attic and into a strange new world. (I eventually learned their names to be Masher, Walt, Slim, and Col, though never which was which.) We passed without pause through the inn—a squalid place that could seldom accommodate civilized guests—and out to the stables at the back, where the true horror of my situation hit me.

I was required to ride.

The boys were astride their own mounts and half-way down the road before they realized I had stayed in the yard, the reins of a massive black brute of a stallion dangling loose in my hand.

"Come on!" cried Slim (or Masher, perhaps). "The day won't wait!"

I made a half-hearted attempt to scale the implacable mountain, but the wall of coarse hair and muscle provided no footholds; with an unseemly squeal of dismay, I slid back to Earth on my rump. In a window above, I saw Kat watching the show, her rosy face unreadable. The horse was staring, too, but his feelings were obvious—pure scorn. Fortunately, I did not have to witness the boys' reaction, for Walt came swiftly to my aid, hoisting me out of the dust and shoving me skywards and into the saddle. The horse skittered about, almost throwing me straight off again.

"Th—Thank you," I muttered, my feet scrabbling clumsily for the stirrups. "I felt all at once... dizzy."

Walt gave me a wink and nodded up at the window. "That little nipper takes it out of you, eh?"

Then he slapped my steed's flank, remounted his own, and together we rode forth towards whatever mischief the boys had planned for me.

This being my first time upon a horse, I had no notion of how to control him, but he seemed to realize this, and spared me further shame by trotting agreeably after his fellows. Still, it took me an age to grow accustomed to the nauseating swaying motion, the dread of falling off, the fear that an overhanging branch might knock me senseless. But the morning was warm and bright, and I began to take a wary pleasure in the dappled sunshine, the smell of fresh air for the first time in days, and watching the world pass by from my lofty new perspective. I might have even enjoyed the ride, had I not been imprisoned in the body of a criminal— a fugitive from the gallows, at that—and compelled to live a life I did not want.

I wondered glumly what was happening in Oxford. Was Serafina still in town? If she'd moved on, I might never be saved. I weighed my chances of turning my steed around and galloping home before the boys could stop me. Not great, I concluded.

When my companions reined their mounts to a halt, my own obligingly joined them. Slim pointed down a grassy bank into a clearing off the road.

"Lookin' good," he said.

"No sign of Jack Martin's gang," said Col.

"We feared the cur might've taken liberties while we were gone," explained Walt.

We descended the bank and held fast in the clearing. I supposed that, from the road, we could not be seen, and though I had previously avoided the purpose of our journey, the reality finally struck me. This was an ambush, and the boys were going to rob a coach. *We* were going to rob a coach.

"I feel unwell," I gasped. "The sunshine, the heat... May we do this another day?"

The boys exchanged glances, and with a sad shake of the head Walt said, "Prison does terrible things to a man. But you'll soon be back in the saddle."

As they sniggered at that *double entendre*, I grimaced, and Col said, "That's more like it. Affright the men, delight their ladies."

I was certain I would be capable of neither. Masher peered at his pocket-watch. "Five minutes. The Tuesday Champion is always bang on time."

Tuesday. I had lost all sense of the passage of time, but now I remembered: today the Philosophical Club would gather as always at Harper's, and top of the agenda would be my wager with Ambrose Bean. I was the victor, but Bean would surely claim the win. Howling silently in Darkin's head, I gnashed his teeth and counted my woes. I'd lost my body and my life, and now a bet I should have won, not to mention membership of my own club. These latter were trifling issues compared with the greater dilemma, of course, but they underscored the wretchedness of my plight. Indeed, so deep was my despair, I again forgot my location, until my thoughts were interrupted by the thunder of many hooves, the rattle of wheel rims in the road, and Masher's exultant shout: "It's here! Let's ride, boys!"

I'd expected them to surge forth like a cavalry charge, allowing me to hang back and perhaps even escape, but instead they all turned expectantly to me, as if I should lead the way or give some signal.

"C'mon!" cried Walt.

I looked from one to the next, bewildered.

"They'll get ahead of us!" hissed Slim.

I flapped my heels, but now the stakes were raised my mount refused to humour me; with a mutinous toss of the head, he dropped his nose to the grass and started munching.

A moment of stunned silence seemed to stretch forever, then Col cursed, pulled on his mask, and spurred his horse up the bank and onto the road. The others did likewise, leaving me below with my recalcitrant steed. From that unhappy haven, my ears were witness to shouts and screams, barked orders, terrified whinnies; all so loud I was certain we could be heard back in Stokenchurch, and would be ambushed ourselves on our return—by forces of a more lawful nature. Again I thought of escape, and jiggled my mount's reins to attract his attention. He snorted and continued his meal.

~ ~ ~

The boys did not speak of my failure to act, and on our return to The Jolly Bull, made no bones about dividing their loot in "the common way". I took leave of their celebrations early, however, and as I dragged Darkin's saddle-sore body up the stairs heard them discussing the changes come over me since my gaol-break, though with concern rather than malice.

I slept fitfully that night; even Kat's tender caresses failed to still my turbulent dreams. I awoke at one point drenched in sweat after dreaming of the imposter in my body; having usurped my *Officina Chimica* post and been lauded by Dr Crouch, he had even won my father's praise. I must have spoken these names in my nightmare, for when I sat up with a gasp, the next words I heard were Kat's.

"You were talking in your sleep. About people, places, things *I* could never dream of."

"I told you once before. I do not belong here."

"But Isaac—"

"I am not Isaac!"

"I heard things did not go well for you today. But 'tis only to be expected, after all you have been through."

"They did not go well for me, 'tis true, but entirely expectable as well. For I am *not* a highwayman."

"Who be you then, if not a highwayman?"

"I am—I am..." With a deadening rush of dismay, I struggled to find an answer. Student, pastry-boy, philosopher, man of science, aeronaut? All I had attempted and none to any account. All my life, I had wished I were something other than what I had been at the time. And now I truly *was* someone else, I had not even flourished at that.

"I am tired," I murmured.

Kat leaned over to kiss my forehead then turned on her side. After a while, I heard her peaceful little snores. 'Twas a long time before I followed her into sleep.

CHAPTER
THIRTY-FIVE

HAVING LEFT JEDIAH TEMPLE to find his own way home, Isaac Darkin continued to ponder Bean's words—all the more so once he had finished the Sadlers' delivery round. Should he follow the showman's advice and embrace his new start? Although, he wondered grimly, would he be able to stand the pace? For he returned to find his maybe-soon-to-be home in the midst of an almighty hubbub, and Oxford Gaol seemed a haven of peace and quiet by comparison.

The instant the tinkle of doorbells announced his arrival, the journeyman, Billy, dashed through from the kitchen and gestured upstairs.

"The Mayor is here," he whispered.

"The Mayor? Of Oxford?" Darkin chuckled to himself at the thought of previous dealings he'd had with that gentleman.

"What other Mayor would there be?"

Then Sadler, Sr. sprinted down the stairs, blaring at Billy: "Close the shutters and bolt the door. Quickly! We cannot be interrupted. This is—James!"

He jerked to a halt, gasping for breath as the sight of Darkin calmed him a little.

"Thank Heavens you are back! The Mayor is here. The Mayor! Here, in our lowly abode!"

"So I gather," Darkin drawled.

"He wants to see you, Lord knows why." The pastry-cook sniffed. "A pity there is no time to clean you up. You will have to do as you are."

He grabbed the empty basket from Darkin, shoved it under the counter, and bustled him straight upstairs and into the parlour. Darkin obliged, if only for curiosity's sake.

The focus of all this kerfuffle was a weasel-gutted cull he remembered well—though from rather different circumstances—decked in a towering powdered wig and massive golden chain. The Mayor had taken Sadler's chair, with an attendant dressed in blue livery standing behind him and Mary in front, serving tea from the family's best pot.

"Here is my son," Sadler said. "He apologizes for his lateness."

Darkin grunted.

Then Sadler squealed, as if stung. "Ah, what a worthless jingle brains am I! I forgot to bring up the pastries. Please do excuse me again, Your Worship."

He bowed and scraped his way out, then clattering footsteps were heard once again on the stairs, and more hullaballoo from the shop. As Darkin passed Mary, he whispered into her ear, "I never took our father for such a fart-catcher." She returned him a bright—if startled—smile, cheeks ablush. With a smile of his own, Darkin offered his hand to the Mayor; that worthy responded with scarcely a nod.

"I hear you wish to speak with me," Darkin said, unperturbed.

The Mayor took a tiny sip of his tea and confirmed that *sotto voce*. Everything about him, in fact, was diminutive, excepting his wig and chain. "Some time ago, your associate Wyndham Rudge contacted our secretary—" He indicated the liveried man. "—with a view to the exhibition of your aerostat at the Town Hall. Having heard nothing since, we decided to follow-up on the business ourselves."

The Mayor appeared offhand, as if speaking of a mere trifle, but Darkin guessed "the business" meant rather more to him than that. Had it not, 'twould have been his secretary haggling over the counter, and no special treats required.

"What will this exhibition involve?" Darkin asked.

"You do not know? We assumed your associate had acted upon your instructions."

"Mr Rudge is my partner, not my lackey."

The Mayor appeared to consider this concept, then promptly dismissed it. "Does *the exhibition of your aerostat at the Town Hall* provide inadequate information? Seems plain enough to us."

Darkin shrugged. "So, we shall bring along our balloon... and lay it flat upon the ground? Or hang it from a pole? I have never attended such an event."

"Clearly not. We doubt a poor show such as that would turn a profit. As we discussed with your... associate, the aerostat will be placed in the Town Hall courtyard—tethered, of course, so 'twill not escape." The Mayor allowed himself a smile.

"You mean," said Darkin, "the balloon will be *inflated?*"

Before the Mayor could elaborate, Sadler returned to the parlour, almost tripping over the threshold in his haste. 'Twas fortunate he did not, for in his hand was a silver tray, and upon the tray sat a magnificent pyramid of chocolate puffs, festooned with pistachio nuts and dried cherries, and mounted on a China plate that matched the tea service.

"Did I hear you mention *business*? And *profit*?" he exclaimed. "Those are, of course, my *forte*. May I be so bold, Your Worship, as to enquire how I might be allowed to assist?"

Darkin took the sweetmeat tray and ushered its bearer back to the door. "The Mayor prefers to discuss the matter in private."

Sadler gasped in disbelief. "In private? With you? But what do you know of business?" He lowered his voice. "Stop this nonsense, James. You are embarrassing us all."

"'Tis you who risks embarrassment, Father."

Sadler whirled beseechingly from Darkin to the Mayor, frustration and fury mounting. Then, with a loud exhalation akin to steam escaping a boiling kettle, he relented.

"I shall be downstairs," he sniffled, "should anyone want me."

The Mayor observed all this without interest, but when Darkin took a seat, remarked, "Our discussion will be of even lesser concern to your sister."

"On the contrary," Darkin replied. "Mary has a far better head for figures than I. I trust her judgement in all affairs financial. In *all* affairs, in fact."

Already on her way out, Mary spun around in the doorway. Darkin grinned at her wide-eyed delight, then stood, offered her his chair, and poured himself a cup of tea.

"Now, let us cut to the chase," he said, with an artful air. "Times, dates, numbers, costs. And the proceeds— they shall be divided well in favour of Rudge and I. 'Tis only fair," he added, as the Mayor began to object. "The Town Hall may be yours, but 'tis the aerostat they will come for—and that is most definitely ours."

CHAPTER THIRTY-SIX

I WAS ALLOWED NO RESPITE in the aftermath of my ordeal, for the boys returned me to work the very next day. And at the break of dawn this time, the Birmingham Mail being our target; 'twas, they assured me, always filled with wealthy Black Country merchants.

We followed the same route as previously for a while, then turned north to join the London-to-Birmingham road, which was not as well maintained as the London-to-Oxford and rather more hazardous to ride. Once more, however, my steed took charge, and I began to feel a grudging fondness for the nag, and even for the boys, who chatted gaily amongst themselves as we trotted along. Most of their banter I did not—or did not wish to—comprehend, but their laughter, mingled with the birdsong and the hum of insect wings, not to mention the gentle balm of the sunlight on my face, lulled me into a tranquil state that refused to admit any troubling thoughts.

As before, at a spot that looked no different from any other but was familiar to my companions, we left the road to prepare our ambush. The air was perfectly still, and almost straight away we heard the rumble of a vehicle in the distance. Walt grinned. "Early today." At this, my heart sank. I thought of all the coaches I had watched from behind the shop counter (and what I would have given to be back there!). The passengers and their various doings had ofttimes fuelled my daydreams. I imagined the Birmingham Mail speeding blindly towards our hiding place, its innocent occupants heedless of what was to come. Was there any way I could warn them? I considered a daring charge up the road—if my mount would oblige. But then I remembered who I now was, and how I was dressed. Mask, pistol, the battle-scarred face of Isaac Darkin. I could be shot before I spoke a word, if the boys failed to shoot me first for betraying them. And if I were not shot, I would surely be overpowered and returned to Oxford Gaol.

And so I stood fast with the boys, gnashing my teeth in frustration as the coach raced ever nearer.

When our prey was in sight, Col hollered, "Let's ride, boys!"

This time they did not wait for me; Walt led the attack, bellowing like a bull. To my dismay, my mount decided to follow this time, and I was bounced around painfully in the saddle as we rode. I forgot all about the impending robbery, being now more concerned with not falling and breaking my neck.

I survived the short gallop intact, however, and caught up with the others as Walt, now dismounted, wrenched open the coach door and yelled at drivers and passengers alike.

"Everybody out!" he shouted.

"We have ladies here!" came a protest from within.

"I'll have you out where I can see you, ladies and all," Walt replied. "If you play along nice, we'll soon have finished our business and you can get back about yours."

"And with a tale to tell," added Masher, who was covering Walt from his horse. "Of how you was robbed by Darkin's boys."

I wondered how they could be so forthright about their identities (or rather, *my* identity), but it was, I supposed, all part of the show.

"You are a liar as well as a thief," cried the driver. "For Isaac Darkin languishes in gaol awaiting the noose—if he hasn't hanged already."

Walt laughed. "You are behind the times in Birmingham. For Isaac Darkin has flown the coop— I know 'cause I was with him. And here he is today!"

He jerked his thumb at me, to gasps of horror from our victims.

"You are Darkin?" demanded a tubby gentleman with a green velvet coat and the look of a banker about him. I tried to say yes, but even that simple word caught in my throat and I could only nod once in reply.

"Then we are done for!" the banker cried. "For 'tis well known that Darkin's gang delights in slitting the throats of their victims."

I sincerely hoped that was not the case, but the banker had his fellows convinced; the men sputtered with outrage, while the elder of the two ladies swooned in fright.

"Nonsense!" This came from the younger woman, stepping out of line as she spoke.

"Do not approach them!" warned the banker. "I have heard they sometimes spare comely young girls, but only for a fate worse than death."

"And I have heard," said the maiden, "that Mr Darkin and his associates always conduct their affairs with the utmost propriety. Is that not true, Mr Darkin?"

She approached me showing no sign of fear, her sky-blue gaze unwavering. Seized with bravado, I leaned over in the saddle and cupped her chin in my hand.

"And how, my dear, would you wish I conduct my affairs?" And how I now appreciated that gravelly baritone voice, hitherto so discordant upon my unaccustomed ear!

The maiden admired it too, for she fluttered her eyelashes shyly. Behind her, I saw the banker flush with anger, and called down to him, "You have something to say?"

The chubby cheeks paled from red to ghostly grey.

"No—not at all—that is, I... No, Mr Darkin."

His reaction startled me, but he must have mistaken surprise for a threat, for he trembled cravenly when Col intervened.

"Back in line now, miss," my henchman ordered. The maiden smiled at me over her shoulder, and Col added to me, in a whisper, "Good to have you back, Isaac."

Having finished searching the coach, Walt turned to its occupants.

"Ladies and gentlemen, my colleague will now pass amongst you." He indicated Slim, who carried an open moneybag. "Kindly turn out your pockets and purses. All donations are gratefully received."

"And no sneaky business, mind," I warned. "For I shall be watching." My steed backed me up with a snort and a stamp of his hoof. Even I was impressed, though not nearly as much as our victims. The banker trembled more wretchedly yet, while the matron was now quite beside herself. The driver bared his teeth in impotent fury. But the maiden blew me a kiss before she unclasped the choker that bound her slender throat; the pearls shimmered in the sunlight as she lowered them into the bag, like the scales of a snake descending a tree.

The banker and the matron fear me, I realized. The driver loathes me. The maiden desires me—or her perception of me, at least. Each one had judged me, right or wrong. To them, I was no nonentity. I was *somebody*—a person meriting judgement, a man to be reckoned with. And the consequences were dazzling.

As Slim strutted past to remount his horse, the bulging moneybag slung on his shoulder, he saluted me. As if I were someone special. I corrected myself. Not *as if* I were special. Because I *was* special.

'Twas hard to admit to myself, but I owed a great debt to Serafina D'Bonaventura and her sorcery.

For by that strange design, I had truly become a man of consequence.

CHAPTER THIRTY-SEVEN

" **. . .A**ND IN PURSUANCE OF THE ABOVE," droned the Town Hall attendant, "any damages charged to the Council, be they through breakage, theft, or loss of life or limb, shall be, by order of the Mayor, deducted at source from your proceeds. Do I make myself clear?" He glared at them one by one, as if undecided who to trust least.

"As clear as the mountain of your Master's self-regard," responded James, "which towers over the molehill of both his person and his singular achievement."

The attendant blinked and rerolled his edict. "I shall be watching," he warned, and turned on his heels, leaving Mary, James, and Rudge alone in the courtyard.

"'Tis a good size," said Rudge.

James winked at Mary. "This place, or His Worship's notables?"

"The courtyard, of course. 'Tis much larger than might be expected, from the outside."

"For the Lady Mayoress's sake, one must hope that also applies to the Mayor."

Mary had contained herself through the endless reams of rules and regulations, but no longer. "Oh James, you are so mean!" she cried, once her laughter subsided enough that she could speak. "'Tis not the Mayor's fault he is tiny."

"You put words into my mouth. Did I ever call him tiny? Although in my experience, the littlest men do tend to hide the biggest of secrets."

"Cease your squabbling, children," said Rudge. "I'm sure our guardian over there would rather be snug in his bed come the morning, not still here and watching after you two."

He waved at the attendant, now stationed not quite out of sight by the exit, then took himself off to the northern edge of the yard. With his back to the Town Clerk's office and his face to the Grammar School building, he embarked upon a slow and meticulous march betwixt the two, his steps planted heel-to-toe while his lips moved in silent count. He seemed to have no immediate need of help, so James offered Mary his arm, and together they joined the gardener on his walk, as folk with no cause to rise early might set out on an evening stroll.

"There you go again, with your *experience*," said Mary. "I do not know where you gained all this worldly knowledge, for I have never encountered it."

"Then 'tis time, perhaps, you sought it out, and stopped waiting for it to find you."

Mary managed a wry smile. "Will you inform Father, or shall I? I fear I am too settled in my common-place life, and must leave the jaunting to Lizzie and you."

"Ah yes, my younger sister..." James paused to straighten his hat, then kicked a clod of earth from his shoe. "...of whom I have heard a little, but still know nothing at all. Will she attend our exhibition?"

"I'm sure Father will write to invite her."

"And I shall look forward to meeting her. Be she merely one-quarter as splendid a woman as you, I shall consider myself a fortunate man, to have two such remarkable sisters."

Such flattery Mary knew well. 'Twas always followed by talk of a favour; or how she must intercede with their father; or why her work counted for naught compared with his, and might be started or stopped at his whim. And indeed, James bore a wicked look in his eye as he charmed her now, but she felt almost certain he meant what he said.

"'Tis up to you to decide, if either of us be 'remarkable',," she replied. "But I must warn you, Lizzie is everything I am not, and I am everything *she* is not. Lizzie is parties, and picnics, and fashionable friends. And shopping for fun, rather than need—can you imagine? My leisure is the Sunday morning service: comfortable but stodgy, and very, very dull. When we were children, 'twas often remarked how different two girls could be, yet share the same blood." James seldom allowed her to speak so many words without interruptions, and suddenly, she ran short. "Father misses her badly," she finished, with a sigh.

They continued in silence. Rudge had finished surveying the courtyard north-to-south, and now went to the centre point of the western edge, behind him the peristyle of the Corn Exchange and over his head the Council Chamber's extravagant balcony, where the Mayor and his worthies assembled to mark each new municipal year, the King's birthday, and other local and national occasions of note.

"And you?" James asked, eventually.

Mary looked upwards, holding her bonnet in place with one hand. 'Twas long after hours at the Town Hall, but the sky remained clear and blue so close to Midsummer. "We must hope it does not rain on the day," she murmured, "nor be too hot, for there is little shelter here."

"Do you miss your sister?"

Of course," she replied, returning her gaze to the ground. "We shared a room for most of my life. All of hers, until she wed."

"And very well, I hear. A physician."

"They met because of you. Do you remember? Even the smallest detail?"

"Not one. But it pains me to learn 'twas I who lost you your sister."

"'Twould have happened sooner or later." She frowned from beneath her bonnet at the familiar lines of his face; so strange and serene it appeared to her now, with its grudges and scorns erased. "As it is, Father's loss is outweighed by his pride. He does enjoy showing her off. For Lizzie moves in prestigious circles, compared with you and I—although that may soon change for you, and then 'twill just be me, all alone."

"I would never leave you alone, my dearest!"

"Do not make promises, James. You are hardly famous for keeping your word."

"As I have learned, to my cost," said Rudge. His survey of the courtyard complete, he was instantly back on the move, his energy boundless as he dashed from spot to spot to explain his designs. "This venue suits us well. We shall inflate our new balloon here, at the centre... its frame extending to here, and here... with space for our generators—and to store the tubes, when we have done with them—in those arches: there, there, and there."

"Those arches are where the wine merchants trade," Mary said, hastily adding, "They love their raisin pies."

"I am sure they will love even more, to trade some space for an increase in business."

"Why, James! If Father could hear you say that, he'd be prouder of you than of Lizzie."

"What are you saying?" he cried, in mock dismay. "Is he not already proud, when I have worked so hard to please him?"

"Any credit you gained on that account, was squandered the instant you banished him from his own parlour."

"As he banished me, from my own home?"

"With good cause, as I remember. 'Tis a shame you do not, for then you would understand how insufferable you could be."

"You mean I am not so insufferable now?"

Mary's smile was broad. "Hardly."

"Well, from now I shall know who my friends are, at least. I trust I can count you among them, Mr Rudge?"

"I take it you are finished?" called the attendant.

He'd been observing them all the while with a disapproving air, but that turned to irritation when James cupped a hand to his ear and pretended to listen intently.

"Is that a tiptoeing mouse I hear? Or simply the Mayor, stamping his tiny foot in impatience?"

Mary burst into laughter again, while Rudge looked on; exasperated at first, then with a bright smile of his own.

"Ah, this takes me back," he said.

Still careless of the attendant's health of mind, James crossed to the courtyard's focal point, at the top of a shallow incline that finished directly beneath the balcony, with the grand façade of the Corn Exchange behind. "You forgot to mention the podium. *That*, we shall place here."

"Podium?" Rudge looked doubtful.

"Where else shall we speak to the crowd? They will want more for their entrance fee, than just a glimpse of a tethered balloon. I could do it alone," James added, mischievously, "if you are feeling shy on the day."

"Me?" Rudge shook his head. "I was thinking of *you*, and your wretched performance in Angel Meadow. You are as poor a public speaker as you are a keeper of promises."

"At the risk of repeating myself yet again, 'tis long past time for a change."

"And 'tis longer still, past my supper." The attendant had suffered enough, and directed them testily to the exit, then fetched a lamp and led the way through the empty maze of lobbies and halls.

"Earlier today—" Mary slowed to speak with James, as far as she dare. "—you set out to look for a woman. Did you find her?"

"I did."

"And did you get back what she took from you?"

She watched him sideways for a reaction.

"No. But I got something else."

"According to your sister," said Rudge, as he, too, fell in step, "you have ruined some poor woman's prospects on the marriage market."

"Have I, now?" James raised an eyebrow.

Mary blushed, but was spared awkward questions by the attendant, for whom this delay meant the final straw; cursing their selfish dawdling, he bundled them into the porter's lodge and from there back onto Fish Street.

'Twas a pleasant amble up to Carfax from that point, but when they reached the crossroads, Rudge stopped.

"Will you walk with us as far as the shop?" Mary asked, worrying that the attendant was not the only one they'd exhausted.

"If you'll excuse me," Rudge said, with a furtive expression. "I have to see a man. About a horse."

"A horse?"

He did not explain, being already on his way to Butcher Row, and pausing only to call to James, "I shall see you tomorrow—early, mind! No slacking!"

"Well!" said Mary. "Why is everyone so *mysterious* all of a sudden?"

And then, as if on cue, she spotted the last person on Earth she might have expected to follow that trend.

"Is that cousin Jediah?"

She had no need to ask, of course. Few townsfolk walked abroad at that time, the workday being done and the night-time not quite commenced, but the Gownsman would have stood out on the busiest market day. He strode up the High from the east, bound for Carfax at an unusual pace for him, his gaze focussed on his feet, regardless of any obstacles he might meet and whether he might avoid them. Mary waved and called his name across the road, but he could not—or would not—hear her.

"He looks unwell," she said. "Don't you think?"

James shrugged. "He looks much the same as he did when I saw him before."

"And when was that?"

"This afternoon, outside the shop. He said he'd come to see me, then he provided me with directions—for the delivery round, that is."

"That was kind of him. He struggles sometimes... to be friendly."

"I noticed no such handicap myself."

"Nor anything else?"

"Nothing else." James took her arm again and tried to usher her onto the High.

"Now I *know* there is something wrong—"

"Why would your cousin confide in *me*? He barely knows—"

"*Shush!* I meant, did you see where he went?"

Jediah had turned onto North Gate Street, but instead of continuing onwards to college, he'd dashed down a turn to the left.

"He went... into that small side-street."

"And you know what lies on that side-street?"

"This city's geography still confounds me," James replied with a breezy laugh. "Except for which parishes eat the most sweetmeats, perhaps."

She continued to stare at the spot where she last saw her cousin, long after the shadows had swallowed his black cloak and hat.

"I have neglected him," she said, "with all that's been happening lately. 'Tis time I set that to rights."

☺

CHAPTER THIRTY-EIGHT

AT THE *MUSÆUM ASHMOLEANUM* the following day, Ambrose Bean and Serafina D'Bonaventura paid their sixpences to a willowy young man tasked with showing them round the collections.

"You are the Keeper?" asked Serafina, bearing down upon him with a vague hint of menace, despite him being a head taller than she.

"Me? Dr Sheffield?" The man laughed. "Oh, goodness no. Dr Sheffield is fully occupied in his chambers today. I am his assistant. Though you will find me well informed on our treasures," he added, seeing the pointed glance that passed from the woman to her companion. "My specialties are the elder Mr Tradescant's mineral species, upon which I have written a treatise highly regarded in the field, if I say so myself. Now, sir and madam—" He gestured up the staircase. "Shall we begin our tour? As we ascend to the main exhibition, we shall first take pause to view our East Indian entomological specimens, and from closer to home, the skeleton of—"

"We prefer to see them alone," said Bean.

Their guide maintained his smile, though his eyelids flickered. "Alone? I'm afraid that is impossible."

"A butterfly the size of a crow is impossible." Bean pointed to the nearest glass case. "All we wish to do, is explore your museum unaccompanied."

"What I mean," the young man persisted, "is that all visitors must be supervised. For the safety of the exhibits, you understand."

Bean frowned. "Are you suggesting we might harm them?"

"Oh, no, no, of course not!" The guide bit his lower lip. "I am sure both you and the lady would be mindful of their fragile and valuable nature."

"Good," said Bean, as he strode towards the staircase. "'Tis settled."

"No—wait—"

Serafina dipped into her pocket and pulled out a shilling. "'Tis so bad, to be paid to do nothing?" She took the young man's hand in her own, placed the coin in his palm, closed his fingers around it, then let his arm drop limply back to his side. "Take a nap, or attend your sweetheart. We shall let ourselves out when we're done."

She patted him on the cheek before she followed Bean up the stairs, pausing on the half-landing to ensure the guide had not followed. But the doors to the Broad had closed already, and she smiled to herself, satisfied.

Bean awaited her in the gallery, tapping his foot on the marbled tiles.

"I thought we would never be rid of him," he grumbled. "Now let's be about our business before he returns."

"You do not wish to inspect the collections? See here—'tis a camel-leopard." Serafina peered at the carcass of a giraffe, its stuffed skin mounted on a plinth at the head of the aisle, its sightless glass gaze looking nowhere. "We have paid for that privilege, after all."

"I fail to understand what people see in this mouldy old rummage." Bean delivered a kick to the nearest exhibit, which happened to be a mighty bull elephant's skull. Hiding his wince behind a snarl, he continued, "Our sixpences would have been better spent, had that sop revealed the whereabouts of his master."

"Patience, dear Ambrose."

She strolled to the wall at the end of the aisle and listened in turn at each door; at the third, she stopped and gestured to Bean. He hastened to join her, for she was now the impatient one and had entered the chamber without him.

"Dr Sheffield, I presume," he heard her say, and from over her shoulder saw a large mahogany desk, and behind it a neat, bespectacled man who'd jumped to his feet in surprise, a stack of papers beneath one hand and a pen still clutched in the other.

"Who are you?" the man demanded. "And where is Glenville?" He stood on tiptoes and bellowed, "Glenville! *Glenville!*"

"I'm afraid he cannot hear you." Serafina stepped aside so Bean could enter, then shut the three of them in.

The Keeper's pasty face grew paler. "Why? What have you done with him?"

Ignoring the question, Bean stamped to the desk. "Are you a Philosopher? A University man?"

Sheffield nodded, beginning to sweat.

"Speak up. I cannot hear you."

"I—I—yes, I am. I am Keeper of the Museum, and Provost of Worcester College."

"Provost? How you Gownsmen love your grand titles. And you have not one, but two! I'll wager life in your Worcester College is *most* agreeable. Snug and safe behind insurmountable walls, sneering down at the rest of us."

Stirred by Bean's discourtesy, the Keeper swallowed his fear and drew himself up to his maximum height. "I am not sure what you mean. But if you think I know nothing of the world, I can assure you that is not the case. This museum is open to all."

Bean laughed without humour. "Open to lecture to all, to improve all. Who says we need improving? Who decides what we need to know—if anything?"

"All men—" The Keeper glanced sidelong at Serafina. "—and women, too, are the better for education."

"So now you wish to better us, eh?" Bean stuck his nose so close to Sheffield's, he could smell the Keeper's defiance melting away. "And if not educated, we are nothing, eh? Is that what you mean?"

Sheffield squirmed. "I do not—I am not—"

"Pah! You are nothing but talk. This is what I think of your philosophy." And with a contemptuous roar, Bean swiped his arms, left and right, across the desktop, flinging first the stack of papers and then an orderly pile of books to the floor. Sheffield's anguished squeal won no mercy, for next he went to the shelves on the wall and began ripping out books one by one, inspecting each volume with disdain before he added it to the chaos. "Pish, pash, flim, flam. Balderdash and bunkum."

"Please!" The Keeper clasped his hands as if in prayer, tears welling behind his lenses.

At this, Serafina intervened. "Enough, Ambrose. You have upset the gentleman—and he is, remember, our host."

Bean bridled, but checked his assault. Still whimpering, Sheffield hurried out from behind the desk.

"Thank you, thank you," he sobbed.

But his gratitude turned to terror, when his saviour shed her saintly smile and drew forth a silver pin.

~ ~ ~

Bean departed a shilling the poorer, but with triumph in his heart, his head held high as the clouds—and Serafina on his arm, to boot—he felt rich beyond mere material wealth. So clement was his mood, in fact, 'twas only slightly dampened by the sight of the Vice Sub-Rector Jediah Temple, who'd installed himself near the foot of the steps awaiting their return. Bean wondered if he had meant to appear inconspicuous. His agitation and hunched shoulders suggested so, though 'twould have been doomed from the start, with that deathly manner of dress.

When the pair reached the street, the Gownsman darted into their path like a third shadow, demanding anxiously, "Is it done? What we agreed?"

Serafina nodded. "Of course. I never break my word. Your Keeper is humbled as promised—reduced to a drooling babe, despoiling his precious books. His inner being now abides within the Soul-Eater." She tapped the pin adorning her *décolletage*.

Temple's eyes opened wide. "You ate his *soul*?"

"Not I. The stone. And not so much ate, as swallowed up whole. Though confined, 'tis quite unharmed."

"That cannot be. No man may direct a soul. Only God—and then only to Heaven or Hell, not into a... a woman's bauble."

"It may have come from your father's loot, but this *bauble* is no work of man." Serafina fingered the point of the pin. "And had you learned more from your teacher, you would know that the soul is a feather-brained creature and easily beguiled by pretty puzzles."

The Gownsman's pallid face took on a sickly hue; prudently, Bean stepped aside.

"He told me 'twas for his infernal machine! He said he would travel to Heaven and see Our Lord's face. 'Twas bad enough, but *this*?" The Vice Sub-Rector choked back a sob then continued, in a whisper, "Had I known, I would never have taken it. 'Tis surely the Devil's work."

Serafina shrugged. "Devil, man, God. It matters naught, for the deed is done. You may go inside and see for yourself, if you disbelieve me."

"This is not what we agreed." He took off his hat and looked to the sky in tearful despair. "All these years, all the nightmares... I thought you must have been killed, for he as good as killed himself. Or worse, he had sent you to Heaven, and God cast you down into Hell for his presumption. Then to see you again, alive, here... I would make amends for the wrongs I did *you*, not visit more wrongs on another."

"I think you delude yourself," said Bean, tiring of the man's wittering. "'Twas only last night you came to beg for absolution. You will not have forgotten already, what we asked of you in exchange: *Advise us where a Philosopher might be found*—a trifling favour, to any observer. Except, you *knew* that whomever you chose, 'twould go badly for him."

"No!"

"You held a grudge against that *Museum Keeper*! You told us yourself—'twas a wrangle over bequests agreed in word but not on paper. In light of which, you should, perhaps, have taken more care when making a deal of your own."

"That is not—"

"But we shall bear no grudges, eh? Come join us, for a celebratory toast." Bean nodded towards The King's Arms. From the Museum 'twas but a brief saunter down to the eastern end of the Broad, though from Temple's expression, he might have been asked to crawl backwards on his knees to the gates of Tartarus.

Before he could refuse, however, the street was shook by a roar from out of the Earth—or rather, Bean realized once he'd regained his wits, from the basement beneath the museum. This truly had to be diabolical in nature, or amplified through some device, for any normal exclamation could not have been heard through the heavy oak door.

"Good God, what was that?" he exclaimed.

Temple scowled. "Alchemists ply their ungodly trade in the basement, transmuting the elements fixed by Our Lord."

"More Philosophers?" Serafina arched an elegant eyebrow at Bean. "I should love to meet them. Will you introduce us, dear Jediah?"

Leaving the Gownsman to his spluttering, Bean offered his arm to his lady once more. As they descended to the yard, they came across Glenville, squatting upon the ash-grimed flagstones with his nose in a halfpenny chapbook. He shoved the pamphlet into his pocket when he heard their footsteps, then recognized them with a conspiratorial grin.

"You again! How went your tour?"

Serafina smiled back. "'Twas educational, if a little dry—all those musty dead things in boxes. I would much prefer to see them in life, conducting their natural business. Which is why—" She pointed at the door in the wall. "—we now wish to view the alchemists in their basement."

"The alchemists? You mean the *Officina Chimica*?" Glenville shook his head. "Oh no, you cannot go in there."

"Did we not discuss this before?" said Bean. "We can go wherever we will, for we are free folk and subject only to the Laws of this Land, not your University rules and regulations."

"But Dr Crouch will—"

"Dr Crouch will agree, as did your Dr Sheffield. Eventually."

Glenville rose slowly to his feet, peering from Bean to Serafina, then asked, a catch in his voice, "What have you done with Dr Sheffield?"

Serafina clapped her hands in delight. "Why, he asked the very same question of you!"

"'Tis touching," sneered Bean. "But fear not—you shall soon be reunited."

~ ~ ~

Cowley Hall could feel cold on the hottest of days, but never so icy as Mary found it that evening.

"What on Earth is Mrs Prout thinking?" she cried, dismayed not just by the temperature in Uncle Elijah's old study, but by Jediah's equally frozen manner. He hadn't responded to her arrival, or given much sign that he'd noticed her presence at all. Instead, he stood unmoving with his back to the empty fireplace, staring silently across the room, at his father's youthful portrait.

"I shall fetch her at once," she added. "This really will not do, Jediah."

"I told her not to," he said.

"Then I shall light it." She tried to edge him aside to reach for the grate, but his slippered feet appeared glued to the unbeaten hearth rug.

"Do not trouble yourself."

"I can't leave you like this! The whole house is filthy, and you will catch your death of cold. Go back to your college rooms and I will set the Prouts to work—myself as well, if needs be."

At last, he looked down at her, with a sorrowful smile.

"Ah Mary, always so kind and ready to help. That self-seeking brother of yours does not deserve you."

"Well..." Mary paused, unsettled. "I find him improved, a little, after all his recent misfortunes. Even Father has noticed, and so would you, if you'd pay us another visit. James said you came to see him yesterday. He was grateful for your help."

"My help?"

"But I am not here to talk about James. 'Tis you who worries me now. Has something happened? Last night, I saw you on North Gate Street. I did not intend to," she added, when Jediah tensed and looked back at the portrait. "You looked upset and I called your name. Did you hear me?"

"Perhaps. I felt myself confounded, as if I were trapped in the depths of the darkest well, and the Heavens spinning about me."

"Shall I fetch... someone?" Mary had no idea who that someone might be, but Jediah shook his head.

"'Tis late. You should return home, to your family."

"You are family as well. I cannot just walk on by."

"Ever the Good Samaritan."

She took hold of his chilly hand. "I'm no Good Samaritan, just... your cousin. I would help you, if you let me."

"Sometimes, tis better not to help," he murmured. "For only God knows the future, and help given today, may on another day have terrible consequences."

"What do you mean?"

But he appeared not to hear her question, saying only, to himself, "How different the lesson would be... had neither the victim nor the Samaritan been what he seemed."

CHAPTER THIRTY-NINE

THE BIRMINGHAM MAIL MARKED a turning point in my new career, though not one of which I am proud. Rather than dreading our next raid, I looked forward to it with childishly eager excitement—more so than any event in years, perhaps in my life. Or should I say, my old life. How frustrating then, when, in response to my pleas to ride the next day, Walt cautioned that we should not become too predictable.

"Better we lie low for the rest of the week," he said. "Keep them wondering when—and where—we'll strike next."

So I waited, ever-more impatient to return to the saddle (where even my steed showed me greater respect, and with regular practice I was becoming a reasonable horseman). Unlike my earliest days at The Jolly Bull, I passed the time, not in the company of Kat, but drinking and gambling in the bar, mixing with men whom James Sadler would not have dared look in the eye, let alone share an ale and a joke with. But as

Isaac Darkin I was their equal; nay, their superior—for 'twas *my* name people feared across the country!

It thus fell to Kat to seek my acquaintance, though the boys would mock me mercilessly and I always cut our encounters short. I saw the hurt in her eyes when I shunned her; I knew the pain I caused. And I did miss her affection. But if such sacrifices were needed, I decided, 'twas how it would be. A man of consequence must be ruthless, to maintain himself in that station.

The coffers by then running low, we rode again the following Thursday. This time I made sure I led from the front, and again the boys rejoiced in my return. Spirits high, we robbed the mid-morning mail coach to Oxford via Maidenhead, then Salter's Charing Cross Swift, then surpassed all with a thrilling—and highly rewarding—pursuit of the Newbury Thunderer. Our moneybags overflowed, as did my confidence.

"We shall drink deep tonight!" cried Slim, as the boys turned their horses for home.

"But 'tis early yet!" I protested. "Shall we not strike the Kidlington Star? Or the London-to-Coventry?"

The boys exchanged glances.

"In this business," said Walt, "it does not do to overextend yourself. We must take what we can while luck's on our side, then get out before it turns."

"Luck!" I scoffed. "This is a matter of skill, not happenstance. Are we not the meanest, mightiest highwaymen in all Oxfordshire?"

The boys cheered and waved their fists in the air.

"Then I say we should go for it. Let us not fear what might be, for that way lies the worst kind of oblivion. And if you wish for omens—look!"

The clear blue skies of the morning had darkened almost to dusk since the Newbury raid; the threat of a storm was, I suspected, the real reason the boys preferred to go home. But a break in the cloud had appeared while I spoke, and our hiding place was suddenly bathed in a sparkling shaft of sunlight.

"Shall we do it?" I urged.

"I have a bad feeling," said Col.

"'Tis the ale you quaffed last night."

"But we never take four in a day," said Slim. "You've always said more than three would be tempting Providence."

"May a man not change his mind?" I replied. "Let us spit in the eye of Providence, and do what we might while we live."

"How long we might live is the problem," said Walt.

"Fortune will smile while ever the Sun does," I said, then I heard a familiar clatter. "Listen! Providence agrees with me!"

Brooking no further dissent, I yelled, "Let's ride, boys!" and charged up the road. After the briefest delay, the boys followed, joining their voices with mine in a battle-cry so glorious, Diomedes would have been shamed.

The driver could hardly fail to notice us. A portly man with more pluck than most, he reined in his panicking horses, then stood in his seat and reached inside his cloak. I shouted to the boys, "I will deal with the cull—you take care of the passengers."

And then, though I'd made no conscious decision to fight, I drew my pistol from my belt and took aim between the coachman's startled eyes. How I did this and remained upright in the saddle, all the while keeping control of my galloping mount with a single hand, I shall never know. I can only surmise that the real Isaac Darkin had done this many times before, and that the memories of the motions required were somehow locked in his muscles and sinews.

"Desist or I will shoot!" I yelled.

The driver hesitated, clearly not believing I could hit him at such a tilt. With no such equivocation on my part, I spurred my steed to a breakneck pace, shifting my sights minutely, and let off a shot that whizzed past the driver's left earlobe. As I congratulated myself on this dazzling marksmanship, I realized that I would somehow now have to reload. But the coachman was even more impressed than I, for he snatched his hands from his cloak and raised them, trembling, over his head.

I stopped alongside, keeping him covered with my empty but still intimidating pistol.

"Get down from there," I ordered. "Slowly, mind."

Now as skittish as his horses, the coachman well-nigh nosedived out of his seat, so eager was he to oblige. I opened his cloak to disarm him, but found only a truncheon looped through a ring sewn into its lining. I shook my head.

"You are either very brave or very stupid," I said. "Now see to your horses. We do not want any accidents, do we?"

"Yes, Mr Darkin. No, of course, Mr Darkin."

He set about calming his team, thanking me all the while for sparing his life, praising my mercy and grace to the skies. I marvelled at what I was capable of, but this was as good as it got. For 'twas then that the day—and my life—took a downturn.

It began with the sound of a raised female voice. Not a scream of fright, nor a plea for the return of some favourite jewel, but a cry of outrage and defiance, followed by a thud and a masculine grunt of pain. I hastened to the off-side of the coach, to find Col clutching his nether parts and Masher wrestling a woman.

"You'll be sorry you did that," he growled.

She pummelled his back with fists clad in dainty lace gloves. "Get off me, you brute!"

"Put her down," I ordered. "That's not how we operate, and well you know it."

But he only glared at me mutinously and clutched his captive tighter still; I would have delivered a stern dressing-down had I not then glimpsed her face.

'Twas Lizzie.

With Masher no match for a man of my strength—or my fraternal wrath—I yanked him off my sister as one might pluck a fly from a jam-spoon, dangled him from his collar until his eyeballs bulged, then tossed him contemptuously into the ditch at the roadside.

"What did I tell you?" I snarled.

But no joyful family reunion ensued, for when I opened my arms to Lizzie, she backed away as if approached by a raving demoniac. I tried to speak her name, to swear I was sorry, but the words would not come. Perhaps I'd forgotten them. Then I recognized Burleigh, struggling with Slim at the door; I supposed that Lizzie and he had been coming to Oxford to pay us a visit. *Us?* Now that *was* madness—there was no *us*. Not since Folly Bridge, nor ever again.

Events now slowed to a crawling pace, though they still moved too fast. Through a fog of despond, I saw Burleigh break free from Slim's grip, tear off his coat, and whip out a pistol. Wondering dully why a doctor would carry a firearm—and why Slim, tasked with searching for weapons, had failed to notice it—I watched my brother-in-law take stock of we four brigands, one by one. His jaw set hard when he made his choice. Then I heard a crack, as of thunder, and a violent blow to the shoulder knocked me flat.

The Sun smiled scornfully as I gasped for breath on the road. Then the break in the clouds closed tight, and its capricious light winked out.

CHAPTER FORTY

IN THE DREARIEST DAYS OF MY SERVI-
TUDE in the Officina's vaults, when the glass-
washing and furnace-dredging had all but broken
my will to live, I had often thought of carving into my
bench, the tally marks I kept in my mind. Fear of Dr
Crouch had dissuaded me. And now I truly was in a
prison, I'd lost all sense of time. No daylight dared the
dungeon of Oxford Gaol, for daylight stands for all
that is good and true, and this netherworld, where I
seemed to have languished for years, was no home to
truth, goodness, or light.

I occupied a large cell with five other wretches: a
horse thief from Faringdon, a coiner from Wantage, a
servant who had broken the nose of his master during
an argument over his wages, a publican said to have
watered down his ale, and a defrauder of rich widows.
These villains considered their own crimes as naught
compared with mine and dubbed me a cutthroat—
which aggrieved me, for Kat had assured me that,
throughout a long career in highway robbery, Isaac
Darkin had never harmed one single victim.

My notoriety did accord me some respect, which
likely saved me from the worst that might have oc-

curred in that stinking hole—the most serious being starvation. Our warders, having families to feed, wasted no expense on their charges; indeed, inmates had to pay (and dearly!) for their own board and lodging, or have their supporters fetch food to the gaol, if they wished to remain alive 'til justice was served. With no money and no friends or family in town—or none that would know me—I would have soon starved to death had my fellow convicts not sometimes tossed me a bit of bread or a morsel of meat to sustain me.

"We shall not cheat the hangman of his fee," explained the fraudster.

There was little conversation in our lightless abode and less that I wished to join, so most of that timeless time I passed prostrate on the damp stone floor, craving the senseless embrace of sleep but unable to shut out the smell, the endless jangle of chains, and the terror that I might die in the stead of another. Would I be judged as James Sadler, I wondered, or as Isaac Darkin? 'Twas a cruel punishment, going to the gallows for the crimes of another man—but how much worse to go to Hell.

I had sworn on my arrival that I was not, in fact, the man I appeared to be; when this earned me naught but ridicule, I fell silent on the matter. Before long I could scarcely speak at all, due to the cough to which so many succumbed while locked up in the cold and damp. At first, I feared I had Gaol Fever; then, I wished I had. Better to perish in private than be hanged for a baying crowd. I had never attended an execution, but I had seen the bloodlust of many who came to the shop to purchase treats "for the show".

'Twas in this degraded state that I received my first—and only—visitor. My spirits had fallen so low, I now seldom stirred except, on occasion, to use the latrine (a fetid, straw-filled hole in the floor) and so infrequently ate the scraps my fellows provided, they had stopped doing so to save them from spoiling.

"You got a guest, Darkin," bawled the warder, a grizzled old man called Wisdom (though wise he was not, for 'twas he who had released the real Darkin—albeit persuaded by some trickery of Serafina's). "'Tis a pretty one."

He leered as the woman approached. To my befuddled mind, it seemed that the light that encircled her came not from Wisdom's lantern but from her own substance, as if she were no mere mortal but an Angel, dispatched from Above to bring succour to the damned. Sluggishly, I realized I knew her. I croaked her name, but so weakly she did not hear me.

She halted a prudent arm's length from the cell, and called with a faltering voice, "Isaac Darkin? Is that you?"

"He says he is not," said the horse thief. "But I will be him, if it please your ladyship."

The others sniggered, and I feared my Angel would be driven away before she could save me. Summoning all that remained of my strength, I raised a manacled hand and cried, "I am here! Over here!"

Wisdom hoisted the lantern higher, for a better view of my ruination. The woman wrinkled her nose, her expression reflecting the downturn in my health since our last encounter. Then she inched closer to the bars, her hands pressed protectively to her midriff.

"I came to thank you." She spoke quickly, as if her courage might run out before she completed what she had come to say. "For what you did. On the Oxford road. Rescuing me from your... assistant. I appreciate your attention was distracted, and you would never have been captured if you hadn't."

"Well, be still my bleeding heart," chortled the publican.

My left hand, shackled to the wall by a length of chain, went gingerly to its opposite shoulder. Burleigh was no marksman; his shot had inflicted naught but a nick, though the wound remained tender, and slow to heal in my squalid surroundings and lacking wholesome food to build muscle and skin.

"Be assured, I shall put in a good word for you with the magistrate—"

"Friends in high places, eh?" grunted the servant. "If only we all had such admirers."

"—I cannot say 'twill sway him, of course." Lizzie's voice grew shriller, her face redder. "But I am certain, when you are judged before God, your kindly act will not be forgot."

All five of my fellows laughed heartily at this.

"Brings a tear to the eye, does it not?" cackled the coiner.

"Is there anything else I can do for you?" Lizzie asked.

More laughter.

She frowned at the leftovers dotting the floor. "Do you need food? Clean water? I could send my maid with provisions. Daily, if you wish. Until..."

Until. Until they took me from this place of confinement and hanged me by the neck until I was dead.

"Lizzie!" I gasped. "I am not who you think I am."

"Here he goes again," groaned the horse thief.

My visitor looked up sharply. "How do you know my name?"

"I am your brother, Elizabeth. I am *James*."

Wide-eyed in alarm, she blurted, "What are you talking about? Are you mad?"

"We tell him so," said the coiner, "though he will hear nothing of it."

"You look—and smell—nothing like him," she sniffed, assuming an uppity air that ill-became her. "Besides, I saw him just an hour ago, and he was a free man then, safe at home amongst family and friends."

I scrambled on hands and knees through the festering straw, further shredding my tattered breeches. Lizzie shied backwards, though long before I reached the bars, I was jerked to a bone-shaking halt by my chains.

"Listen—"

"I think I shall not. Goodbye."

She gestured to Wisdom and whirled away, pursued by a chorus of catcalls from my companions.

I bellowed after her: "Lizzie! *Lizzie!* Do you remember the day our mother died? You'd been sent to the kitchen, with that crabby old matron from Horsemill Lane. The one who made off with lost children—so Jediah said—and boiled their bones for glue in a giant kettle. You were crying, and I didn't care why. Mary was furious. *What was it that made you so selfish, James?* That's what she said—do you remember?"

Lizzie had stopped, but not turned about. Perhaps she dare not.

"*I* remember," I cried. "And I remember because I was there."

Still she failed to act.

"The man you saw an hour ago is not your brother. You have to believe me, Lizzie."

I tried to rise, but overcome for want of food and fresh air, I toppled back to the ground, saved from fainting by the sting at my wrist as the manacle gouged my skin. I yelled in pain and frustration—which roused my sister from her stupor, for she gathered up her skirts at the sound and curtly shouldered Wisdom aside, so urgent her wish to depart.

As the flinty click of her heels faded away, I thrashed about on my back in the filth, bawling like a fractious babe. "Lizzie! Come back! Please come back! I am James! James Sadler! Son of Thomas Sadler, Pastry-cook and Confectioner of the High!"

"If you *are* James Sadler," mused the coiner, "why do you not employ your balloon to fly yourself out of this hellhole?"

"And the rest of us with you," grunted the fraudster.

They mocked me more cruelly still, but my spirit was spent. Shrivelled within and without, I subsumed myself in their laughter, which seemed like an incoming tide, and I of no greater consequence than flotsam adrift in the flow. In the eyes of these men—all men, and women too—I was a criminal, and as a criminal I would soon die. For Isaac Darkin, there would be no last-minute reprieve. The hangman's fee was due, and no one would save me now.

PART VII

CHAPTER FORTY-ONE

ATHER'S SULK DRAGGED ON FOR DAYS. On the very morning of the aerostat's exhibition, he still refused to mention it; all the more pointedly so, when James arose at dawn to meet with Rudge for their final arrangements. Without voicing a word, he made plain his affront at his son's "special breakfast", Mary's good-luck wishes, and most of all, the rapturous cheers to be heard on the High at James's departure. When Mary suggested they might attend the Town Hall later, he ignored her.

Mid-morning, a band of confectioners and pastry-cooks arrived at the shop uninvited. Father smiled for almost the first time since the Mayor's visit, for the Guild Master's election was but a few days away.

"You must all come upstairs at once," he declared. "Mary will prepare us a spread, and we'll talk sweetmeats and pies until dinner."

"You are most hospitable," said Mr Twigg of the Turl. "But we are not stopping. We are on our way to the Town Hall, and thought you might escort us."

"Me? Escort you?"

"We hoped we might save our entrance fees, by arriving with a relative of the exhibitor," explained a bombon-vendor from out of town whose name Father failed to recall.

"Frankly, I am surprised you are not there already," added Mr Robinson, of Robinson & Robinson of Ship Lane.

"I am sure he wishes he were," said Mrs Winstable. "But even the proudest papa must always consider his customers first."

"Aye, that is so," Father sighed. "I would have dearly wished to accompany my only son on this, his greatest day. But through no fault of his or mine, the timing is inconvenient—I must toil every hour God sends, for the Bursar of St Alban's requires his comfits early this year."

The confectioners and pastry-cooks marvelled amongst themselves at their colleague's devotion to duty, while Mrs Winstable took his hand in hers.

"Poor Thomas!" she cooed. "Of course, this settles the matter. You must take pause before you wear yourself down to a crumb. You will be no good to business nor family, collapsed like an undercooked sugar puff."

Father nodded, raising a cheer from the Guildsmen. "Perhaps you are right." As he fetched his coat and hat, he called up to Mary, "I am off to the Town Hall. Leave the ledgers for later and come mind the shop."

Mary appeared at the top of the stairs, red-eyed from lack of sleep and the hours she'd laboured already that day checking credits and debits, expenses and profits, all chronicled in her father's tiny hand. His colleagues, however, mistook her fatigue for despair.

"Have pity on the girl!" they demanded. "She must come too!"

"Our pastries are exceptional," said Father, "but not so clever they will sell themselves."

Mr Robinson regarded him earnestly. "Surely 'tis the Sadlers' finest hour, at least since you were appointed Supplier of Comfits. Will your daughter be denied a seat at the table?"

Father shuddered at the thought of that particular Benefaction—and that posterity might know the family best for balloons instead of its pastries. Nonetheless, he wavered.

"What of our customers?"

"Come, Thomas," chided Mrs Winstable. "What is a few hours' trade compared with your daughter's happiness? She weeps like a babe, look!"

Mary scrubbed at her eyes, abashed. "'Tis but a speck of dust," she tried to explain, but her words were drowned by another cheer, when Father surrendered again.

"Very well, very well. But she must return once the speeches are done. We are pastry-cooks, not adventurers, at heart, and no Sadler—nor anyone else—should ever forget so."

~ ~ ~

The confectioners' march up the High was sluggish, being conducted at the pace of their most ancient and laggardly member. Mary itched to run on ahead, and might have done so when at last they turned onto Fish Street, except then they were stopped altogether.

A huge mass of people had clogged the road, converging from north and south along the outer Town Hall wall, all bound for the same narrow entrance like a gigantic camel wringing itself through the eye of a minuscule needle. Those who failed to gain admittance were buffeted backwards into the road—to the vexation of passing waggoners and coachmen, though these drivers' remonstrations were barely heard above the tumult. Some disaster was surely at hand, and indeed, as the Sadlers' party joined the throng, a lady fainted ahead of them, and shouts went up that the crowd stand back for fear she might be trampled.

"No pastry-cook or confectioner's shop has ever drawn such a queue!" shouted Mr Robinson.

"Perhaps we were too hasty to condemn him," mused Mr Twigg.

"Your boy is a hero!" cried Mrs Winstable, grasping Father's arm.

"I should have liked to meet him," grumbled the bombon-vendor, "but at this rate we shall still be here next Tuesday, and I have a business to run."

"You cannot leave now. See how far we have come!" Mr Twigg pointed first to Carfax and then to the entrance, which in truth looked no nearer than when they'd arrived. "Think of the tale you will tell your grandchildren."

The elder Sadler spluttered at this, though his words—perhaps for the best—were indistinct. Meanwhile, the bombon-vendor decided to stay after all, which was a fortunate choice, for minutes later an Alderman arrived with a team of helpers to organize the crowd and the queue began to advance more smoothly. As they funnelled down Fish Street, Mary managed to move ahead of her companions, though she won her freedom only when they finally reached the courtyard.

The Town Hall could have never seen so many visitors—not for the annual Corporation Ball nor even the busiest polling days (My Lord Spencer and Capt.

Bertie being safe in their seats for several Parliaments now and, unlike a certain Tho. Sadler of the High, having no need of electioneering). The horde of Town and Gown had been further swelled by Corn Exchange traders, while at Mr Nixon's Free Grammar School, the clerestory windows were crammed with youthful faces, all jockeying for the clearest view.

The focus of their attention had been inflated the previous night to its maximum, majestic girth and was tethered to a scaffold in the centre of the courtyard, straining at its reins like a high-strung colt. James stood close at hand, as if his presence might calm the balloon, and had attracted no less attention than his handiwork. Supporters vied on all sides to engage him in trite conversation, or pat him on the back, or praise him for his derring-do—along with the odd naysayer. Mary heard one bracket-faced gent explaining how misfortunes always insist on occurring in threes, and that Sadler's exploits, coming so close upon the Brick Tax and the loss of our American Colonies, were undoubtedly doomed to disaster.

Despite the hubbub, James noticed Mary straight away, and greeted her with a genuine kiss on the cheek. Mary blushed; he had never done *that* before.

"You came after all," he whispered.

"We should thank the Guild for that. Father would swear black were white if it won him a vote. But what about you? How are you coping with all this to-do?"

He gave her a lopsided smile. "The to-do I can cope with. My problem is the people—everyone claims to know me, while I know the name of none. How am I to distinguish my true friends, from those who hope to gain some advantage through flattery?"

"I can help you with their names," Mary said, "but not their motivations, I'm afraid."

He squeezed her hand. "You are such an innocent, dearest."

She had no idea what to say to that, but was interrupted by the swaggering arrival of a Gownsman she knew all too well.

"This is no friend," she muttered. "'Tis Edwin Osborne, of your Philosophical Club."

Before she could explain further, the student was upon them. James offered his hand, but Osborne ignored it.

"You have pulled quite a mob," the student sneered. "A pity your wager with Bean is already lost."

James grinned affably. "From what I have heard of *your* mob, the loss was all yours."

With a scowl, Osborne retreated into the concourse.

"Oh James!" Mary giggled. "That showed him. But you loved that club. You called it your own."

James shrugged. "What you have never known, you cannot miss." Casting about for familiar figures, he spotted one lurking beneath the peristyle of the Corn Exchange; he had the look of a man lying low, with his hunched shoulders and downcast gaze, but even clad in his cleanest trousers he appeared glaringly out of place amongst the nattily turned-out traders. "Has Rudge fallen out with us? He seemed happy enough when I got here."

"I expect he saw Father arrive." Excusing herself from her brother, Mary returned to her father, who was swapping handshakes and gossip with all who would share. Behind the banter, she detected a grudging respect for James's accomplishments—albeit swayed by the views of his peers.

"How lucky you are, to have such a son!" gushed one.

"'Tis not luck," averred another. "For behind every great man, stands an even greater father."

"Tell us your secret, Thomas—how did you come to raise such a sterling heir?"

Father beamed like a beacon, until someone else enquired, "Now James is a famous aeronaut, who will take over the shop when you are retired?"

His smile became more forced after that, his manner a little less merry, and it seemed his day had soured 'til the entrance of Lizzie and Burleigh revived him.

"'Tis my younger daughter and her husband," he announced, adding, "Burleigh is a physician, you know—a professional man of great learning and skill. His practice is the most renowned in all of London—"

"Shush, Father!" scolded Lizzie. "His head is already quite swollen enough."

"With good reason," Burleigh grumbled.

As the three of them exchanged embraces, Sadler cried, "It has made my day, having you two here!"

"'Twould not have been so, had Isaac Darkin got his way," said Burleigh, adding for the benefit of his father-in-law's associates, "This Thursday past, we fell afoul of that notorious highwayman and his gang on the Oxford road."

Sadler laid an arm around his shoulders. "Burleigh is too modest to tell the full tale. The truth is, he dared to defy the villains' demands, and with his quick thinking and steady aim saved the lives of all present, not to mention their valuables. Thanks to Burleigh, Darkin shall never again terrorize innocent travellers. For the wretch was returned to gaol, and will soon meet his well-deserved fate—and be judged by his Maker."

A round of applause ensued, and it occurred to the watching Mary that her father's praise flowed more freely for his son-in-law's deeds than his son's.

"You must be so proud of your husband!" Mrs Winstable squealed, but Lizzie's response was a shudder.

"I would rather be ashamed of a living husband than proud of a dead one. 'Twas a dreadfully foolish thing to do. The man was armed, for goodness sake! But Burleigh has promised to be less brave the next time we are assaulted. Now, let us change the subject—please!"

"Death and disaster," said Mr Twigg, "man's constant companions. They never stray far from our side, be we enjoying our leisure, natural or unnatural—" He indicated Burleigh and Lizzie as an example of the first; the aerostat for the second. "—or simply about our gainful employment. Consider those various Gownsmen—colleagues of your brother, in fact—so queerly struck down in pursuit of their studies—"

This tale was no news to Mary; a succession of customers had acquainted her with the details, each retelling more lurid than the last. She slipped away to find James again. Escaped from his admirers, he had also taken himself off alone, and reclined against the rear wall of the school, oblivious to the ogling boys in the windows above.

"Would you mind if I were to sit with you?" Mary asked. "Just for a moment?"

"Why in Heavens' name should I mind?" James fanned the flags with a rolled-up sheet of paper, cleaning a space for her in the dust. "I was practising my speech. Rudge insisted I write it down, lest I forget the best parts. I told him I would speak better without restraint—*extempore*, as they call it—but he made plain that I do as he say..." He stopped and regarded his sister. "What troubles you, dearest?"

"'Tis nothing. Or if not nothing, then less to me than to others."

"I have known you only a little while—or so it seems to me—but long enough to read your temper. Do tell me. It may lighten your load."

"I did not intend to spoil your speech."

James smiled. "Well, now you have *me* worried, too. Better tell me, or I may lose my nerve when I mount the stage, and perform drier than a box of Father's parched almonds."

Mary almost laughed. "Then perhaps I must, before you hear it from someone else."

"Go on."

With a nervous glance from beneath her bonnet, she began: "People have been talking about a... mishap at your laboratory. Dr Crouch, Nugent, Wilkes, and the rest are all done away with. Not dead," she added. "Nor even injured, but lacking all rational action and speech, as if trapped in a waking dream, they say. Dr Sheffield was stricken as well, and his assistant. 'Tis said a poisonous air of Crouch's design infested the building, having escaped from its container. There were no townsfolk in the collections at the time, thank goodness, but some accuse the University of endangering the whole city, and are demanding they close the laboratory."

James watched her intently, but not with the shock she'd expected; his expression, if anything, said, *Is that* all? When he spoke, he sounded indifferent.

"You are right. 'Twas quite a mishap."

Even on the best of days, Crouch could be, Mary knew, a right-royal botheration. But James might have been talking of strangers.

"You really don't remember, do you?"

"I am glad I do not," he replied. "For then I would know how badly I treated you, and that would pain me greatly." He brushed her burning cheek with the back of one hand, then said, "We will talk later. For now, my audience awaits." He nodded towards the crowd, now massing around the podium on the far side of the courtyard. "Wish me luck."

She watched him stride boldly through the horde, this man who looked like her brother and sounded like her brother, but spoke and acted and moved nothing like him. And she, too, felt far from her usual self. For her heart had begun to flutter, and it had never done that before.

CHAPTER
FORTY-TWO

W HEN NEITHER COLLEGE AFFAIRS
nor pacing the cloister provided the peace
he craved, Jediah Temple took himself off
into town, though he had no errand to run, nor acquaintance to meet, nor distance to cover in mind; he
had no aim at all, in fact, save the silencing of thought
with senseless action.

His wanderings took him to Fish Street, where he
was startled by a sudden, tumultuous clamour. Had
God taken pity upon him at last, and chosen to strike
him down? When the noise subsided a little, and he
found himself unharmed and still stopped in the road,
he realized it had come, not from Heaven, but from
the Town Hall, and comprised not Divine wrath but a
multitude of human voices raised in some violent emotion, be it ecstasy, terror, or worse.

"What—what was that?" he exclaimed, addressing
no one in particular, though a doorman chose to
respond.

"Have you been sleeping these several days past? 'Tis the aeronaut James Sadler and his famous globe, of course."

"James Sadler? My cousin?"

"*This* James Sadler is a Townsman. I doubt *you* would know him."

The doorman did not trouble to hide his disdain; normally, Jediah would have rebuked him for lack of respect.

"He is here?"

"Aye, that is what I said."

"With his globe?"

The attendant rolled his eyes. "Pay tenpence like everyone else and you may find out for yourself."

Meekly, Jediah fumbled for the fee. He did not need to ask where to head once inside, for the commotion, though diminished, rumbled on. He lurched blindly towards its source, as if impelled by an unseen hand—until, upon taking a corner, he collided with a woman travelling just as fast in the opposite direction, and with no more attention than he.

"Beg pardon, sir!" she gasped, red-faced. "I did not mean to— Jediah! What are you doing here?"

Jediah steadied himself against the wall, feeling all at once lightheaded. "I do—I am... not sure. An urgent need for fresh air, perhaps? A walk to stretch my limbs? I have been... not myself, of late."

"I was right to worry." Mary directed him into the chamber from which she'd emerged. One wainscoted wall housed an ornate oaken fire-piece, above it a shelf of tankards and flagons fashioned in pewter and silver-gilt; a low wooden bench ran the length of the opposite wall, and here she sat him down, her coaxing and nudgings gentle but insistent.

"When last I saw you, you seemed very... distant. Almost as if you were not fully there."

Jediah struggled to recall it, though he knew 'twas the day his perdition began. "Forgive me if my mood disturbed you. I did not intend so."

"I am a Sadler. It takes more than a testy mood to disturb me. I'm just happy to see you out and about—and feeling a little better, maybe?"

"Hardly better." Jediah sighed. "Today I tried to draft my St Alban's Day sermon, but no benedictions would flow from my pen, only guilty recriminations. I feel I am living a nightmare—one of my own design, from which I shall never awake."

Mary frowned, but not at him, as if briefly caught up in another concern. Then she stirred herself and said, "If you cannot remember... we talked of parables, and morals depending on motives. Such ominous things. What has *happened* to you, Jediah?"

"A great weight has fallen upon me."

"You may share it with me, if that would help."

"I shall share the beginning of it, if you wish, for I would not trouble you to hear the full story."

"I would not mind," she said, with a squeeze of his hand for encouragement.

"Very well." Several moments passed before he spoke again, and then reluctantly. "'Twas the spring of the year I first went up to St Alban's. My father wished me to meet my tutor-to-be, come that Michaelmas Term. He'd been my father's tutor as well, and they'd become friends, of a sort. On the way, I passed a young girl in Alban Lane, lying in the kennel, bloody and beaten. I dearly wished to walk by, for I would be late for my appointment if I stopped, and she appeared in every way so thoroughly filthy, so contemptible. And besides, she could have been dead, and then whatever I did, 'twould be pointless."

He glanced up at the silverware over the mantel, catching sight of his reflection in the fat, polished belly of a loving-cup.

"Then I heard her speak," he went on, closing his eyes. "Barely a whisper, begging for help. 'Twas no one else around, and even if there were, I expect they would have felt the same as I. She opened her eyes, and I knew straight away I must do as she asked. She was younger than I and had barely no flesh on her bones—'twas easy to carry her up to the porter's lodge. There, I found the tutor, awaiting me. He took the matter out of my hands, and I felt such relief. We would meet a different day, he said, for the girl's condition was perilous. So he took her away, and I returned home."

Mary frowned at this conclusion. "It seems to me, what you did was entirely proper. You hesitated at first, but 'tis understandable. You were not much more than a child yourself, in an alarming situation, and you made the right choice in the end."

"Did I?" Jediah continued quickly, before he could think the better of it. "Later, I learned 'twas the girl's father who had assaulted her. They were vagabond folk—members of a troupe of fairground conjurers and other tricksters. Such people, I have heard, live by a harsh code of honour, which she, though a child, had somehow conspired to break. Knowing all too well what her father was capable of, she had run away to save herself."

"Oh Jediah, I do not know what to say—"

"I also learned, that when her father discovered her whereabouts, he sought out my tutor and offered to sell her to him, so she might be taken off his hands and he could recoup but a small portion of his expenses for bringing her up. A deal my tutor accepted."

"'Tis a terrible story. That poor, poor girl, to have such a father, and then to fall into the clutches of... well..." Mary shuddered. "But I still see no fault in *you.*"

"As I said, 'twas only the start."

She leaned closer, but Jediah flinched away, unable to meet her gaze.

"Whatever has happened," she said, "you could not have predicted it when you saved the girl. No man could—you said so yourself, last time we met. Only God knows the future."

"Last time we met, I fear I did not make much sense."

"'Tis not so long since your father died. We might believe the blows of the past lie safe behind us, but they can strike us again any time, whenever we least expect it, and more painfully than before."

Jediah realized he had removed his hat at some point, and had been thoughtlessly warping and winding its brim. He smoothed out the fabric and returned it to his head, with a smile of his own. "You talk good sense, as always. When we spoke at Cowley Hall, I do remember talk of a visit. It seems a long time since I saw you all together."

"You must come by whenever you wish."

"I had feared I would not be welcome. 'Twas wrong of me, to betray your brother's confidence—more so, since it seems to have been the start of his recent troubles. I wished to apologize, but he clearly remembers nothing of it."

"I am sure, if he remembered, he would say there was naught to forgive. He is different now."

Jediah jumped at yet another roar from the crowd; even louder than the first, and very much closer. "They are cheering... for *him*?"

Mary glanced towards the source of the ructions. "Who knew he could speak so well?" she said, with an unexpected hint of despair.

"He speaks of his aerial globe?"

"His globe, and the future, and all that men shall achieve on this Earth and beyond it."

Jediah tugged a handkerchief from his cloak and pressed it into her hands, though she did not use it.

"Then why the tears?" he asked. "Are you not pleased by your brother's achievement? If that is what you consider it."

At the far end of the chamber, a man of official appearance peered in; at Mary and Jediah first, then at the silverware.

"I fear 'twill take him away from me," Mary said when the man had passed by. "That his head will be turned by success. Or worse still... well, ballooning is not the safest of occupations. 'Tis selfish, I know, but I could not bear to lose him, just when I seem to have found him for the first time."

Jediah smiled fondly. "Love bears, believes, hopes, and endures all things. It seeks not its own, and rejoices in the truth. Truly, no man can love God, who fails to love his brother."

"I think..." Mary whispered, "I love him a little *too* much."

Jediah's smile froze on his face.

"Forgive me. I shouldn't bother you with my family troubles, when you..." She stood awkwardly and brushed herself down, though the bench was not dusty. "I must get back. I do not suppose I'll be missed, but I'd like to be there when James finishes."

She kissed him on his cheek before she departed.

"Thank you for listening. And do not forget to visit us soon."

Jediah touched his fingertips to his skin; gingerly, as if he'd been burned. Then he fled the way he had come, the truth unfurling before him like a sickly scented bloom.

"Seen all you wanted?" the doorman remarked.

"All that I needed," said Jediah.

~ ~ ~

Back in the courtyard, the crowd packed ever more tightly around the podium, all clamouring for a closer view of their hero; James held his own, but precariously, like a shipwrecked sailor clung on a rock in a storm. When Mary first saw the scene, she feared for his safety, shocked to realize that fame carried risks on the ground as well as in flight. She skirted around the edge of the crowd, to the far side of the courtyard so she might see her brother face on and judge how he fared.

'Twas then she saw Edwin Osborne and one of his cronies, scrambling like huge ungainly spiders up the tethers securing the aerostat. Given their location, and with the crowd's attention focussed on the podium, Mary realized she was the only one aware that they were there. The only one who had seen the glint of the knife in Osborne's hand.

"Stop!" She picked up her petticoats and raced to the aerostat's rescue. "Stop that at once, I tell you!"

A few people at the rear of the crowd turned when they heard the commotion.

"'Tis sabotage!" she shouted. "Look—they are on the aerostat!"

She grasped one of the ropes and tugged it fiercely, as if to shake them down like bad fruit from a tree. But before she could dislodge him, Osborne descended by himself and grabbed her by the shoulders, shaking her savagely.

"Shut up!" he snarled,.

She struggled, yelping in pain as his fingers dug deeper. Then the hands were ripped away, and James stood between them.

"How dare you!" he yelled. "How dare you lay your filthy paws on her!"

"'Tis pitiful," Osborne jeered, "to see the dog so quick to jump at the bitch's bark."

Without reply, James smashed a fist in his face—to cheers and hoots of laughter from their audience.

"Is this part of the show?" someone shouted. "Had I known, I'd have stumped up a shilling."

Osborne was back on his feet in an instant and would have come at James again without the good sense of his crony, who hastened to hold him back.

"Leave it, Edwin," the Gownsman hissed. "He's not worth the trouble."

Osborne shook him off and collected himself with a scowl.

"We shall thank you to leave now," said James.

Osborne spat a bright bead of blood in the dirt. "The pleasure shall all be mine, I assure you. Ten-pence?" He snarled at the aerostat. "I wouldn't spend the horseshit on my shoe. But I *will* get my money's worth."

"Let's go, Edwin. If the Bulldogs—"

"Stuff the Bulldogs. Shall I slink away in disgrace like a scolded cur?" He fixed James with a steely glare. "My honour is offended and I therefore demand satisfaction."

"Is that a good idea?" his associate murmured.

"Of course, the very best." Osborne raised his voice so all could hear. "James Sadler, pastry-boy of the High, I challenge you to a duel—the time and place to be arranged in the usual fashion, the matter decided by death. What say you, Sadler? Are you man enough to accept?"

"My God, James," cried Mary, her heart pounding its fiercest yet. "You cannot agree."

"I can and I will." An odd smile played about James's lips, as boldly he declared, "Edwin Osborne, windbag of no significance, I accept your challenge. A duel to the death 'twill be. And I trust the best marksman will win."

~ ~ ~

When Jediah came to the shop, the Sadler party had not yet returned, having been, as their journeyman informed him, "Delayed by the flummery of the Mayor and his worthies, who know a vote-winner when they see it."

"I shall wait upstairs," Jediah replied.

"They could be some time."

"I have plenty of that."

He bypassed the parlour and climbed to the attic.

'Twas darker than he'd expected. At this hour of day, though the sky remained bright, the tiny rooflight admitted the barest sliver of sunshine, so he kindled a rush and waited, perched stiffly upon the unmade bed.

383

He'd known this house so well as a boy; now he realized he'd entered the attic not once since Anne Sadler's funeral. Dusk had come so early that evening. He remembered the smothering gloom, that foolish struggle; James rejecting the Lord for human vainglory. The Sadlers, he decided, had always been prone to ungodliness. Even Mary, whom he would least have expected to fall. He shuddered to think of the look in her eyes when she spoke of her brother. In fleeing one monstrous sin, he had stumbled upon another worse still—yet this surely meant that God had not abandoned him. For by saving his relatives' souls, he might atone for his own transgressions.

As the journeyman promised, time passed, and Jediah's restlessness increased. He dwelled on St Alban's Day and his unwritten sermon, then paced about the floorboards, his frustration mounting until, on taking a left turn instead of a right, he came upon another memory hidden away in the shadows—this one in physical form. A dusty, aged book, discarded upon a heap of odds and ends in an overlooked corner.

After all those years, James still had it. Jediah took the book and blew a thick cloud of dust from its cover. He had lied—another sin to be weighed against him—when he'd said he had read the last page. Despite his schoolmaster's efforts, his Latin had been weak when he went up to college; he'd invented his claim that the author had failed in his quest and was mocked to his grave. The story might well have ended with a spectacular success, though Jediah doubted it. Men would never ascend to the Moon. 'Twas impossible.

He laid the book aside, with a final glance at the fly-leaf. However misguided Anne Sadler's beliefs, she always put her son first. Would that the Temples had done half as much...

And with that single thought, other memories he'd tried to forget were tossed up, like great jagged rocks in a storm. The mother he barely knew. Wyndham Rudge, dearer to him than his father, until... He squeezed shut his eyes, as if sightless he might forget again, but the scene was seared on his soul and he would never be free from the shame. His father's new wife and oldest friend, the breathless heat of the desert, the stench of sweat—

"Stop!"

He grabbed Anne Sadler's book and flung it hard and fast at the wall; it hit a crossbeam with a thud and dropped to the floor, where it sagged like a broken dead bird, spine snapped and boards sheared from its carcass. And there, amidst the muddled leaves, a letter poked out from the binding, its withered wax seal smashed to bits by the fall.

The ink, when he dared to open the letter, was faded, the hand and style unschooled. But the voice it evoked in his head sounded oddly familiar. He did not read far, before he realized why.

Then he raised his face to the rooflight, eyes burning with furious tears. In his fist, the letter crumpled. If only he could, by force alone, crush the news it contained from existence.

CHAPTER FORTY-THREE

T HE SADLER PARTY HAD HAPPIER NEWS at the end of their hectic day. 'Twas an announcement from the Guildhouse, where (having seen which way the wind had blown) all candidates for the Mastership had withdrawn themselves to a man, and thus was Thomas Sadler, Pastry-cook and Confectioner of the High, returned unopposed.

To celebrate his victory, the Master-Elect had brought his allies back for tea, and with his three offspring and his son-in-law by his side, he could not, he declared, have been one iota happier had the Prince of Wales himself dropped by for a cup.

"Which can only be a matter of time," Mrs Winstable remarked. "Your praise will soon be sung throughout the land—and to top it all, 'tis St Alban's Day tomorrow, where your rise to fame began."

"I have had a marvellous idea!" exclaimed Mr Twigg, with a start that jiggled a chocolate puff from his tea-plate onto the carpet. "When James constructs his next aerostat, be sure to paint your name and profession in tall, bright letters upon the surface of the globe—with a likeness of your cheesecake, perhaps. So when he flies about the country, everyone will see it, and your fame will truly be boundless."

Mary grimaced—at both the mess and the idea—expecting a scornful response from her father. But he raised his teacup to Mr Twigg, and said to James, "Perhaps that can be arranged, eh son?"

James smiled and nodded. "Perhaps."

"I would not risk it, if I were you," cautioned Mr Robinson. "Birds might mistake the painting for a genuine cheesecake, and by pecking at the globe bring its flight to a tragic halt. And imagine the panic if simple folk on the ground made a similar error. Such persons, I would hazard, are ill-prepared for the sight of a flying sweetmeat the size of a waggon."

The Sadlers, father and son, exchanged sidelong glances then burst into laughter. Not since Mother died had Mary seen the pair so at ease with each other. Were the years of bad feeling forgotten, she wondered, now James's deeds might prove to his father's advantage?

Scolding herself for that uncharitable thought, she restocked the refreshments and took the tea tray back to the kitchen. She busied herself with the dishes, 'til Lizzie slipped into the room, her modish dress jarringly out of place with the pots and pans.

"Will you rejoin us?" she asked, with a look of concern. "You are quiet today."

Mary almost snapped, *Am I not always?* but stayed her tongue; at least her sister cared to ask.

Then Lizzie continued, "James asked that I attend you. Our self-centred brother, so caring. Not like him at all."

Mary shrugged and returned to the dishes.

"But that is the least of it, don't you think?" Lizzie pulled up a chair and sat at the table, her elbows on the well-scrubbed top and her chin propped in her hands, as if she were a child again. "He seems... *different* since I last saw him."

"Different?" Mary laughed a little giddily. "I have not noticed."

"You see him every day, so maybe you would not."

"Yes, that must be it."

"Though even you must admit—he has never before fought a duel."

"What he did this afternoon," Mary murmured, "was rather brave, I think."

"Of course, that student was unforgivably beastly to you. But accepting his *challenge*... What was James thinking?"

"I expect it will not come down to a fight. He will find a way around it."

"Well, we must hope so." Lizzie tapped a fingernail on the table, then picked at a knot in the wood. "Speaking of James... Well, not of *him*, exactly... I had a strange experience at the gaol the other day."

"You went to the gaol?" Lizzie lowered her voice. "Do not mention it to Burleigh, but I wished to thank Isaac Darkin for saving *me* from brutish behaviour. I thought if I confronted him with the glimmer of good in his heart, he might be consoled while he dwells on his fate."

Mary turned away so Lizzie would not see her face. "That was... thoughtful of you."

"I almost wish I had not, for he frightened me after that."

"What did he do?"

"'Twas not what he did, but what he said. He told me—he *insisted*—that he is not Isaac Darkin at all, but James Sadler."

"*Our* James Sadler?"

"The very same."

"I expect he hoped to talk himself out of his cell— 'twas how he escaped before, I have heard. Or perhaps he is simply mad."

"His cellmates think so. As did I, until..." Lizzie hesitated. "He knew my name. And certain details from James's past."

Mary continued washing the dishes. "'Tis the nature of fame, I suppose. Everyone presumes to know your business."

"But these were private details, things only James and I could possibly know."

"Our brother has kept some strange company lately, so who can say what might have been said, or to whom?"

Lizzie sighed. "I suppose you are right." She stopped picking at the knot and spread her hand upon the table; from her station by the basin, Mary spied a gleam of gold.

"I think Father may pass the shop to him soon. 'Tis time he retired, and now James is in favour again... But what will *you* do, sister? Will you continue to keep house here?"

"Do I have a choice?"

Lizzie hesitated. "Well, I don't know. Is there—is there anyone I should know about, perhaps? Anyone special?"

A teacup slipped from Mary's grasp and splashed back into the basin. "What do you mean?" she demanded, wheeling about with such uncommon fire that Lizzie was briefly struck dumb.

"I did not mean—I simply thought... It seems to me that *you* are different, too. You have a look about you... a restlessness I have not seen before." She dropped her gaze, embarrassed by Mary's reaction. "Forgive me, I did not intend to pry. Burleigh and I were concerned for you, that is all."

"You and Burleigh discussed my private life?"

Lizzie pursed her lips. "We discussed nothing. 'Twas only mentioned in passing."

"*In passing?* And that should make me feel better?"

"Of course not! I mean, that is to say—"

"Say nothing Lizzie, for I am hardly worth even that small effort. You just said so yourself."

"I said no such—"

"And if you are short of time to attend to *my* business, you may gain more if you mind your own."

Lizzie began to respond, though with apologies or objections would never be known, for then they heard the bang of a door flying open overhead, followed by footsteps down the stairs. Together, they turned in time to see a tall, gaunt figure in black descend like a raging storm upon the parlour.

"Was that cousin Jediah?" Lizzie brightened at the sudden change of subject. "I wondered if we would see him today. But what was he doing upstairs?"

"I don't think Father invited him," Mary said, with a stab of guilt.

"In that case, we must make him extra welcome!"

They found the occupants of the parlour in a state of uneasy bemusement. Jediah stood centre stage, scrutinizing each in turn with the beady eye of a carrion crow picking the tastiest morsel. He greeted Lizzie and Mary with a bleakly distracted smile.

"Come, nephew—join our celebration," said Mr Sadler, proffering a teacup and saucer. "'Tis a day for cheesecake, shared amongst our dear friends and family alike!"

"*Family?*" Something seemed to snap, and Jediah snarled when he rounded on his uncle. "*You* dare speak of family?"

Sadler frowned. "Everyone knows my family is more precious to me than... anything."

His pastry-cooks and confectioners confirmed this as one; his offspring, meanwhile, looked nervously between themselves. Jediah smirked.

"I see your children are unconvinced. But... *are* they your children? We both know one is not, but perhaps that is true for the others as well. Perhaps your wife adopted every passing bastard that stirred her pity."

Sadler staggered backwards into his armchair.

"What is he talking about?" Lizzie added a shrill cry to the gasps of shock sounding all around. "Father? *Father?*"

Burleigh leaned in close to murmur, "Perhaps 'tis time we were leaving, my pet."

"'Tis time you knew the truth," Jediah growled. "All of you—dear friends and family alike!—must hear it." Seeing Burleigh motioning Lizzie towards the door, he added, with indecent glee, "Do not fear, good Doctor—your wife at least is no more than she appears: the shopkeeper's girl passing off as a lady. 'Tis your brother-in-law you will find inconvenient."

All eyes turned to James, who responded with a smile.

"Inconvenient? Kinder than most of the names I've been called."

Jediah turned again on Sadler. "You never told a soul, did you? The deal was done between you, your wife, and my stepmother, and they both took the secret to their graves."

Sadler buried his face in his hands. "I am sorry, so sorry," he moaned. "Your mother wished to tell you when you were older, but then she was gone, and I did not dare. 'Twas all for the best, I swear. Or so I believed... What else could we do? They were family..."

His Guildsmen gazed embarrassed in all directions: at the wilting spread on the tea-table; at the knick-knacks and lacy doilies; at the mantle-clock, deaf and blind to the cares of men, as it counted down their brief and troublesome lives. Anywhere, in fact, except at the faces of the players in the drama. Apart from Mr Twigg, who could scarcely contain his excitement.

"In Heaven's name, Thomas, what does this mean?"

"It means," said Jediah, relishing the moment, "this so-called *aeronaut*–" He spat the word at James. "–is not, as all have assumed, Thomas Sadler's son and heir. As Jacob learned with Esau, appearances can be deceptive."

And before anyone could enquire further, he snatched a crumpled paper from his cloak, and began a contemptuous declamation.

"*Dearest James. When you read these words, you will already know the truth, so I shall not speak any more of the past, except to say it is done with and now we must look to the future. I have given this letter to Mrs Sadler, so she might give it to you when she thinks you are ready. The decision is hers, for she has raised you and knows you best, and I am only your Aunt Rebecca, though I hope we are friends, and that you understand why I had to give you up, and forgive me for what I have done. Be certain your Uncle Elijah can never know what has happened, for that would be the end of him and he is a good man who does not deserve what I did, and what your daddy Wyndham did too, being his companion for so long. But I pray to the Father of us all that you will bear me no malice, and that we can still have visitings together and be as cordial as our circumstances allow. The exchanges I most long to share must go unspoken, but you shall always hold a special place in my heart, for you are my firstborn and naught shall ever change that. And now I must say goodbye, dearest James, for your new mama is waiting. Perhaps we shall abide together in Heaven, but wherever Fate may take us in this unhappy life, be sure I shall ever remain... Your true and affectionate* Mother."

Jediah paused, his audience stunned into silence. "I do not know which is worse—the ill-formed calligraphy or her cumbrous way with words. Regardless, my stepmother is doubly guilty, compounding her adultery with a deception no less devious than that of her Biblical namesake, and with the aid of my traitorous relatives."

Withered away in his favourite chair, Thomas Sadler whimpered, "Anne only wished to protect your father."

"The road to Hell is paved with good intentions," Jediah said, with an air of finality. Then, he turned to Mary. "Cousin, you do not seem upset that your parents misled you. Although, this news suits you nicely, does it not?"

Mary jumped in alarm, while James, who had somehow remained unruffled throughout, moved to stand beside her protectively.

"Leave her alone," he said. "She has no argument with you."

Jediah responded with a sinister chuckle. "Ah, the power of brotherly love! Not something *I* have ever known, of course. Or... is there more to it than that?"

James and Mary exchanged glances, while Mr Twigg implored, "There is *more?* Tell us now, man, and be done with this needless prevarication."

With immense satisfaction, as if a plan forever in the making had finally come to fruition, Jediah folded his arms on his chest and regarded the entire room with a look of disgust, as if all were somehow culpable in what he would now divulge: doilies, teacups, and humans alike.

"Very well, I shall say it plainly. And let the good name of the Sadlers—if they still have one—be ground forever into the dust. For their elder daughter and mountebank son are embarked upon a relationship most inappropriate for a man and woman who, until this evening, considered themselves brother and sister."

The hushed unrest turned to gasps of horror.

"As spake the Prophet Isaiah: *Your iniquities have separated you from your God, and your sins have hid His face from you, that He will not hear.* 'Tis assured," Jediah continued, twisting the knife a little further, "this monstrous pair will burn in Hell—for he who makes himself a crooked path shall never know peace."

"Can this be true?" Sadler whispered, his face a blank and bloodless mask as he looked from Mary to James, though he met the gaze of neither.

Mary saw the same question, unspoken, in James's eyes.

"How can you believe that?" she cried, and weeping, fled from their sight.

CHAPTER
FORTY-FOUR

W HEN OUT TO TAKE THE AIR that afternoon, Serafina D'Bonaventura and Ambrose Bean's leisurely pace belied the sinister drift of their converse.

"How many of them are there, do you suppose?" Serafina wondered.

'Twas hard to count even the modest crowd that obstructed their walk down the Turl. The squawking, squabbling, formless mass of ermine and Ottoman silk seemed utterly lacking in singular features.

"They appear to me, more numerous than the stars in the sky, or grains of sand on all the world's beaches," said Bean. "I fear 'twill take a lifetime to oust them all—if so many will even fit within the Soul-Eater."

He peered at the gem at Serafina's throat, as a younger pair of students pranced into view from Market Lane, resplendent in their velvet caps and scarlet and gold-brocade gowns.

"When you obtained it from the old *roué*, did he indicate its... capacity, so to speak?"

"Really, Ambrose! Did you think I would leave him in any position to *talk*? But you are right about the Gownsmen. We cannot hope to deal with them one by one. Which is why I have been wondering..." She drew Bean a little closer. "...if we might use the Thanatoscope to speed the process. Imagine the mayhem, were demonstrations arranged for Philosophers alone, perhaps one within each of their colleges."

"'Tis a marvellously devious idea. However, as we already know, the Gownsmen are a law unto themselves, and their rules will never permit such a show on their premises. 'Tis a wonder my Golden Cross performance proceeded without interference, for they meddle in the townsfolks' affairs as well."

Serafina scowled. "Why do the townsfolk allow this? Why do they not overthrow the Gownsmen and take back control of their city? The University is large and wealthy, but the Townsmen are more numerous, and they have strength and worldly wiles on their side, while the Gownsmen's only weapons are their words."

"'Tis a mystery," agreed Bean. "Perhaps they are all mesmerized? 'Twould explain their docility."

Serafina appeared thoughtful for a moment, then they came upon their destination.

"Here we have it," she said. "St Alban's College."

"The Gownsmen call them *alma mater*—their nurturing mother."

"I saw not much of either of those." Serafina stood back, hands on hips, to regard the stately timber gate with its round-headed rivets and iron strapwork, the coat of arms affixed to the keystone, and the hulking gatehouse above. "I should have returned a long time ago."

"So many scores to settle, so little time?"

She grimaced at Bean, then opened the wicket and entered the porter's lodge.

"You may go no further, madam," was the shoddy style of her welcome, but she gritted her teeth and enquired with forced gentility, "We are here to see Mr Temple."

"The Vice Sub-Rector is out," said the porter. He offered no further details and was clearly resolved not to do so, given the chary look he gave Bean.

"I cannot say I shall miss him," Bean whispered to Serafina. "Although I admit, his unique *joie de vivre* added a *je ne sais quoi* to our previous sport."

As they turned to depart, he stubbed his toes on a crate unmindfully stored between the porter's seat and the door. "Do you wish to cripple your callers?" he snapped. "A slower-witted man than I might suffer a broken ankle or worse." Then he spied the name *Sadler* stamped upon the crate's lid, and demanded, "What is this death-trap?"

The porter did not apologize for Bean's injury, but deigned to reply to his question: "'Tis the first consignment of our St Alban's Day comfits, lately delivered by their maker's journeyman." Observing Bean's blank expression, he added, "You know of St Alban's Day?"

Bean sighed. "Enlighten me."

With evident pride, the porter continued: "Each Midsummer noon, we mark the feast of our namesake by dispensing these sweetmeats—" He pointed at the crate. "—from the roof of Old Crab's Tower. A great crowd of townsfolk assembles below, each to claim his share of the college's boon—or the Amphibalian Benefaction, as we call it—which by tradition is funded from the Master's own purse. 'Tis the centrepiece of the college calendar."

"How quaint," murmured Bean.

Once back on the Broad, however, he laughed heartily, and loud enough that the porter might hear. "How I long to escape this tedious town and its brow-beaten, witless inhabitants."

Serafina appeared less amused. "I cannot understand it. Is it not, to them, a dishonour—to jump for scraps like dogs?" She shook her head at the sight of the commonplace folk abroad on the street, all meekly pursuing their commonplace business. "Why do they not rise up and seize the sweetmeats for themselves, if they like them so much?"

Bean followed her gaze with a sneer. "We must depart for someplace more thrilling, my dear, else we soon waste away from sheer boredom."

~ ~ ~

They arrived back at The Crown to learn that a visitor waited upstairs.

"If that is Jediah Temple again," growled Bean, "let us send him away. I've had my fill of that cold fish and his oily excuses. *I only wanted to* help. *My teacher never told* me *of his evil intentions, or his shortage of subjects. Or the purpose of that Devil-spawned device of his. 'Twas a gift to him from my father, but how was that* my *fault? And the stone. I know I stole it, but he* asked *me to.* Such people never accept the blame for their deeds. 'Tis always someone else's fault."

"But without him," said Serafina, "how shall we know which Gownsmen are Philosophers, and which are not? Or where, precisely, to find them?"

"Take them all, I say. Each one is surely every bit as pompous as the next."

'Twas not the dour Gownsman they found, however, and Bean's lodgings—normally steeped in fusty odours from the bar—bore a sweet and unsullied scent redolent of dewy meadows and fresh-mown hay. The source of this sylvan idyll occupied his only side-chair: a fresh-faced young woman, simply clad in a clean if well-patched gingham frock and a once-fashionable straw *bergère* trimmed with cornflowers and yellow ribbons. Her work-worn hands lay clenched upon her lap, sturdy fingers knitted as nervously as her brow.

"Do I know you from somewhere?" Bean enquired.

Before the girl could reply, Serafina shunted him aside and breezed into the room like a summer squall. "Why, 'tis Kat!" she exclaimed. "Little Kat from Stokenchurch. Isaac Darkin's doxy."

The girl's cheeks flushed, but she met Serafina's gaze with a pleasing fearlessness.

"What brings you here, my dear?" Kat stood to attention, her chin jutted forwards. "I knew you had come to Oxford, Miss, and asked all who I encountered here for news of a beautiful stranger. 'Twas not so hard to find you, for no one who meets you forgets you."

"And you are too bright for a blockhead like Darkin," said Serafina, enjoying this encounter more by the minute. "So, that is the how—but what of the why?"

"Wh—why I am here, Miss," Kat stuttered, "is to plead for your assistance in a matter of the greatest importance."

Serafina arched an eyebrow. "'Tis a personal affair?"

Kat nodded and swiped at a tear.

"I shall speak with Kat in private," said Serafina, turning to Bean.

Bean scowled. "I was about to retire."

"'Tis barely teatime. You are not a babe, in need of his afternoon nap."

"But where shall I go?"

Serafina's smile became strained. "We stand above an inn, my dearest. Where do you think you might go?"

Bean scowled again but departed, leaving Serafina to motion Kat back to the side-chair.

"'Tis so long," she sighed, "since I enjoyed intelligent converse. Now—what is it you wish to ask?"

Kat swallowed hard and said, "I ask you to save my Isaac. Though he be not Isaac now, not since he broke out of gaol, and I think you know that. I think you know what happened to him, because you were the one who made him that way."

Serafina chuckled. "You get to the point quickly. I like that." She took a seat at the dressing-table and began her toilet, observing Kat's reflection in the glass. "But news travels late to Stokenchurch, for Isaac Darkin was re-apprehended and at once returned to his cell, where most people say he belongs."

"I know that well enough." Kat's fists clenched tighter still. "He looks like Isaac, but I swear he is not. He is another man, trapped in Isaac's body. At least, that is what he said. And I believe him. I have heard him talking in his sleep, about the life he has lost."

"A sorry state of affairs, if true, but how am *I* to blame?"

"I've seen you play at The Bull." Kat frowned at the door, as if Bean might be skulking behind it. "I've seen how he works his box of lights, so that the crowd, at your direction, might make fools of themselves for their own entertainment. I've seen that big stone, too—the one you call a diamond, though it cannot possibly be. For if you owned a jewel so huge, you would not be performing in coaching inns for pennies."

Serafina chuckled as she opened up her patch-box and searched amongst the taffeta circles and stars. "Quick to the point, and sharp too. You keep your light well hidden, little Kat." Settling on a simple disc, she moistened it with a dab of her tongue and applied it onto the corner of her left eye. "Ambrose gave me this." She tapped the gilded lid of the box. "He says he acquired it from the *Dame d'Atour* to the Queen of France, but *I* do not believe *him*, I'm afraid."

Kat refused to be distracted. "'Tis said that through the stone, you can read a man's thoughts like a book, then trade them for another man's, so a simpleton becomes a sage, or a curate curses like a tar. That such men be in thrall to the stone, senseless to aught that befalls them—as if 'twere a maze in which they are lost. 'Tis different to your tricks with the showman's box, and the key to all my troubles, I am certain. That stone is a snare for the soul, and while the soul is trapped, you toy with it as you will. And that is what happened to Isaac and the man who he is not, only you traded *them* for good."

"You have a fertile imagination." With a dash of rouge to each cheek, Serafina completed her make-up and turned an appraising eye on her high piled coiffure. "But even if all you say were true, what would you have me do now?"

In the glass, she saw Kat bow her head. "You must save my man from the gallows, Miss Serafina.

403

He will be hanged on Midsummer's Day—and that is tomorrow."

"Midsummer's Day—tomorrow? Of course..." The seed of a plan already sown began to germinate as Serafina teased out her hairpins, one by one. "That's an ill-timed lot if there ever were one. For Midsummer's Day is a holiday here—a day of good cheer, when a great mass of townsfolk gathers to honour their betters. They call it the Feast of St Alban."

Kat met her reflected gaze with a frown of frustration. "I know nothing about St Alban, but I do know the man in Isaac's body is a good person and does not deserve to die. Why, even if he *were* Isaac, he should not be killed, for Isaac never hurt no man nor woman and only ever took their valuables, which were more use to us, who had nothing, than to them, who had so many more."

With a toss of her head, Serafina showered her shoulders with ebony curls.

"You have *power*," Kat persisted. "You can save him somehow."

"Perhaps. But what shall I have in return?"

"Your conscience?"

Serafina squealed with oddly girlish delight. "Little Kat, you are as blunt as you are sharp. Come—" She replaced her hat upon her unbound tresses and turned to regard her visitor face-to-face. "We shall collect Ambrose—'tis unavoidable, I'm afraid, for I shall need him for the scheme I have in mind. Then you will show us the lie of the land, and I shall reveal to you the true identity of your *Isaac*. I make no promises, mind," she added, forestalling Kat's tearful thanks. "For this feat will be unrivalled in the history of my art. But this much I guarantee: Oxford will have a St Alban's Day that no one, Town or Gown, might ever forget!"

CHAPTER FORTY-FIVE

MARY SHUT HERSELF INTO HER ROOM, crouched behind the door at first, as she listened to Father's guests take their leave— their voices hushed, as if someone had died. Then Lizzie and Burleigh departed as well, bound for their rooms across town; Lizzie had promised to call upon Father tomorrow, to delay her return to London, if he desired. As if he were the one most in need of consolation. Only after sundown did she hear a knock on the door, but she left it unanswered and took to her bed, where she tossed and turned, wishing Lizzie were there. That they'd never grown up, and that life could be simple again.

Once the house had fallen still, she crept downstairs to the shop, where she pulled the seconds-jar out from the back of the counter. Second-rate pastries, stored in the hope they might be sold before they went stale. 'Twas fitting, she thought.

They did not assuage her guilt, but the sweetmeats provided senseless relief for a while; she had to remind herself not to empty the jar. At which thought, she almost laughed aloud—as if, after all that had happened, a few missing cast-offs would cause a stir. She resealed the jar nonetheless and trudged upstairs.

Quite how far the world had been knocked out-of-tilt became clear at the parlour. 'Twas signified by a sound—or rather, its absence. Every night of her life, and on every night before that, Father had fetched the key from his bureau and wound the clock on the mantle at ten o'clock sharp, no sooner or later. And tonight, the clock had stopped. Mary wondered if she should wind it herself, for the house felt as dead as her heart without its beat.

But when she stepped inside, she found James, standing as clear as day in the moonlight, and with him the family moneybox, open on the table amidst the half-drunk cups of tea and half-eaten cakes.

"What are you doing?" she gasped.

Startled, he moved away from the table, a sheaf of banknotes clutched in his hand.

"You are stealing from us!" she hissed. "From your own family!"

He shrugged. "If cousin Jediah's claims are true, this is not my family. Nor one I would care to mention in polite company."

"How dare you!" Mary raised a hand to slap him, but the will departed 'twixt thought and action, and she pressed her fist to her mouth instead. "I thought you had changed. We all did."

"I *have* changed," he said, regarding her keenly. "And I was not stealing."

He offered her the moneybox, as though this might prove both claims, but she shoved it aside—more violently than she'd intended—and it crashed onto the floor, spilling coins on the chocolate-stained carpet. From above, they heard a drowsy call—"Who goes there? Shall I never know peace, not in life nor in sleep? Cursed I am. *Cursed...*"—then a single, thundering snore, followed by silence.

James headed for the stairs.

"Wait! We must talk."

"Talk?" he replied, with a snort of laughter. "Whatever is there to talk about?"

They glared at each other over the fallen moneybox, all that simmered between them unspoken. Then James was gone, to a fanfare of tiny brass bells, as the door to the High opened and closed behind him.

~ ~ ~

Darkin reached Angel Meadow barely moments before the time he'd been told, locating the Gownsmen by light of the Moon and the glow from their lantern upon the damp grass. He arrived short of breath and discomposed—not the best state for duelling, but given the opposition, he still highly rated his chances.

"We thought you had cried off," Osborne remarked as he approached.

Darkin laughed. "I have never yet dodged a challenge, and will not begin with a loll of your sort."

Osborne started towards him, murder in his eyes; in his hands too, perhaps, if his seconds had not restrained him.

"You must keep your pet under better control," Darkin sneered. "Or I shall have to put him down where he stands."

"Ignore the dog," said the taller of the two Gownsmen, as Osborne snapped and snarled in their grip. "'Tis naught but bluster and bluff. He has never duelled before."

409

Osborne nodded and steadied himself; straightened his waistcoat, squared his jaw. The smaller Gownsman produced a glossy walnut case, inside which rested two pistols, spotlessly clean and sparkling on a pillow of plush black velvet.

Osborne gestured towards them. "I presumed you would have no weapon, and so took the liberty of providing one for you."

"Considerate," Darkin said. He took one of the pistols and tested its weight and feel in his hand; 'twas a fussy thing—more a toy, or the weapon of a woman, than a real firearm. He raised it and squinted along the barrel.

"I presume you have never used a pistol," said Osborne, removing its twin from the case.

"You presume a lot," Darkin murmured.

"Just point and pull the trigger," advised the taller second.

"I shall try to remember that."

The Gownsmen exchanged amused glances. Then Osborne checked his pocket-watch and declared, "Time marches on, and a chill descends. Let's finish this wretch and withdraw to my rooms, a good fire, and the splendid Yorkshire ham I received from my aunt this afternoon. 'Tis a beauty!"

"As you wish," Darkin said. "I prefer a thick slice with a little fat on the side and some mustard if you have it."

The Gownsmen sniggered again, though less cock-sure than before.

"But first," Darkin continued, "I would ask you one question."

Osborne sighed. "Very well."

"What is it you have against this man, James Sadler? A puffed-up dandiprat he may be, but of no especial importance in the greater scheme of life. Surely 'twould be better to simply ignore him, not take all these pains to extinguish him?"

"You put it a strange way," said Osborne. "But your lack of importance is *why* you must be returned to your natural station. You fell so eagerly for the wager I planned with the showman—you were never intended to *win*. And this is where you have brought us. If only you had stayed down, 'twould never have come to this, and you'd still have your life."

"I lost my life a while ago," said Darkin. Then he turned to the shorter Gownsman and said, "Please continue."

The Gownsman raised a hand. "You may begin. And may the better man win."

"I am sure he will," smirked Osborne.

Darkin did not reply, focussing instead on the task ahead.

They took their stations back to back, then advanced across the turf, ten paces apiece. Darkin closed his eyes, held his breath...

"At my signal," called the second.

...exhaled, steady and slow...

"Now!"

...and realized his fatal mistake. He'd assumed he retained *all* of his highwayman faculties, not just his memories and mind. Now, as he failed to spin on his heels and fire, he knew he did not—that as well as James Sadler's puny body, he had acquired his lack of coordination, speed, balance, and aim. Everything, in fact, that would make the difference between him winning the duel and lying dead in the mud.

411

Two eventualities saved his life: the first being Edwin Osborne's marksman skills, which proved even less deadly than Sadler's, and the second, a terrified "*Stop!*"

'Twas Mary, running blind out of the shadows in a daze of tears and splashes of dew. Darkin started to scream a warning, but Osborne had turned at last, his finger upon the trigger; with a yell of triumph he fired, and reflexively Darkin returned. Mary froze between them, then with a cry of surprise more than pain, she dropped to the ground and lay still.

Darkin tossed the pistol away and fell to his knees at her side. She moaned softly, her eyelids flickered but once, then silence.

"Mary? *Mary?*" He scooped her into his arms, warm wetness slicking his hands. To Osborne, he yelled, "What have you *done?*"

"You fired too," Osborne whimpered. "It could have been either of us. Isn't that so?" He looked to his men for support.

"'Tis so," said the taller. "Besides, she came out of nowhere—no warning, no care on her part, and certainly no consideration. 'Twas her own doing."

Darkin screamed in wordless fury, buffeting Osborne backwards; the Gownsman slipped and landed on his arse in the grass, where his gaze at last alighted upon their victim.

"Come—we have no time to sit around." His taller crony kicked over the lantern, snuffing out the flame so only the moonlight remained. "If the Bulldogs find us here, we shall be finished."

But Osborne held fast, his horrified gaze fixed as obdurately on Mary as his left fist was clenched in the grass, and the right still clutching his pistol. The shorter Gownsman detached him from all three, then the taller hauled him erect.

"Hurry, Edwin!"

"Of course. Yes. We'd be fools to stay..." With hushed voice and faltering steps, Osborne allowed his cronies to lead him away.

Darkin snapped out of his own trance when Mary moaned the name of her brother.

"Don't give up on me," he whispered. "I *have* changed—I shall show you!"

With rather less decorum than Osborne's men, he manhandled Mary into a roughly standing position, and with his arms around her shoulders and waist to support her, commenced a gruelling quest for help.

"Nearly there," he wheezed as he staggered up onto the bridge—as much to himself as to her, for his hold upon her was slipping. "When you're recovered... there will be no more pastries... no more pound cakes, nor biscuits... I shall forbid them from the house... every custard, every damn cheesecake..."

The Plain stood deserted, the church in darkness, the tollhouse long ago closed for the night. Half-hidden down a wooded turn to the south, Darkin spotted a muted light; a lone sign of life—and a source of help, he prayed.

Mustering the last of his strength, he stumbled down the track until he located a house, alone and neglected—but occupied, for a candle sat on the sill of an upstairs window, and the acrid smell of a wood fire drifted around from the rear of the building. Letting Mary slide to the ground in the porch, he pounded on the door with both fists.

"Open up! I have an injured woman here!"

No one came.

413

"Open up! I beg you!"

He hammered and shouted again, and again; forever-and-a-day slipped by before the door at last cracked open.

"I'd thank you to cease your banging," grumbled the weasely face's owner. "Don't you know what hour this is? Shame on you, rousing a hard-working man, worn out from a long night of hammering, chopping, and burning."

Darkin suppressed an urge to wring the servant's skinny neck. "Did you not hear? Can you not see?" He jabbed a finger at Mary; at her pallor, at the damp patch on her arm that grew ever larger.

"Oh," said the servant.

Once stirred into action, however, he proved more useful than he appeared, first helping Darkin carry Mary inside, then guiding them through a strange assortment of whatnots that cluttered the hall, to a dusty reception room, where they placed her upon a sofa. Like the exterior of the house, there was a chill about it all, an air of abandonment.

"I shall light a fire," the servant said.

"No—fetch help!" Darkin cried.

He scampered from the room, while Darkin knelt by the sofa, chafing Mary's hands in his own, as if this might warm her whole body right through.

"Do not leave me," he whispered. "Not now that you know who I am."

Sooner than he'd expected, the servant returned—with a physician, Darkin hoped, spotting the lofty figure behind him. His spirits sank when he saw who it was. Not help, but Jediah Temple, bizarrely dressed in a quilted banyan and cap.

"Why are *you* here?" Darkin demanded.

414

Jediah regarded him curiously; half suspicious, half darkly amused. "You were expecting someone else? Why should I *not* be here? This is my house, inherited in the usual way from my father, and he from his. I think you carry this lapse-of-memory charade a little too far, dear *brother.*"

"Never mind that," Darkin cried. "Attend to your cousin! She is wounded."

Jediah nodded. "Yes, 'tis plain to see."

"She needs treatment—quickly."

"Again, I cannot disagree."

Darkin would have flattened him where he stood, if he hadn't needed Temple's help, but instead he reined in his fury and tried to speak in a reasonable tone: "Whatever grievance lies between you and James Sadler, you have no quarrel with this woman. Fetch a doctor. Please. Her brother-in-law—Burleigh—"

Jediah remained unmoved. "I do not believe in doctors. If it be God's will that she pass from mortal life upon this night, who are we—mere men—to meddle?" He sniffed. "Though I doubt 'twill be in Heaven that her eternal soul abides."

And with that, he left the room.

"No!"

Darkin sprang after him, slamming a shoulder into his back as he entered the hall. They fell to the floor together, Darkin atop. He gave no quarter, pummelling his foe upon his meatless shoulders and ribs until Jediah mewled like a babe, the banyan scant protection from such an assault.

"What is wrong with you?" Darkin shouted. "What harm did these people do you?"

As he spoke, he spied a movement at the corner of his eye, but with James Sadler's torpid reactions slowed to a crawl by his state of mind, he realized what was happening far too late to do something about it.

For he had forgotten the servant, and though a meagre physical specimen, the man stood surrounded by a slew of potential weapons. He made an unlikely choice, but turned out handy enough with a Pontian bagpipe. Darkin felt a crack behind his left ear, then nothing.

PART VIII

CHAPTER FORTY-SIX

S T ALBAN'S DAY DAWNED AS DARK as any other in my lightless cell.

I had ceased to count the days of my confinement in Darkin's body, but I guessed the date when Wisdom arrived, unlocked my chains, and led me away from the cell to a minister, waiting with Bible in hand. Then I knew for sure, that this was the Twenty-First Day of June; a festival for the good folk of the city. For me—as my cellmates informed me in ghoulish jest—'twas 'washing day'.

The day I was scheduled to die.

"Good luck!" shouted the horse thief.

"And don't forget to smile nice for the crowd," warned the publican. "They hate a sniveller."

I gazed wistfully back at that filthy hole as two warders grasped my arms and dragged me away. How I longed to be back there, shackled to that sturdy iron ring, with straw for my bed like a beast and villains my only company. While entombed, I had yearned to see the Sun, but now out of the pit and at last emerged into daylight, I was blinded by its brilliance, its heat searing my chilled and bloodless skin.

"Keep moving, Darkin. We haven't got all morning." Wisdom tugged me onwards. "There's a big crowd today, and they want to see you swing in good time—'tis the Benefaction at noon."

The Benefaction. I thought of the comfits, and of Father. Had he missed me? Had Mary? Or Rudge? Dr Crouch, even? Nugent? It occurred to me that, given the way I had ofttimes treated them, none had much cause to regret my disappearance.

Our little procession reached the prison yard, where a boisterous crowd of townsfolk, and no few Gownsmen—all in holiday mood and many drunk already—had gathered in the shadow of the Tower of St George. I remembered the tale of the Empress Maud (a bedtime favourite of Mary's), besieged within the tower by the army of King Stephen, facing capture or death by starvation until a violent snowstorm blew in, during which three valiant knights won her freedom, all clothed in white so no one could see.

But no white knights for me—just a cheer from the crowd when I entered the yard. That dismal space was crammed full, save an aisle that the guards had cleared before my arrival. At its end, raised up on a platform, stood the gallows, the noose swaying gently in the breeze as if waving in welcome.

I close upon screamed at the sight, my vitals contorted in terror. Then I recalled the publican's words. Perish I must for another man's crimes, but I refused to die a sniveller. Beside me, the minister took up his Bible, and turned to the Gospel of John; then, without further niceties, we set off on the path to my doom.

I swallowed down my fear and tried to heed the minister's words, though I could scarcely hear a thing above the shouting. Many taunted me, but I also heard wails and sobs, and women shrieking Darkin's name and begging I blow them a kiss. They conjured up thoughts of the power I'd felt when we robbed the Birmingham Mail. Is this how a man of consequence dies? I wondered.

And then, a chance overhearing ruined my hopes of a dignified end. 'Twas a comment passed from a man to his wife; they stood to the fore of the mob on the edge of the path, but were well behaved by that standard. No calls in hope of a lingering death, or that I hand over my neckcloth for them to remember me by. They seemed, indeed, to be hardly watching at all.

"...a hanging is *entertainment*, I cannot deny," contended the man, "if you enjoy that sort of thing. But the aerostat show—now that was *educational*."

"A grand young man he was," agreed the wife. "If folk revered James Sadler as they do this fellow Darkin, we should have a more civilized country."

I struggled against the warders' grasp. "You, there!" I cried. "You saw James Sadler?"

They viewed me with shock, as if the sight of the condemned man at his own execution were something surprising.

"That we did," said the husband, quickly recovered and hooking his thumbs in his waistcoat. "And his flying globe and all. At the Town Hall. 'Twas a spectacle like no other, and an inspiration to man and boy. I hear 'tis still on show, for those who could not attend yesterday—a pity you cannot see it for yourself, being hanged as you are."

Here, at the very last, came confirmation of what I had feared: Isaac Darkin had stolen my life, as I had been forced into his. With that truth, came a horror worse than any I had known; starker even than the terror of my fast-approaching death. A highwayman now lived my life, pretending he was me. He had my balloon, and would soon become the first English aeronaut. He would become the man of consequence I should have been, and all that I had done was more than forgot—'twas as though I had never existed.

I shrieked and fought my captors like a fiend, and jeers from the crowd erupted on all sides; this was not how they'd expected the brave Isaac Darkin to go to his Maker.

'Twas not yet the end of my torment. In my writhings I glimpsed a woman amongst the respectable folk at the back of the crowd. She had exchanged her veil for an overweening hat and her widow-weeds for a frock the colour of flame, but there was no mistaking *her* identity.

"See that woman?" I bawled. "Ask her! She knows who I am!"

Serafina—if 'twas indeed her and not a figment of my frenzied imagination—made no move to save me, and before I could shout again, we had reached that fateful platform, where a Magistrate's man had already begun reciting the list of my crimes.

"I am not Isaac Darkin! I am James Sadler. James Sadler the aeronaut!"

The jeers turned to guffaws as I was bundled onto the platform and a bag pulled over my head; I gulped for air, fearing I would suffocate before they had chance to hang me. Then the minister started upon the Lord's Prayer, and I felt the weight of the noose on my neck. Time after time I swore my innocence, but unlike the catcalls, my cries were now stifled. What torment was this—that the last sound I would hear should be laughter!

But not *quite* the last sound. For suddenly, a chorus of whoops and cheers replaced the hilarity. Although I could not see, it seemed the crowd's attention had shifted, and I heard first a clumping upon the steps to the platform and then a familiar voice at my side.

"Ladies, gentlemen, one and all! What a pleasure it is, to see so many faces here today, having come to see justice dispensed."

Dear Lord, were my sins so depraved that I merited death as a backdrop to Ambrose Bean's prattle? The crowd cheered again and I raged like a madman. Bean had upstaged me at my Philosophy Club, where all my troubles began; now he'd upstaged me at my own execution. I wondered how he had managed to get on the platform, why the magistrate's men or Wisdom had not pulled him down.

"For Oxford is an ancient seat of the Law, albeit unhappily famous for the Black Assize, which no one might ever forget, though ten score years and more have passed. 'Twas the trial of one Rolande Jenckes, a treasonous pedlar of books in the employ of certain Gownsmen—proof, as if 'twere needed, that no good has ever come from the printed word—"

I heard the squeak of a turning crank handle, my guess that Bean had brought his Thanatoscope confirmed a moment later when the crowd emitted, as one, a gasp of astonishment.

"This saucy fellow dared to curse not just his accusers, but everyone present. Judges, jury, witnesses, women, and babes... All succumbed—except for Rolande Jenckes himself and his University friends!"

More gasps—of horror this time—and cries of "Stop this show, you are frightening the kiddies!" But the shouts for it to continue sounded louder and more numerous still; Bean's spectacle, it seemed, made the perfect prelude to a hanging.

"Before the day was out, thousands had died. Horribly! Their bodies consumed by fever and pustulent boils. Their minds driven to madness, wracked by convulsions, tortured by demons. Demons such as these—"

Screams now joined the gasps and shouts. I began to wish my execution was over and done with, for I could bear to listen no longer. And indeed, I heard the magistrate's men behind me discussing the need to be finished and all cleaned up in good time for St Alban's, and how long would this pantomime last, and who had invited Bean anyway. Then the Lord's Prayer resumed, the minister starting from where he'd left off, and Bean's patter took on a more urgent edge.

"What caused that malignant contagion? Why— 'twas a roiling cloud of foul air, belched forth from the entrails of Hell. No different, in stripe, from the fumes of the so-called Philosophers—lately released upon the city, by University men!"

So frenzied was the response to this, no one could have been watching when the floor beneath my feet was whipped away. For an instant I felt I was flying, but only for an instant, my first and last voyage cut brutally short. Before I could catch my breath, the rope around my neck jerked tight and however hard I heaved for air, none would come. I thrashed my shackled legs, sending my body into a sickening spin; a fierce white pain flared behind my sightless eyes and swelled to fill my head, 'til the blackness turned to light and the pain devoured me. Then I fell again, down a bottomless pit, and screaming and shouting and thudding feet chased me down.

I heard a single, stricken wail—"'Tis the Gaol Fever, sent by the Gownsmen! Run!"—before I hit the floor with a thump, and screaming and shouting and pain were all I knew.

CHAPTER FORTY-SEVEN

WYNDHAM RUDGE, IN ALL HIS LONG LIFE, had never once observed St Alban's Day. 'Twas not his notion of fun, so while his colleagues made the most of their junket, he alone remained at work. It went quicker that way, and he'd double-dug a whole bed before he allowed himself a break to stretch his back, and spotted a plume of smoke arising from over the trees across the Cherwell, south of The Plain. As he wondered what this might signify, a shadow fell upon him, shutting him off from the warmth of the Sun.

"Good morning, Wyndham."

His unease at the sight of the smoke turned to shock, then delight, then returned to foreboding.

"Jediah! I cannot guess what brought you here, except good timing perhaps." He pointed towards the haze beyond the river. "Is that Cowley Hall, do you think?"

Jediah showed scant concern.

"Perhaps we should take a look?"

427

Again he got no response, beyond a shrug and a faraway look.

"'Tis your house, I do not dispute, and you may do with it as you wish. But what of your father's collections? They are priceless!"

Jediah's curt laugh did little to calm his fears. "I am disposing of some unwanted rummage, nothing more. Prout has it under control."

"If you are sure."

"Quite sure."

"'Twould be a tragedy to lose Elijah's legacy."

Then silence fell. Rudge waited in trepidation to hear the cause for Jediah's visit; when none came, he brightened again.

"Well, whatever your business be, or none, 'tis fortunate you happened by. For I have something to show you—if you wish to see it."

Neither snub nor quarrel ensued, to Rudge's cautious relicf; Jediah followed in silence through the ranks of flowers and herbs, to a wilder realm of the garden, set apart in the southernmost corner and seldom disturbed by Rudge's colleagues. As they walked together, he thought of happier times.

"I have wondered for weeks how to broach this," he said, "or if I should do so at all. I knew you wouldn't receive me gladly. But this, too, is your father's legacy, as much as Cowley Hall and all that is in it. And now you have come of your own accord, so Fate smiles upon us, it seems." He halted at a small plot of soil, surrounded by brambles but cleared of weeds, and freshly dressed with steaming manure. "See here!"

Jediah stared long and hard at the spindly sapling. No higher than his hip, sparsely dotted with leaves and buds; fortunately, 'twas bound to a stake, for it looked so frail, the slightest puff of air might blow it down.

"'Tis a tree," he said, at last.

"Ah, but *what* a tree!" Rudge beamed with conspiratorial joy. "You remember those special seeds? I swore I would raise one, one day, though for years 'twas naught but frustration. Plants can be as particular as people in their likes and dislikes, and learning their inclinations is a matter of trial and much error. But I persevered. And now... Isn't she beautiful? If only Elijah were here, to see her as well."

Jediah remained stony faced, and with sudden apprehension Rudge remembered the ravaged garden at Cowley Hall.

"Come away, I should not have brought you here."

"To the contrary, 'tis most fitting you did."

"Then I beg you..." Rudge rubbed his weary brow. "Stop talking in riddles. Tell me why you *are* here and be done with it."

"I shall speak my piece, never fear," said Jediah. "As I failed to speak, so many years past. How different life might have been... But I was a boy, and what could I do? Not warn my father, for certain, for whom would he believe? The son who meant nothing to him, or the wife who had bewitched him and the servant he called his friend?"

"Why, Jediah? Why?" Rudge groaned. "Why bring this up again, now?"

"You thought to forget it." Jediah marched back and forth, wringing his hands in his cloak. "It happened oh, so far away, and when the whore died, no one was left who knew. Except I, of course."

"And I am forever indebted, that you did not tell your father what you saw." Rudge reached out his hand, but Jediah shoved it away.

"I did it for my father, not for you. God knows why he loved that woman."

Rudge hung his head. "As did I."

"If that be the truth, it may please you to learn that your love did, after all, bear fruit—albeit quite spoiled."

He continued to pace, his gaze first on the sapling, then on the spade that Rudge had earlier left by the wall. Rudge tensed.

"What do you mean?"

"She had a son. Your son."

"That's impossible." Rudge laughed, incredulous. "I would have known."

"Would you? *Think*—when did she die?"

Rudge hesitated. "Before Elijah and I returned from China. Of a fever."

"Not fever. She died giving birth to your child."

"Then what happened to him?" Rudge demanded. "Where is he now?"

"Your lover conspired with Anne Sadler—my father's own sister!—and her gutless husband. 'Twould have been obvious to my father that any offspring could not be his. So they claimed Anne was with child, then entered a lengthy lying-in, with my stepmother playing her sister-in-law's companion. No one knew the truth, for they stayed outside the county, at the house of a distant and doddering aunt. They planned to pass off the baby as the Sadler's child." He paused to drive the news home. "As events fell out, your lover died giving birth—they passed that off as well, as a fever caught in the cold and damp of the Fens. But the whelp lives on today, still a Sadler. *James* Sadler."

Rudge clenched his fists, as though to strike Jediah for the lie, but his eyes brimmed with tears.

"I see you are convinced," Jediah said.

"My son," Rudge moaned. "Becky's son." He covered his face with his hands, then abruptly put them down again and swiped away the tears. "Does James know this?"

Jediah shook his head. "He knows his true mother, but not the name of his father. Nor will he ever."

"I must see him. I must explain." Forgetting Jediah, and the sapling, and even the spade, Rudge made for the gate, but Jediah grasped his shoulder and spun him around—and again he saw the smoke.

"You are too late," Jediah said. "For your son will soon burn to death, and my father's legacy with him."

"You would not dare!" Rudge choked.

"Would I not? I have nothing to lose."

Rudge charged him with an anguished roar, but his knees gave out beneath him and he crashed amongst the brambles.

"You murderer!" he shrieked.

"Enough," Jediah said, and snatched the spade from the wall.

"No!" With the last of his strength, Rudge flung his body in front of the sapling, but the spade was not for the tree. Without pause, Jediah grasped the shaft and swung the blade at the gardener's head.

He watched Rudge moan and twitch. Then he dropped the spade, wiped a splash from his cheek, and took leave of his oldest friend, while the sapling, the only remaining witness to Rudge's fate, wept drops of the gardener's blood from its shivering branches.

☉

CHAPTER
FORTY-EIGHT

WHEN ISAAC DARKIN WOKE feeling dizzy and bilious, he grinned to himself nonetheless, convinced he'd spent the night in his cups with the boys, toasting their latest haul. But when he tried to yawn and stretch, he realized that he was not safe and sound in his bed, nor even slumped under a table in The Bull. The pain in his head was a wound behind his left ear, and he could not move because his wrists and ankles were bound, the rope chafing his skin.

He prised open his eyes, and when the world had stopped revolving saw he reposed upon his back, on a rug, on the floor of a room unknown—though he could guess its owner, for Jediah Temple loomed nearby, his head almost touching the ceiling. Darkin gasped in consternation, then realized 'twas naught but a portrait, and not of Jediah himself, but of a man who bore Mary's cousin a striking resemblance.

Mary.

She lay just an arm's length away, sleeping upon a chaise-longue near the hearth. At least, Darkin

433

thought, they did not toss *her* on the floor like a stick of dead wood. He shuffled across the rug towards her, heartened to see the colour returned to her cheeks. He saw, too, a bandage about the wound in her upper arm; not applied by Jediah Temple, he assumed, and it looked too capably done to have been his man-servant's work.

"Mary." He spoke her name softly, wary of alerting their captor. "'Tis me—" He stopped. Who *was* 'me', exactly? Not James, for sure, but now he scarcely felt like Isaac Darkin, either.

Mary groaned and opened her eyes.

"Thank God," Darkin whispered. "You are back."

She winced and tried to raise a hand to the opposite, injured arm, but her wrist was secured to the frame of her seat by a grubby strip of white linen—the manservant's doing, this time; 'twas, for certain, his neckcloth.

"What—What has happened to us? Is this Cowley Hall?"

Darkin could not help but smile. Awake and aware was a promising sign, and though the tightly shuttered windows admitted scant daylight, 'twas sufficient to judge her wound far less grave than he'd feared last night.

She stared down at him on the floor, still awash with confusion. "Why are we here? Why am I—Why are *we* tied up?"

Darkin grimaced. "Your cousin's petty grievances seem to have taken a drastic turn—Talk of the Devil!" he cried, as the man himself strode in, a tight roll of papers in hand.

"And he doth appear," Jediah responded. "Though you are a fine one to speak of the Author of Evil."

434

"Evil is as evil does. Going somewhere?" Darkin added, for Jediah had swapped the banyan for his more usual sombre attire, including his cloak and hat.

"Indeed. But not to the same place as you—or her." His scornful gaze alighted on Mary. "I see you survive, dear cousin. But death can never be cheated for long."

Darkin tested his bonds, desperate to wring the breath from this cold-blooded monster.

"I expect you wish me harm." Jediah's smile had all the warmth of an open grave, if rather less charm. "Be assured, naught will save you from the fate that you have brought upon yourself."

"Would you still feel this way," Darkin asked, "if I told you that I am *not* James Sadler?"

"Excellent speech becometh not a fool, much less do lying lips a prince—or a pastry-cook. If that is the best you can do, the Father of Lies has not taught you well."

Darkin tried another tack. "Very well, if I *am* James Sadler, and what you announced yesterday is true, then I am the closest thing you have to a brother. Would a reasonable man treat his sibling like this?"

Jediah's smile disappeared, his marbled cheeks set hard. "Not if that sibling be born of betrayal. And that is the least of it. *Think*, James Sadler—of all you have had in your life, and did not want. Your loving parents, your sisters, your place in the family business. Then think on all that Jediah Temple did *not* have. No mother, no playmates. A father who even when present, cared more for his work than his son. A friend who—" He shook his head. "I would have cherished the meagrest scrap of your life, had you tossed one my way. And now, I discover 'twas all obtained, not through God's ineffable will, but through treachery

435

and deceit. You should have paid for your mother's sins..."

He had begun to set a fire during this speech, using the roll of papers as kindling; they uncurled in the flames, and Darkin glimpsed faces and places unknown, in the instant before they blackened and burned. He welcomed the heat, for his hands and feet felt chilled to the core; less welcome was their captor's increasing abstraction.

"The irony is," said Jediah, still crouched in front of the grate, "you would have fitted in perfectly here, at Cowley Hall. Always wishing you were somewhere else. Up at college. In the atmosphere. On the Moon." He shuddered. "My father was the same. His visits home were naught but plannings for where he'd go next. Like you, he talked of the Moon, and how by unholy means it might be conquered. Like you, he was led astray by another—"

"Jediah." Mary raised herself as best she could on one elbow. "When we were children, James never once turned you away. You were part of the family to him—to us all. We knew you were lonely."

"Lonely?" Jediah stood and rubbed the soot from his palms. "That explains the endless visitings, the meals, the excursions. You felt sorry for me."

Mary frowned. "No, that was not it at all—"

"But now we are grown, and must put away childish things." He crossed the room and reached for the portrait above the desk, taking it down and gazing solemnly into its eyes.

"You called me your Good Samaritan," Mary said. "Will you not be mine?"

"I also said, 'tis sometimes better *not* to help."

"You cannot keep us captive forever," growled Darkin.

"'Tis true, I cannot."

"So what now?"

Jediah nodded, as if concluding a conversation with someone else. "I have always hated this house. As a child, I thought it too empty. Now, 'tis too full—of unwanted memories. Today, I shall erase them all."

He returned to the hearth, and almost nonchalantly, dipped one corner of the portrait into the flames. When the gilded frame began to blister, he placed it on a sofa against the side wall, so that was soon burning as well.

"What are you doing?" Darkin demanded, although 'twas all too clear.

Jediah ignored him and made for the door.

"Jediah!" Mary cried.

"Kill me if you must," Darkin yelled. "But not your cousin—I beg you!"

Jediah seemed not to hear them; perhaps he no longer knew they were there. He slipped from the room like a father leaving the side of his sleeping child, treading softly, and with a tender smile.

CHAPTER FORTY-NINE

'TWAS WITH GREAT SURPRISE I returned to my senses, not in Pandæmonium, where I'd seemed to be headed, nor any other circle of Hell, but in Heaven. Or at least, some part of Heaven that basks in sunlight upon a riverbank, with birdsong and burbling waters, and a soft, cooling hand to soothe the brow. I revelled in the sensation; all too briefly, before a hammering headache assailed me, and burning both inside and outside my throat. What poor sort of Heaven is this? I wondered. 'Twas far from what the Rev. Slade had promised.

Then I opened my eyes and saw, not an angel, but Kat. My Kat.

"You are dead too?" I mumbled. "'A pity for you, of course, but better for me."

Kat's mouth fell open in stunned indignation. "I should kill you for saying that, if you hadn't been half-strangled already."

My hands went to my neck, feeling the bruises left by the noose and the specks of dried blood where the rope broke my skin. In a rush, the memory returned, and I gulped for air, for the sweet breath of life. This time, it came. To my shame, I sobbed like a babe, though Kat did not hold it against me; instead, she returned my hands to my sides, saying I had to rest to regain my strength, then moved her fingers in calming circles upon my chest, her tender whispers enfolding me, as I drifted back into darkness.

"You must sleep while you can, dear James."

At that, I started awake. "You know my name."

Kat smiled. "Serafina D'Bonaventura told me. She told me everything, in fact."

"You've seen Serafina?" I sat up, ignoring the strain on my shoulders and neck, and with a pang of horror identified our location.

"My God, this is where it began!"

"'Twas the furthest they would take us." Kat slipped a comforting arm around my waist. "But the gaol was in such a flap—no one could have seen us escape, or which way we went. You are safe now."

"*Safe?* They tried to hang me! And will succeed, I expect, when they catch me again." I peered up and down the towpath. "How long was I unconscious?"

"You are not going to ask how I rescued you?"

I coughed. "Of course I am! 'Twould have been my next question."

"'Twas Serafina's doing, really. I remembered you blaming all that had happened on her, and wanting to go to Oxford to set her straight. I thought she was your lover," she added, blushing.

"God forbid," I muttered.

Kat grinned. "So I came to Oxford myself, and found her lodging with that dandy showman."

"Ambrose Bean," I muttered again. "I cannot imagine a pair more deserving of each other's company."

"I begged her to help you. She said she couldn't give you your body back if she didn't have Isaac's as well. But she said she would come to the gaol and cause a distraction while Bean cut you down."

"What sort of distraction?" I asked, thinking of the commotion I'd heard as death almost claimed me.

Kat shrugged. "I cannot say. They were baying for your blood, then racing this way and that of a sudden, screeching like a barnyard of petrified hens. Some shouted that a huge black cloud had arisen from under the ground, but I could see nothing."

"Gaol Fever," I said, as another piece of the puzzle slipped into place. "Serafina made them see Gaol Fever."

"How did she do that?"

"I know only 'tis some species of mesmerism. She can make a man see impossible things and swear they be true."

"I meant, how could she fool so many at once? There were scores in that yard."

"Maybe not all were convinced, but enough to cause panic to spread. People believe what they see, and see what they believe."

Kat pondered this for a moment. "That might explain what she said to her man."

I stretched out once again on my back, enjoying the warmth of the Sun on my face. 'Twas not my true face—and I knew I must soon resume my false life on the run—but I clung to this moment of pleasure and peace a while longer.

"He asked Serafina why she would help you. He sounded suspicious—perhaps he believes you are lovers, as well." Kat chuckled, then continued "Serafina said 'twas a means to her ends. She said working such

441

a huge audience—that's what she called the crowd at the gaol, her audience—would be her greatest performance. Then Bean got huffy and said 'twas also his show, and wouldn't be happening at all without him and his Than—Than—"

"Thanatoscope?"

Kat nodded. "She jollied him up after that, told him how his little shows had opened the way for the big one. And when I asked her what the big one was, she smiled and said they would cause the greatest stir since St Schol—Schol—"

"St Scholastica's Day," I said. "'Twas a terrible riot, long past but never forgotten. The townsfolk went mad, and many Gownsmen were murdered." I frowned. "What did she mean? Does she plan to disrupt the Benefaction?"

"All these saints and strange words... 'Tis a curious place, this hometown of yours. But whatever her purpose be, she will leave town a little lighter than she arrived." With an impish look about her, Kat delved into the folds of her petticoat, where nestled a singular trinket, fashioned from silver and sparkling stone.

I gasped in delight. "How did you get hold of that?"

Kat grinned. "I am not just a pretty face, you know. I was a pickpocket in my Newbury days, 'til the magistrate's men got wise. You are not the only gaol-breaker here."

I hugged her tight, to many loud protests of pain from my arms and chest. "You truly *are* an angel, Kat!"

"I do not know about that, but I do know I want you away from here, safe and sound."

"As do I. But wherever I go, 'twill be done in my natural body. Your Isaac wears my face, but not for much longer. With this—" I pointed at the pin. "—I can get it back."

"How will you find him? He could be anywhere by now."

Thirsty for action, I lurched to my feet. "Worry not, dear Kat," I said. "I know exactly where he will be."

Hand in hand, we left Folly Bridge behind us, turning north towards Fish Street and whatever the Fates decreed for us next.

"'Tis deathly quiet," said Kat. "I've heard Oxford be a merry town."

I had to agree; the road up from Grandpont and Abingdon, the tollhouse, even the barges in the wharf—all seemed deserted. "It must be the Benefaction."

"That strange word again. What does it mean?"

"It means my hanging was only the start of the day's entertainments." I grimaced. "The townsfolk will go to St Alban's next, where they'll stand at the foot of the bell-tower while the Master and Fellows drop comfits to catch."

"That must be good fun."

"Not always. The comfits are made by my father. He has supplied them for years, in fact, being Oxford's premier pastry-cook and confectioner."

"That be fortunate, for I love sweetmeats! Cheesecake is my favourite, though we don't see much of it out in Stokenchurch. You must be proud to burst."

"I was, once."

She asked me what I meant by that, but my thoughts suddenly shifted from the past to the here-and-now—and worse, what might occur in the very near future

"He will be there as we speak, accepting the Master's thanks—and his remittance. And Serafina... will she be there too? What is she planning?"

"I told you before," said Kat. "'Twill be bigger than St Schol— St Scholastica's Day."

I halted so abruptly, she'd raced several steps ahead before she realized I had stopped, and had to scurry back to rejoin me.

"I must save them," I said.

She gaped at me, aghast. "You want to save them? *They* want to hang you, for goodness sake. And when you have saved them, they will do it."

"'Tis a chance I must take," I replied, before I could change my mind. "I have to see my father safe. Go back to the towpath and wait. If I do not return... well, I suppose what you do then is up to you."

I planted a kiss on her forehead, then resumed my march up Fish Street. 'Twas not long, however, before I heard running footsteps.

"You'd only go getting yourself into trouble," Kat puffed, with a sly little wink.

CHAPTER FIFTY

ELIJAH TEMPLE'S PORTRAIT BURNED SWIFTLY: paint charred and canvas frizzled 'til naught but a fiery frame remained, feeding the blaze on the sofa. When a stray lick of flame caught a tassel attached to a swag in the window behind it, the fire began to take hold.

"We have to get out!" Mary cried.

Darkin rolled to his knees and tried to push himself upright against the chaise-longue, but the blow to his head had dazed him more than he'd realized, and with use of neither hands nor feet, he soon lost his balance and fell alongside it. Mary twisted around to see him, the hems of her petticoats skimming his face.

"Last night..." he groaned, "what the Devil were you thinking?"

"I saw the money," she said, in short, panicky gasps. "You were putting it *in* the box. I saw it the instant I looked, but you'd already left. So I followed."

"'Twas money I'd made on the side at the exhibition. James Sadler raised it, not I, so I reckoned his kin should have it. If only you'd let me speak."

"I would not have believed you."

"You would not trust the word of your brother?"

445

"I would not trust James... as far as I could throw him. But you are not James." She turned her face from the fire and fixed a fearful gaze upon Darkin's. "I guessed long ago, but dared not believe it."

"I felt the same way. 'Twas wickedness of a sort, that brought me to you, but I'd wish nothing different. 'Til now."

For Fate had again decreed he would die, but now, an innocent with him, and no one to witness their end, save a column of clay figurines with empty eyes of stone and shell. Shut in a case on the wall, their lump-en bodies contorted in a dance of smoke and flame, as if they had sprung into life, moments before their extinction.

Never a man for prayers or petitions, Darkin offered one up as the pelmet collapsed and the flames crept onto the ceiling. And someone listened, for he straight away glimpsed an object beneath the chaise-longue.

"Can you reach under the seat?" he gasped. "I see a pair of scissors."

Mary had screwed shut her eyes and clenched her fists in the couch's upholstery—perhaps saying a prayer of her own—but now she stretched as far as her tether and wound would allow, her fingers fumbling blindly in empty space.

"I cannot find them!" Darkin swivelled about to angle his feet beneath the couch and swept the scissors into the open.

"Save yourself," he ordered.

'Twas a simple task made hard by its deadly urgency, and excruciating seconds of hacking, sawing, and ripping ensued before Mary pulled free from her binding. Darkin's initial relief turned to horror, for instead of heading straight for the exit, she dropped to her knees beside him and set to work on the rope round his ankles.

"Leave me!" he cried.

She ignored him and continued, snipping the fibres one by one 'til the rope was easily snapped. Before she could move to his wrists, he pushed her away and towards the door.

"That can wait. Let's get out."

But if they were destined to escape, 'twould not be via the hall. A dense black cloud of smoke rushed in when Mary opened the door, and towers of flame barred their passage from study to porch. Within them, cracking and spitting, burned the strange assortment of objects Darkin had seen the previous night. He wheeled around.

"Try the window."

'Twas equally fruitless, the shutters nailed down.

"He planned this all along!" Mary despaired. "How *could* he?"

She coughed on a spume of filth, and Darkin watched in a stupor as gobbets of fire from the ceiling spattered the rug upon which he'd awoken, lighting new blazes wherever they fell. Benumbed in body and mind by the smoke and heat, he felt he was burning already.

It seemed they were finally done for when a hail of blazing plaster announced the ceiling's impending collapse. Then Darkin felt Mary's hand upon his, guiding him gently but urgently forwards.

"Where—What—?"

"Follow me," she said, her words clear and calm above the Hellish roar of the flames. "We can get out through the sunroom."

447

He clutched her hand and stumbled behind her, his streaming eyes all but blind—into the scorching hall at first, then swiftly pulled to the left, pursued at every turn by screeching timbers and shattering glass. But the smoke thinned as they ran, and suddenly sunlight dispelled the darkness. Blinking, he saw they'd entered a room with a glazed double door giving onto a terrace outside. Mary rattled the handle, then grabbed a brass candelabra from a sideboard and threw it with all her might. The glass cracked and the wooden frame buckled, surrendering completely when she attacked its remains with a side-chair. Darkin simply looked on in dazed admiration.

She led him through the splinters and shards, across the terrace and onto an empty patch of soil that might have been a garden, had it contained any living plants. Darkin relished the cooling breeze on his face, but the air smelled no fresher outside than in, for yet another fire blazed at the end of the garden, and it had not been the first—behind a low colonnade sat a pile of ashes and charred bits of wood.

Exhausted, he collapsed upon a sculpted sandstone bench and looked back at the house. The inferno raged on, and now he saw its full extent: the upper floors had also been put to the flame, with even the attic afire.

"Your cousin is thorough," he rasped. "But there must be simpler ways to dispose of one's clutter." Mary joined him on the bench, and having kept hold of the scissors throughout their escape, now applied them to the rope around his wrists—more carefully than she'd attacked the manservant's neckcloth, Heavens be thanked. The finger-rings and blades were needlessly dainty; Darkin guessed they belonged to whoever had dressed Mary's wound.

"That was a stroke of luck, eh?"

"Perhaps someone left them on purpose," Mary said. "I'd like to think we had one ally in there." A weary smile lit her sweat- and soot-stained face. "Jediah was right about one thing—"

What that one thing might be, Darkin would have to ask later, for they heard the clang of a gate at the side of the house, followed by an anguished shout as the wreckage of a man lurched into the garden. It took Darkin far too long to put a name to the blackened face streaked with tears and blood.

"James! The door was locked, I broke a window, but the fire... too fierce. I thought he had killed you!"

His hands and arms were badly slashed and covered with burns—as was his face, and his chest beneath the torn and scorched shirt, and the side of his skull that wasn't already encrusted with blood. If he'd had the head wound before he arrived, as Darkin suspected, 'twas a miracle he had made it as far as the house.

"What kept you so long, old man?" he said, with a studiedly casual air as he hawked and spat a gobbet of phlegm.

But Rudge was long beyond banter. Mary helped him down to the ground, then sat alongside him and lifted his head on her lap.

"Ignore my boorish brother," she said, as Rudge began to breathe in stutters and starts. "Lie still, and I shall send him for help." She looked at her hands, then at Darkin, her eyes betraying her feelings. Darkin shook his head, and sat with her by Rudge's side.

"What was all that about, eh? You should have known that Mary would have things in hand."

449

Rudge made a fearful, grating attempt at a laugh. "Be a man of consequence, James," he whispered. "But never forget where you came from. And do not weep for me."

"'Tis the smoke," Darkin grunted.

A smile cracked the gardener's blistered lips. "I did nothing more than any man would do. For his son."

Then his head dropped back, he let out a sigh, and his body fell limp in Mary's embrace.

"He is gone," she said.

"Did you hear that? He *knew...*"

A hush descended despite the quickening fire, broken only when Jediah's runtish servant appeared, hurrying into the garden from the same direction as Rudge. He joined them all a-jitter, his agitation multiplied when he saw the man on the ground.

"'Twas not my idea," he babbled. "'Twas Master Jediah's doing, I swear. Not me, not the missus—"

With a silent word of farewell, Darkin patted Rudge on the shoulder, then snapped at the terrified servant, "Pull yourself together, fool!" When the weasel stopped sniffling, Darkin pointed at Rudge. "Treat this man with all the respect he is due. Do you hear? The fate of your immortal soul depends upon it. Mary will help you."

Mary frowned. "What about—Wait, where are you going?"

"Away," Darkin said.

He turned aside, unable to watch as her grief was compounded by shock, then confusion, then hurt.

"You can't go away. Not now."

He gritted his teeth. "That has always been the plan. Since the day I first heard of your brother's balloon. Why do you think I took such an interest? 'Tis my chance of a change in direction—to fly far away and find a new place, a new life."

Mary laid the old gardener back on the soil, then, as furious with Darkin as she'd been gentle with Rudge, confronted him with gore upon her petticoats, and a curse upon her lips.

"What about James? Where is *he*? Is he even alive? You have stolen *his* body, *his* life—don't you care?"

"They are not the first things I have stolen," Darkin muttered.

He turned his back on the burning house and strode towards the track that led to The Plain.

"And what, pray, do you think you are doing?" he said, increasing his pace.

"I am coming with you."

He stopped. "I forbid it. Wherever I be going, 'tis no place for a woman. And look at you—you are in no fit state to travel."

Mary pressed a hand to her wound with a wince, but her mind was clearly made up. Darkin considered her for a while before he relented, first with a sigh, then the ghost of a playful grin.

"Then come along if you must. But I warn you— the ride may be bumpy."

CHAPTER FIFTY-ONE

'TWAS NOT FAR TO THE TOWN HALL, where the eerie silence persisted. No ne'er-do-well at the butter-bench, no kitchen maid at Carfax; not a greasy parcel of meat to be seen, nor the babble of gossip or idle blather heard. A waggon trundled west from the High, but both the farmer and his horse appeared so slumberous, they barely counted as life. The road was otherwise empty. And the Town Hall door was locked.

"Is *everyone* at St Alban's?" I cried, then bellowed up at the window: "Hey! Hey! Let us in! 'Tis a matter of life and death!"

Kat added her voice to mine, and at this the door creaked open. Being on a chain, however, the gap was only a foot or so wide, and most of that occupied by a whiskery scowl.

"Cease that racket at once or I shall fetch the bailiff," it growled. "Can't a porter sleep in peace?"

"Let us pass and you may sleep all you wish," I retorted. "For this is a grave emergency."

The whiskers ventured out a smidgen further, suspiciously scanning the empty street. "Don't look like an emergency to me."

"Who be prattling there?" a new voice barked. Then the whiskers were jerked aside, and the Mayor of Oxford himself barred our entrance.

"If you don't let us in right now," I said, "a terrible fate will befall us all."

The Mayor frowned. "Do I know you?"

"Of course you do—I am James Sadler!" I cried. Then I realized that, of course, I was not, and that he might well have recognized me as Isaac Darkin. I took a step backwards. But the Mayor was now looking over my shoulder, a smile on his powdered face.

"Sadler—what a coincidence!" he exclaimed. "This man just said he is you!"

I turned about, enraged at the interruption—and of all the unnatural experiences I'd endured in the past several weeks, this surpassed even the man in the mirror. For though I saw myself approach, 'twas not as in a looking-glass. No cold, flat reflection this, but a living, breathing man, so familiar yet at once alarmingly alien. I could tell from my likeness's pallor that he felt the same, and in that moment our expressions, at least, were mirror images.

'Twas the newcomer—Isaac Darkin, I presumed—who recovered first, and demanded of the Mayor, "Let us in, man. This is urgent."

The Mayor's convivial smile turned to annoyance. "Enough of this nonsense!" he snapped, his hands upon the door.

"I want my aerostat!" shouted Darkin.

"So do I!" I yelled.

The Mayor paused and said, "It cannot be moved. Not today. I am reopening the exhibition this afternoon. With the holiday crowds, the takings will be prodigious."

"You cannot keep it from me!" Darkin cried. "What about our agreement?"

"'Tis *my* aerostat," I insisted. "And no one does anything with it without my permission."

The Mayor scratched his chin, appraising each of us in turn. Then to Darkin, he said, "Very well. I shall allow you to take back possession of your aerostat—*against our agreement*, I might add—on condition that you relinquish one-half of all your proceeds accrued. And not a penny less—do you understand?"

"That is daylight robbery!"

So focussed was I on my mission, I had been 'til now only vaguely aware that Darkin had not come alone, and when his companion thus drew my attention I could scarcely believe my eyes.

"Mary! What are you doing here? Why are you bleeding? Have you seen your clothes, your hair, your *hat*?"

"Forgive me," my sister grated, her scowl most uncouth. "How slovenly of me, not to wash before we came out. Regardless that I've been shot, then almost burned to death, then..." She glanced down upon her petticoats, and her sarcasm swiftly subsided. "James... if that be you... though of course it must, for who else might it be...? Brother, I have terrible news—"

"'Twill have to wait, I'm afraid." I raised a hand to silence her and returned to the closing door. 'Twas fortunate for us all that they made it so weighty, and the Mayor so small. "I do not have all day."

"Nor I," harrumphed the Mayor.

"People will *die* if we dally much longer."

As the Mayor wavered, Darkin impatiently shoved me aside and seized the front of his waistcoat.

"Stop that," I hissed. "Think of my reputation!"

455

The Mayor wriggled feebly. "Release me, Sadler. I shall report you to the magistrate for this."

"Then fetch him quickly," Darkin said. "For I, too, have misdeeds to recount." He hoisted the Mayor off his feet and jammed him fast betwixt the frame and the almost-closed door, as if inclined to haul him straight through, and Heaven help his arms, legs, and other protuberances. "It concerns one night in Stokenchurch, and an inn—The Jolly Bull. A strange place for respectable men to meet, but unrespectable business was done that night: a deal between two worthies, one from this very borough. Most profitable it was—to the conspirators. Less so for the good folk of Oxford, who might expect the taxes they pay to be used for the weal of all."

The Mayor's cheeks blanched, then turned a blazing shade of puce—a disconcerting display beneath the white powder. "How—how did you—?"

Darkin jerked him further through the gap, so close the tips of their noses were almost touching. "Let us say, a very old friend told me so. You should be more careful who you sing to in your cups. Now—will you open the door or shall *I* fetch the magistrate?"

"Of course! Of course! 'Twas never in doubt!" All fingers and thumbs, the Mayor released the door-chain, then fled as the four of us entered, his wig slipping down on one ear and his own, golden chain jangling.

"So 'twas you who stole my body." Darkin glowered at me as I latched the door behind us. "You might have taken better care of it."

"And you of mine," I growled, for he was as filthy and soot-stained as Mary. "My sister's, too."

Darkin glanced at her, then flashed Kat a roguish smile. "Mornin' Kat. Good to see you."

Beside me, Mary bristled.

"The pleasure's all mine," said Kat, taking my arm.

"May we save these happy reunions for later?" Mary urged. "The Mayor might fetch reinforcements."

"Agreed," Darkin said. "Let's go get my aerostat."

"*My* aerostat."

My body—and its objectionable occupant—took the lead as we passed through the building; I scurried behind like a pup, but my hackles were raised. "What could *you* possibly want with it?" I demanded.

"I wish only to escape the many woes of my troublesome life."

"That is a fine plan," I said. "But you forget one tiny detail. The aerostat—like the life you so unfairly disparage—is *mine*."

Darkin shrugged. "Your body, your aerostat, your sister... I admit, some might call it unfair."

I glowered at Mary. "Is it true? You are with this... ruffian?"

"'Tis a long story," she sighed.

"Not as long as ours, I'll bet," said Kat.

"I'd be careful who sees you about," I continued, archly. "For people will think you are courting your brother, and I shudder to imagine what Father might say to that."

When Mary failed to reply, I returned to Darkin. "But even were the aerostat *not* my property, virtue dictates I should have it, for my need is nobler than yours. By means of her unholy art, your friend Serafina D'Bonaventura would spark a deadly riot at the House of St Alban the Martyr—"

"St Alban's?" Mary cried. "Father will be there!"

"Indeed," I said. "Which makes this all the more urgent. The globe is fully inflated, yes?"

Mary nodded.

"Then fortune is on our side. I shall board the aerostat—you will all help me launch it—and rise above the town. From there, I'll shout down to whomever I see, though I doubt I shall want for attention. The small balloon I launched with Rudge caused a stir that shook the city. Seeing a far larger globe—and a man raised beneath it!—the townsfolk will be astounded, and forget all notions of violence."

Darkin snorted. "I should like to see it. But I shall be long gone by then."

Mary grasped his arm, forcing him to a standstill. "And our father? He took you in, cared for you like a son."

"I *was* his son!"

"You have to help us—please!"

I gave him no chance to prevaricate further, for the obvious means of persuasion had suddenly struck me.

"If you help me with the aerostat," I said, "I will give you back your body."

"What if I'd rather keep yours?" Darkin grunted, though he was plainly interested.

"I am sure you would rather have your own. In every way, 'tis so much... *more.*"

"Supposing I did," said Darkin, "how would we do it? We need Serafina's accursed hatpin."

"Look what *I* have," giggled Kat.

I reached out to take it from her, but Darkin stayed me. "Be careful with that. 'Tis called the Soul-Eater, for it swallows whole the minds of men—and women, too, I would hazard, though Serafina's taste is for the former. Woebetide any man who crosses her, in business or love, or any man she loves too much, for 'tis her pleasure to trap them in here—" He tapped the glistening stone. "—and keep them close forever."

I heard Mary gasp, but being focussed on my own grievance, offered her no chance to speak. "She told me 'twas a family heirloom," I said. "That her people have owned it for generations."

"'Tis older than that," said Darkin. "And no one owns the Soul-Eater—it passes through human hands where, when, and how it might wish. Owning them, if anything."

I gulped, my offer now less tempting than it had seemed a moment ago. "'Twould be madness, don't you think?" I gabbled. "To wittingly give ourselves up, having already suffered so much against our will? 'Tis not as though we have to. Not now, at least. Nor can we guarantee success, for we are hardly experts in the procedure."

"I thought you wanted your body back," Darkin sneered. "'Tis after all, in every way, so much *less*."

Kat giggled again, and my cheeks began to burn.

"Not least," I muttered, "'the Town Hall is an ill-suited venue for surgery."

"Stop snivelling, James Sadler!"

This outburst came from Mary, who confronted me with a spirit she had never shown before.

"Do it or do not," she said. "But whichever, choose quickly. For Father needs us now, not next week!"

I looked from her to Kat to Darkin and back, my face hotter still. "Very well."

With a shiver, I closed my eyes, and bared my surrogate chest. When a moment passed and nothing transpired, I opened them again to see a bemused expression on Darkin's (my!) face.

"Is this not how it's done?" I grumbled.

"Everything is a show to our Serafina." Darkin seized my hand and showed me the pin. "Even this serves for appearances only, though it makes a convenient pricker." Then he jabbed the pin in my thumb, and repeated the same on himself. "Perhaps I should tell you now," he added.

I frowned. "Tell me what?"

"Later," Mary commanded.

Darkin shrugged and grabbed me again—this time in a firm handshake, with the stone between our palms and smears of our blood mingled upon it.

I'd felt no pain at the needle's prick, but now a wintry chill overtook me; a sense of time standing still, and that Darkin and I, though two, were bound as one in a single substance. I heard once again the ceaseless chatter of bird-like beings, then a violent gust of wind threw me backwards. I staggered against the wall behind me—now facing the opposite side of the hall, and a tall, muscular man with a grizzled chin and dirty black hair.

I heaved for breath like a babe just born, and as weak as a babe in my newly diminished anatomy. Darkin, meanwhile, was swiftly recovered, and already pressing his suit with my awestruck sister.

"Allow me to introduce myself, Miss Sadler—Isaac Darkin is my name, gentleman of the road, and forever at your service. *Former* gentleman of the road," he added, catching Mary's frown.

Not to be outdone, Kat flung her arms about my neck and delivered a vigorous kiss to my cheek. "Pleased to meet you too, James Sadler. And my, you are so pretty!"

And flimsy with it, for that kiss almost knocked me flat. Isaac Darkin, I feared, had never been felled by a woman.

I grasped the highwayman's arm both to steady myself and to gain his attention. "Did you see them, too?" I wheezed. " In the stone? The birds?"

"Not birds," said Darkin. "Souls. You may have recognized some of them."

Mary glowered at him. "You knew about this, didn't you? You should have told me."

"I've had much on my mind," he said. "If you have noticed."

Mary then gave a wretched sigh and pulled me close. "Oh, James! Dr Sheffield, Dr Crouch, all your colleagues at the laboratory... 'tis *them* in there. I am certain Serafina has trapped them, and how we might get them back without her aid, I do not know."

"This is your news?" I asked—and what harrowing news it was.

"Some of it," Darkin replied.

I paused to collect my thoughts. "Then once we have dealt with St Alban's, we shall find Serafina and deal with *this* as well."

Kat beamed at me, and I allowed myself a twinge of delight at the pride I saw in her eyes.

Thanks to all this chatter and general to-doing, we had made little headway, having barely moved beyond the lodge and its whiskery porter. But now I urged the party on.

"I presume the aerostat is in the courtyard?"

"No—it be in the council chamber," said Darkin.

"Mary and Kat will help me with the basket, then as soon as I am installed, Darkin will cut the ropes—"

"Darkin will do as he chooses," he snarled. "You do not control my actions now, *pastry-boy.*"

"Mind your tongue, *convict.* Or I may lose control of *my* actions." I clenched my fists, not a little dismayed to see how puny they were.

"Will both of you shut your potato-traps?" cried Mary.

I gaped at my sister in shock, as, to his credit, did Darkin.

"Some colourful language you've learned," I muttered. "What else has he taught you, I wonder?"

Then daylight dawned ahead, as we came upon the courtyard, and all our petty quarrels were forgot.

"You said you inflated it." I jerked to a horrified halt.

"We *did,*" Darkin said.

"Is it meant to look like that?" asked Kat. She crossed to the centre of the courtyard and poked at the mass of fabric, collapsed upon its basket like a dollop of sunken dough.

Mary clapped her hands to her cheeks. "This is Edwin Osborne's doing—he climbed upon it during the exhibition. But I thought he'd had no chance to do any harm..."

"A slow puncture," Darkin sighed, then tut-tutted and turned for the exit. "That is that, then."

From the street, we heard the bells of Old Tom sounding the three-quarter hour.

"'Tis nearly noon," said Mary.

"There must be *something* we can do," I cried.

And then I did indeed lose control of my actions, for my feet, with scarcely a prod from my conscious mind, took me speedily out of the courtyard. Before I knew where I was, or what I was doing, I'd stormed straight through the building and burst onto Fish Street. The others followed behind, calling my name in consternation, but I focussed on staying upon my feet and moving ever forwards at pace. In my unfamiliar body, 'twas the best I could do.

CHAPTER FIFTY-TWO

I BOLTED DOWN NORTH GATE STREET: past the Conduit, The Crown, and the Golden Cross; past the pillory opposite Bridewell Lane, where I'd strolled with Jediah lifetimes ago. There I encountered the first living soul I had seen since I left the Town Hall: a lad, wide-eyed and anxious, his face pressed to the window in the room above The Plough, a cloth held tight to his mouth. The casement opened a fraction and the boy called down to me, though I struggled to catch his words.

"You for St Alban's, Mister?" Denying me a chance to reply, he continued, "Then your belly be bigger than your brains, 'tis what my Ma says. And bigger still when the Gaol Fever gets you, for then it be puffed up fatter than Sadler's balloon."

I had to smile. "Is that why you're hiding up there?"

The boy nodded.

"Are there more of you?"

"Everyone! We're all of us indoors, 'Cept those gone to Alban's for their sweeties. My Ma says—"

Then a woman—Ma, I presumed—appeared, a cloth fastened about her face like a highwayman's mask, and the child was snatched from my sight as the casement slammed shut.

Although 'everyone' might indeed be indoors as he'd claimed, when I reached the Broad 'twas obvious Oxford had no shortage of foolhardy gundiguts. Not as many as in a normal year, but enough—crammed like cattle in Alban Lane and around the foot of Old Crab's Tower. Even the City Waits had turned out, if diminished in number. 'Twas the holiday mood that fell short; as I approached the rear of the crowd, all I heard was gripes and groans, and bitter talk of the pestilence that the Earth had so recently spewed.

"'Tis fine for *them*," a brawny cove expounded. "Safe up there in their tower, untouched by the hand of death that bedevils us common folk."

"Perhaps that is their wish," added another. "To watch us all die for their pleasure."

"Nonsense!" cried a third. "For who would butcher their meat, and sew their gowns, and mend their walls, if we were gone? Who would run the city?"

"'Tis not so far-fetched," said an elderly man. "One year, I remember, the sweetmeats were poisoned."

"I remember that, too."

"And I!"

"And I," confirmed the brawny man. "My father was near choked to death that day. They have tried to murder us once, now they do so again."

"But why?"

"Why not? Were we gone, they could take the whole town for themselves—it'd save them the trouble of tossing us treats now and then, to keep us in line."

On cue, I caught sight of black robes on the roof of the tower, moving into position between the merlons. The Master glanced down in his hooded disguise, then a bran tub hove into view. A bran tub containing Sadler's finest comfits. The boneheaded rabble responded with menacing jeers, and seized with terror, I pounced on them: elbowing, shoving, kicking—and bawling all the while.

"Go to your homes! All of you! *Now!*"

They elbowed and shoved and kicked me back, as if I were nine years old again. *Stop! The sweetmeats are poisoned!* Grabbing any and all that I could, I tried to drag them away one-by-one, but then I was grabbed myself and flung rudely back to the street, where I crashed upon the cobbles. On the opposite side of the road, near the museum, I saw Darkin, Mary, and Kat.

"Where is Father?" Mary yelled.

As I pointed with trembling hand towards the tower, 'The Maid of Llangollen' began—this year in an unusual minor key, owing perhaps, to the City Waits' want of performers.

More dreadful still, were the bells of Old Crab's Tower, striking twelve.

~ ~ ~

Thomas Sadler waited in what had become, over the years, his usual station. Out of sight of the crowd in Alban Lane, but able to watch with satisfaction as his sweetmeats—*his* Benefaction, as he liked to think of it—were dispensed to their grateful recipients. 'Twas the highlight of his year, a time to reflect on his blessings and look to the future, though this St Alban's Day, he found nothing to celebrate.

"Strange it is, how life moves in circles," he mused to the Bursar, who by tradition escorted him onto the roof and stood with him during the ceremony. "On the first occasion my comfits were strewn from this spot,

I believed my world had ended, that my family's reputation was fatally wounded, and would forever lie in
ruins."

The Bursar, a normally talkative man, nodded and
grunted.

"'Twas not the case, of course—far from it!—
but now I truly have reached the end. Unthinkable
disgrace has befallen my family. Immoral subterfuge
laid bare, my children embroiled in scandal. What be
it all for, eh? We labour a lifetime for kith and kin,
and then...? Naught but dust, and none to remember
us."

"As you speak of dust," said the Bursar, springing to
life, "'twas suggested at our Fellows' meeting this morning, that the College conduct a grand *spring cleaning*,
not only of our buildings, but of our traditions. In the
words of the Dean, *St Alban's will take a brave new
broom to the dusty cobwebs of habit!* You will be no-
tified, of course, but I thought I might apprise you of
this... renewal, in advance. You, of all men, are aware
of the critical need to move with the times."

"Indeed?" Sadler digested this information with
care. "I shall be more than happy, of course, to help
facilitate your... renewal."

"I am afraid," said the Bursar, "the renewal does
not appertain to the Benefaction."

'Twas warm in the sun upon the roof, but Thomas
Sadler felt a chill in his heart. "You would sweep away
the Benefaction?"

The Bursar straightened his gown upon his shoulders. "Ah, no. Perhaps I should have said, the renewal
does not appertain to your *contract.*"

When Sadler did not reply, the man continued, in a
happier style, "For sure, the Master and Fellows will

bestow some special gift to mark your many years of service. A painting of Old Crab's Tower has been suggested, which you may hang in your home to remember us by."

Sadler glanced towards the battlement, where servants were fixing the bran tub in place, high above the heads of the crowd. He imagined dashing across the roof, taking everyone by surprise; grabbing a handful of comfits and then—what? Petulantly throwing them away? They would be thrown away whatever he did.

"If it please you, sir," he said. "I think I should like to leave."

But his chaperone, who usually stuck to his side like a gum-cake, had gone to look over the battlement—along with the Master, the Fellows, and everyone else upon the roof. All were staring down into Alban Lane, with an air of no little alarm.

When his curiosity overcame his pride and he joined them, Thomas Sadler realized why.

~ ~ ~

In the gatehouse above St Alban's lodge, Ambrose Bean raised a two-pint silver chalice charged with a generous portion of well-aged Madeira—the former a tiny part of the college plate, the latter freshly liberated from its cellar.

"To the future," he said.

"To the suggestible townsfolk of Oxford," replied Serafina.

He laughed and returned to the window, with its excellent view of the street below. "You chose our vantage point well."

"'Twas all down to you, my dearest. Had the porter not seen your show, or its effects been not so long last-

ing, we would still be waiting out there, for those dull-
ards to get us inside."

Bean basked in a warm glow of pleasure while he
sipped his wine and watched events unfold. Several
Townsmen continued to fume at the foot of the tower,
shouting and waving their fists at the unfortunates
trapped on the roof, but many others had moved to
the gate, to hammer and yell for admittance.

"See that building?" he said, as a smaller group detached and crossed the street. "The oddly shaped one,
with the lookout on top. What is it, do you think?"

"They call it a theatre, though it has never once
seen a show, only the flatulent ceremonials of the
Gownsmen."

"And those stone heads, upon the wall around it?"

"Likenesses of Philosophers, I believe."

"How exquisitely apposite. 'Tis heating up down
there," he added. "Look—they are fighting amongst
themselves! I shall hate to miss the finale."

"And I. But I fear 'twill get a little *too* hot before the
final curtain falls. Best I be done with my business
here, then we shall both take a bow."

"A pity, but sensible thinking." Bean drained the
chalice with a last, lingering look through the window.
"Strange to say, I shall miss Oxford. 'Tis a handsome
place."

Serafina smiled. "But at this time of year, I have
heard, Paris is *beautiful*."

~ ~ ~

I picked my bruised body off the cobbles and ran
across the Broad to join my strange little band of
companions.

"'Tis hopeless," I said, my shoulders slumped in defeat.

"We have to do *something*!" Mary gazed up at the tower, suddenly rigid with fear. "My God, is that Father? I can see him, looking over the battlement. James!"

Darkin took hold of her shoulders and turned her aside.

"Why? Why did she do this?" I cried. Hearing their insults and threats of dire violence, the crowd seemed to me barely human. "Why St Alban's?"

"She bears them a grudge." Mary spoke from Darkin's embrace, her composure recovered a little. "One of their Fellows held her here as a child. I don't know why—Jediah would not say—but 'twas certainly for horrible purposes. Her father sold her, like chattel."

"Jediah told you this? How would *he* know such things?"

"There is much you have missed," said Darkin. "Especially concerning your... cousin."

I frowned at that weird hesitation. "Perhaps you could summarize. If it be of any use, that is, and not just salacious tittle-tattle."

"Watch out!" shouted Kat.

Several Townsmen had broken away from the rest and stampeded across the street. For an instant, I truly believed we would all be mangled. But then the mob veered east—their target not us, but the Sheldonian Theatre, and in particular the thirteen stone heads upon its wall.

These statues had never been treated kindly, and the mob took no time to topple the first in the row. It fell from plinth to street with a crack, then they picked

471

it up between them—it being half as long as a man is tall and very much weightier—and dashed back towards St Alban's. As they neared the college, they picked up their pace further still, and with naught but a last-second warning that their colleagues should move aside, rammed the head straight into the gate. It took just three such blows, before the wicket was knocked off its hinges.

A cheer went up and the rioters swarmed the lodge like angry bees. 'Twas fortunate only the wicket was breached and not the whole gate, for the narrow gap ensured no more than one at a time could pass, and in practice not even that many. The mob's fury, impatience, and lack of organization led to many becoming stuck and needing their colleagues to pull them out or push them in to resume the invasion.

"'Tis dangerous here," said Kat. "We should go somewhere safer and *then* make a plan."

"You are right." Seizing the moment, I pointed towards the museum. "Get inside, bolt the door, and let no one in. Not even I—the face might be mine, but the intention someone else's." I turned to Darkin. "I would be indebted if you delayed your escape a while longer. To see all goes safely here."

He nodded.

"And I would have that accursed stone."

"What are you going to do?" whispered Kat.

"I am sure something will come along," I replied, with what I hoped was a dashing smile.

CHAPTER
FIFTY-THREE

I FOUND THE LODGE DESERTED save for the porter, who had hidden beneath his overturned booth when the townsfolk broke down the door. Seeing him shaking with fright but unscathed, I dared to hope Father might also be spared—though neither Town nor Gown would be safe, if the rioters reached the overcrowded roof of Old Crab's Tower. Besides which, I supposed 'twas my duty to rescue the Master, Fellows, and Scholars as well—and even save from themselves the rioting townsfolk.

Venturing into the front quadrangle first, I encountered a panicking crowd of cooks and scullery boys; the college kitchens were breached, yelled one, and their pots and pans assaulted. Not even Dr Crouch could miss *that*, though besides the immediate racket, more muffled celebrations suggested they'd breached the wine cellar, too. Several Townsmen seemed as full as goats already; I spotted them through the dining hall windows, lolling about at High Table with their feet up on the cloth and making sport with pilfered tidbits, while the brawny man from Alban Lane strutted upon the refectory tables, the lid of a soup tureen on his head and a ladle clenched in his hand like the Chancellor's mace.

Matters took a more serious turn in the back quad, where the college's Undergraduates lived and the rioters, not content with trampling the grass, had laid siege to the students' staircases. 'Twas alarming to hear the abuse the townsfolk hurled, but worse to witness their targets' retaliation. I tried to console myself as I fled the scene—dodging stray volleys of books and chamber-pot contents—thinking that if a riot had to happen, 'twas better it did so in summer, with fewer true scholars about.

I knew where the next arch would take me.

To my surprise, fewer than half a dozen had found their way to the tower. They had assembled in the corner of the cloister, shouting and whistling, but making no real attempt to get in. I guessed the Master had sent his servants to hold the door until help arrived, and I thought of that Midsummer's Day when I'd climbed those steps to the roof myself. Then as now, Father had been my prime concern, except then I'd tried to escape him, not save him. In my mind's eye, I saw myself stumble through the gloom, dazed and desperate; the dead beneath my feet, secret paths and invisible threats all around, a blue satin ribbon, a nursery rhyme. *The Moon shines bright. The Stars give a light...*

'Twas fitting to see Serafina D'Bonaventura at that instant, clad in the black cloak and veil she had worn the evening we met—and the one we parted, as well.

"Isaac!" she cried, with apparent delight. "'Tis wonderful to see you again! Especially after we parted on not such good terms at those flea-bitten lodgings of Ambrose's. But... what are you doing here, exactly?"

Of course, to Serafina I was still Darkin, and when I'd recovered from my initial confusion, I wondered if I might turn that to my advantage.

"I have come to thank you," I said, affecting the highwayman's forthright manner as I strode around the cloister. "I hear Isaac Darkin escaped the noose yet again, and so outrageously, it had to be your doing."

"'Tis the second time I have saved your neck—so yes, I think I am due a dividend." Her eyes sparkled behind the veil. "You have something specific in mind? Although, I am afraid, your original body would make a more pleasing reward... Which reminds me— I have some bad news concerning your Kat."

My inadvertent alarm must have shown on my face, for Serafina chuckled. "Oh dear. 'Tis serious, then? In that case, I shall let you down gently. It seems Kat, too, prefers her men more manly, and less..." She looked me up and down. "...just, less."

I managed a flinty frown. "'Tis an old joke, Serafina. Do you think I've not heard it before? As for my thanks... Well, the best reward I *can* offer, is to persuade you to call a halt to all this." I gestured towards the rioters, still clamouring ineffectually at the tower.

"A novel idea of reward, you have. How would I benefit?"

"You would have your conscience."

She laughed. "You and Kat are two of a piece. Perhaps you are made for each other after all."

"This morning, you saved one innocent man condemned for another man's crime. Why are these Gownsmen *and* Townsmen any different?" Encouraged when she did not protest, I pushed further. "You

475

do not have to forgive, Serafina, but 'twill be easier for all if you forget. In the name of aught that lies between us, I beg you—stop this riot now, before anyone is hurt."

She gazed into my eyes and pressed her hand over my heart, as she'd done in the Golden Cross Yard. "Why, Isaac... I never knew you felt—" Then she gasped. "You are not Darkin! How—"

"I am, as you see, James Sadler." I pointed at the tower. "My father is up there, and though I have often wished we were unrelated, I would rather not lose him now."

She tried to pull her hand away, but I held it in place.

"We have been here before. You sang to me."

"*The Moon shines bright...*" Serafina smiled sadly. "My mother taught me that song. She died when I was very young."

"My mother died too. She tried to teach me many things, though I hardly ever listened. She once said that when I was ready, I would understand. I still cannot say what she meant me to understand—maybe I never will—but I *do* know, now, who I am and who I am not. Not everything is a show, Serafina."

She did not respond with violence as I had feared, or even much irritation, so I continued. "You wanted to be remembered for this day. To create a spectacle none would ever forget—bigger than St Scholastica's Day, you said. That *day* was actually three, not one. It began with a brawl in a tavern and ended with half the town burned down, and dozens maimed or killed. When men from around the county came to fight for the townsfolk's cause, students barricaded the city gates, to fight for their lives. Even King Edward called for peace, but he was ignored and the fighting went on. And every year since, to mark the first day of the riot, the town's highest worthies have to swallow their pride and pay penance. That riot is remembered because it had consequences, then and ever after. How does *this* compare with *that?*"

I gestured across the cloister at the increasingly temperate Townsmen. I had worried that reinforcements might soon arrive from elsewhere in the college; now that notion seemed absurd.

"Your rioters are too busy having fun to do much rioting—they prefer to eat, drink, to play the fool. But 'tis *you* who made them fools. No one will remember this day for long, and to anyone who does 'twill be just a party that got out of hand. Your spectacular show never happened, Serafina. You have failed—and maybe, like me, you failed because your heart was not in it. Because this is not who you are."

She closed her eyes for a moment, then sighed and called to the Townsmen.

"You, there!"

One of them spun about and lurched towards us the instant she spoke, as if hooked on a fisherman's line.

"We must... stop the Gownsmen..." he croaked, straining to break Serafina's invisible grip and return to his colleagues. "We must..."

"You must do nothing." She placed her open palm on his chest.

"The comfits are poisoned!"

She shook her head. "The comfits are not poisoned. They never were. Go tell your friends so. 'Tis time you all returned to your homes and families."

The man recoiled as the line snapped, then he raced back to his colleagues, shouting and pointing.

"Thank you," I said, with feeling.

"I cannot guarantee 'twill work. It takes no less than two men to begin a riot, and more than one to stop it."

"I just hope—"

The arrival of Ambrose Bean interrupted me.

"Here he is at last," said Serafina, plainly annoyed.

He swayed like a ship in a squall, though 'twas hard to tell if that were because he was drunk, or merely over-encumbered by both his Thanatoscope and his coat; sagged almost off his shoulders, the latter clinked merrily as he shuffled around the cloister to join us.

"I hoped we had seen the last of you," he muttered.

"Do not fret Ambrose—'tis not Isaac, but James!" Serafina beamed. "I hope your return to the cellar was worth this tiresome waste of my time?"

Bean grinned slyly and opened his coat, revealing many capacious pockets and bottles in all of them. "Those barbarous townsfolk could not tell a *Château d'Yquem* from a flagon of horse piss."

Serafina stared long and hard, barely concealing her disdain, though I doubt Bean noticed. "Come along, then. I have business to finish."

"What do you mean?" I followed behind her in consternation, Bean trailing us both. "Where are you going?"

She stopped by a door and smiled at me. "Dear James. Are you not a little curious, to see how this all began?"

She opened the door before I could ask further questions—and all were swiftly forgot anyway, for the room we had entered upon was the one where I had awoken, dazed and injured, so many years past. It remained exactly as I remembered it, as if not one day had elapsed between then and now. I saw the sofa, the plump cushions, the carpet in which I had curled my bare toes, the books—so many books! The window where I heard two Gownsmen deride me. *No one of any consequence.* The trestle-desk beside the window remained as well, and the strange contraption upon it, which I now knew as an orrery—a mechanical representation of the Heavenly realm and its contents.

Indeed, throughout the whole room, the only differences I identified were a side-chair placed close to the desk and its occupant: an aged man, stick-thin and wasted, dressed in Gownsman robes, his liver-spotted scalp dotted with random tufts of white hair. His skeletal fingers clutched the chair's armrests as if in a rictus, yet his face hung slack-jawed and devoid of expression, his skin dried-up and paper-thin. Only his eyes seemed alive, for they were open and staring, but his gaze was fixed on the orrery, and he did not react when the three of us entered. Twas a long time, I suspected, since he last reacted to anything.

"So this is your gaoler." Bean leaned the Thanatoscope against the wall behind the door and went to inspect the old man as if he were one of Tradescant's exhibits. He snapped his fingers in the vacant face, with no response. "Has he been this way all the time?"

"They couldn't decide what to do with him." Serafina looked pleased with herself. "So they chose to do nothing at all. They keep him fed, watered, washed when he needs it, and wait for Father Time to call and take him off their hands." She turned to me and added, "I keep contacts in Oxford. In many towns, in fact. 'Tis good to know the lie of the land, before I move in."

479

Then I, too, came around the chair for a closer look.

"I know this man," I breathed.

"Of course," said Serafina. "He is the man who brought you here, for this is his study. 'Twas the first time I saved your life, when I tempted you out of this room with my song. Do you remember? I told you to run. I knew he would try to take you, as he took me, and would use you for his investigations as well."

I'd been too dazzled to see his face that day, but I heard his voice loud and clear. *Might he rest here a little while longer?...I shall return him when he's recovered...*

"He thought to make me disappear, and that no one would notice or care." Thought 'twas long in the past, I trembled with fear for my nine-year-old self. "Maybe he hoped to give Father money for *me.*"

"'Twould surely have been an unthinkable fate," said Bean.

"Indeed," said Serafina. "But not in the way you like to imply. In the months I spent trapped in this maze of mazes, nothing of *that* nature occurred, though it might have seemed to some, the obvious motive. Even had he wanted to, he'd have baulked at it, I am sure. For his whole life was governed by fear— so much so, it seemed odd to me, that he'd crave any more of it."

"He planned to live forever, you see," said Bean, as if I needed a clarification.

"He was your cousin's father's teacher and friend," said Serafina. "The Thanatoscope, you know, was a gift between them, for my gaoler loved to tinker."

"I know, I saw it here," I said.

"*He* first saw the Soul-Eater at their home, though he knew what a soul-eater be from his readings. *I* never saw him so thrilled as when he told me—and he told me everything, for I was not just the star of the show, but its only audience, 'til your cousin saw things he should not... All I *felt* was dread. Your cousin stole the stone at his request. He would have done aught for that man, I believe. 'Twas perhaps out of missing his father. Then my gaoler swore him to secrecy, and after that poor Jediah's troubled mind was thoroughly knocked out of balance."

"For good—or rather, bad—it seems," said Bean. "Having met him in person quite recently."

So much I saw more clearly now, but much I still wanted to know. "What was the Soul-Eater's purpose?" I asked.

"Using the stone, he hoped to transport his soul to a new, youthful body once his own became too old. And to do so forever, leaving behind him a trail of young souls trapped in soon-to-die bodies, robbed of their lives. I would not let that happen. I was only a child myself, but I was a prodigy, and I knew what to do. I overthrew my gaoler, and fled with the tools of my torment—but not until I had put him away, in a special small prison I made just for him."

She wound the orrery's key by a couple of turns, and the spheres began to move in their preordained paths. The Gownsman's eyes swivelled in his motionless face to follow them—or rather, to follow *it*. For as I watched, I realized the object of his attention was not the orrery itself, but the small, translucent gem representing the Moon.

"You have heard the tale of the princess who pricked her finger, then slept for a hundred years? In

481

our story, 'twas not a princess who fell asleep, but a king."

As the orrery slowed to a halt, Serafina reached out with finger and thumb, and plucked the Moon's orb from its mount. I glimpsed a bright, sharp golden pin left behind, then by some sleight of hand, she replaced the orb with another of similar nature. The Gownsman's gaze never wavered throughout, so when she lifted her veil and raised the glassy gem to her own eye, 'twas as if they regarded each other through its interior.

"Eternal life was not the least of his plans. He talked of sending his soul to the Sun in a gem, leaving his body unharmed by the journey. Which is why, of course, I put him in the Moon—it being the lesser light, forever subject to the motions of the greater orbs."

"This is all very well, but getting us nowhere." Bean indicated the window, with a scowl. "Those blasted Proctors have arrived, and in force. If your gloating is done, let us leave while we can."

"Patience, dear Ambrose. For we are upon the final act." Serafina dropped the Moon-gem onto the carpet, and with the solid wooden heel of a black-velvet Louis shoe, first smashed it into fragments, then thoroughly ground it to dust.

This took even the Gownsman by surprise, and he was the first to recover. His hands flew to his throat, and he coughed and gasped as he ripped his horrified gaze from the ruined gem to the smiling woman who'd just destroyed it.

"I hope you have learned your lesson," she said.

The Gownsman struggled to reply, his mouth clicking open and shut like the hinged jaw of a toy.

"'Twas a long wait for me, and a longer one for you, I expect. All of these years, shut up in there—" She pointed at the Moon-dust on the carpet. "—and now you are free, but shut up again, in a frail and feeble body that will very soon wither and die."

The Gownsman continued to claw at his throat, disjointed whimpers and mewls emerging, but still no words.

"I brought *this* fool with me—" Now she indicated Bean, who spluttered in outrage. "—to show you what he has done with your Thanatoscope. So you might know how it feels, but also so I might see inside your mind and add a few nightmares. Perhaps you would have come to long for death... But on reflection, I think I shall not. 'Twould be a punishment too far even for you, and I must consider my own conscience now, thanks to him." She glanced at me, accusingly.

"You... do... not... dare..." croaked the Gownsman, his words as insubstantial as an echo from the depths of an empty tomb.

Serafina patted his shoulder. "Make the most of the time you have," she said, then straightened and moved towards Bean with a practical air. "And now I shall deal with *you...*"

"'Tis about time you did. We must leave at once, my dear. My display at the Golden Cross turned a decent profit, but the show is not so inviting *sans* you, and your *indecent costume.*"

He grinned and slapped her behind as he spoke, then busied himself with the Thanatoscope, so missed her reaction.

"First, we shall collect my effects from The Crown."

Serafina raised a hand to stop him. "I prefer to travel light."

"What are you talking about? Serafina?"

"Darling Ambrose," she purred. "Did you believe I'd forgive and forget? I took the opportunity to finish my business here, and I enjoyed your petty vendetta against the Gownsmen. Why, I even learned the difference betwixt a Philosopher and a *Natural* Philosopher—although too late, I am afraid, for those *particular* gentlemen. But in the end, I would never have been here at all, were it not for you."

Quicker than Bean could protest let alone defend himself, she wrenched aside his shirt and delved in her cloak. Then she froze and glared at me, the truth of her own carelessness dawning.

"What have you done with it?"

Bean used this distraction to shove her aside; she struck the desk as she fell, tipping the orrery onto the floor, while Bean stumbled to safety. Trembling from head to toe, he glared at her from the doorway in wordless fury, his torn shirt clenched to his heart, his purpling face puckered up like a babe about to bawl.

"You—" he gurgled. "You—"

'Twas the last we heard of him, save the clinking of his coat as he bolted. Serafina yelled after him in frustration, and I decided I should also take my leave—whether she'd found her conscience or not.

She got herself up on her elbows, beneath her a wreck of twisted gold wire, and gems thrown from their orbits rolling around on the carpet like marbles. Her hat had come off and her veil knocked askew; she raised a hand to straighten it, then stopped and stared at her palm. 'Twas smeared with blood.

In the side-chair, the Gownsman cackled.

When she turned her baleful glare on me, I fled.

⬡

CHAPTER FIFTY-FOUR

I DID NOT GET FAR, however, for I ran straight out of the cloister into the azure-robed arms of a Proctor—with not just a Pro-Proctor in tow, but a Bedel as well. 'Twas clear the authorities took the riot rather more seriously than the rioters did.

"Hold!" ordered the Proctor, while the Pro-Proctor hastened to stand in my path and the Bedel brandished his mace.

"You must let me pass!" I cried. "'Tis a matter of life and death." Although, I thought as I said this, was any matter *not*, nowadays?

"Thought you could riot with impunity, eh?" barked the Proctor, as they began to march me away— in the direction of the lodge, it appeared, which was at least where I had been heading. "Thought you could run from the harm you've caused, and no one would stop you?"

"Do I look like a rioter?"

The Proctor and the Pro-Proctor glanced at each other.

"You look like a Townsman," said the latter. "And you look to be running loose on college property, with no obvious reason for such."

"That is because you neglected to ask! I came here to *stop* the riot. And I succeeded!"

A hollow-sounding claim, I had to admit, as we passed the shredded books and human filth in the back quad, and the empty bottles and vomit adorning the front. I'd thought I might make a run for it at the lodge, but an especially large and fearsome Bulldog guarded the gap where the wicket had stood.

"Take him down," said the Proctor.

A second Bulldog appeared, and together they seized my arms and took me outside. I got a glimpse of the museum from the Broad—brief and uninformative—before we arrived at the Printing House, where the Bulldogs kept their cells. With an interlude only to take my name, I was manhandled down to the basement and into a windowless room containing numerous townsmen; some drunk, many nursing lumps, bumps, and wounded pride. 'Twas an infinitely pleasanter prison than Oxford Gaol, being of fairly recent construction, and built to accommodate printers and their presses rather than criminals—but a prison nonetheless, and I paced anxiously back and forth, cursing the bad luck that had brought me there.

"Stop your prancing, 'tis hurting my head," groaned one of the men.

That blasted brawny fellow again! He peered at me with bloodshot eyes. "I know you, don't I?"

"Of course you do," I snapped. "I am James Sadler, the aeronaut."

The brawny man sniggered, as did several of his colleagues.

"I heard your balloon is not the only thing going up." He gave me an exaggerated wink, and elbowed the man beside him. "If you know what I mean."

"I have not the faintest idea what you mean," I growled. "I am James Sadler, the aeronaut, and I demand to be released straight away!"

While I hammered upon the door, the brawny one whispered to his companions, eliciting a strange mix of reactions: mirth, embarrassment... *disgust?* Unnerved, I hammered louder, until the Bulldogs must have tired of the racket, and sent one of their force to investigate.

"I must get out, please! I swear I am not a rioter."

"Be you a rioter or be you not," said the Bulldog, "a man of your sort should *never* get out."

And with that meaningless riddle—and to further scandalized whispers and laughter from the Townsmen—he locked the door in my face. *Dear God*, I thought. I knew not how he'd done it, but that highwayman had destroyed my reputation.

~ ~ ~

"So, you are saying that James works here—"

"Not quite here," said Mary. "In the basement."

"In the basement then, and in your shop, and on the delivery rounds, and he builds his balloons, and exhibits and flies them as well." Kat shook her head in admiration. "Why, he must be the hardest-working man alive!"

"I am sure he would say so," Mary murmured.

"These grubs are pretty—" Now Kat inspected a case of large and glossy beetles. "—but so enormous. Are they all like this in Oxford? I should not like to meet one myself... I wonder what has happened to him?" she added, for the dozenth time. "He's been gone so long."

From his post balanced upon a windowsill, Darkin looked over the shutters and onto the street. "'Tis all over, I think. Those Gownsmen in the fancy blue robes are turning out the stragglers now." He laughed. "One of them has a shiny stick that he waves about to impress. Even those bacon-fed rioters could snap it in two like a twig, but they submit to him meek as mice."

"'Tis called respect for authority," Mary said. "Father rates it most highly." She sighed and stood to stretch her legs, cramped after sitting so long on the cold marble staircase. "I hope James got him safe."

"Probably downing a shot of medicinal rum as we speak." Spotting a chance for action at last, Darkin jumped back to the floor. "I shall go see what is afoot."

Mary gasped. "But James said—"

"He said not to let anyone in. But I am going out."

"Then you will not mind if we refuse you when you return?"

Darkin laughed and pulled back the bolt.

'Twas calmer since they were hidden away. The small crowd that had gathered to watch spoke only amongst themselves in hushed tones, though various Gownsmen still to-ed and fro-ed in agitation. Darkin drew the attention of a student hurrying past.

"The riot is quashed," the young man gasped without prompting, "and the ringleaders taken away by the Proctors. But many townsfolk have injured themselves whilst drunk, and a Fellow of the College lies dead in his study. I have heard he bore no wounds—'tis thought his heart gave out in pure shock!"

The student could have gone on, Darkin was sure, but he excused himself when he spied a familiar figure, standing apart from the watching crowd.

"Serafina." He came upon her warily, as if she might strike; she regarded him with a blank look at first, then an equally wary smile.

"Do I–" she began, then said, "Isaac Darkin."

"I could say you are looking well, but 'twould be lying." Besides her agitation–plain to see through the rents in her veil–she seemed crumpled and dusty all over, with her hat knocked out of shape, and untidy black tresses hanging loose upon her shoulders where her curls had come free from their clasps.

Darkin gestured across the street. "Would you come inside, take a seat, and recover yourself?" When she hesitated, he continued, in a jolly manner, "You called me Darkin, so you must know we reversed your soul-swapping trick. And you must have seen Sadler, as well. Is he here?" He glanced around the crowd. "I suppose I must apologize for the loss of your stone... but I am sure we can make some arrangement. What be the market rate, do you think, for such a trinket?"

"I would rest," she interrupted. "Lead the way."

Darkin did so until they arrived outside the museum, where he stopped to allow Serafina to mount the steps first, struck by how uncertainly she moved. He got no reply when he rapped on the door, though the top of Mary's head bobbed about at the window, her eyes just visible over the shutter.

"Let us in, will you?" he called. "'Tis only I. And Serafina."

Her indisposition, he thought, was surely obvious– and Mary seemed to agree, for she disappeared from the window. But several long moments ensued, and the door still failed to open.

He gave Serafina an embarrassed smile. "They obey me a little *too* well."

She raised a hand, but not to knock. Instead, with no stone head in sight, the heavy twin doors burst apart with a deafening bang, while the bolt, blown off its fix-

489

ings, smashed into the opposite wall in a shower of paint and shattered plaster.

"You could have tried knocking again," Darkin gasped.

He stumbled inside, relieved to see Mary and Kat at the foot of the staircase, shocked but unharmed.

"I hear you have the stone," said Serafina.

"If I had the stone," said Darkin, skirting around the hall so he could edge between her and the staircase, "do you think I would still be stuck in this highwayman's body, a price on my head?"

"He speaks the truth," said Mary.

"None of us has it," said Kat. "And we do not know where it has gone, if you were going to ask."

Serafina looked at each of them. "One of you must have it. You said you had used it, and 'twas not upon Sadler, or I would have known."

Kat moved closer, a tremor in her voice. "What do you know about James? What have you done with him?"

But Serafina did not say. Instead, she flung back her head and reached upwards, straining her arms and hands to their fullest extent, as if grasping at motes of sunlight. Then starting with her fingers, a flicker about their tips became a shimmer that coursed down her body like molten gold, 'til every inch of her form was engulfed—and 'twas no longer Serafina who stood before them, but a man, in Gownsman robes. Tall and sturdily built, as far as they could tell, but the flicker remained about him, blurring his motions, and 'twas hard to read his expression, for his features appeared as blank and coldly flawless as those of a statue.

He remained where Serafina had stood for a moment, curling and uncurling his fingers, shrugging his shoulders, flexing his elbows and knees, like he'd just woken up from a very long slumber.

Darkin turned to Mary and Kat. "Get upstairs. Both of you—now."

Mary began to protest, but Kat took her arm and dragged her as far as the first half-landing.

"I know you know the stone's location."

The Gownsman moved closer, his voice deep and demanding attention, resounding to fill the whole breadth of the hall and every inch of its height, from the polished stone floor to the bright stucco ceiling. 'Twas an uncanny sight, however, for while his lips moved in the normal way, the sounds he made lagged behind them, so Darkin found himself watching rather than listening.

"I can see it in your mind," the Gownsman added.

"If you could read my mind, you would see I speak the truth when I say I know not."

"The word of a highwayman. Who would trust that?"

"Former highwayman."

"Indeed?" The Gownsman paused, as if to consult with himself on the matter; his lips moved, but his words seemed inwardly aimed. Then, he again spoke aloud: "'Tis of no interest to me what you do with your life. But if you wish to continue enjoying that life, you will give me what I want."

"How many more times?"

"Don't, Isaac," called Mary.

"'Tis of no interest to *me* who you are, what you want, or why you might want it." Darkin spoke in a dangerous growl. "But if you would rather not feel my boot so far up your arse, it kicks out your teeth, I would get the hell out of here—now!" He pointed furiously at the doorway.

Without a word, the Gownsman raised a hand. Darkin glimpsed a palm that looked carved from white marble, the only blemish a smear of dried blood on the thumb, then 'twas as if he'd been hit by a horse. He flew across the floor dazed and winded, to exclamations of anger and fright from the staircase.

"Insolent dog."

As he lay groaning upon his back, he saw Mary staring down at him from the landing, her golden-brown eyes wide in terror.

"Leave him alone, you great bully!" Kat yelled.

"Give me the stone and I might."

Something small, hard, and jagged shot from the staircase, striking the Gownsman a ringing blow on his seamless forehead. Before he could raise an arm to deflect them, a second missile whizzed in, and another in rapid succession.

"You want stones? We have a whole room of them up here!"

Kat fought until she had naught left to throw, though he'd taken her measure long before then and easily warded her best-aimed endeavours. The floor of the hall became peppered with broken rocks and splinters of crystal. Then silence fell, while she caught her breath and the Gownsman brushed himself off.

"Is that the best you can do?" he crowed, with a laugh that chilled the soul all the more, for him surely lacking his own.

~ ~ ~

'Twas but a short while before I did gain my freedom, though it seemed a long time to me, so anxious was I to break out Crouch and the rest.

During that time, as further rioters arrived, the room became uncomfortably crowded, especially given the lack of facilities—and even Oxford Gaol provided those. Amongst the miscreants, I heard much talk of regret for the riot, though some disbelieved it had happened at all. The mood swung from fear over what might be done to them; to denial that the Proctors held any power to punish a Townsman; to blind faith (soon to be scotched, I hoped) that the plan was simply to "give them a fright" before they were sent on their way.

My pacing now curtailed by the number of bodies around, I leapt at the door when it opened, desperate to state my case once again.

"James Sadler!" called the Bulldog before I could speak.

He jumped when I replied from right under his nose, then informed me I had a visitor; as he led me out, I had a horrid recollection of Lizzie at the Gaol, and when I saw my latest caller, my hopes first soared, then plunged.

"This is your son?" said the Pro-Proctor who had accompanied him.

My father perused me at his leisure, as if not quite decided.

"Aye. This is my son, James Sadler."

The Pro-Proctor, an officious sort with a cap too small for his head, consulted the papers in his hand. "'Tis reported that when approached, he attempted to evade apprehension—"

"That is a blatant lie!" I cried.

The Pro-Proctor glared at me. "—having been found within St Alban's College this day, in the environs of an unlawful disorder, and offering no valid cause for his presence." The Pro-Proctor paused and looked at Father. "You are well regarded in this city, your Benefaction enjoyed by all, from highest to lowest. 'Twas a surprise to see your son listed here, although of course, there is only so much a parent can do."

"You are right there," said Father.

"To whit," said the Pro-Proctor, "we are keen to resolve this problem without further fuss. We need only be reassured, that when your son entered St Alban's, his intentions were honest and not at all bent on destruction."

Father inspected me again.

"Father? You must get me out. I beg you."

"He was there because I had told him to be," he responded, at last. "Our normal business does not cease, not even for the Benefaction. Other orders were due at St Alban's today."

The Pro-Proctor nodded and consulted his papers again. "May I confirm—what you are saying is, your son was delivering pastries?"

When Father did not reply straight away, I blurted, "Yes, yes! I was on the delivery round. One of the rioters seized my basket for himself, which was why I had nothing to show when they caught me."

Father's expression was no more friendly then, than the one he had worn the last time I saw him, throwing me out of my home.

"Aye, he was on the delivery round."

The Pro-Proctor heaved a sigh of relief at these words. "Excellent! One fewer to deal with..."

The Bulldog showed us back to the street, with an obvious air of reluctance. I immediately turned left towards the museum, while Father veered right for Catte Street and the High. We both stopped and turned to look at each other.

"I heard you had been arrested." Father scowled. "Rioting, is it now? Not the worst of your sins in God's eyes, but another to add to the roster."

"I think," I said, "I have much explaining to do, and you may not believe a word of it, though I swear it all be true."

He frowned. "Tell me now and I shall decide."

"I shall, but I cannot do it now."

"Cannot or will not?"

"Father, please! I have to go. Lives depend upon me."

"I pity them, whoever they be, if they only have you to rely on."

I imagined I heard the faintest glimmer of humour in these words, and took this as a signal to run up the Broad.

"I shall be back as soon as I can," I called behind me.

"I shall not wait up," he called back.

~ ~ ~

When Darkin could finally struggle no more, the Gownsman left him lying where he had fallen and crossed to the staircase.

"Perhaps you will prove more talkative?"

"I'm not afraid of you!" 'Twas Mary's voice.

"You will be."

Darkin stretched out a hand, protesting, imploring...

Then a new voice spoke. "Excuse me, sir—'tis six-pence to view the collections."

"You are alive!"

Stirred by Kat's jubilant shout, Darkin raised his head off the floor. James Sadler stood in the doorway, framed in sunlight like some scrawny avenging angel. But only for an instant, for he suddenly turned and ran. Darkin could not blame him; he would have probably done the same. He closed his eyes and laid back his head once again, too spent to do aught but await the inevitable.

Hours or instants later, he awoke again to various happenings: shouting, cursing; a billowing gown and hood flying past; a fleeting flutter of gingham and yellow ribbons; then Mary tugging his arm, shaking with fear as she urged him to stand.

"They are heading down to the basement!" she cried. "What is James doing? He'll be trapped, wherever he goes."

Darkin allowed her to help him up and outside. While Kat remained sobbing on the street, the pastry-boy had continued descending into the basement yard, the Gownsman following after him, and naught else down there save a door and a huge pile of ash.

"You have backed yourself into a corner, you fool. If you wish to leave this place alive, direct me towards my property."

"Of course." Sadler plunged his arm into the ash-pile—and pulled out the Soul-Eater, the gem covered with soot but still sparkling darkly.

The Gownsman held out a hand. "You will give me that now."

But Sadler dashed for the door, ducking beneath the Gownsman's arms when Kat yelled a warning, then grabbing a handful of ash and flinging it into the face of his foe at close quarters. As the Gownsman choked and clawed at his eyes, the flicker surrounding his body seemed to dim, and for the briefest heartbeat, a faint image of Serafina appeared to writhe in his stead. Sadler did not take pause to ponder and darted into the basement.

"Come take your damned stone, if you dare," he shouted. "But I warn you—you will not get it lightly."

"Don't you hurt him!" yelled Kat.

She bolted down the steps to the yard, followed and then overtaken by Darkin, but the Gownsman had already gone. As they reached for the door, it slammed shut, though there was barely a draught in the yard.

"'Tis locked!" Kat cried.

"How can that be? They had no key."

Darkin battered the door, to no avail.

~ ~ ~

My plan had both succeeded and, I feared, already failed. I had the stone, the laboratory, and my opponent's attention in hand, but faced a far more potent threat than I had expected from Serafina.

'Twould have been madness to turn aside, so I inched backwards from the door towards the chymical stores on the wall. Was it I—I thought—who once so neatly scribed such instructive labels? Who arranged their bottles and jars with such orderly care? Or was it the work of some other man? 'Twas as if I'd begun to exist only that morning, when I awoke beneath Folly Bridge, with Kat by my side.

"You are wondering—" said the Fellow, when someone banged on the door. "—why your friends do not simply open it and come after you."

I had, indeed, been wondering—but more on how the lamps had managed to light themselves when the door slammed shut. 'Twas fortunate they had, for I would have got nowhere in darkness.

As I continued my retreat—slow and steady, for fear of tripping—I glimpsed further signs of that other man's life: an ear trumpet, abandoned upon the flagstones; an impeccably tidy work-bench; then another, bearing an order book, its legs knocked out of true as if from a fall.

"They cannot because it is locked," the Fellow declared, clearly miffed I had not attempted an answer myself.

"'Tis not locked. It does not *have* a lock."

"They believe it is locked. I made them believe. And more than that—I reshaped their sensible world, to accord with those beliefs. That baseborn girl had no notion of the true extent of her powers." He gazed in exultation at his fingers, spreading them wide before his face. "Reading and writing the surface of the mind is barely the start."

"*I* do not believe it is locked."

The inhumanly faultless face stretched in a smile. "Then come past me and see for yourself."

"I would rather stay here, if that please you."

"What would please me is the return of my property." The Fellow held out his hand, palm uppermost. "Then we might part as friends, as we did on Old Crab's Tower. You remember me, of course."

I had to shudder. "I did not see your face, but yes, I remember you."

"Until I acquire a body better suited to my needs, I must occupy the girl's. However, I assumed this glamour so you might know me—"

At last, an explanation for the artifice of his form; 'twas a show, like so much else. Then I thought of that other man, who would have scoffed at such dubious flim-flam.

"—and perhaps feel more... comfortable, also."

"Comfortable? You would have used me for your foul *investigations*, as if I were not flesh and blood, but a—a bottle of chymicals, to be measured and mixed, and tossed in the waste when broken."

"I could have offered you more than that."

"I thought you did. My father seemed so *small* compared with you, so inconsequential. I was wrong."

"Yet that was not the only time you ran from him. You would have left with the girl and never returned, for she made you think you loved her. It did not go well, of course."

I stumbled, caught off balance. "How do you know that?"

"I begin to feel her memories—as if they not only abide in the soul, but are etched somehow in the physical form. 'Tis not aught I'd considered before, but be certain, I shall learn more—and make *very* good use of that learning. As I was saying..." He opened his hand again. "My stone."

"Never. 'Tis a prison for innocent souls."

He laughed. "No one is innocent."

Then he tired of talk and unleashed the attack I expected, though not in any manner I had feared. No blow was thrown, no tooth bared like a beast; just one twitch of a shimmering finger, then a thud of pain in my skull as though he had shot a bolt straight through it. From out of nowhere, I saw sunset on Shotover Hill, and my mother, her face sketched in moonlight. 'Twas so real, I reached forth to touch her, but the phantasm fled and my hand closed instead on the arm of a dried-up shell on its deathbed.

You have failed me, James, rasped the carcass. You shall never amount to much. Better had it been you who died at birth, and Baby Temple lived.

"No!" I choked. "That was Mary, not her."

The carcass expired a puff of dust in my face and withered to naught, then another illusion took form in its place—and this one truly impossible. For without explanation, cause, or warning, a hole had appeared in the ceiling above the reverberatory, and the ensuing deluge of rubble smashed my least-favourite furnace to bits. A roiling cloud of flame and ash spat forth, and from this maelstrom emerged a nightmare.

In some last remaining rational part of my mind, I labelled it as the skeleton of a dragon from the museum, before it descended upon me at speed, slamming me flat upon the flags with its bony claws and fleshless tail. Despite this perilous turn of events, the irony was not lost on me—for 'twas it not the *Officina Chimica* that had been deemed a deadly menace, and the museum in need of protection?

While I lay winded, the Fellow wrested the pin from my grasp and drove the shaft at my heart. I grabbed his wrist with both of my hands but could barely restrain him, and as we struggled, the stone slipped free from its mount, as it had on the night I fought for my life with Potato-face and Turnip-head.

The Fellow shrieked in frustration and shot out an arm, lightning-fast, to grab at the stone as it rattled away. I was swifter still. Back on my feet in a heartbeat, seconds later I had the stone in one hand and a glass of Aromatic Spirit Vegetabilis in the other. I offered my thanks to Dr Crouch, so unfairly trapped in the stone; for had he not made me tidy the stocks, I should never have found what I needed so quickly.

"Give me my stone," the Fellow demanded, all trace of indulgence gone.

'Twas my turn to smirk. "This glass contains a chymical that will dissolve whatever it touches. Even your stone. *Especially* your stone. Do not come any closer, or I will destroy it."

"I do not believe you."

I shrugged. "Come here and see for yourself."

He took a step closer.

"Do not say I failed to warn you," I said, and dropped the stone in the glass.

He gaped at me, thunderstruck.

But my triumph proved short-lived, for with the dread wail of a banshee, the skeletal dragon sprang back into play, sweeping me clean off the floor and through the still-smoking hole in the ceiling, then up the stairwell into Tradescant's collections above. I thought it might stop at that point; when it did not, 'twas grimly clear it intended to smash through the roof.

I closed my eyes, covered my head, and awaited a wretched death, crushed like a bug on the rafters. Then I felt a rush of fresh air on my face, and peeked from beneath my arms to see that we'd passed through the roof intact, and that the dragon continued to climb—into Heaven, perhaps, though I feared 'twould not be its ultimate destination.

I noted too, that with every beat of its bony wings, the dragon enlarged a fraction. It brought to mind an air-pump, as if the beast were an operation in a pneumatic chymistry lecture. 'Twould dwarf even the Countess of Westmorland's lodestone—in stature as well as renown, for the dragon was soon as big as a horse, as a house... as big as an elephant. And as it swelled in size, it gained in substance too: sprouting golden eyes and a serpentine tongue, and muscle and sinew to dress its dry bones, and a shimmering pearly skin.

We circled once, twice, thrice about the city, my mount's wings clicking and clacking, its throat emitting an endless shriek so piercing, I would have clamped my hands to my ears, had I not needed them to cling to its scaly back. I was glad of the practice I'd had with Isaac Darkin's nag, though that had been riding a dove compared with my latest steed.

When I dared to look down, I saw we'd flown east— to the River Cherwell where it crossed Angel Meadow, its meanderings a counterpoint to the Physic Garden's regimented plots. I thought of Wyndham Rudge, with a pang of regret that we argued the last time we met. But the higher we rose, the further such cares receded, 'til I could no longer distinguish Town from Gown, the best of them being no more than a column of ants, scuttling upon a handkerchief to no purpose.

I could hear not one sound from the Earth, and the dragon had by now ceased its shrieking. All in all, I decided, 'twas not so bad as it could have been, and thus reassured I began to relax. I stopped fighting the dragon's motions, moving with it instead, and closed my eyes; not in fear this time, but with a sensation akin to bliss. I gorged myself on the clean, sweet air that no man had tasted before, and noticed how 'twas cooler up here than below, though we be nearer the Sun— giving the lie to the story of Ikarus.

I did not even startle when the dragon began to speak. in a voice not unlike the Fellow's.

"Daedalus warned his son not to fly too high, but Ikarus also knew not to fly too low, lest the seawater weigh down his wings."

I did not respond, for the beast was surely reading my thoughts.

"Follow *my* path," it said, "and you will have no need of *human* contrivance."

We spiralled higher, and higher still, 'til Oxford shrank to a distant smudge, and I knew I would soon spot Newbury, and Winchester, and Southampton. Overwhelmed, I hollered in joy; had I not, I think my heart might have burst.

Should I do as the dragon required? 'Twas possible that I might, one day, raise myself to a higher station, but naught could be certain. With the dragon, I'd fly so high, even the loftiest man of consequence would seem no taller to me, than an ant on the ground appeared now.

"'Tis impossible to fly too high," hissed the dragon in my mind. But its voice was then joined by my mother's; her own this time, not the Fellow's false memories.

Nothing of worth is gained without work.

"Will you let me in? Let me in, and we shall share the power of flight."

"That is not yours to offer," I said, overtook by a strange serenity. "For you cannot fly yourself."

We dropped a fathom or more at those words, as the dragon's steady cadence abruptly faltered—a sickening sensation, yet I persisted, still at peace. "You cannot fly because you are a dragon. And there never was such a thing as a dragon. They exist only in stories for children."

It shuddered and bucked as the beautiful rainbow scales began to fall apart.

"But I am grown," I said. "And I know you are only a lizard, condemned to crawl on the ground all your life."

Tattered skin sloughed in shreds off mouldering flesh; golden eyeballs boiled in their sockets. With a final shriek of disbelief, the dragon's tongue crumbled to dust. Then the wings that had brought us so high melted away, and clutching a pile of old bones, I plummeted back to the Earth.

~ ~ ~

Darkin, Mary, and Kat continued to pound the recalcitrant door—until it opened as it had closed, of its own accord. Kat dashed in first, heedless of the danger.

'Twas quiet inside. Not a work-bench nor furnace nor test-glass disturbed, as if naught at all had occurred, and all three had imagined the struggle they'd heard.

Real enough, however, were the motionless forms on the floor.

CHAPTER FIFTY-FIVE

BESIDES TWO DEATHS FROM SHEER FRIGHT (one unsurprising due to great age, the other of dubious pertinence), the St Alban's Day Spree, as it came to be known, cost no one their life directly, though it caused consternation amongst many Gownsmen. At the University Chancellor's command, the Corporation of Oxford made good all damages, with further compensation to be paid each Midsummer's Day for a full ten years thereafter, despite protestations from the Mayor (who should have been grateful he stayed in office, and his profiteering concealed).

As for the source of the riot, 'twas ascribed to poisoned sweetmeats by a few—though never in the presence of Tho. Sadler, Grand Master in Perpetuity of the Oxford Guild of Pastry-cooks and Confectioners. Others suggested the culprit truly had been poisoned air—not Gaol Fever (which was swiftly exposed as a hoax), but a noxious gas escaped from the *Officina Chimica*, which had already been blamed for the stupor observed in the occupants of that building and their neighbours. When Drs Sheffield, Crouch, and the rest regained their reason (by coincidence, on the very day of the riot), they all denied such a mishap had

505

ever occurred—although, as many muttered darkly, they would say that, wouldn't they?

'Twas also wondered what might have befallen St Alban's Vice Sub-Rector, believed to have fled to a safer town for fear of future riots. That he had razed his own house (and with criminal disregard for the safety of innocent passers-by) was testament to the state of his mind—as were his frankly bizarre allegations concerning his relatives' doings. Given the Sadlers' reputation, these slanders were roundly dismissed.

No one wondered where Ambrose Bean had gone, except the innkeeper at The Crown, who found his rooms unexpectedly emptied, and no trace of the next week's rent.

Remarkable it is, how quickly people forget. With the damage repaired, the kitchens and cellar re-stocked, and everyday life resumed, an event that might have forever divided the city was seldom re-called, and Town and Gown turned out together to wit-ness my first ascent. Angel Meadow being reckoned too humble a venue, my aerostat would be launched from the meadow at Christ Church (by personal in-vitation of the Dean, no less)—within sight of the Physic Garden, where all had begun. I did not resurrect the punctured balloon. Instead, I built anew: a craft powered by heat-ed air, a larger incarnation of the one that Rudge had glimpsed, so many moons ago, from Magdalen Bridge.

Various notables and worthies came to the Meadow to see me off, but none as gladly received as my family.

"I am sure you will not need it," said my father, shaking my hand. "But I wish you good luck—son."

"Providence smiles upon us." I squinted into the spotless sky, tasted the westerly breeze; conditions were perfect. "'Tis most definitely a day for cheesecake."

"Not cheesecake," Father said. "'Tis a day for aero-nautics—Sadler's finest. Though I shall be sure to raise a slice upon your return."

With a catch in his voice, he hugged me, then returned to the more capacious embrace of his guest for the day, Mrs Winstable.

That everyone present might see me, men of the Corporation had put up a platform beside the balloon; as I climbed upon it, I thought of 'washing day', and my mood darkened at all that had passed. Then the City Waits tootled a merrier tune, and my spirits rose again—especially when I heard a strident miaow from inside the basket. 'Twas Buttons the cat, perched atop my crate of Champagne (a shrewd gift from the Mayor), impatiently swishing his tail.

"Do be careful, James!" Lizzie waved from the front of the crowd.

"I shall, never fear!" Burleigh raised a hand in salute, his other arm being about his wife's waist—which was (as Kat had pointed out to me earlier) grown somewhat thicker than before. And Kat was there as well, of course, blowing kisses and fizzing with excitement.

"I'll be waiting for you!" she yelled.

This raised bawdy *Hurrahs!* from the crowd; I blushed, and was glad to be distracted by Mary, who joined me on the platform with lowered voice and downcast gaze.

"Is Isaac here?" I asked, scanning the crowd.

"Yes, but you will not see him."

I grinned. "He is, of course, a master of disguise."

Mary returned my smile, belying the sadness in her eyes. "We leave today. I am here to say goodbye."

I had known this time would come, but it hurt nonetheless.

"For Plymouth?"

"And then to America. It must be done, for Isaac's sake. We shall both have a new beginning." She glanced over her shoulder at Father. "I just worry how *he* will manage alone."

"He will manage as he always has," I said. "And he does not want for company. 'Tis embarrassing to behold, the way he canoodles like a lovestruck cub with his sweetheart."

This time, Mary's laughter was sincere.

"You have the stone?" I added.

She opened the pocket in her petticoat so I could see the pouch inside.

"'Tis in here. And I collected every last splinter of the Moon-stone. Although I must say," she scolded, "I did not appreciate being treated like a charwoman, especially by you."

"I would have done it myself, I swear, except... How could I? Everyone knows me." I laughed, then continued more seriously, "We know any larger part of the stone might have powers all of its own. But those tiny pieces, the fragments no bigger than dust...?" I shrugged. "Better safe than sorry."

"I found this, as well." From beside the pouch, she pulled out another small gem. "Amidst the broken orrery. 'Twas the largest of all the spheres, so must have been meant for the Sun. It looked different somehow, compared with the rest."

She held the stone to the light, angling it this way and that for a moment. Then she dropped it onto the platform, and crushed it with a sharp stamp of her travelling boot.

"When we reach the deepest part of the ocean," she said, as an unexpected breeze caught the smallest specks of the Sun-stone and whirled them away, "we shall drop them from the side of the ship, as we agreed."

"And then we shall begin our new lives." I kissed her upon the forehead. "Tell that brute, he must answer to me, if he fails to provide you with all you so richly deserve. I shall know if your hopes be dashed, and I am a half-way decent marksman. Or at least, I never shot my own sister."

"And I shall always be your sister, whatever Jediah said."

This took me by surprise, for we'd hardly spoken about it 'til then. "You do not believe him?"

"I do not know what to believe. No one else read the letter he claimed to have found. And I still remember talk of him having a brother, before you were born..." She sighed. "I suppose we shall never know."

"Are you ready, Mr Sadler?" called the *Jackson's Oxford Journal* man.

"As I shall ever be!" I cried, and vaulted into the basket, to cheers from the crowd.

There, I made a great show of my trusty assistants releasing the tethers, 'til Father shouted, "Speak up! They want to hear you as well as watch!"

I gazed aghast at the mass of expectant faces.

"Come on, boy—stir their souls! Like you—*he* did at the Town Hall."

"I—I... *I* do not give speeches," I croaked.

And if that were not reason enough to depart, William Tench appeared at that instant, waving above the heads of the crowd his Bacon's *Opus Maius*, recently returned but not, perhaps, in the pristine state I had pawned it.

"Cut the ropes—quickly," I hissed.

509

My assistants obliged, and the basket lurched as the globe took up the slack. Caught unawares, my audience gasped; in surprise at first, then in fear, then delight.

From the platform, Mary shouted, "James! Can you hear me?"

"My ears are working as yet," I replied. "As are my other faculties—though I have only been airborne a moment. According to Professor Charles, there should be no untoward effects until at least ten thousand feet—"

"Do you remember that St Alban's Day, the one when you fought with Jediah?"

"How could I forget?" I called back.

"I know who poisoned the sweetmeats."

Perhaps Prof. Charles was wrong and I had already lost my wits. Could I trust my own senses at all, aloft in this airy realm? Though when I gazed upon my shrinking sister, I was certain I'd heard her words and not imagined them.

"Who?" I yelled, bewildered.

But 'who' would be another story, for the fire had lifted me into the sky and the wind now swept me abroad. Beneath me the world awaited, and all that was in it: Southampton, America, China. And if not I, then men of the future would fly around the world and beyond it—though their exploits would never eclipse my achievement that day. For by dint of natural philosophy, and not a little good fortune, I had become the first English aeronaut, and a man of consequence at last.

THE END

Acknowledgements

If I should thank you, I am sure you
know that I do.

Except the cats. Thanks to the cats.

And to Lorna Fergusson of Fictionfire, who
encouraged me to do better. It took a while, but
(I hope) I got at least part-way there in the end.

Typographical errors are my own.

Anachronisms, inconsistencies, and blatant
fabrications I must blame on James Sadler,
who related this account many years after the events
described herein.

About the Author

Wendy A.M. Prosser lives in Oxfordshire, UK with her husband, cats, and many interests, including wildlife gardening, Egyptology, cosmology, particle physics, and learning other languages. She was born in Singapore, grew up in Kingston upon Hull, UK, and studied zoology at the University of Oxford, where she was also awarded a PhD for her research on intracellular symbionts in aphids. Wendy worked in market research before moving into publishing. She is now a freelance science editor.

Visit Wendy's blog: https://wendyamprosser.com

Printed in Great Britain
by Amazon

30115551R00292